MARMAI

Exit, Pursu

GW01238318

Keira Willis was born in Manchester i ＿＿＿＿＿＿＿＿＿＿＿＿
she was going to grow up to be both a writer and a barrister (Reader, this did
not happen). She graduated with a degree in English Literature, followed by
studying for an MEd at Queens' College, Cambridge while teaching English
and Drama at a secondary school. She eventually decided that it was time to
get back to writing stories.

Exit, Pursued by Death is the second instalment in the *Tib Street Ballroom*
series. Despite the title of the series there is (regrettably) no dancing contained
within.

EXIT, PURSUED BY DEATH

KEIRA WILLIS

MARMALADE PRESS

Published by Marmalade Press
www.marmaladepress.co.uk

First published 2024

A CIP catalogue record for this book
is available from the British Library

Printed and bound in Great Britain by
Clays Ltd, Elcograf S.p.A.

Typeset in Adobe Garamond Pro and Futura by Spike-E

ISBN 978-1-9997645-3-1

MIX
Paper | Supporting
responsible forestry
FSC® C018072

To Mummy
with love
(I'm very sorry for giving you nightmares…)

ONE

Detective Inspector Andrew Joyce had somewhat naïvely assumed that by the time his mid-thirties rolled around he'd be settled into a comfortable, straightforward period of his life.

For years, it had seemed like everything was heading in the direction he'd expected it to; he'd been promoted to Detective Inspector at thirty-three, owned his own house and a very sensible car, and he'd even managed to have a couple of serious girlfriends in his late twenties.

So, it did take him a little by surprise that at almost midnight on the eve of turning thirty-four, he found himself neither surrounded by family at home, nor in the pub with friends, but instead hauling himself out of the Rochdale Canal and onto a freezing towpath in Ancoats.

Andrew swore loudly as his fingers scrabbled uselessly on the uneven surface in the dark, until he found enough purchase to be able to drag his legs out of the water, cursing the day he'd decided to become a police officer.

'Andrew!'

'Sir!'

'Oh good, an audience,' Andrew griped as he struggled to his feet, canal water draining out from his suit and shoes until he was standing in a large puddle.

The two women who'd been calling his name were running up the towpath towards him. The weak moonlight was just bright enough for Andrew to pick out their silhouettes, and the sound of their shoes slapping against the ground was almost obscenely loud in the otherwise still night.

Peggy Swan reached him first, hair flying out wildly behind her before she skidded to a halt a couple of feet from where Andrew stood.

Detective Sergeant Jen Cusack arrived only a second later, already reaching for her radio as she frowned in concern at the sodden figure before her.

'Lloyd, it's Jen,' she said into the radio. 'Can you bring the car further down Henry Street, please?'

Andrew missed whatever Lloyd said in reply because Peggy was doing that thing again; that thing where she looked like she was staring intently at an empty patch of air, but at any moment would launch into what sounded like a one-sided conversation. It had been nine months since he'd had to somewhat grudgingly accept that Peggy could have conversations with ghosts, but Andrew still wasn't entirely sure that he'd ever be completely comfortable with the concept.

'Sir?' Jen said. 'Lloyd will be here in five minutes.'

'He only parked at the other end of the road,' Andrew grumbled in annoyance, keeping one eye on where Peggy's frown was deepening. 'What's taking so long?'

'He says he went for chips, sir,' Jen replied sheepishly.

'Chips,' Andrew repeated, almost devoid of any emotion.

'Chips,' Jen confirmed. 'He was at the front of the queue. If it helps, he did say he'd get enough for everyone.'

It was in moments like this that Andrew was forced to stop and consider what his life might have been like if he'd just stayed at CID. If he *had* stayed, it was unlikely that he'd now be dripping wet, and equally unlikely that he'd probably just contracted a water-borne parasitic disease while waiting for his DC to finish getting a takeaway.

'So, DI Joyce ending up in the canal had absolutely nothing to do with you?' Peggy asked the patch of nothingness, shaking her head in disbelief. '*Really?*'

She turned to face Andrew a few seconds later and grimaced apologetically. 'Arthur says he's very sorry. He got a bit carried away with running after you. The nudge was accidental.'

Andrew tried to glare in the direction of wherever the elusive - and very dead - Arthur Havers, was standing. '*Nudge*? He hit me hard enough to nearly end up on the other side of the canal!'

Peggy held up her hands in a silent reminder that it wasn't her fault.

'You said he wasn't strong enough to physically do anything,' Andrew added, feeling, that despite Peggy's assertion to the contrary, this actually was at least a little bit her fault. 'I'd say trying to drown me is proof otherwise.'

Peggy rolled her eyes, and Andrew felt overwhelmingly like he was being judged.

'He wasn't trying to drown you, Andrew. Anyway, Arthur says that it's all a bit clearer to him now.'

'Oh, *does* Arthur?' Andrew replied, gritting his teeth.

He was still fairly convinced that ex-convict and notorious thief Havers was playing silly buggers. This was the third night that they'd spent on this very stretch of the towpath, and each time, Havers had eventually announced that he apparently couldn't quite remember where the final hoard of stolen diamonds had been stashed. According to Peggy, Andrew should be showing Havers a little more patience, given that minutes after the diamonds had originally been hidden, Havers had been brutally killed by a former associate only a few hundred yards up the road.

'He says that you'll find the box behind the wall on the edge of the towpath, just in line with the lock,' Peggy added, overlooking Andrew's frustration. 'You'll need to go over the bridge first.'

'A whole case of stolen jewellery is just hidden behind a wall?' Andrew shook his head in incredulity. 'And nobody's happened upon it in the ten years since it was put there?'

'It's bolted down, and it should be well covered by plants,' Peggy replied, gesturing towards the empty space next to Andrew again. 'Can you not shoot the messenger, please? I'm only repeating what Arthur's said.'

'Fine, I'll go and have a look,' Andrew said, running a hand through his hair and grimacing as his fingers collected a combination of what felt like grit and slime. He was glad that it was far too dark to see it in any detail. 'Can you ask your little friend to stay away from me this time though?'

For just a second, Andrew thought that Peggy was going to say something snappish, but instead, she just took a deep breath through her nose and shot him a sardonic smile. 'As you wish, Detective Inspector.'

Ugh, Andrew hated it when Peggy got all prim, because it usually meant that he'd said something to really irritate her, and he could look forward to pursed lips and pointed silence. In his defence, he'd just been dunked in the Rochdale Canal in the dead of night, on the eve of his birthday.

He decided that it would probably be best to stay quiet, and instead of commenting further he slowly made his way up the towpath and over the red-panelled footbridge towards the lock, keeping his head held as high as it was possible to do so when every single step he took resulted in a terrible squelching sound.

True to Peggy's description, there was a low brick wall jutting out onto the towpath in line with the lock gate. He could hear Jen's footsteps just behind him, which meant that Peggy and whatever remained of Arthur Havers probably weren't too far away either. If Havers was taking the piss about the location of the jewellery, Andrew was going to work out exactly who he needed to speak to about arranging an exorcism.

'DS Cusack, would you like to do the honours?' Andrew asked tightly as he tried to rid his cold hands of cramp by

4

repeatedly clenching his fingers into fists.

'Sir,' Jen said with a short nod before she knelt down on the tow path and switched on her torch.

'Here, let me hold that for you,' Peggy said, brushing past Andrew to take Jen's torch and hold it high enough that the vegetation growing behind the wall was bathed in light.

'Thanks, Peggy.' Jen reached down to tug at the long grass-like planting until it came free from the soil and then laid the remains next to her.

Andrew hoped that the wall wasn't a popular dumping ground for the kind of questionable, and sometimes dangerous, detritus that covered the edges of the towpath all the way through the city, but he knew that Jen would be careful to protect her hands as best she could.

When Jen had pulled out enough plant debris to create a small pile at her side, she looked up at her companions in surprise. 'It feels like there's a metal box in here. Just as Havers said, sir.'

Andrew knew that he probably looked like he'd just swallowed a whole net of lemons. 'Alright, very good, Jen. Take some photos before we do anything else.'

Jen nodded her assent and reached into the large bag she'd been carrying all evening as they'd traipsed up and down the towpath.

Andrew was relieved that he'd be able to tell Higson that they'd finally used the camera. He'd spent almost a month practically begging his DCI to pay for it out of the minuscule Ballroom budget, and even when Higson had finally relented, he hadn't seemed entirely convinced by any of Andrew's arguments for why the department needed a camera in the first place. Hopefully seeing photos of the stolen jewels in situ would mollify him, at least a bit.

Once she'd taken a couple of photographs, Jen looked back

over at Andrew, 'How do you intend on getting it out of here if it's bolted to the wall, sir?'

'Well, if *someone* had told us about this little detail before we came down here, we'd have come prepared,' Andrew replied, being careful not to catch Peggy's eye. Andrew was happy to continue making snippy comments, but he'd be less happy if he ended up in the canal again.

'Arthur says there should be a combination lock on the side of the case,' Peggy said to Jen, patently ignoring Andrew. 'He's just trying to remember what the combination is.'

Any retort Andrew had balancing on the tip of his tongue was swallowed quickly when he heard hurried footsteps behind him. He spun around, ready to face whoever thought they had any business being down here at this time of night, and then relaxed almost immediately when he came face-to-face with his wayward DC.

'Sorry, sir!' Lloyd called, jogging towards them, white paper-wrapped parcels held tightly in his arms. 'Thought I'd bring the chips down.'

Andrew knew that he should berate Lloyd for bringing food to a crime scene, but the smell of salt and vinegar drenched oil made him pause, almost unconsciously. Lunchtime seemed so very far away.

'Hang on, wait for me! I've got Lilt for everyone!'

Andrew's mouth dropped open as another familiar figure appeared on the Kitty Bridge. He whirled back round to glare at Peggy. 'What the bloody hell is your brother doing here?'

'I'm not his secretary, Andrew,' Peggy replied firmly, wrinkling her nose at her brother's approaching figure. 'I have no idea. I haven't seen him all day.'

'Bugger!' Charlie Swan yelped as he displaced the stack of cans in his arms and the topmost one plummeted heavily onto the towpath before rolling straight into the canal.

'Whoops!' he added, as he adjusted the four cans he was still holding. 'Sorry, chaps, two of you will have to share. Bagsy not me, I'm parched. Peg, you'll share with Joycie, won't you?'

Andrew glared at Lloyd. 'Explain!'

Lloyd pulled one side of his mouth down in a show of contrition. 'Sorry, sir. Charlie was in front of me in the queue in the chippy. He's been out with some friends.'

Andrew closed his eyes and pinched the bridge of his nose.

'Joyce, why on earth do you look like a drowned rat?' Charlie laughed as he placed the remaining cans of Lilt by his feet.

'Charlie!' Peggy snapped warningly, and Andrew almost thanked her for that.

'Sir?' Jen asked loudly, trying to get everyone to focus on the reason they were all huddled on a dark towpath even as she shot a longing look at Lloyd's stack of chips. 'What do you want to do? Come back tomorrow?'

Andrew shook his head. 'Not a chance. We end this tonight, or we close the case unsolved. We're not wasting any more time on this. Havers is obviously a dead end.'

'One-seven-eight-three,' Peggy said suddenly.

'Sorry, what?' Andrew asked, blinking in surprise.

'Try that for the lock,' Peggy clarified. 'One-seven-eight-three.'

Andrew nodded at Jen, and he watched as she carefully moved yet more planting out of the way when Peggy held the torch a little closer to the wall.

'What have I missed?' Charlie asked, noisily popping open a can as he wobbled slightly on his feet.

'You're not even supposed to be here,' Andrew said for what felt like the hundredth time in their acquaintance.

Whereas Peggy's presence was officially sanctioned by Higson on what now seemed to be an almost-weekly basis – whether the case really required her or not - Charlie just made it his business to appear on investigations whenever the mood struck him.

Higson didn't seem to care at all, which just made Andrew feel even more put-out.

'He's right, Charlie,' Peggy added. 'You're not supposed to be here.'

If there was only one thing that Andrew could always count on, it was for Peggy to back him up when Charlie was behaving like a particularly annoying arse; he could continue to count on this even when Andrew himself was being a particularly annoying arse.

Charlie just grinned as he always did and took another gulp of fizzy drink. 'I was bored!'

'Sir!' Jen exclaimed in surprise. 'It's opened.'

Andrew hurried over to crouch next to Jen as she awkwardly forced the lid open, metal scraping against metal noisily as the slightly deformed box protested at being disturbed after so long.

The crooked lid tilted back far enough for the light of Peggy's torch to catch on something that sparkled so obnoxiously that Andrew immediately had no doubt that they'd found what they'd been looking for.

'Photos, Jen, please,' Andrew instructed firmly. 'I want photos of the scene as it is now, and I want every single piece of jewellery categorised separately, both here and then again back at the Ballroom.'

Jen complied, taking a few photos before she laid some evidence bags on the ground and gingerly started removing the jewellery from the box, one item at a time.

'If you wouldn't mind, Peggy,' Lloyd said, thrusting the stack of wrapped chips at her as he took the torch from her hand. 'I'll make a list of everything we've got.'

'I think we might be here a while, sir,' Jen said dejectedly as Lloyd passed her the torch and she looked down into the illuminated box. 'There's loads of tiny things in here.'

Andrew sighed. Well, there went any chance of getting home

soon. He wouldn't leave until they had a record of everything though, no matter how long it took. News of the recovered diamonds would get back to CID quickly enough, and since Andrew had spent the last nine months living with the deeply paranoid sense that his former colleagues would eventually try to use the Ballroom's upped success rate against him, he wanted to ensure that everything was done by the book. He needed everyone on Higson's team to be above reproach if their own re-investigations were scrutinised at any point in the future.

'Alright,' Andrew sighed tiredly, and he shivered as a light breeze caught his wet clothes. 'Jen, Lloyd, hold it there for a second. Let's eat first, and then get back to cataloguing everything.'

He turned his attention to Peggy, who seemed to be having a hushed conversation with Havers.

'Thank you for your help this week, Peggy. You can take your brother home now,' Andrew said, and winced at how formal he sounded. He really hadn't got any better at swallowing his pride.

'Arthur says he can tell you where everything came from,' Peggy said, waving away the stilted gratitude. 'Would that help?'

Andrew wanted to say 'no' because that would mean that Peggy would have to leave, and Andrew could momentarily go back to pretending that a significant number of the cases they'd closed recently had been down to careful police work and excellent deductive reasoning, rather than because of their resident ghost expert. He wouldn't say 'no' though, because at the end of the day he still took an enormous amount of pride in his job, whether ghosts helped the success rate or not.

'Alright, yes, that would help,' Andrew agreed, and Peggy looked surprised, as though she'd been waiting for an argument.

'Charlie!' Andrew then snapped. 'If you want to be useful, you can go and get coffees for everyone.'

Charlie saluted with a hiccup, sloshing fizzy pop all over his hand as he walked backwards.

'Jesus Christ, get yourself at least two,' Andrew replied disdainfully, turning away with an eye roll.

'Can we have the chips now, sir?' Lloyd asked hopefully. 'Please?'

'Yeah, alright.' Andrew looked down at his fingers and wondered whether it was actually safe to put them anywhere near food right now.

'Oh, come on, you won't die,' Peggy said as she caught Andrew staring at his hands. '*Probably*.'

'Thanks, that's really reassuring!' Andrew shook his head and reached for a portion of chips anyway.

Peggy glanced at her watch and smiled. 'Oh, hey, it's gone twelve. Happy birthday!'

'Thanks.' Andrew paused, chip halfway to his mouth. 'Oh God, you're not going to sing, are you?'

Peggy snorted. 'No, but I can't promise that Charlie won't try when he gets back.'

'Can't wait for that then.'

Andrew looked up at the sky and thought about how his Nana Joyce used to loudly encourage him to make wishes when he blew out his birthday candles. He doubted there would be any cake and candles for him this year, so instead he picked a random star and stared at it intently. Surely stars worked just as well as candles did.

All he really wanted was a year that went a bit more smoothly than the last one had.

That wasn't too much to ask for, right?

TWO

Peggy cracked open one eye and gingerly lifted her head from where it had been pillowed on her folded arms. It took a good few moments of staring down at her own body for her to even begin to understand that she was slumped in a chair in the Ballroom, with her arms resting on the desk in front of her. Based on the discarded concert tickets and the half-empty packet of gingernuts being used as a paperweight it was Lloyd's desk.

She sat up a little straighter and looked around, spinning the chair so that she didn't need to concern herself with how stiff her neck was. The light pouring in through the wall of windows looked bright enough to suggest it was a civilised time of the morning, and a quick squint at her watch told her that it was nearly half-seven.

A loud snore erupted from Charlie, who was face down on the blue sofa against the opposite wall with the knuckles of his left hand scraping the floor. He snorted a second time, mumbled something incomprehensible, and then resettled into silence.

Charlie's wheezing had disturbed the only other person Peggy could see. Even though his eyes were still closed, Andrew looked distinctly unimpressed to have been disturbed. He scratched the top of his head and then blinked himself awake. When he caught sight of Peggy he jumped in surprise.

'Christ,' Andrew said through a yawn, rubbing his face with his hands. 'You scared the hell out of me.'

Peggy waved a hand tiredly and didn't really care whether it was interpreted as an apology or a brush-off. She yawned widely too, stretching her arms above her head as she stood up and tried to rid her right foot of pins and needles.

'What time is it?' Andrew grumbled, also standing up and picking at his wrinkled shirt in disgust. He wrapped the threadbare blanket he'd found in a cupboard the night before more tightly around his shoulders.

'Half-seven,' Peggy replied just as one of the double doors opened.

Lloyd appeared, carrying a tray with four mugs. 'Oh good, you're all awake!'

He kicked the door, and it slammed closed behind him.

'We are *not* all awake,' moaned Charlie, his voice muffled by the sofa cushion in his mouth. 'Christ, Lloyd, keep it down.'

Peggy gratefully accepted her mug of coffee from Lloyd. 'Thanks.'

'No problem,' Lloyd replied with a grin, handing a mug to Andrew, and then placing one on the floor next to the sofa for Charlie. 'Jen left an hour ago. She was going to pop home for a shower but promised to come back with breakfast. She shouldn't be too much longer.'

As if on cue, the door opened again.

It wasn't Jen, but DCI Higson, who was in the Ballroom far earlier than Peggy had ever known him to be. He often didn't make an appearance until well after nine.

'Sir?' Andrew asked, staring in confusion at his boss over the rim of his coffee mug. 'What are you doing here?'

Higson raised his eyebrows at Andrew. 'Oh, I'm sorry, Joyce, I was under the impression that I worked here. Is my presence disturbing you?'

Peggy tried not to laugh as it took Andrew's brain a lot longer than usual to catch up with the fact that he'd possibly just insulted his DCI.

'I didn't mean that,' Andrew stammered slightly. 'I just meant, er, well-'

'Shut up before you do yourself an injury,' Higson said as he lowered himself into his chair with a mild groan. 'Now, Joyce, do you want to explain to me why it looks like I'm running a B&B?'

Before Andrew could formulate a reply, Higson looked at Lloyd. 'Give me Charlie Boy's coffee.'

Charlie made a feeble attempt to grab the mug before Lloyd swiped it and handed it over to Higson as requested.

Peggy watched as Andrew used this little interlude to compose himself, taking one large gulp of coffee and shaking his shoulders a little.

'Well, sir, we were working on locating the jewellery stolen by Arthur Havers and Jacob Selsby,' Andrew explained once Higson had put the mug down, professional mask firmly back in place. 'Miss Swan was able to give us the location of the jewels after speaking to Havers.'

'Good work, Miss Swan,' Higson, raising his coffee mug towards Peggy in a toast. He looked at Andrew's desk, where the jewellery was all laid out after being photographed again. 'I take it that's all of it?'

'Yes, sir,' Andrew replied. 'DS Cusack and DC Parker catalogued and photographed each piece in turn. We also have a full record of where every item came from.'

'Courtesy of Arthur Havers, I presume?' Higson grinned smugly. He was fully aware of how Andrew still felt about the 'spooky' side of his job and took great pleasure in making him squirm whenever it came up.

Andrew nodded once; he didn't have the energy to rise to one of Higson's taunts.

Higson just smiled again and gestured towards Peggy. 'Miss Swan, throw those biscuits over here, would you?'

Peggy picked up the gingernuts and tossed them towards Higson, who caught them neatly in one large hand.

'But, Joyce, you still haven't explained why you, Parker, and Their Majesties One and Two are all here so early,' Higson continued as he noisily untwisted the top of the biscuit packet.

'We didn't actually finish cataloguing everything until just after four o'clock,' Andrew said with a grimace. 'There didn't seem much point in going home at the time.'

'And you look like you were recently drowned, because…?' Higson prompted.

'I, er, was pushed into the canal,' Andrew admitted sheepishly, the tips of his ears reddening slightly in embarrassment as he tried to subtly discard the blanket he'd been clinging to.

'You were *pushed* into the canal?' Higson repeated. 'Who by? Swan? Either of them.'

Andrew scowled. 'By Arthur Havers, sir.'

Higson was silent for a long moment, before he laughed loudly, coffee sloshing threateningly towards the rim of the mug. 'Well, that's a bit of a shame when you've got a meeting about a new case in an hour. *All of you.*'

Charlie moaned in distress again.

'Well, no, actually not you, Swan,' Higson corrected. 'Though as you're here you might as well make yourself useful. Greggs will be open in a bit; go and get me two of anything you think I'll like.'

'Sir, I'd really appreciate the opportunity to run home and get changed first,' Andrew said, looking a little desperate.

'No need,' Higson replied, waving a biscuit airily. 'I'm sure nobody will mind that you look bloody terrible.'

Peggy glanced over at a very disgruntled Andrew, and she might have been inclined to feel sorry for him if she hadn't also slept in her clothes.

'But sir-' Andrew began his protest in earnest but stopped immediately when Higson held up his hand.

'It's alright, mate,' Lloyd said cheerfully.

His eyes widened at Andrew's glare, and he cleared his throat as he attempted to look contrite. 'I mean, *sir*. I've got some spare clothes downstairs. You can borrow them if you like.'

Based on the face that Andrew made in response to that offer,

Peggy thought that borrowing Lloyd's clothes was the absolute last thing he wanted to do. When Andrew's expression finally morphed into pained resignation, she had to cover her mouth to stifle the laugh trying to claw its way out.

'Thank you, Lloyd,' Andrew replied tightly, and Peggy had to disguise her giggle with a cough.

She wasn't quite quick enough though, and Andrew glared at her as though she'd committed the most serious of betrayals.

'I don't know why you're laughing,' Andrew snapped, folding his arms. 'You look like you've been dragged through a hedge backwards.'

Peggy couldn't help it. As Andrew's face grew even stonier, a desperately hysterical bleat of laughter - the sort that only comes from the truly exhausted - bubbled from Peggy's lips. She laughed so hard she had to sit down again a few seconds later.

'Peg, I love you, but can you keep it down?' Charlie grumbled as he struggled into a sitting position.

'I'm sorry,' Peggy said, wiping her eyes. 'I'm so sorry.'

Peggy clamped her eyes shut until Higson started speaking again. As long as she didn't catch anyone's eye, she'd be fine.

'Right, well, before it bloody well turns into *The Clothes Show* in here, can everyone just sit down and shut up for a second?' Higson griped.

The Ballroom door opened once more, and Higson threw up his hands in annoyance.

This time it was a freshly showered Jen carrying a paper bag that Peggy hoped contained breakfast, because by that point she was seriously considering just asking Higson to hand over one of Lloyd's biscuits.

'What's going on?' Jen asked as she frowned, looking around at everyone.

'Oh good, a grown-up's finally arrived,' Higson said, shaking his head. 'Sit down, Cusack. You've got a new case.'

Jen sat down, but only after passing out custard tarts to everyone first. Higson looked positively delighted, and even Andrew managed to crack a smile in thanks.

'Right,' Higson said, spraying crumbs everywhere again. 'What can any of you tell me about Lady Bancroft's Rose?'

'What?' Lloyd asked. 'Is this like a *Gardener's World* thing? Because I don't think any of us are Geoff Hamilton.'

'No, you utter nonce,' Higson said, rolling his eyes. He looked directly at Andrew. 'And I thought you were supposed to be bright, Joyce!'

Andrew looked so put out that Peggy had to breathe through her nose to avoid dissolving into giggles again. She seriously needed to get a grip; and some sleep. She *really* needed some sleep.

'*Lady Bancroft's Rose* is a play,' Higson explained, looking around at all of them in expectation. 'Nothing? From any of you? Uncultured swine!'

'Er, do you like this play, boss?' Lloyd asked carefully. He'd eaten his custard tart so quickly that Peggy thought it might have been inhaled in reasonable fear of Higson suddenly demanding it for himself.

'I couldn't give two hoots about the play,' Higson replied, obviously offended by Lloyd's suggestion. 'But I do care that it's supposedly cursed.'

'Cursed?' Andrew groaned disbelievingly. 'Oh, come off it.'

Peggy added 'curses' to her ever-growing list of things that Andrew was terribly sceptical of, placing it right between 'wizards' and the 'Beast of Bodmin Moor'.

Higson folded his arms, custard tart fully consumed. 'The Manchester Curse. The play's only been performed three times in Manchester since 1932, and each time one of the actors has died in suspicious circumstances on opening night.'

'What happened to them?' Lloyd asked, leaning forward on

his elbows in anticipation.

'The first was electrocuted on stage in his final scene,' Higson replied, lowering his voice as though telling a ghost story. 'The second fell down a flight of stairs and broke her neck during the interval, and the last one, back in seventy-three, had a heart attack five minutes before the curtain went up.'

Andrew's eyebrows performed a complicated little wiggle that Peggy recognised as a sign that he was about to transform into Captain Cynicism. She fleetingly wondered when she'd developed the ability to read him like an open book.

Andrew folded his arms in a mirror image of Higson. 'Right, so there was an accident, another accident, and a death from natural causes. Yet somehow that all adds up to a curse?'

'Well, they do say the Scottish Play is cursed, don't they?' Jen said.

'You mean *Macbeth*,' Andrew corrected impatiently. 'Why does everyone get so het up about this sort of thing when it comes to plays? Theatres are dangerous places. Plenty of opportunity for something to go wrong. It's not cursed.'

'Stow your pessimism, Joyce,' Higson ordered pointedly. 'Now, a production of *Lady Bancroft* is due to open at the Court Theatre next Wednesday.'

'Oh, I own the Court,' Charlie piped up from the sofa, nodding his head consideringly. 'Well, I *will*.'

Andrew stared at Charlie silently until the younger man looked suitably chastised.

'I was just saying,' Charlie mumbled, terribly offended.

'The cast's getting a bit twitchy about it. There've been a few unexplained events that have them on edge,' Higson added.

'So, they all think it's cursed, but they're putting on the play anyway?' Andrew laughed disbelievingly.

'You can't stifle art, Joycie,' Charlie said, as though imparting a great wisdom.

'Are you still here, Charlie Boy?' Higson asked sharply. 'You should be at least halfway to my next breakfast by now.'

Charlie grimaced at Peggy, and she just shrugged in return.

'You said you wanted to be helpful,' Peggy argued.

'This isn't exactly what I meant,' Charlie complained, checking his pocket for his wallet. 'Ugh, fine. I'll see you later.'

Peggy waved as her brother trudged out of the room, muttering under his breath.

'What's this all got to do with us though?' Jen asked Higson. 'Are we supposed to look into the three deaths before the play opens? Because that sounds like a lot for six days.'

Higson shook his head. 'No. The director of the play has approached GMP multiple times in the past few days, concerned about a possible threat to his actors. Nobody else seems to think it's worth investigating though, so it's ours.'

'Hang on, you want us to investigate a *current* case?' Andrew asked, and he suddenly looked an awful lot brighter than he had a moment ago. He obviously didn't even care that said case had been deemed so obviously pointless that literally nobody else wanted anything to do with it.

Higson flapped a hand dismissively. 'Don't get carried away.'

'Do you think it's a serial killer?' Lloyd asked, looking a combination of excited and terrified.

'That's unlikely when the murders span fifty years, and it's been nearly fifteen years since the last one,' Jen said, clearly thinking it through. 'Unless we have a very sprightly killer.'

'You're not spending a week chasing a serial killer, Parker, so relax,' Higson sighed.

Andrew frowned again. 'What are we supposed to be doing?'

'Well, Joyce, I'm glad you asked,' Higson replied, clasping his hands on his stomach and leaning back in his chair.

Uh oh, thought Peggy as she watched Higson's feigned casualness not quite cover the spark of amusement in his eyes. It was clear that whatever he was about to say was something likely designed to irritate Andrew beyond belief.

'You'll be making sure nobody tries to off one of the actors,' Higson said as his smile widened. 'So, it looks like you'll get to do some *real* police work after all.'

Andrew's mouth dropped open in horror. 'Babysitting?'

'Call it what you like, Joyce,' Higson said with a shrug. 'But you'll be shadowing the cast whenever they're in the theatre for the next six days, until opening night is over and done with.'

Then Higson turned his attention to Peggy.

'Yes?' she asked, aiming for confident and fighting the urge to fidget. Up to then, she'd thought that she was just going to have to pop to the theatre, say 'nope, nothing useful' and then she'd be able to head home to get some sleep, but something about the sharpness in Higson's eyes suggested otherwise.

'And you, Miss Swan,' Higson continued, 'are contractually obliged to lend your specific skills to this case. The cast believes they are being haunted by a restless spirit.'

'Haunted?' Peggy repeated as though she'd never heard the word before.

'You know, ghosty-ghosty spooky-spook,' Higson replied, obviously very amused with himself as he waggled his fingers towards her. 'There's been stories of an active spirit in that place since the day it was built. You need to make sure that it isn't a murderous ghost looking for vengeance, alright?'

'You want Peggy to contact a potentially murderous spirit?' Andrew asked, clearly alarmed. 'That's a terrible idea!'

'Perhaps, but you don't really believe in the potentially murderous spirit anyway, Joyce, so you don't need to worry about it, do you?' Higson said with a mocking widening of his eyes.

Peggy knew that Higson's conclusion was slightly incorrect. It wasn't that Andrew didn't believe in the idea of a murderous ghost; it was that he didn't *want* to believe in it. She reasoned it was probably quite a bizarre feeling to be worried about something you could never quite accept as real.

'I'm certain that Miss Swan is perfectly capable of handling whatever she uncovers,' Higson added.

'What makes them think that there's a vengeful spirit?' Jen asked, salvaging the situation as always.

'Things being moved, props being smashed; that sort of thing.' Higson had another biscuit.

'So let them all quit and then cancel the production,' Andrew said with the complete confidence of someone stating what they believed to be the only obvious conclusion. 'Problem solved.'

'Well, yeah, but only until the next time someone tries to put on the play in Manchester, right?' Lloyd asked. 'If it is a vengeful ghost, I mean, wouldn't we just be looking at a death being delayed, rather than prevented?'

Higson looked at Lloyd in astonishment. 'Well, Parker, that was actually approaching insightful.'

'Thank you, boss.' Lloyd grinned.

'Which is why Miss Swan will be joining you all at the theatre to find out whether there is a spirit or not,' Higson concluded with a loud clap of his hands. 'Right, off you all pop to the Court. Oh, the director - *Cohen* - might have a bit of a sore head this morning. He didn't seem to be coping too well with the vat of whiskey he was downing last night.'

'Hang on,' Andrew said incredulously. 'Did you meet this guy in the pub?'

'Where else would I have met him?' Higson asked. He somehow managed to make it sound like Andrew was asking a terribly unreasonable question.

'Where else indeed?' Andrew sighed and pinched the bridge of his nose. 'Alright, let's go then.'

'I'll get those clothes out for you, sir,' Lloyd said as he hopped out of his chair. 'You're a bit taller than me, but I'm sure it will be fine.'

Peggy glanced between the two of them. There was a height difference of a good four inches, so she thought 'fine' was probably pushing it.

'Oh, and Joyce?' Higson called as Andrew slowly followed Lloyd like he'd been condemned to death.

'Yes?' Andrew asked with all the enthusiasm of a bone-tired man being led towards his own inevitable demise.

Higson smiled benignly. 'Happy birthday.'

* * *

'You look fine, sir,' Jen assured Andrew when he paused for the third time, his hand raised, ready to knock on the stage door at the rear of the Court Theatre. 'Honestly.'

Maybe if she hadn't added that 'honestly' Andrew could have just about believed her.

Actually, no, he couldn't, because he'd still have Peggy shooting him amused glances whenever she thought he wasn't watching. That, and the fact that he was fairly certain that the smell of dank canal water wasn't just in his imagination.

Andrew looked down at himself one last time with a sigh. He was wearing jeans to work for the first time in his entire career; jeans which were at least three inches too short. At least Lloyd had come up trumps with a plain white t-shirt, rather than something emblazoned with some obscure band logo, as Andrew had feared. The only saving grace was that his suit jacket had been tucked up safely on the backseat of his Belmont when he'd taken his little swim in the canal, so at least he had that to remind him that he was supposed to be a Detective Inspector.

The trainers, however, were just as bad as the jeans. Lloyd had seemed unreasonably hesitant to hand them over, behaving as though they were some greatly prized possessions, and Andrew would have gladly avoided accepting them if it weren't for the fact that his own loafers were still sodden. He'd had no choice but to wedge his feet into the far too tight, far too white monstrosities.

To be fair to them, Lloyd and Peggy were both still wearing the same clothes as the night before, so at least Andrew wasn't entirely alone in the subpar appearance department.

Andrew steeled himself and finally knocked on the door, still feeling underprepared and off-balance about the whole morning.

Almost immediately, the door opened to reveal a tall, lanky man in his late forties, perhaps a little younger. He had the faintly glowing tan of someone who'd recently been abroad, but the tightness around his eyes suggested that there hadn't been any relaxation in his life lately.

'Albany Cohen?' Andrew guessed.

'Yes,' Cohen replied, raising an eyebrow.

'Detective Inspector Andrew Joyce,' Andrew stated as he showed Cohen his identification. 'These are my colleagues, Detective Sergeant Jennifer Cusack, and Detective Constable Lloyd Parker.'

Andrew then gestured towards Peggy, hesitating, as always, over what label to give her this time round. 'This is Margaret *Jones*. She's consulting on this case for us.'

'Ah, the consultant!' Cohen said in a thick New York accent, eyes sparkling suddenly as he reached out to shake Peggy's hand enthusiastically. 'Yes, DCI Higson mentioned you. Come on in, come on in. Please.'

Before Andrew could blink, Cohen had ushered Peggy through the door and into the dimly lit corridor beyond.

By the time he, Jen and Lloyd had followed, Cohen was already leading their 'consultant' up a staircase to the first floor, chattering at her the whole time.

'We can talk in my office,' Cohen called back to the stragglers as he gestured towards a room halfway down the hallway.

Cohen's office was bright and airy, in direct contrast to the sepia-tinged dinginess of the inner hallways of the Court. An enormous, walnut desk dominated the space in front of the window, which itself looked out over the city. Every single flat surface held bundles of papers covered in unintelligible scribbles, and there was even a pile of paper stacked on top of a lampshade in the corner in what had to be the most flagrant fire hazard Andrew had ever seen.

'This is Vic Hill, my stage manager,' Cohen said as he gestured towards where a woman with dark hair and even darker eyes was leaning against the far wall.

Andrew nodded to her and quickly recapped their introductions as he shook her hand.

Peggy attempted to tuck herself away behind Jen and Lloyd. She was never one to welcome enthusiastic interest in her 'talents', and by now Andrew was used to seeing Peggy make efforts to conceal herself.

Cohen was having absolutely none of it though, and he doubled back across the room to steer Peggy to one of the chairs on the opposite side of the desk to where he then sat himself a few seconds later.

Andrew took the vacant seat next to Peggy as Jen and Lloyd hovered nearby. The cuffs of his borrowed jeans hiked up even further and Andrew shifted as subtly as possible, trying to find a comfortable way to sit that didn't make him look like a poorly dressed teenager at Parents' Evening.

'Are you alright over there?' Peggy whispered to him as Cohen fussed with a pile of papers, clearly looking for something.

Andrew just grimaced in reply and tried to stop fidgeting. He was very aware of Vic's questioning gaze on him.

'Ah, here,' Cohen said, producing a page from the stack and sliding it across the deep desk towards Andrew. 'These are the details of the cast. Names, addresses, etcetera. I can get that for everyone attached to the production if that would be useful.'

'Thank you, yes it would,' Andrew said as he scanned the page in front of him. He frowned as he turned the paper over to find nothing on the back. 'Only four names?'

Cohen nodded. 'Only four characters. It was quite an experimental work for its time.'

Andrew could tell that Cohen was about to launch into an enthusiastic presentation about the play, which he didn't have the energy to listen to just then. 'Of course. Mr Cohen, would you mind explaining exactly why you've contacted the police regarding the production next week? I know you've already spoken to DCI Higson, but I'd appreciate hearing the details directly from you.'

Any sort of detail would be better than the vague rundown they'd had from Higson, but Andrew was going to keep that thought to himself.

'Sure, no problem,' Cohen replied, clasping his hands together on the desk, enthusiasm only partially dimmed. 'So, the play was written in 1861 by Dylan Hopkins. It was first performed that year, and there's no record of any problems with a single production in the nineteenth century, of which there were many.

'I don't know how familiar you all are with the history of British theatre, but back then audiences were showing a lot of love for dramatic comedies. *Lady Bancroft's Rose* was incredibly popular; the small cast and simple staging meant it worked just as well in smaller theatres as it did in more impressive surroundings.'

'I'll be honest, Mr Cohen, I've never heard of it,' Andrew said, neatly folding the piece of paper he was holding.

'Most people haven't,' Cohen replied with a shrug. 'As things do, it fell out of favour over time, particularly once the twentieth century hit. It was still popular enough that the Court wanted to stage a production in the summer of 1932, with Clarence Wright in the role of Sebastian. Sebastian's the young hero of the story, and Wright was like the Tom Cruise of the theatre world. So far, so straightforward, right?

'Anyway, the production was going down a storm on opening night, even though the character of Sebastian was actually being performed by Wright's standby: a local kid named Alistair Tunham.'

'What happened to Wright?' Andrew asked.

'Well, nobody really knows,' Cohen said with another shrug. 'He claimed that a family tragedy took him back to London that afternoon. However, there was also a rumour that Wright had been involved in a tryst with the leading lady, and that her husband was planning to confront Wright about it on opening night.

'Whatever the reason, Alistair Tunham was on stage that night instead, and the audience loved him, even though he wasn't the great Clarence Wright.

'In the final scene, Sebastian re-enters the Bancroft house in search of his lover Isabella. He's expecting a full house because the family had been planning to host a party, but he finds the rooms in darkness instead. In the original stage directions he lights a lamp, but with the way theatres were nervous about fire back then, the director had chosen a more contemporary staging: Tunham was supposed to flick a light switch.

'The switch wasn't supposed to be connected to anything. It was a dummy, so when he flicked the switch the stage lights would be brought up.'

'And that's not what happened?' Andrew asked, even though he already knew exactly where the story was heading.

'Tunham came on stage to rapturous applause, delivered his line in the dark and then hit the light switch. He was electrocuted right there in front of six hundred people,' Cohen replied sombrely. 'The audience thought it was part of the performance until the lights didn't come back on.'

Andrew raised his eyebrows. Okay, that had all been suitably dramatic so far. 'So, the switch was accidentally connected to the power for some reason? And then what? A loose connection? Faulty wiring? It *was* the twenties.'

Cohen shook his head slowly. 'No, Detective Inspector. The switch had been tampered with and hooked up to the electricity supply. Alistair Tunham's death was premeditated. Whether it was meant for him, or for Clarence Wright, that switch was meant to kill.'

Andrew looked around at his colleagues. Lloyd was staring wide-eyed at Cohen, as though he were listening to a particularly gripping bedtime story, and even Jen looked entirely absorbed. Andrew couldn't deny that Cohen was a good storyteller.

'And then there's the note, of course,' Cohen added.

'What note?' Lloyd gasped out, and then winced apologetically at Andrew when he received a sharp glare.

'This note,' Cohen replied as he opened a drawer in his desk with a definite flourish. He pulled out what seemed to be a photo frame and handed it to Andrew. 'They found it in Tunham's dressing room. The theatre's kept it ever since.'

Andrew frowned at the object he'd just been handed. It was a wooden frame, no bigger than a notebook, holding a piece of paper behind the glass. The paper was ragged and torn on one edge, and scribbled in black ink was a phrase Andrew recognised:

The deceitfulness of the wicked shall destroy them.

'It's from Proverbs,' Cohen explained before Andrew could. 'Nobody at the time could explain why. It didn't seem to have any relation to Alistair Tunham whatsoever.'

'Was Tunham's death ruled an accident?' Andrew asked as the frame made its way to Jen and Lloyd.

'Unexplained,' Cohen said. 'Which is probably the best anybody could have hoped for back then. They tried to pin it on one of the maintenance guys who worked here at the time, but it looks like that was mostly out of desperation for someone to point the finger at than anything concrete. He was never charged. I mean, the police didn't even keep the note, did they? I don't think they took it too seriously. It might have been a different story if Clarence Wright had been the one to die.'

'And the two other deaths that occurred?' Andrew asked because he needed more to work with than a half-baked ghost story.

'One in forty-seven. The play was on at the Palace that time,' Cohen confirmed with a nod. 'Henriette St. Clair had the role of Lady Bancroft. She'd actually been the standby for the Isabella role in the thirty-two production. A week before opening night she apparently started seeing what she described as a 'man made of shadows' following her around the theatre.'

Peggy shivered slightly next to him, and Andrew couldn't blame her. He didn't think it likely that anyone would enjoy trying to find a murderous 'man made of shadows', no matter how unlikely.

'Opening night was going well for everyone but Henriette,' Cohen continued, firmly back in storyteller mode. 'A note had been left in her dressing room that afternoon.'

'Another passage from Proverbs?' Andrew asked.

'Bingo!' Cohen slapped his palms down on the desk. 'She obviously knew the story of the note on Alistair's door, and by all accounts could barely get her lines out, she was trembling so much with fright. When the interval came, it looks like she went up one of the narrow staircases at the back of the theatre – nobody knows why, as she had no business being there – before falling down it and breaking her neck. Her standby performed the second half of the play, mostly to avoid panic, I think.'

Andrew made a face of distaste at the thought.

'Henriette's note was significantly longer than Alistair's,' Cohen added. He flipped through a notebook in front of him. 'I've got it here somewhere. Here: *Haughty eyes, a lying tongue,* hands that shed innocent blood. A heart that deviseth wicked plots, feet that are swift to run into mischief. A deceitful witness that uttereth lies, and him that soweth discord among brethren.'

'Hefty,' muttered Lloyd.

'Exactly. Anyway, it all came out in the papers, of course,' Cohen explained. 'That's when the rumours of the play being cursed began. People love a good curse, don't they?'

Andrew didn't, but he magnanimously ignored the comment.

'The play wasn't staged in Manchester again until seventy-three, and that was back here at the Court,' Cohen continued. 'That time, the victim hadn't even made it to the stage. The actor playing Lord Bancroft – Peter McClellan – was already pretty well known for being a heavy drinker, but in the final week of rehearsals he was, by all accounts, paralytically drunk from morning to night.'

'Had he reported seeing anything strange?' Jen asked. Andrew suspected that it was because he hadn't kept the disdain away from his expression as successfully as he'd thought, leaving his DS to salvage the situation.

Cohen nodded. 'He said that a man had come out of his mirror and told him that he was going to die.'

'*Out* of his mirror?' Andrew asked. 'What?'

'Yeah, in his dressing room,' Cohen said. He shivered slightly and then laughed at himself. 'God, sorry, I've always thought that bit was really creepy.'

He held his hands up. 'Anyway, just before the curtain was due to go up, he dropped dead of a heart attack in his dressing room.'

'Was there a note that time?' Peggy asked, surprising Andrew enough that he turned away from Cohen to look at her instead. On the few occasions that she'd accompanied them to speak to anyone connected to a case – anyone still living, anyway – she'd kept quiet.

'It was written on the mirror, in black lipstick, of all things,'

Cohen confirmed grimly as he reached for a notebook on his desk and read, '*He that gathereth treasures by a lying tongue shall stumble upon the shades of death.*'

Andrew shivered slightly, and then puffed up his cheeks to blow out a noisy breath to cover it. 'Even if an actor questioned the validity of the curse theory - which, to be clear, I also do – why would any of them jump at the chance to be in a production of this play? I'll be candid, Mr Cohen, I'm unsure why you'd even try to put this on here in Manchester.'

'Well, that's not entirely down to me,' Cohen replied. 'It's come up a few times over the years as an option, but last summer, we'd just finished *The Importance of Being Earnest* here, and the bigwigs reached out to request that I open their fundraising season with *Lady Bancroft*.'

Vic grimaced as she took a step away from the wall. 'I think they were hoping that the papers would dig up the previous issues with productions, and it would generate interest, which would then generate ticket sales. The producers are thrilled.'

'You can't stifle art,' Andrew muttered to himself, repeating Charlie's words.

'Sorry, what?' Cohen frowned.

'Oh, nothing, Mr Cohen,' Andrew said, pasting on a professional smile. 'Tunham, St. Clair and McClellan were all playing different characters, correct?'

'That's right,' Cohen confirmed. 'So, I can see why Lavinia is more than a little jumpy, as her character is the only one left.'

'Lavinia?' Andrew asked aloud before unfolding the cast information to scan the names again.

'Lavinia Heathcote. She was my Cecily in *Earnest* last year, and a perfect fit for Isabella in *Lady Bancroft*. Lavinia's a real professional, you know, she's been doing all this since she was a little kid. She doesn't believe in any of the curse rumours, and she jumped at the chance to be a part of this. At first, at least.'

'So, what's happened to change her mind?' Andrew asked. Finally, a question with an answer he was actually interested in because this was where there might be something for him to investigate.

'It started with a few things being moved around on Tuesday morning; scripts, notes, that sort of thing,' Cohen said. 'There are people in and out of backstage all the time, so it's not unusual for things to get misplaced. But then after lunch, one of her costumes was cut into ribbons and left on the floor of her dressing room. We'd only been in the theatre for a few hours; we'd been in a rehearsal space until this week.'

'Disgruntled castmate, maybe?' Jen suggested.

'Always a possibility in this business,' Cohen admitted. 'But that doesn't explain last night.'

'What happened last night, Mr Cohen?' Andrew asked. Whatever it was, it must have been only hours before Higson had encountered Cohen at the pub.

Cohen smiled grimly. 'Last night, just as she was heading home, Lavinia swears that she saw someone at the other end of the hallway, even though nobody should have been up on the second floor but her.'

'Who?' Andrew pressed.

'She doesn't know,' Cohen replied. 'She said that she could only describe it as the figure of a man, but that he looked like he was made of shadows; like he couldn't really be there. Vic saw him too, and she's really not the flighty type.'

There was a loud knock on the door, and everyone jumped in fright.

'Jesus Christ.' Andrew chastised himself for getting caught up in the story.

Cohen cleared his throat. 'Come in!'

The door creaked open, and everyone turned to face it.

A young woman appeared, confusion creasing her face as she

realised that everyone was staring at her.

'Um, hello?' she said in a high, tinkly voice that made Andrew think of fairies.

'Ah, Lavinia, come in,' Cohen said with a smile, rising to his feet. 'We were just talking about you.'

'All good things, I hope?' Lavinia smiled, and Andrew realised that while the fairy description still held, Lavinia Heathcote actually spoke like a much, much gigglier version of Peggy.

'Always,' Cohen said, beaming at her before pointing at Andrew. 'This is Detective Inspector Andrew Joyce, Lavinia. He and his colleagues are here to make sure that everything goes smoothly this week.'

'Oh,' Lavinia said brightly as she crossed the room towards Andrew, holding her hand out.

Andrew stumbled to his feet, once again mortifyingly aware of the way he was dressed and shook Lavinia's hand. 'Nice to meet you, Miss Heathcote.'

'Hi,' Lavinia said, directing her smile to everyone individually, before returning the full wattage of it to Andrew. 'I'm sorry to interrupt, but I just need to give Albany a message, if that's alright?'

'Go ahead.' Andrew then realised that he probably should have let go of Lavinia's hand a good few seconds earlier. He practically snatched his arm back and ignored the way that Lloyd was pretending that he wasn't laughing at him.

Lavinia gave him one more smile before turning to Cohen. 'I was on my way to the auditorium when Katie asked if I could get you to pop down to see her. It's about the opening night gala.'

'More bureaucratic nonsense, I imagine,' Cohen said with a loud sigh. 'You'd think people running a charity would feel more charitable towards the people putting on a production for their benefit.'

'The theatre?' Andrew asked.

'Oh no,' Lavinia replied, shaking her head. 'The gala opening night is always for a local charity. Last year it was the children's hospital. This year it's for the Winshire Foundation.'

Peggy made an odd, strangled sound, and Andrew turned to look at her. She was staring at Lavinia as though something was terribly wrong. *Christ*, he hoped the so-called Shadow Man hadn't appeared somewhere.

'Sorry,' Peggy choked out, 'did you say the Winshire Foundation?'

'Yes.' Lavinia replied slowly. She was still smiling, but it looked slightly strained in the face of Peggy's intense stare. 'It's for deprived m-'

'Yes, I know what it's for,' Peggy interjected, rising to her feet so quickly that the chair legs scraped noisily along the floor. 'Excuse me.'

Peggy bolted from the room.

'Is she alright?' Lavinia asked, looking around at everyone else, utterly mystified. 'Did I say something wrong?'

'Excuse me a moment, Mr Cohen,' Andrew said hurriedly. 'You too, Miss Heathcote.'

Andrew left the office without waiting for a response and jogged down the staircase as quickly as the pinch of his too-tight shoes would allow. He hoped that Peggy had gone in that direction because if she'd disappeared off into the theatre itself, he had no idea how he'd find her.

He pulled open the door they'd come in through and was gratified to see that Peggy was just outside.

He was less gratified to see that she was sitting on the filthy concrete, with her head between her knees as though she thought she might be sick.

'Jesus, Peggy, what the hell was that about?' Andrew asked as he crouched down in front of her. He tapped her on the elbow lightly when she didn't initially respond. 'Hey, seriously, what's wrong?'

Peggy finally raised her head, and she definitely looked more than a little green around the gills. Maybe it was the late-night chips?

'What's wrong?' Andrew repeated, somewhat concerned that if she didn't say something quickly, he was going to have to move out of this squat before Lloyd's ridiculous jeans tore at the seams.

'The charity night opening gala,' Peggy said, swallowing heavily.

'Yeah, the thing for the Wiltshire whatever?' Andrew said, shrugging.

He was still confused about why she looked so distraught. Maybe Peggy didn't like charity? No, that was patently ridiculous even if you didn't take into account the fact that she'd basically adopted a ghost or hadn't yet killed her brother; surely those two things alone made her virtually saintly.

'The *Winshire* Foundation,' Peggy corrected him, as though that were somehow important.

She smiled, but it wasn't really a smile at all. 'It's a charity founded by Caroline Winshire, Countess of Acresfield. It's my mother, Andrew.'

Oh, thought Andrew.

Bollocks.

THREE

After the announcement she'd just made, Peggy expected that Andrew would want to ask her more questions about her mother, and about the unmitigated disaster that was the Peggy/Caroline relationship these days. She'd come to understand early on in their association that Andrew really hated it when questions went unasked, so she was more than a little surprised when he just silently unfolded himself from the crouch he was in and sat down on the floor next to her with nothing more than a heavy sigh.

For a long moment, the quiet between them was broken only by the muted sound of traffic passing by on the other side of the Court.

'Sorry,' said Peggy eventually, the beginnings of embarrassment creeping up on her. Jesus, she was thirty-five years old; that surely meant she should possess enough maturity to deal with the mere mention of her mother.

'You don't need to apologise.' Andrew nudged her shoulder with his own. 'I'm sorry we didn't know about her involvement before we got here. I would have told you if I'd known, you know that, right?'

'I know you would have,' Peggy said, and that was the truth. 'It's not like she's actually in there, is it? I shouldn't have run out like that.'

'We'll have it all wrapped up by opening night,' Andrew promised. 'You won't have to cross paths with her.'

Oh God. Peggy hadn't actually got that far in her thinking. She'd heard 'Winshire', and her brain had ground to a screeching halt. The unexpected possibility of being in the same place as her mother was enough to make her stomach clench again.

'I thought she'd gone back to London before Christmas anyway,' Andrew added, clearly unable to stop himself from prying just a little. The predictability was almost enough to make Peggy smile.

'Oh, she did,' Peggy scoffed, 'but she's never been one to miss an opportunity to be the centre of attention; a charity gala is right up her street. Plus, she needs to introduce Edgar to the whole Cheshire set properly.'

The bitterness burned like acid in her mouth when she uttered her former fiancé's name, flaring as she corrected herself with a sneer, 'Well, *reintroduce* him, I suppose.'

'Peg,' Andrew sighed, and with one word he managed to sound so sympathetically miserable on her behalf that Peggy had to wrench herself back towards neutral ground before she did something awfully humiliating like burst into tears.

'Look, it's fine,' Peggy said, shuffling slightly further away in a bid for self-preservation. 'Like you said, we'll be well done before opening night. Fingers crossed for no signs of a murderous ghost, right?'

Andrew frowned as Peggy stood up. 'You're sure about going back in there right now?'

'Of course,' Peggy hoped that she sounded suitably nonchalant. She didn't really have a choice anyway, did she? It's not as though she wanted to have a conversation with DCI Higson about why she'd decided to remove herself from the case.

'Alright,' Andrew agreed eventually. He had a look on his face that suggested he wasn't even remotely fooled by Peggy's sudden show of indifference as he struggled to his feet.

'Andrew?' Peggy grasped his arm to stop him before he could head for the stage door.

'Yeah?'

'Can you not tell anyone, please?' Peggy asked, swallowing heavily. 'About Caroline being my mother, I mean.'

'Of course I won't,' Andrew replied. 'But you'll tell Charlie about this?'

Peggy nodded in agreement. 'And maybe I can be just plain old Margaret Jones this time? Nobody in there needs to know about the title thing.'

'As you wish, Your Highness,' Andrew replied, making an obvious effort to lighten the mood.

Peggy's answering smile was small, but it was there. 'Thank you.'

'Come on,' Andrew said, pulling the door wide and gesturing for Peggy to lead the way. 'We should get back before Cohen completely terrifies Lloyd with another one of his stories.'

'I think we need to have a really good look around,' Peggy said, as they slowly ascended the stairs. She politely chose not to comment on the slight hiss of discomfort Andrew made with every step. 'I haven't seen a single hint of anything odd since we got here, which I think is a bit odd in itself.'

'You do?' Andrew asked as they reached the first floor again. They could hear voices carrying down from the open door of Cohen's office.

'It's an old building, Andrew,' Peggy explained, 'and, alright, that doesn't automatically mean that there'll be ghosts, but it's a theatre. It's the kind of place that people can become really attached to. I'd be surprised if there aren't quite a few spirits in here somewhere. Actors can be the most superstitious people of all.'

'I really don't want it to be a ghost this time,' Andrew grumbled, pausing just before they reached Cohen's office.

'I know.'

'Miss Jones, is that you?' Cohen called from the office.

'Looks like you've got yourself a fan,' Andrew said, raising his eyebrows.

'Don't,' Peggy said, and she thought maybe it had come out a little sharper than she'd meant it to when Andrew recoiled slightly.

Andrew, wisely, remained silent as he followed Peggy back into Cohen's office.

'Are you alright?' Lavinia asked, rushing over to Peggy immediately, eyes wide in concern.

Peggy reeled back in surprise, stepping on Andrew's foot as she did so.

'Oh, yes, I'm fine, thank you. Sorry about that,' Peggy replied sheepishly. 'Custard tarts for breakfast. You know how it is.'

Evidently, Lavinia *didn't* know how it was, as she only blinked in confusion and turned to Andrew, who still looked pained. 'Are you quite well, Detective Inspector?'

'Great, thanks,' Andrew said tightly, hobbling towards the chairs, grumbling as though Peggy had purposefully tried to break his foot.

'I'm so sorry, I didn't catch your name before, Detective...?' Lavinia said to Peggy.

'Oh, I'm not a detective. Margaret Jones.'

'*Not* a detective?' Lavinia tilted her head in obvious bewilderment.

'Peggy's a colleague of ours,' Jen explained, and Peggy took the opportunity to duck away from Lavinia and reclaim her seat.

'She's a consultant,' Andrew added.

'A consultant?' Lavinia looked even more perplexed. Peggy, perhaps uncharitably, thought that at least some of it was feigned.

'Yes,' Peggy confirmed. 'I help with some of the more, um, *inexplicable* aspects of certain cases.'

'Miss Jones is an expert in spirit activity,' Cohen announced, looking as delighted as Higson always did when he got onto this subject.

'Spirits,' Lavinia repeated slowly. 'As in ghosts? You're not serious, are you?'

'Oh no, I am,' Peggy replied evenly. She didn't like talking about what she could do, but she liked it even less when people questioned the validity of it.

'Detective Inspector?' Lavinia turned to Andrew, blinking furiously. 'Surely not?'

Oh sure, ignore me and ask the *man*. Peggy just about stopped herself from rolling her eyes. She wasn't being fair, she knew that. It wasn't Lavinia's fault that Peggy was having a personal crisis, nor was it Lavinia's fault that Peggy had the oddest talent possible.

'I can assure you that we're a much more effective team with Peggy as part of it,' Andrew replied, and Peggy decided that she'd probably forgive him for the overdramatic limping after all.

Lavinia held up her hands towards Peggy. 'Oh, I meant no offence.'

'None taken,' Peggy replied. If Charlie had been there, he probably would have said something about his sister's tone.

'I think we need to do a walk-through of the theatre,' Andrew announced. 'That will give us a chance to understand the layout of the building, and to see any locations where unusual activity has been reported.'

Peggy nodded, pushing herself to her feet.

'Everyone else is downstairs,' Cohen said, glancing at his watch. 'We start work on stage in thirty minutes, so you may want to meet them first. They'll be tied up for a few hours at that point. It would help them to know that the police are taking their concerns seriously.'

'It might be prudent for us to take a look around the stage first then,' Peggy offered, glancing at Andrew for support. 'You know, just in case.'

'I agree,' Andrew replied. He looked over at Jen and Lloyd. 'DS Cusack, can you and Peggy take a good look around the theatre? DI Parker and I will speak to the cast, and we can all meet back in the stalls in half an hour.'

'No problem, sir,' Jen replied. She nodded her head towards the door. 'Peggy?'

'Coming,' Peggy replied.

'Be careful,' Andrew said quietly as Peggy passed him, lightly brushing his fingers against the sleeve of her jacket. 'I'm serious. If there's anything even remotely weirder than the usual, you and Jen get out of there immediately, alright?'

'I thought you didn't believe in curses.'

'I don't, but I do believe that if anyone's going to find one, it's probably you,' Andrew replied seriously.

Peggy wasn't sure whether that was supposed to be a compliment or not, so turned away without comment and followed Jen out of the room.

'Are you alright, Peggy?' Jen asked as she led the way down the corridor. 'You disappeared pretty quickly earlier.'

'Honestly, I'm fine, Jen, thanks,' Peggy replied. She liked Jen a lot, but that didn't mean that she wanted to hash out her personal life with someone else right now. 'It's nothing to worry about, I promise.'

'As long as you're sure.'

Andrew had told Peggy plenty of times that he thought Jen was a particularly good detective, and she'd often proved it when she managed to read people like a book when they were working on a case. Peggy knew that Jen was likely deducing all sorts from Peggy's silence.

'Honestly, it's nothing.' Peggy tried for a big smile. She wasn't naïve enough to think that it would fool Jen entirely, but she hoped it would be enough to put the issue to rest for the time being. 'Now, let's see if we can find someone to talk to.'

'Alright,' Jen agreed reluctantly.

Peggy kept a watchful eye as they twisted through the labyrinthine corridors and down a staircase that led to the stage itself, but there wasn't a hint of anything out of the ordinary.

'There's nothing, Jen,' she said as they stopped. If the numerous signs reminding them to be quiet with increasingly heated punctuation were anything to go by, they'd reached the final door to the stage. 'Absolutely nothing.'

'It does seem odd,' Jen said, pursing her lips. 'I mean, how many spirits did you see at that old cinema a few weeks ago? Four? Five?'

'Something like that. I would have put money on a place like this having significantly more.'

'Maybe they're all on the stage,' Jen suggested. 'Perhaps that's the only place they've ever wanted to be.'

Peggy didn't think that was a completely insane theory, and it was confirmed, to a degree, almost immediately when she swung open the door and saw a figure sitting at the front edge of the stage, legs swinging down into the orchestra pit at the front of the auditorium. 'Oh.'

'Someone's here?' Jen asked, looking around wildly as though maybe this time she'd be able to see them too. After the miracle that was Marnie Driscoll and her ability to appear as solid as you like, most other ghosts were quite a let-down to the Ballroom team.

'Mmhmm,' Peggy confirmed quietly. 'Jen, would you mind staying here for a minute?'

'Peggy, I th–'

'Please.'

'Alright,' Jen agreed eventually, apprehension obvious. 'But you know that if any ghost so much as looks at you the wrong way, DI Joyce will have my head.'

Peggy bristled. 'I won't do anything stupid.'

'Oh, I know,' Jen replied seriously. 'You know what the boss is like, though. He can't help worrying.'

Peggy grumbled to herself as she turned and walked towards the edge of the stage. It was nice to hear that Andrew didn't trust her not to do something he would deem as idiotic. *Well*, that was just brilliant, wasn't it? She'd thought that they were past that.

'Well, someone's in quite the mood, aren't they?' the ghost said, standing up and smirking as he looked Peggy up and down.

'Very observant,' Peggy replied drily, and she watched as the ghost's expression morphed into one of pure surprise.

'Wait, you can see me?' he asked hesitantly before his face broke out into the widest smile Peggy had ever seen on anyone. 'Really, truly?'

Peggy nodded, and the smile grew impossibly larger.

The man whooped loudly. 'This is the best day of my life! Or, *not* life, I suppose!'

Peggy blinked in surprise. She didn't usually get quite such an enthusiastic reaction from the spirits she interacted with; other than Marnie, obviously, but Marnie was a very, very special case.

He appeared to be younger than Peggy – mid-twenties, maybe - and he was as neat as a pin in a double-breasted grey tweed suit. With a straw boater perched on his head he was only a bowtie away from being a convincing extra in *The Great Gatsby*.

The man's lips were stretched so wide it was almost grotesque. 'Are you a mystic? A fortune teller?'

The man's effusive delight reminded Peggy of her brother.

'I saw a fortune teller when my mum took me to the seaside once. Blackpool, I think. She had a parakeet!' the man added, as he clapped his hands together

'Sorry, no parakeets here,' Peggy replied, and she looked around when Jen made a vague snorting sound. 'Just me. Well, my friend Jen is over there. She's a detective.'

'A woman detective!' The man's eyes were now even wider. 'Can she see me too?'

'No, she can't.'

The man shook his head wonderingly. 'What year is it?'

'1987,' Peggy replied.

'Eighty-seven?' The man's eyes bugged. 'Has it really been that long?'

41

Peggy thought back to everything she'd heard from Higson and Cohen earlier that morning and looked hopefully at the young man in front of her. 'Alistair Tunham?'

The man's eyes grew even larger in shock, and he blinked in surprise. 'How on earth did you know that?'

'Your reputation precedes you.'

'I've seen them rehearsing *Lady Bancroft*,' Alistair replied sadly. 'I couldn't believe it at first. Not after what happened to that poor man last time. Are you here because of that? Has something bad happened again? Is that why you're here with a detective?'

Peggy thought carefully about how to answer those questions. 'Well, we're just looking into a few things at the moment.'

'I'm sorry, miss, but I haven't spoken to anyone in such a long time!'

Peggy frowned. 'Nobody at all?'

'Nobody real like you. I suppose I mean nobody *alive*,' Alistair explained grimly. 'The others – the ones like me that were here when I first came back to myself, as it were – had been here for such a long time. Once the war came, and the stage went dark, most just gradually faded over time. The theatre was shut for thirty years after the war ended, you know.'

Oh, Peggy knew all about the closure. She'd heard her father complain about the upkeep costs for the empty shell of the theatre plenty of times when she'd been younger. He'd refused to sell it though, no matter how exorbitant the offers he'd received from interested parties had been. He'd said that he needed to 'safeguard the property for future generations of the Swan family', as though a crumbling structure with no purpose was somehow worth more to him than every offer to revitalise the space could ever be. Peggy was fairly certain that the only reason her father had reopened the theatre in the seventies was because a financial advisor somewhere had presented him with a convincing argument to do so; William Swan was unlikely to agree to anything that didn't ultimately benefit him more so than anybody else.

Peggy had no intention of sharing any of that with Alistair, of course, so she just did her best to look surprised by that fact. 'Gosh, I see. But you've stayed. Why?'

Alistair shrugged. 'I don't think I'd know how to leave even if I wanted to. I love watching the productions, you know, and I've learned a lot in the time I've been here, just by watching and listening to the people who work here, and the audiences that fill these seats. I've heard of the wonderful ways that the world has changed, but I can't leave the building itself.'

'So, you've tried to leave?' Peggy asked carefully.

'Oh yes,' replied Alistair wistfully. 'Once, years ago, bombs were raining down on the city, and all I could do was stand and watch as buildings around me were hit. I was so scared that the theatre would be destroyed. Not because I was in any danger of being killed again – surely that's impossible – but what would happen to me if the theatre wasn't here anymore? Would I be free, or would I just cease to exist?'

Alistair seemed like he might be much more into existentialism than the other ghosts Peggy had encountered. She wondered if she should try and introduce him to Marnie, given that she was still fully convinced that she could live a relatively normal 'life', despite the apparently insignificant fact that she didn't actually *have* a life anymore.

'I'm not entirely alone, I suppose, even though I can barely see the others now,' Alistair continued, face tilted towards the stalls as though he were delivering a soliloquy. 'There's Celia, even if there's not much left of her these days; and the Taylor brothers too, of course. They were perfectly nice chaps once you got past the ventriloquist dummy that Percy always carried with him – *Hercules*, apparently – but I haven't seen either of them in months now.'

Alistair's face darkened suddenly. 'Then there's *him* as well. Though I'd hesitate to call him a person.'

'Who?' Peggy thought she might know already.

'We know him as Jock.' Alistair's voice wavered as his eyes drifted back to Peggy. 'He's not like the rest of us.'

Peggy shivered. 'Who is he, Alistair? Who *was* he?'

Alistair shook his head helplessly. 'I don't know much. They say he's from a time before the theatre even stood here. He does not really speak, and I've never truly seen his face. He always hides in the dark. I fear he is more like the blackest part of a soul, left behind when any goodness or compassion has been removed. People always used to call him the Shadow Man, and now I understand why.'

Alistair laughed, a harsh self-deprecating sound that didn't echo as it would have done if he were alive. It made Peggy uneasy.

'Don't you think it's funny that a *ghost* should be scared of something?' Alistair asked.

No, Peggy didn't think it was funny at all. 'Has this other spirit – this *Jock* - been anywhere near the cast this week?'

'I don't know,' Alistair said again. 'Probably. He does tend to appear in the days before a show. Although even he isn't as active as he used to be.'

'Did you ever see him yourself?' Peggy asked. '*Before?*'

'Back when I was alive you mean?' Alistair raised his eyebrows. 'No, never. I was the standby, you see. I was only told that Clarence Wright had left the production on the morning of our opening. We were all so shocked at the news. I'd been here for every rehearsal, just in case, but the cast looked strong. I'd never dreamt that I'd ever get on stage as Sebastian.'

Alistair paused and screwed up his face. 'I assume that you know the story of the performance that night? Do you know what happened?'

Peggy grimaced. 'We're trying to find out what really happened to you, Alistair.'

'Do you remember anything about that night at all?' Peggy asked. 'Or the days before? Was anyone acting suspiciously?'

Alistair shrugged apologetically. 'I'm sorry. My memories of those days have always been hazy, but, no, I don't believe there is anything useful I could tell you.'

It wasn't surprising to Peggy that Alistair didn't have clear memories of his final moments. She knew from Marnie that for some spirits it was too difficult to remember the circumstances of their own death unless they were really pushed into doing so. Peggy wouldn't push Alistair though; not yet.

'Everything okay, Peggy?' Jen asked.

'All fine,' Peggy replied, and then turned back to Alistair. 'We're going to be here for the next few days, until the gala performance of *Lady Bancroft* is over, so if you want to speak to me about anything you can just come and find me, alright?'

'Thank you.' Alistair was back to smiling widely. 'I'm so sorry, I didn't catch your name, miss?'

'Jones,' Peggy replied. 'Margaret Jones. You can call me Peggy though.'

'Thank you, Miss Peggy.'

Alistair tipped his hat politely and faded slowly until Peggy was looking out into the auditorium.

'He's gone, Jen.'

Jen hesitantly approached where Peggy was standing. 'Did I hear you call him Alistair?'

Peggy nodded. 'Alistair Tunham. The first victim, from 1932.'

'Poor lad,' Jen said, shaking her head. 'What a horrible thing to happen to someone.'

'He doesn't seem to know the specifics of anything that's happened this week,' Peggy explained. 'He's confirmed that we might have a problem though.'

'What?' Jen sounded apprehensive.

'Alistair has given me the names of three of other spirits who are here – they seem to be previous performers, and not particularly active by the sounds of things. However, there is also one more.'

'One more?'

'Yes.' Peggy grimaced. 'Alistair's confirmed the existence of the Shadow Man. He called him Jock too, just in case that helps in working out who he could be, or how long he's been around; Alistair seems to think that he's from a time before the theatre even stood here. From his description, I think it's safe to say that whoever or whatever it is, they're not benevolent.'

Jen shuddered. 'I really don't like the sound of that.'

'Neither do I,' Peggy agreed. 'And now we're going to have to go and tell someone who'll like it even less.'

* * *

Admittedly, he had been the one who'd sent Jen and Peggy off together to seek out anything unusual, but that didn't mean that Andrew was delighted about it. He knew that Jen was an exemplary police officer, and he certainly trusted her more than Lloyd in the event of an unanticipated crisis, mainly because Lloyd still seemed to equate 'dangerous' with 'exciting'. When it came to Peggy, however, Andrew still felt like he was personally responsible for her whenever she worked with them. He was the superior officer, so of course he should be accountable for the safety of every member of the team, but he was also still a bit on edge after the whole kidnapping/blazing inferno situation they'd all been through last June, even if he wouldn't admit that to anyone but himself.

Andrew also knew, however, that Peggy would kill him if he gave her even the slightest cause to think that he didn't trust her judgement and conduct as implicitly as he trusted Jen's. To him, it wasn't a question of trust though. At the end of the day, no matter how helpful she was, nor how loyal to the Ballroom she'd become, Peggy still wasn't a police officer.

He also thought that Peggy was unlikely to have her mind entirely on the job right now, which didn't help his nerves about the whole possibility of a malevolent spirit lurking in the wings.

Up until that morning, Andrew had been working under the assumption that Peggy's mother and wayward ex-fiancé would likely show up in her life again at some indeterminate point in the future, but that they'd be unlikely to possess the gall to parade themselves so publicly - and *so soon* - after everything that had apparently gone down at Butterton House the summer before last. It was at moments like this that Andrew was reminded that he really did not understand the behaviour of the apparent upper echelons of society at all.

At least he felt that he understood Peggy better these days. After Marnie's case, it had been simple for them to fall into a fairly regular routine of dinner or drinks after work a couple of times a week. Sometimes Lloyd and Jen would join them, or maybe even Charlie if he were in town, but more often than not it was just the two of them.

Andrew had spent enough time with Peggy to know that she was far smarter and more pragmatic than he was an awful lot of the time, but that didn't mean he wasn't worried that she'd find herself in a precarious situation if she were distracted by something in her personal life. The reappearance of her thieving mother and utter bastard of an ex-fiancé would definitely count as a possible distraction in Andrew's eyes.

He hadn't had much time to dwell on any of that though, as Peggy and Jen had barely disappeared from view before he and Lloyd were led from the room in the opposite direction by Vic.

'The others will be in the foyer,' Lavinia explained as they all trooped down the staircase.

'They've taken to having their morning coffee there, rather than in their dressing rooms,' Cohen added. 'Not that I can blame them. What happened to Lavinia's dress the other day really freaked them out.'

'And that's not even mentioning the warpath that Wardrobe's been on since it happened. They're furious that they've had to remake one of the key costumes with only days to go,' Lavinia said, hopping off the bottom step onto her tiptoes. 'We're all hiding from them in case they want to do another last-minute fitting. Ben was stabbed twice yesterday; he had blood all over his shoulder.'

Andrew saw his own horror mirrored on Lloyd's face.

'He wasn't *stabbed*, Lavinia!' Vic's face creased in exasperation as she pulled open a set of double doors that led into the plush red and gold foyer. 'It was a minor injury from a safety pin, detectives, as you can see from the fact that Ben is alive and well. He's sitting right over there.'

Sitting on a chaise against the opposite wall were a man and woman, both holding mugs, heads pressed close together as they talked quietly. There was also another man, younger than the first, sitting on the crimson carpet; he seemed entirely engrossed in puzzling out the Rubik's Cube held in his hands.

'Everyone,' Cohen called, causing all three to stop what they were doing and look up at him. 'As you know, I spoke to a DCI from Greater Manchester Police last night, and he agreed to send a team over to look into what's happened this week.'

'I hope he sent the fucking Ghostbusters,' said the younger man gravely. 'That's what we actually need!'

'He has!' Lavinia announced, and, to Andrew, she sounded rather giddy about it even though she apparently didn't believe in that sort of thing.

'What?' Seriously?' The man looked at Andrew and Lloyd critically. 'They don't look like they take down ghouls.'

Andrew wondered if he looked more or less likely to 'take down ghouls when dressed like Lloyd than if he'd been wearing his usual suit.

'Detective Inspector Andrew Joyce.' Andrew smiled tightly at the three of them. 'This is Detective Constable Parker. Our colleagues are currently elsewhere in the building.'

'Looking for ghosts,' Lavinia added, nodding sagely.

'Lavinia!' Vic pinched the bridge of her nose and sighed again.

'They're looking for any evidence of suspicious activity,' Andrew corrected. He found this display a little disheartening as he'd found Lavinia's blatant scepticism somewhat refreshing.

'So, you believe in the curse?' the older woman on the chaise asked.

Given that lying was frowned upon in his chosen profession, Andrew instead chose to circumvent the truth. 'We're looking for any human involvement in the first instance, but we're also considering more unorthodox theories.'

There, he thought to himself, that statement allowed for the inescapable fact that ghosts *did* exist - he really couldn't deny that they did at this stage, no matter how much he wanted to - but it did not mean that he had to commit to believing in curses. That wasn't going to happen. *Ever*.

He found Lavinia looking at him shrewdly though, so maybe his statement hadn't been quite as opaque as he'd intended.

'Here we have our Lady Bancroft, Marion Price,' Cohen stated, waving a hand towards the woman who'd spoken. 'Next to her is Lord Bancroft, Ben James. And finally, down there on the floor is our Sebastian, Edward Smeaton.'

'Call me Teddy, please,' the younger man said as he returned his attention to the Rubik's Cube.

Andrew wondered what had happened in his life that meant he seemed to be almost constantly surrounded by people who sounded like they'd fallen out of an Enid Blyton novel. It gave him a dark sort of amusement to know that his mother would have been livid about it all: Agatha Joyce had never been one to approve of what she saw as 'airs and graces'.

'Teddy? Like the bear?' Lloyd asked, and *Christ*, Andrew could hear the smirk without looking at him.

Thankfully, Teddy didn't seem to take offence. 'Yes, just like the bear, Detective Constable.'

'Cool,' Lloyd replied.

Andrew was *really* going to have to have that conversation with Lloyd about the use of 'cool' as a response during working hours.

'So, how exactly are you planning on dealing with our problem?' Marion asked, in obvious judgement of the two men standing before her. 'As Teddy said, you don't very well look like ghost hunters.'

'That's because we aren't ghost hunters, Ms Price,' Andrew replied tightly. 'We're police detectives, of that I can assure you, and at this time our priority is looking into any human involvement in the events of the past week.'

'So, they're *not* looking for ghosts?' Teddy said, raising an eyebrow at Lavinia and Cohen.

'Detective Joyce and his team will look at every possibility, Teddy,' Cohen said placatingly.

'This 'curse' thing is all Lavinia's fault anyway,' Ben added, taking a large sip from his coffee mug.

'How is it *my* fault?' Lavinia cried in dismay. 'I don't even believe in curses or ghosts!'

'Well, neither did the rest of us until Tuesday,' Ben replied, shaking his head at her. 'You made such a point of being all 'oh, there's no such thing as curses', and then *bam*, two days later, we get here, and weird shit started happening.'

'Regardless of the cause,' Andrew cut in, before the heated discussion could turn into an actual argument, 'we will be looking into all possibilities, as Mr Cohen said.'

'Hmm,' Ben replied mulishly.

Andrew longed a little for the days he used to spend dealing with actual criminals, and actual cases.

'Did Lavinia tell you about the supposed ghost she and Vic saw?' Marion asked, pursing her lips.

'Oh, for God's sake, Marion, it wasn't a ghost!' Lavinia protested loudly. 'I got a little dramatic in my description of a man dressed in black, that's all.'

Lavinia turned to Andrew. 'A man who absolutely should not have been anywhere near the second floor, by the by.'

'Did you see the man's face, Miss Heathcote?' Andrew asked. 'Could you give us any description that would help us to identify him?'

Lavinia shook her head. 'No, I'm sorry. He was facing away from me, and it was dark up there. I got such a shock I just turned and ran down the stairs. Vic came running, but only saw the back of him.'

'Lavinia, you missed out the part where you were shrieking like a banshee,' Teddy added from the floor.

'I was not shrieking!' Lavinia snapped.

She then smiled politely at Andrew. 'I was not shrieking, Detective Inspector. I merely had a fright.'

'A natural reaction,' Andrew replied diplomatically. He'd definitely shrieked on several occasions when Marnie had popped up in the Ballroom unannounced, but nobody here had to know that.

Lavinia looked pleased, and Andrew was almost certain that he saw Lloyd roll his eyes.

Cohen cleared his throat. 'Look, I'm sorry to cut this off here, but we do need to get started ASAP this morning.'

Marion sighed loudly as she got to her feet. 'I suppose we'll need all the time we have to make sure that Teddy actually gets though his lines today.'

'Oh, do piss off, Marion,' Teddy replied, finally putting the Rubik's Cube down.

'Charming, as always,' Marion muttered, turning away.

'They're always like this,' Lavinia whispered conspiratorially to Andrew as she fell into step beside him on the walk back towards Cohen's office. 'Incredibly professional when we're working, of course, but at each other's throats any time we're not on stage.'

Andrew hadn't yet revised his view of actors being far too melodramatic for his liking.

As they reached Cohen's office, Lavinia stopped Andrew with a hand on his arm. 'Detective Inspector?'

'Yes, Miss Heathcote?'

'*Lavinia*, please,' she replied, smiling again. 'I was hoping that I could sit down with you later and talk through everything that's happened this week. Everyone else is so caught up with curses and all that ghost nonsense, I'd really like to speak to someone who clearly has their feet on the ground.'

'Of course,' Andrew replied, casually skipping over the point that unfortunately ghosts weren't, in fact, nonsense.

'Fantastic,' Lavinia's smile grew impossibly brighter. 'Perhaps we can go out for something to eat after we're finished here for the day?'

Andrew was ready to tell Lavinia that while he was very happy to have a conversation with her, there were professional boundaries at play here and that he couldn't accept a dinner invitation, regardless of how innocent the intention may be.

Lavinia, however, didn't give him a chance to say any of that, and she accepted the momentary silence between breaths as agreement.

'Fantastic,' she said again, and turned away with a swish of wavy hair to hurry after Cohen. 'I'll see you later.'

Lloyd looked like he was about to start laughing.

'What?' Andrew snapped.

'Absolutely nothing, sir,' Lloyd replied, snorting slightly as he made a beeline for the short staircase that led to the auditorium doors.

Andrew shook his head and followed his awfully cheeky DC. He hoped that Jen and Peggy hadn't found even the slightest suggestion of something ghostly in nature. Andrew would much prefer just being able to track down a human suspect for once.

When Andrew reached the auditorium, he spotted Peggy and Jen sitting about halfway back in the stalls, both at the end of a row on opposites sides of the aisle. Lloyd was already bounding towards them, and Andrew realised that he'd better get a move on if he didn't want Lloyd to start telling tales.

'What did you find out?' Andrew called loudly, before he'd even reached them, effectively cutting off whatever Lloyd had just opened his mouth to say. 'Please tell me that there is a zero chance of a murderous ghost actually being a thing.'

Jen's lips twisted into apology. 'Sorry, sir. Not sure we can do that.'

Christ, here we go, thought Andrew as he looked over at Peggy.

Peggy looked about as delighted at the prospect of sharing her information with Andrew as he felt about hearing it.

'Alistair Tunham is here,' Peggy said, wrapping the end of her hair around her finger in a nervous motion.

'Dead guy number one?' Lloyd asked loudly.

'*Lloyd*!' Andrew growled.

'Sorry, sir,' Lloyd muttered, giving a little nod of contrition. 'I meant, the first victim.'

'Yes,' Peggy confirmed. 'He can't tell us anything particularly useful regarding his own death though, or the events leading up to it.'

'Typical,' Andrew muttered under his breath. Though, if the sharp glare Peggy gave him was anything to go by, he hadn't been quiet enough.

'He *was* able to share something pertinent to the case though,' Peggy continued, still visibly annoyed with Andrew. 'The Shadow Man isn't just a story.'

'Shit,' Andrew growled, because really, what else was he supposed to say to that?

'Quite.' Peggy raised one eyebrow. 'Unfortunately, it sounds as though he isn't particularly talkative, nor is he the friendly type.'

'What else?' Andrew asked, because he could tell that Peggy wasn't finished yet.

Peggy wrinkled her nose. 'Alistair confirmed that the Shadow Man tends to appear in the days leading up to a production, which means that we're probably going to see some further, um, activity.'

She looked at Andrew pointedly. 'Before you say anything, please remember what I said last night about not shooting the messenger.'

Andrew groaned loudly. Were you allowed to have tantrums when you were thirty-four? He felt like one would help him enormously with venting his frustration.

'What do we do?' Jen asked.

Andrew regretfully pressed pause on his plan to sulk dramatically. 'I think we tell Mr Cohen that his production's off.'

'I don't think he's going to go for that, sir,' Jen replied with a grimace. 'When you and Peggy popped out earlier, Cohen went off on this ramble about how he'd turned down loads of offers for productions elsewhere so that he could do this one. He was also complaining about how much pressure is being put on them all by the charity that's involved. Apparently, the chairwoman is – and please remember, these are Cohen's words, not mine – a 'total bitch'.'

Andrew glanced at Peggy, and she gave him the barest hint of a smile in return.

'What?' Lloyd asked, of course choosing that moment to be more perceptive than usual.

'Nothing,' Andrew and Peggy replied in unison.

'It's really freaky when you two do that, you know,' Lloyd said, as he put a hand in his pocket to retrieve a Mars Bar.

'Well, if he won't cancel the production, we're just going to have to do everything we can to make sure that everybody on that stage is safe,' Andrew said, looking over his shoulder to where the four actors, along with a handful of other people Andrew hadn't met yet, were forming a semi-circle around Cohen and Vic.

'How do we keep people safe from a ghost, if that really is what's happening here?' Jen asked.

It was a perfectly reasonable question, and it was also one that Andrew had hoped wouldn't be asked quite yet, as he didn't think the answer poised on the tip of his tongue just then was a particularly good one.

Still, it was all he had, so he thought he might as well share it:

'I haven't got a bloody clue.

FOUR

'Is it just me, or does this play not make any sense?' Lloyd asked from the row behind Andrew, emptying the last couple of Minstrels directly from the bag into his mouth. 'Like, what's a rose got to do with anything?'

'It's not an actual rose,' Jen replied, and Andrew could hear the eye roll. 'The rose is her daughter, Isabella.'

'What?' Lloyd screwed up his face.

'Jesus, never mind, Lloyd. Just shut up and watch it.'

'But it's so boring,' Lloyd hissed in disgust. 'It didn't make sense the first time we watched it this morning, or the second time, and I think it actually makes even less sense now.'

Andrew was pleased that they were sitting far enough away from the stage that the actors were unlikely to hear Lloyd, but he would have to secretly agree with his DC on this one. Thank God this was the last run through of the day.

His attention had already wandered off into thoughts of possible suspects when they were about ten minutes into the latest rehash of the same scene. By the time he'd returned to the present, two problematic things had occurred:

1. He'd realised that as hard as he might try to think otherwise, the most likely suspect responsible for the odd happenings at the theatre in the preceding few days may actually be a ghost, and therefore Andrew still wasn't exactly sure how they were meant to 'protect' the cast. As far as he was aware, nobody on his team had recently qualified in Exorcism Management.

2. Peggy had obviously been about as enthralled by the play as Andrew. At some point she'd fallen asleep and was currently snoring lightly on the detective's shoulder. He had absolutely

no idea what he was supposed to do in such a situation, and therefore was dealing with it by doing absolutely nothing.

'I think Peggy's got the right idea, don't you, sir?' Lloyd asked, alongside the unmistakeable sound of another bag of sweets being torn open.

'You better not even be *thinking* about charging those sweets to the department,' Andrew hissed, keeping as still as he could. 'How are you still hungry after the amount of lunch you ate?'

'Well, that was lunch, but these are snacks, sir,' Lloyd replied. 'Sustenance for the investigation. Plus, we're at the theatre, so there's got to be sweets, right?'

A sudden crash on the stage surprised everyone, and Peggy startled awake when Andrew jumped.

'Sorry!' Cohen called, waving a hand towards his little audience. 'Teddy's apparently forgotten how to walk in a straight line!'

'Me?' Teddy cried, looking aghast as he clambered to his feet. 'Who put that bloody table there? It wasn't that close to me when we started.'

'I hope you're not blaming me!' Marion said, hands on hips, when she realised that Teddy was glaring at her.

'You're the only person standing anywhere near it!' Teddy replied.

'Right, but when exactly did you see me heft a bloody great table towards you?' Marion sniped.

'I *didn't* see you, that's why I collided with it!'

'Oh Christ,' Andrew said, getting to his feet. 'Maybe one of them will strangle the other right now, and that will be this year's murder out of the way.'

'Alistair!' Peggy shouted suddenly, looking slightly alarmed. She was wide awake now, and shoved Andrew out of the way so that she could slip past him and out into the aisle.

'Watch it!' Andrew called half-heartedly as he wobbled against the folding seat. 'Hang on, *Alistair*?'

Andrew ran towards the stage, trying to catch up with Peggy.

'Miss Jones, what's going on?' Cohen asked in surprise as Peggy began to clamber – very inelegantly in Andrew's honest opinion - up onto the stage via the empty orchestra pit.

Andrew reached the stage just as Cohen helped Peggy to her feet again. No help was offered to the detective, and Andrew thought that he actually managed to do a worse job of climbing up than Peggy had done. *Bloody ridiculous jeans.*

'Are you alright Detective Inspector?' Lavinia asked, frowning down at Andrew from across the stage.

'Fine, Miss Heathcote, thank you,' Andrew managed to grind out politely, while plotting myriad ways to kill Lloyd for not just having sensible clothes like any normal person would.

Peggy had already made it to the far side of the stage and appeared to be deep in hushed conversation with a grandfather clock.

'What on earth is she doing?' Marion asked. Andrew recognised the judgemental tone from earlier.

'Mr Cohen, perhaps it would be sensible to briefly remove the cast from the area,' Andrew suggested, hoping that it was clear that it actually wasn't in any way a *suggestion*.

'We're in the middle of a run through, Detective Inspector,' Cohen replied, though he kept his eyes on Peggy.

'And I'm in the middle of an active police investigation,' Andrew responded as politely as he could. 'My job is to protect your cast, and right now I want them all off the stage.'

'Alright,' Cohen agreed, although he didn't look happy about it. 'Everybody, backstage. Now.'

Andrew nodded his thanks, and then made a series of hand gestures at Jen and Lloyd, which, were they to be translated correctly, suggested that his two colleagues go and make sure that everyone stayed away while he got to the bottom of whatever Peggy was up to with the mysterious Alistair.

Jen followed the cast out through the door, and yanked on Lloyd's arm when he didn't immediately understand Andrew's instructions.

'Peggy?' Andrew tried quietly, staying on his side of the stage. He still didn't love being part of a conversation where he couldn't see or hear one of the other participants.

'It's okay, Andrew, you can come over,' Peggy replied, before she whispered something in the direction of the clock again.

'Yes, he is a detective,' Peggy was saying very quietly as Andrew approached. 'No, he doesn't normally wear clothes like that to work. No, no, trust me, he really isn't happy about it.'

Andrew cleared his throat and Peggy smiled guiltily at him.

'Andrew, this is Alistair Tunham,' Peggy added, gesturing towards the clock.

She'd taken to doing that whenever she was trying to include Andrew in a confab with a ghost; she'd give him a clue where to look so that he wasn't staring in completely the wrong direction. He'd told her it was a weird thing to do, but he secretly thought it was actually quite clever. Given that she'd kept on doing it anyway, Andrew thought that it was probably a safe bet to think that Peggy knew that he appreciated it really.

'Hi,' Andrew said, 'I'm sure Peggy's already explained that she's the only one who can, er, do her *thing*.'

'We're still explaining it like that, are we?' Peggy rolled her eyes.

Andrew had actually once asked Peggy how she'd describe what she did, and she still hadn't given him an answer. Therefore, was it really fair that she judged his description?

'Anyway,' Peggy continued, turning back to the clock. 'This is Detective Inspector Andrew Joyce and, despite his unusual attire today, I promise you that he'll do everything he can to find out what happened to you. You can trust him.'

Andrew twitched, slightly taken aback at Peggy's display of faith in him. He knew she trusted him to direct the team, and to keep them all safe and in line, but it was still nice to hear that she'd vouch for him to a complete stranger.

'Yes, I *promise*,' Peggy said, nodding.

'Excuse us for just one second, Alistair,' Andrew politely addressed the clock. 'Peggy, why exactly did you come flying up here like a bat out of hell?'

Peggy suddenly grinned delightedly.

'What?' Andrew asked, completely baffled.

'Sorry, Alistair just said that he likes that song,' Peggy replied. '*Bat Out of Hell*. Apparently, he used to hear it on the radio a lot when they were cleaning up the auditorium after a performance.'

Peggy, to Andrew's great relief, then seemed to remember that she wasn't supposed to just be having a casual chat with a murder victim.

'Sorry,' she said again. 'No, what happened was that when everyone on stage was yelling at each other, I could see Alistair looking distressed.'

'Right?' Andrew hadn't been blessed with the patience for getting information like this through to him in dribs and drabs.

'According to Alistair it wasn't Marion who moved the table,' Peggy continued with a grimace. 'He says it was the Shadow Man. Jock.'

Andrew tried very hard to stand still and not start looking around wildly. Even though he knew it was completely irrational, he felt the hairs on the back of his neck stand to attention at the thought.

'He's not here anymore,' Peggy said, because apparently she could read Andrew's thoughts now. 'Alistair said that he vanished when I called out to him.'

The way that Andrew's blood ran cold at that statement was

not irrational in any way. 'So, this *thing* knows that you can see it?'

'I didn't see it, Andrew,' Peggy replied, shaking her head. 'I didn't see anyone but the cast, Mr Cohen, and Alistair.'

'But it saw *you*, and it knows that you saw Alistair.'

'Right, but it also saw you, and Jen, and Lloyd, and everyone on this stage,' Peggy said calmly.

'I don't like this, Peggy,' Andrew replied, voice wound tight with concern.

'I don't think anyone likes it.' Peggy raised her eyebrows. 'Look, we just need to carry on as normal. We need to find out what happened to Alistair, and the others, and work out why it's *this* play, and only in *this* place.'

'Oh, well it all sounds so straightforward when you put it like that,' Andrew scoffed. 'Why didn't I think of that?'

'Don't be a dick, Andrew, it doesn't suit you,' Peggy replied primly and turned back to the clock.

'Sorry, Alistair,' she said, 'it sometimes takes Andrew a little time to accept that he's dealing with things he doesn't quite understand.'

The little flair of self-confidence that had appeared when Peggy had told Alistair to trust him fizzled out entirely. He might grudgingly admit that he deserved that.

'Alistair, I promise we'll do everything we can to find out what happened the night you were killed,' Andrew said with as much politeness as he could muster.

'He says 'thank you',' Peggy added. 'He's gone, but he said he'll go and have a look around for us.'

Andrew nodded. 'Is it safe to let everyone back out here?'

'I think so,' Peggy replied.

'Though with the way Marion and Teddy were at each other's throats I'm not so sure,' Andrew commented.

'What? When?' Peggy asked.

A second later her eyes widened in horror as Andrew saw the realisation click into place. Under the bright stage lights there wasn't a hope in hell that she could hide the fact that her cheeks were turning pink with embarrassment.

Andrew tried not to laugh. 'It's alright, Peggy. I won't tell Cohen that you fell asleep in the middle of his precious play.'

'Oh my God,' Peggy whined, closing her eyes.

'Detective Inspector?'

Andrew turned as Cohen called from behind them. 'Mr Cohen, it looks like everything's fine. You can return to your rehearsal now.'

Cohen shook his head. 'We've got a half hour left, but I think Marion might actually quit if she has to spend another second with Teddy today. I've told them all to go home early.'

'Probably for the best,' Andrew said. 'We'll be back first thing in the morning.'

'Thanks,' Cohen said solemnly, before he smiled toothily. 'Goodnight, Miss Jones.'

'Goodnight,' Peggy replied, still borderline beetroot.

Andrew did not scowl.

'What's that face for?' Peggy asked, frowning as Cohen left with a wave.

'What face?' Andrew asked. 'It's just my face.'

Peggy rolled her eyes at him. 'Well, whatever face it is, I think we've just been told that we don't have to watch any more of that bloody play today.'

'Thank God for that,' Andrew replied, as he helped Peggy hop down off the stage.

Peggy grinned at him as they headed back to the stalls to grab their things. 'Are you ready to go now then? Lloyd's been practically salivating about the thought of steak all day.'

'Go where?' Andrew frowned, pulling at the hem of his borrowed t-shirt again.

Peggy's smile faded slightly. 'Dinner?'

Andrew had no idea what she was talking about. 'What?'

'For your birthday. My treat for all of us, remember?' Peggy replied slowly as she picked up her jacket and handbag, eyeing Andrew as though he might have recently suffered a head injury.

Oh, hang on, hang on, Andrew *did* remember agreeing to Peggy's suggestion a couple of weeks ago. 'Shit, I forgot.'

'That's alright,' Peggy laughed as she shrugged her jacket on. 'I suspect they'll still let you in, even if you're dressed like an extra from *Footloose*.'

'No, no, I mean I forgot, and now I can't go,' Andrew corrected.

'You can't go?' Peggy's frown was back. 'What do you mean?'

'Lavinia wants to talk to me about some of the things that have happened this week,' Andrew replied. 'I've agreed to meet her later. She's really concerned about it all.'

'Oh,' Peggy replied, and she looked rather taken aback.

'It's work, Peggy,' Andrew said with a shrug. 'You know that has to take priority, right?'

'Right, of course,' Peggy replied after a long moment. 'Work. Got it.'

'You should all still go out though,' Andrew encouraged. 'You'll probably have way more fun without me anyway.'

'Bit pointless having a birthday dinner without the birthday boy, isn't it?'

Peggy wasn't being in any way outwardly hostile, but there was definitely an edge to her voice that hadn't been there at the start of the conversation.

'Wait, are you angry with me?' Andrew raised an eyebrow.

Peggy shook her head. 'Why would I be angry with you?'

Andrew sighed loudly. 'Peggy, it's *work*. Lavinia might be a target, and it's my job – *our* job - to make sure that she's safe.'

Peggy made a complicated facial expression that Andrew

couldn't interpret, before she dipped her hand into the bag hanging from her shoulder. She pulled out a small, neatly wrapped gift and shoved it unceremoniously into Andrew's hand.

'Of course. Anyway, here,' she said, all in a rush, already turning away. 'Happy birthday, Andrew.'

Andrew was still processing the fact that he was holding the only birthday present that he'd received that year when the door at the edge of the auditorium slammed shut with an echoing sense of finality.

He was left with the sneaking suspicion that he might have just done something wrong.

* * *

Peggy kept her foot on the accelerator as she guided her poor little car up the driveway towards Butterton House. She shot past the lake on her left and wasn't above taking an immature pleasure in how the little flock of pigeons at the edge of the water scattered in surprise.

It was childish behaviour, she knew that, but she didn't slow down until she screeched the car to a halt right outside the front door. She climbed out and slammed the driver's door behind her, growing more irritated when that didn't actually make her feel any better.

Timothy would go absolutely berserk when he saw that she hadn't parked the car in the garage, but she'd have plenty to say to him if he so much as hinted that she might want to move it. In fact, she rather hoped that the butler complained to her father, because she had even more she'd like to say to *him* at this point.

'Alright, what on earth has got into you?'

Peggy looked up, startled, to see Charlie leaning against the open front door. He had his arms folded and was looking at his sister as though he'd never seen her before.

'Nothing,' Peggy replied with as much dignity as she could manage, knowing that Charlie was likely to have seen her little sprint up the driveway. She walked to the door slowly, carefully arranging her features into disinterest.

Charlie's eyes widened, and he looked like he desperately wanted to laugh. 'Try again, Niki Lauda.'

'Oh, piss off, Charlie,' Peggy snapped, pushing past her brother and stalking up the stairs.

'Okay, now I really am intrigued,' Charlie said, bounding up the staircase behind her. 'What the hell happened today?'

Peggy whirled around as soon as she reached the landing and Charlie stopped short a few steps lower, reaching out to grab the bannister to help him balance.

'Well, *firstly*, that play they're putting on at the Court next week, is a charity production.'

'And charity somehow insults you these days?' Charlie asked mildly.

Peggy glared at her brother. 'It's for the fucking Winshire Foundation, Charlie.'

Charlie blinked hard, as though Peggy had slapped him. She didn't often swear at her brother, and she'd done it twice in under a minute. On top of that, she'd just uttered their mother's name within the very walls they tried to keep her out of.

'I hope you told Higson that you're not working the case anymore,' Charlie said eventually, absolutely furious. 'And how dare she put something on in that theatre!'

'I suspect she knows that it will drive Father mad,' Peggy replied. 'But I expect his silence on the matter will be killing her.'

Charlie let out a string of expletives, and Peggy felt better about her own mood.

'What else?' Charlie asked once Peggy had moved out of the way to let him finish climbing the stairs. 'You said that was 'firstly', so what else?'

'Nothing,' Peggy replied again, but far, far quieter this time. 'Look, I'm just tired. Sleeping at the Ballroom was a terrible idea, and I'm pretty sure I fell asleep on Andrew's shoulder in the theatre this aft-'

Peggy clamped her lips together and her eyes bugged as she turned away from her brother and headed for her bedroom.

'What did you just say?' Charlie asked, bounding past her and blocking the door. Dear Christ, he looked far too gleeful for a person who'd been swearing like a sailor a moment ago. 'Did you just say that you fell asleep on *Joycie*?'

Peggy quickly moved her hand past Charlie's side and turned the doorknob viciously enough that the door opened and Charlie stumbled backwards into the room.

Charlie landed on the carpet with a heartening thud and a yelp of shock. Unfortunately, Peggy was unable to truly appreciate the joy of the moment as she was too busy being surprised by the fact that Marnie and Emmeline were both sitting on the end of her bed, staring at the small television perched on top of a VCR player on the dressing table. A television and VCR player that definitely hadn't been there that morning.

'Oh good, you're back,' Marnie said to Charlie, dropping the remote control she'd been holding in her right hand. 'I was going to press play again if you were much longer. Emmy wouldn't have stopped me.'

'It's true, I wouldn't have.' Emmeline nodded sagely.

Marnie then smiled at Peggy. 'Oh, hiya. We thought you were out tonight.'

'Oh yes,' Charlie said, drawing out the words as he stood up and studied his sister shrewdly. 'You *are* supposed to be out tonight.'

'Well, I'm quite clearly not out,' Peggy snapped. 'And why are you all in my bedroom anyway? Do you know how many rooms this house has?'

'We're watching something called *Neighbours*,' Emmeline replied with a wide smile, ignoring Peggy's later questions. 'Marnie tells me that it comes all the way from the other side of the world. Can you believe that?'

'*Neighbours?*' Peggy asked, shaking her head as though she doubted her own hearing.

'Yes, it's all very exciting,' Emmeline continued. 'We've been watching for a few weeks now.'

'Right,' Peggy said slowly, still not entirely sure what was going on.

'Now, I'm sorry to be Peter the Repeater here,' Charlie said, chuckling at his own apparent cleverness, 'but I am just going to ask you again why you said that you fell asleep on Joycie, alright?'

'You did *what?*' shrieked Marnie, jumping off the bed and clutching her clasped hands to her chest.

Emmeline just raised one judgemental eyebrow and pursed her lips.

'On his shoulder, Jesus Christ,' Peggy whined, flopping backwards onto her bed. 'In public. It was horribly embarrassing. I would like to die quietly now, so please go away.'

'*And?*' Charlie asked. 'I mean, yes, I can see how that would be mortifying for you, but that doesn't explain why you flew up the driveway at a hundred miles an hour.'

'It obviously wasn't *a hundred*,' Peggy sniped, pulling her pillow over her face. Now that she was surrounded by three other people – well, 'people' might be a bit of a stretch – she felt completely moronic, and also like she was being judged at a teenage sleepover.

'Peg?' Charlie patted her ankle. 'Seriously, what's going on?'

Peggy sat up slowly and grimaced. 'Nothing, honestly. I just took something the wrong way, that's all. I'll be fine. I just need a good sleep.'

'You're supposed to be out tonight,' Marnie repeated Charlie's earlier words, slower this time as though turning the thought over carefully in her mind.

'Yes, and I'm not, alright?' Peggy snapped. 'So, I'm sorry that I've ruined your evening plans, but you can bloody well blame Andrew Joyce for that as well, okay?'

'Okay,' Marnie said after a solid few seconds of deafening silence. 'Right, Emmy, I'm so sorry, we'll catch up with Ramsay Street tomorrow, I promise. I'll make sure I don't tape over it before you've seen it. Also, Charlie, you can just piss off now, yeah?'

Charlie looked offended, and Emmeline looked downright miserable.

'*Goodnight*, both of you,' Marnie said sternly, looking between them. 'Seriously, shoo.'

Charlie opened his mouth to reply, but eventually just narrowed his eyes at Marnie and backed out of the room silently. Emmeline dissolved dramatically, as though trying to make sure that everyone knew of her great and immeasurable sorrow.

'Peggy, what's going on?' Marnie asked the second Charlie had closed the door behind him. 'And don't say 'nothing', alright?'

Peggy sighed. 'Marnie, look, I appreciate your concern, really, I do, but there's nothing wrong.'

'Oh, okay,' Marnie shrugged, taking a seat in the window. 'That's fine then.'

Peggy looked over at her, confused. She'd been expecting resistance. Yet, Marnie just sat there, perfectly quietly, looking out over the grounds as the evening sun bathed the estate in a golden wash.

Shaking her head, Peggy climbed off the bed and wandered into her bathroom, taking her pyjamas with her. She didn't care that it was obscenely early; after three solid nights of wandering the towpaths of the Rochdale Canal she was more than ready to crawl into her own bed.

She brushed her teeth and stared at herself in the mirror while she did so. *Jesus*, Andrew had been right, she really did look like she'd been dragged through a hedge backwards.

Not that she should care, of course. She wasn't a self-conscious adolescent, and she wasn't trying to impress anyone by having neat, shiny hair or wearing pretty dresses. She was a grown woman, and she absolutely did not concern herself with what other people thought of her anymore. She'd done enough of that, and it hadn't got her anywhere particularly pleasant, had it?

Still, she was a grown woman, and if she wanted to be unreasonably pissed off about something, then she was absolutely allowed to be.

And, if she also just wanted to go back into her bedroom and listen to Billy Joel while screaming into her pillow in frustration then she was absolutely allowed to do that too.

She practically threw herself into the shower, and washed her hair as quickly as she could manage before drying off and pulling on her pyjamas.

Heading back into her bedroom, with her face slathered in moisturiser that smelled far too strongly of cucumber, Peggy felt truly clean for the first time in two days. Her almost-irrational level of annoyance at Andrew had dimmed significantly and she thought that she might actually venture in search of a stack of buttered toast before heading to bed.

Marnie, however, clearly had other ideas.

'Peggy, don't take this the wrong way, but you're being a bit mental tonight,' Marnie said, with absolutely no preamble whatsoever as she turned from looking out the window to stare at Peggy in that unnerving all-knowing way that she had.

'Wow, thanks,' Peggy said, closing the bathroom door behind her and reaching for the jumper thrown over the armchair near the wardrobe.

'Why don't you tell me about the case?' Marnie suggested.

'*You* want to talk about a case?' Peggy asked in surprise as she sat on the end of her bed with her hair soaking her shoulders.

'Yeah, why not?' Marnie replied. 'Come on, you know I love the theatre! Charlie told me it's about a really old unsolved murder, but not much else.'

Peggy knew that Marnie loved *musicals*, that much was true. She'd already spent the past few weeks wishing that she hadn't caved to Marnie's desire to own *The Phantom of the Opera* cast recording. If Peggy had to listen to *The Music of The Night* even one more time, she was going to personally hunt down Andrew Lloyd Webber and throw the album at him.

'Alright,' Peggy sighed, knowing full well that Marnie wouldn't stop asking until Peggy explained anyway. 'A man was electrocuted on stage in the final scene of a play back in 1932. He was the standby for a famous actor. I met him today, actually.'

'Ooh, a new ghost! What's he called?'

Peggy was fairly certain that Marnie was the female equivalent of Lloyd in many ways; they both got terribly overexcited about the smallest hint of anything out of the ordinary, and Peggy knew for certain that Andrew was never quite sure how to deal with either of them.

'His name is Alistair,' Peggy replied. 'Alistair Tunham, and he seems to be the only active ghost at the Court.'

'Only one ghost at the *theatre*?' Marnie asked in surprise, wrinkling her nose. 'Doesn't that seem a little odd to you?'

Peggy was pleased that everyone found this fact a little disconcerting, but that also made her wariness of the situation ratchet up a little more.

'Yes, I do,' Peggy replied. 'Though technically that's not correct. There have been reports of another spirit in the theatre; one that has been seen by various people just before two other deaths occurred, both connected to the same play as Alistair Tunham's. He's been described as being 'made of shadows', which is more than a little creepy.'

'So, the play is *cursed*?' Marnie asked, sounding awestruck. 'Oh my God, this is actually worth missing *Neighbours* for.'

'I don't know if I believe in curses, Marnie,' Peggy replied. She rolled her eyes. 'And Andrew *certainly* doesn't.'

'I don't think he really believes in *me*, Peggy,' Marnie scoffed.

'Hmm.' Peggy prodded the duvet by her leg.

'What are you going to do about this creepy, shadow guy?' Marnie asked. 'He actually sounds pretty terrifying. Did he kill those other people?'

'I don't know,' Peggy replied, 'but Alistair confirmed that he exists. He was there today, apparently, but I couldn't see him at all.'

'You should let me come to the theatre with you tomorrow!' Marnie looked like she'd just struck gold at the idea.

'Absolutely not,' Peggy replied, horrified at the thought. 'It's bad enough that you swan about here making Timothy think that we've got some sort of pseudo-houseguest who only has one outfit. You can't come to a possible crime scene with me!'

In the nine months that Marnie had been 'living' at Butterton, she and Peggy, along with some input from Emmeline (helpful) and Charlie (utterly useless), had come up with a range of experiments to test Marnie's skills.

They'd concluded that Marnie was able to quite easily travel to anywhere that Peggy currently was, or was strongly attached to, within a reasonable distance, or to places that Marnie herself had been very connected to when she was alive. Other locations required more effort, but as long as it wasn't *too* far from Peggy it seemed to work just fine. Much to her chagrin, however, she couldn't just do a jolly day-trip to Paris or somewhere, no matter how hard she tried.

They were also sure that once the location conditions were met, Marnie could make herself appear as human and as perfectly alive as you like, so long as Peggy, or someone connected closely to her, was in the vicinity. Marnie had really enjoyed popping up at the Ballroom when Andrew was there alone in the evenings, just to scare the living daylights out of him.

'No, no, no, Peggy, seriously, think about it,' Marnie said, waving her arms excitedly. 'You said that you couldn't see the shadow guy, right?'

Peggy definitely hadn't said 'the shadow guy', but she nodded exasperatedly at Marnie anyway. 'Yes, *and*?'

'But this Alistair can see him, which means that I can probably see him too!' Marnie declared triumphantly. 'Even Andrew would have to agree with that logic.'

Oh Christ, Marnie was right. If Peggy couldn't see Jock, then they had no way of knowing where he was, unless Alistair was around.

'See!' Marnie hissed, her eyes bright with excitement. 'It makes perfect sense.'

Peggy groaned loudly. 'Andrew won't agree to it, Marnie.'

'Like he has to *agree* to anything,' Marnie scoffed, plopping down next to Peggy.

'It's his case, Marnie, not ours. We're not actually the police, remember?'

'Maybe not, but you're as much a part of that team as Andrew is,' Marnie said, raising an eyebrow. 'Which reminds me; I thought you were all going out for Andrew's birthday today?'

'Change of plans,' Peggy replied, hoping that would be the end of it.

'Why?'

'Does it matter?'

Marnie raised an eyebrow. 'Now that you're basically avoiding the answer, yeah, it does.'

'Andrew forgot,' Peggy said simply. 'He made other plans.'

'*Andrew* had other plans?' Marnie wrinkled her nose. 'Since when has he got a life outside work?'

'That's not very fair, Marnie,' Peggy chastised her friend.

'Oh my God, Peggy, it's so true though.' Marnie folded her arms. 'Name one thing that Andrew does outside of work that doesn't involve either you or one of the others from Tib Street.'

Peggy opened her mouth, and then had to close it again immediately when she realised that she didn't have an answer.

'Exactly! So, what plans does Andrew have?'

Peggy sighed. She felt like she was fifteen again. 'He went out for dinner with one of the actresses from the case we're working on.'

Marnie instantly looked outraged. 'He did *what*?'

'She wanted to talk to him about the things that have been happening at the theatre,' Peggy said, shrugging.

'Oh, I *bet* she did!'

'It's for work, Marnie,' Peggy added, and it sounded like a lame excuse even to her own ears.

'Sure it is.' Marnie rolled her eyes, but then her face softened dramatically. 'Are you alright?'

'Why wouldn't I be?' Peggy asked immediately, and, yes, perhaps that was a little too defensive.

Marnie just looked back at her shrewdly. 'Right.'

'Look, Marnie, it's fine, Andrew can do whatever he wants.'

'Did you give him the present?' Marnie asked carefully.

Peggy nodded, tugging on her earlobe self-consciously and twisting the small diamond stud round and round.

'And he still ditched you?' Marnie was back to outraged.

'He didn't *ditch* me, Marnie,' Peggy muttered. 'Anyway, he didn't actually open it. I just sort of shoved it at him and left.'

Marnie didn't look any less annoyed.

Peggy blew out a loud breath of frustration. 'Look, can we just leave it now, please? It's been a crap day from start to finish.'

Marnie perked up again. 'Why? What else happened?'

Peggy considered not telling her, but she knew that Marnie would probably just go after Charlie for information instead, which would probably be worse for everyone involved.

'The play is being staged for charity,' Peggy explained. 'My mother's charity. There's going to be a gala performance on Wednesday, and I expect she'll be there.'

Whatever version of antagonism Marnie had shown for Andrew's actions was pitiful compared to the fury that crossed her face at Peggy's words.

'What? Do you want me to go scare the crap out of her?' Marnie asked dangerously.

Peggy knew full well that Marnie was still making it her business to occasionally torment Athena Hughes in prison - which seemed entirely fair given that Athena had murdered Marnie in a jealous rage – so she had no doubt that Marnie would take haunting Caroline very seriously.

'No, God, please don't do that!' Peggy wasn't above begging in this situation. 'It's bad enough that Andrew knows, and he quite clearly doesn't trust me to focus on the job because of it. Let's not make it worse.'

Marnie frowned. 'Andrew trusts you.'

Peggy scoffed. 'He doesn't want me questioning anybody by myself, and Jen outright said that she'd basically been sent with me to make sure I didn't do anything stupid.'

'No way did *Jen* say that to you,' Marnie said doubtfully.

'Her exact words were that Andrew would have her head if a ghost so much as looked at me the wrong way,' Peggy replied.

'Right, so, you took that and still somehow came up with Andrew doesn't trust you?' Marnie asked slowly.

'Well, it's obvious, isn't it?'

'No, Peggy, I really don't think it is,' Marnie said, and she patted Peggy's knee before she stood up.

'Best get some sleep anyway,' Marnie added with a sudden grin. 'We have a really big day tomorrow!'

Peggy had an awful feeling that everything was about to go to hell again.

FIVE

The walk from where Andrew had parked his car on Tib Street to the Court shouldn't have taken more than quarter of an hour, but Andrew's journey was currently running to forty-six minutes and counting.

When he'd reached the top of Peter Street with the grand façade of the theatre visible in the near distance he'd turned abruptly on his heel and started walking back the way he'd come from. That had been a perfectly good plan until he'd seen Jen and Lloyd crossing the street further ahead and he'd jerked quickly to the left and taken shelter behind one of Manchester Central Library's imposing columns.

It wasn't that he was hiding from his colleagues. No, it was that he simply wasn't quite yet in the frame of mind to deal with anyone.

He was not *hiding*. He was just giving himself some space to think.

When Peggy had left him in the auditorium the day before, he'd stood there for a good few minutes, wondering whether he was supposed to have gone after her or not. She'd said she wasn't angry with him, after all, but he really would have needed to be a complete idiot to believe that was entirely true.

He'd been contemplating opening the surprise birthday gift she'd practically chucked at him when Lavinia had all but skipped back onto the stage, beaming at Andrew as she stood right on the edge, her hair catching the light and making Andrew think about fairies again.

'Ready to go?' Lavinia had called brightly.

Andrew had awkwardly stuffed the present into his jacket pocket to deal with later, and they'd headed out to a small Italian restaurant further up the street that Lavinia swore had the best pasta she'd eaten outside of Italy.

Andrew had never been to Italy, so he didn't have the experience for comparison, but he would happily admit that the food he'd eaten was far better than anything he'd have been minded to make for himself at home.

Dinner had been very pleasant. Lavinia had been all pretty smiles and amusing anecdotes about her life on stage, but she'd made sure to give Andrew plenty of opportunities to make himself look good by asking him questions about his job and then duly flattering him further by reacting at all the right points in his stories.

Halfway through dessert he'd let his imagination settle over the scene briefly. He hadn't had a girlfriend since the utter disaster that was the situation with Kate the year before and, even though he was fairly certain that blame for problems in that relationship should be equally apportioned, he couldn't remember them ever just having a pleasant dinner date together where Kate had smiled at him from start to finish. Not that this thing with Lavinia was a date, of course. Like he'd said to Peggy, it was *work*.

The slight problem, however, was that they hadn't really talked about the case at any point. Any time Andrew had tried to bring it up, Lavinia had batted the topic away with such skill that, even after a full evening ruminating on it, Andrew still couldn't work out how she'd done it.

At least he'd firmly rejected the idea of a bottle of wine when they'd arrived at the restaurant. It had definitely been the right choice, even if Lavinia had looked slightly put out for a second or two.

After dinner, he'd politely declined the offer of a nightcap at the bar, and he'd driven Lavinia to the hotel she was staying in for the duration of rehearsals and the production. He'd spent the drive marvelling at how anyone could just afford to stay somewhere that fancy for such a long period of time. Apparently even knowing the Swan siblings for almost a year hadn't completely desensitised him to the concept of huge reserves of cash.

Lavinia had chatted happily the whole time they'd been driving, only stopping for breath when Andrew pulled the car up outside the hotel and came round to open her door; he was still going to be a gentleman, even when it was *not* a date.

'Thank you for a lovely evening,' Lavinia had said, before she'd kissed him on the cheek and smiled at him coyly.

Andrew had very, very firmly reminded himself for the umpteenth time that it was still not a date, and he'd climbed straight back into the car and driven home with nothing more than a hasty 'goodnight'.

He'd been so wrapped up in his thoughts that he'd entirely forgotten about the birthday present from Peggy until he'd parked outside his house and looked up at his brother's old bedroom window, just as he did every day. Thinking of Rob had reminded him of Peggy, and he'd taken the gift out of his pocket and passed it from one hand to the other a few of times before carefully ripping the tidily sellotaped seam of the wrapping paper.

Whatever Andrew might have guessed would be the kind of present that Peggy Swan would buy him for his birthday, he would have been utterly incorrect.

He hadn't been expecting the neat, gently curling handwriting on the insert of the cassette tape box - *Andrew Joyce, This is Your Life '87* - followed by the titles of four songs on each side.

Peggy hadn't bought him a present at all. She'd *made* him one.

Andrew had laughed, despite himself, as he looked at the songs that Peggy had picked out. Side One started with *Superstition* by Stevie Wonder, and Side Two finished with Kate Bush's *Wuthering Heights*.

He'd stopped laughing almost immediately and groaned loudly.

'Oh, Joyce, you are a complete git,' Andrew chastised himself as he tapped the tape on the steering wheel.

By the time he'd opened the front door and chucked the house keys onto the kitchen counter he'd decided that it probably wasn't too late to call Peggy at home to thank her for the present.

But then all the lights had started flickering and so instead he'd spent half an hour quietly pleading with his dead brother to please just stop it.

Ever since Peggy had told him about Rob's ghost the previous summer the number of slightly odd occurrences in Andrew's house had ratcheted up tenfold. Not to mention the fact that Andrew felt like he was being watched most of the time whenever he woke up in the middle of the night.

He knew that he probably should mention it to Peggy at some point, but right then, he had more pressing matters than being haunted by his brother.

Pressing matters like the fact that he should have been at the Court already; and like how he was going to explain to his team that he'd learned nothing useful from Lavinia the night before; oh, and like how he had to apologise to his team for blowing them off, and to Peggy, specifically, for being a complete tit.

He really needed to get a move on.

Andrew turned away from the cold stone he'd been leaning against and headed for the theatre, reminding himself that he was supposed to be both a grown man and a professional, career-focussed Detective Inspector.

When he started crossing the road in front of the theatre, he nearly stopped dead in the middle of the traffic.

'Oh, for fuck's sake.' He glared at the familiar Aston Martin parked right outside the Court. If that car was here, then Charlie Swan was here too.

He balled his fists and wondered if he could pull in any favours any arrange to have the car towed. To be fair, he could probably get Higson involved; the DCI liked Charlie well enough, but he'd also find inconveniencing him terribly amusing.

Andrew did actually like Charlie too, even if he was loath to admit that to anyone, but he did not like Charlie anywhere near his cases. While the youngest Swan had proved himself useful in the past, he was often just an irritation, save for the occasional bout as a certified menace. Andrew was going to have to get rid of him pretty swiftly.

When Andrew reached the Stage Door, he found it propped open, despite his repeated requests to Cohen to improve security the day before.

Andrew sighed as he ascended the stairs towards Cohen's office, trying to mentally prepare himself for both an exuberant aristocrat and a day of sitting through that bloody play again. He was going to have to send Lloyd on a coffee run as soon as possible.

He reached the first-floor landing just as Cohen stepped off the staircase from the second floor.

'Good morning, DI Joyce,' Cohen drawled, yawning widely.

'Mr Cohen,' Andrew greeted the director, clenching his jaw and fighting against the urge to yawn himself in response.

Andrew was struck with sudden inspiration. Rather than immediately eject Charlie from the theatre, he was going to force him to sit through at least one run through of the play first. That would probably ensure that this was a one-time visit. That thought made Andrew feel instantly better.

'Miss Jones and her associate are currently on the stage,' Cohen replied, pulling Andrew out of his plotting.

He gestured for Andrew to lead the way down the corridor. 'After you.'

Andrew didn't move. 'Sorry, what did you say?'

'Miss Jones is on the stage already,' Cohen replied slowly.

'With her *associate*?' Andrew wanted to just check that he'd heard Cohen correctly. Oh Jesus Christ, what the hell sort of story was Charlie feeding people?

'Yes, I'm sorry I didn't catch her name,' Cohen replied frowning.

Andrew's mouth dropped open. *Her* name, Cohen had said. He wasn't talking about Charlie.

'Is there a problem?' Cohen asked.

Yes! Andrew wanted to yell. Yes, there was a problem, because he was coming to a terrible realisation about what was going on here, and it was a much bigger issue than just Charlie making a nuisance of himself.

'No, no, problem at all,' Andrew said aloud, hoping that his pasted-on smile looked appropriately reassuring.

Cohen's frown deepened, so Andrew had to assume that the smile hadn't worked well enough.

'Would you just excuse me for a few minutes?' Andrew asked politely, even as he was already backing away. 'I just need to check something with Miss Jones before she gets too far ahead in her investigation.'

'Oh, I'm heading that way anyway,' Cohen said mildly, falling into step beside Andrew. 'Don't worry, I'll stay out of your way.'

By the time they reached the door to the stage Andrew had been grinding his teeth so hard he thought that he might have loosened a filling.

Andrew had no idea what expression was on his face when he stepped under the stage lights, but the one that popped onto Peggy's face when she saw him approaching was priceless. In all his years of being a policeman he didn't think he'd ever seen someone look so immediately guilty.

'Um, hi?' Peggy managed with a grimace.

'Miss Jones.' Andrew said through gritted teeth as he stopped in front of her, with Cohen only a few feet away.

'Oh, hiya, Andrew!' Marnie called cheerfully from the front

row of seats. Then she waved at him with a smug little grin.

'Explain *now*,' Andrew hissed to Peggy when Cohen dipped back into the wings.

Unusually, Peggy didn't try to circumvent Andrew's request for an answer.

'Yesterday, I had no idea that this Jock character was anywhere near the stage, even though Alistair could see him,' Peggy started. 'Marnie suggested that maybe only ghosts can see him all of the time.'

'You're talking to Marnie about cases now?' Andrew snapped. 'Why? Don't you think it's already bad enough that your brother gets bored enough to tag along?'

Peggy looked taken aback by Andrew's particularly bad-tempered response. 'Charlie gave me a lift into town. He's not 'tagging along.' Saying that, I think it's perfectly reasonable that my brother wants to be nearby, given the *family connection* to this case.'

Bugger, thought Andrew. He'd momentarily forgotten about Caroline Winshire.

'Well, either way, you can't bring a bloody ghost to an investigation Peggy!' Andrew added crossly.

He turned to Marnie and shook his head. 'You're not supposed to be here.'

'Well, well, you're in quite the mood this morning,' Marnie said, slouching down in her seat and folding her arms. 'What's up? Didn't your date go very well?'

Andrew's eyes bugged.

'Marnie!' Peggy yelped in shared outrage.

Marnie just rolled her eyes. 'Oh, right, sorry, yeah, I forgot. I mean, didn't your *work meeting* go very well?'

Andrew was furious.

'Right, that is it!' He made towards the edge of the stage, ready to hop down and tell Marnie in no uncertain terms that his life was absolutely none of her business.

'Woah, woah!' Peggy said loudly, grabbing Andrew's arm and tugging him back across the stage away from where Marnie was making faces at him. 'I think maybe you two need to just stay out of each other's way for the rest of the day.'

'Right, so you can both can just go off for a gossip like two little old ladies?' Andrew scoffed. 'Peggy, you better get her out of here right now.'

'No,' Peggy said firmly in obvious irritation. 'Marnie's staying, because she might be able to help here. I know that you can see that, Andrew.'

'What I can *see* is how insane it is to bring a dead woman out in public,' Andrew snapped. 'Look, I know this might be normal to you, but you're *not* normal. It's more than a little grotesque to everybody else, alright?'

Peggy looked hurt. 'You know you're being a complete arse right now, don't you?'

Andrew did, actually, but that wasn't the point.

'Is everything alright over there?'

Andrew and Peggy turned in unison to see Cohen staring at them apprehensively. Peggy let go of Andrew's sleeve, and he, in turn, straightened his jacket accordingly.

'All fine, Albany,' Peggy replied, doing a much better job at faking a smile than Andrew had.

Oh, so apparently Peggy was on first name terms with Cohen now.

'Just testing out a theory,' Peggy added, lying through her teeth. 'DI Joyce is very keen on supporting the unusual methods we need to employ sometimes.'

'That's right,' Andrew muttered grimly.

'Right,' Cohen replied slowly. 'I need to get my actors out here pretty damn soon. Like, *immediately* actually. Is that okay?'

'Fine,' Peggy answered before Andrew could. 'No problem at all.'

'Thanks.'

Cohen left, still looking unsure about the pair of them.

'Look, just let Marnie have a look around, alright?' Peggy sighed when it was just the two of them again. 'How am I supposed to help keep anyone safe if I can't see the thing that's apparently the problem?'

Andrew dearly wanted to point out that Peggy had just described how Andrew felt most of the time since he'd transferred to the Ballroom. He held his tongue though and made himself consider what Peggy was proposing. 'She still shouldn't be here, Peggy.'

'She can help, Andrew. Just trust me. *Please*?'

'Alright, fine.' Andrew sighed, long and loud. 'But I can't even begin to think about what would happen if anyone found out that Marnie isn't...'

He trailed off and waved his hands. 'You know.'

'You're right,' Peggy replied seriously, 'but, I promise that nobody will find out.'

Andrew looked over at where Marnie was now smiling placidly at him, and he scowled in response.

'Good morning, Andrew!'

Andrew turned to see Lavinia striding towards him, smiling just as coyly as she had done the night before.

'Oh, I'll leave you to it,' Peggy said hurriedly, taking a step backwards.

'What? Why?' Andrew asked, but Peggy was already making a beeline off the stage towards Marnie.

'Andrew!' Lavinia repeated, louder this time.

No, not louder; *closer*. She was standing in front of him.

'I almost didn't recognise you dressed like this,' Lavinia laughed lightly. 'You look different in a suit.'

Andrew reminded himself to have that serious conversation with Lloyd about what constituted proper backup clothes at work. He'd made sure to put a couple of spare sets of his own clothes in the car that morning, because he'd realised that he could never be entirely certain that he wouldn't end up in that bloody canal again.

'I had a really lovely time last night,' Lavinia said, brushing a speck of something - possibly imaginary - from Andrew's tie. 'Maybe we could do it again over the weekend?'

'Lavinia, please!' Cohen snapped. 'We're starting.'

'I'll see you at lunch,' Lavinia said, finally removing her hand from Andrew's tie as she turned away.

Andrew shook his head slightly. He thought that he might have just been part of a whole conversation that had happened without him saying anything at all.

He looked down at the stalls and found Marnie glaring at him, even though Peggy seemed to be doing her level best to tug the wayward ghost away from the front row and towards the back of the auditorium where Jen and Lloyd were waiting.

'Excuse me, Detective Inspector,' Marion said, suddenly appearing next to him. 'I'm afraid that you're in my way.'

The words were polite, but Marion's tone was nothing short of waspish. Andrew shuffled out of the way quickly and went to join his team.

'Alright there, boss?' Lloyd grinned, handing over a thermos of coffee for Andrew to take.

'What?' Andrew said, inhaling the smell of coffee gratefully.

'Good evening, was it?' Lloyd asked with a wink.

Andrew burned the roof of his mouth on the coffee and swore loudly just as Jen smacked Lloyd on the arm. Peggy was whispering furiously to Marnie a few rows further back.

Lloyd seemed to remember who he was talking to. 'Er, right, well, I had a little chat with a couple of the Wardrobe girls this morning, and apparently nothing actually weird happened until Lavinia had a huge barney with Marion about whether the play was cursed or not.'

'Marion believes in the curse, right?' Jen asked, tactfully avoiding looking at where Andrew was staring balefully at the coffee marks on his previously white shirt.

'Even though she's still a bit sceptical about the *ghost* part, yeah, she does. They all do,' Lloyd replied, raising his eyebrows. 'Except Lavinia Heathcote, of course.'

'There's no such thing as curses,' Andrew said sternly.

'I think the three dead people would beg to differ,' Marnie offered, even though she wasn't supposed to be part of this conversation.

Andrew ignored her and kept looking at Lloyd. 'Anything else?'

'Nothing yet, sir,' Lloyd said. 'Not much has happened to anyone but Lavinia, and even though she's convinced it must be a stalker, or a disgruntled cast member sh-'

'Stalker?' Andrew asked, horrified.

'Yeah,' Lloyd replied slowly. 'She gets weird fan mail all the time apparently. Did she not mention it last night?'

Andrew was very aware that everyone was looking at him. 'No, no, she didn't mention that.'

'Fair enough. I suppose she's worried though, what with her technically being the standby, just like Alistair Tunham was, right?' Lloyd continued.

'What?' Andrew said again, and it felt like the twentieth time he'd said it that morning.

Lloyd looked at Jen and then back at Andrew with a frown. 'Lavinia wasn't originally playing the part of Isabella. Cohen had cast someone else.'

Andrew shook his head. 'No, that's not right. Cohen said that she was his first choice to play Isabella.'

Jen shook her head. 'I think that's the official story.'

'What's the *unofficial* story?' Andrew asked.

'Cohen cast a girl he'd never worked with before,' Lloyd explained, flicking through his notes. 'Emma Allen. Everyone I spoke to says that she was perfect for the part, but then she heard about the curse during early rehearsals, got spooked, and left the production. Enter Lavinia, who, by all accounts, isn't a fan of playing second fiddle to anyone.'

'Well, she sounds like a right catch, Andrew,' Marnie muttered darkly.

'Peggy!' Andrew barked.

Peggy, who was clearly pretending the rest of them didn't exist, jumped about three feet in the air at being addressed so loudly, and Andrew felt momentarily bad about taking his irritation out on her.

'Can you and Marnie go and see if you can find anything out from Alistair, please?' Andrew asked much more quietly.

Marnie slowly shook her head at him as she and Peggy wordlessly stood up and headed for the door.

'What?' Andrew asked again, this time to Jen when he noticed that she was frowning at him.

'Nothing, sir,' Jen replied tightly. 'Just thinking, that's all.'

'I think it's brilliant that Marnie's helping out,' Lloyd added, unable to read the room, as always.

'Well, I'm glad someone does, DC Parker,' Andrew snapped, sitting down heavily in the uncomfortable folding seat next to him.

Andrew looked over at the stage to where Marion was glaring at Teddy and Lavinia.

'We need to find out more about that lot,' he said, gesturing towards the actors. 'Barring the table being moved yesterday there's not been a hint of anything ghostly about this, has there?'

'Well, Lavinia saw that shadowy figure too, right?' Lloyd piped up. 'Outside her dressing room.'

Andrew shook his head. 'Which, by her own admission, was

probably just a man in dark clothing. Vic agrees, remember?'

'Maybe.' Lloyd didn't sound convinced.

'Plus, I don't think there's any love lost between any of the main cast, do you?' Andrew said, pointing at where Ben and Teddy now seemed to be arguing over something.

'Mad as a box of frogs,' Lloyd said, noisily unwrapping a lollipop and shoving it in his mouth. 'The lot of them.'

'What if one of them is just using the so-called 'curse' as an excuse to cause trouble?' Andrew asked.

'I can look into everyone's background,' Jen suggested. 'Including this Emma Allen girl, just in case.'

'Vic and Cohen too,' Andrew added as the director tried to break up the argument.

'You think *Cohen* could be behind it?' Lloyd asked, unconvinced. 'Even though he called us in?'

'Oh, come on, he even admitted himself that the theatre was hoping that the threat of a 'curse' might increase ticket sales,' Andrew said rolling his eyes. 'He'll have a completely sold-out production if word gets out about all this.'

'Does that mean we should also be looking into this woman from the charity who seems to be pulling all the strings?' Lloyd asked around the lollipop. 'Whatsername?'

'Caroline Winshire,' Jen confirmed, checking her notes.

'No, no, I think we should leave Caroline Winshire out of things for now,' Andrew said quickly.

'Any particular reason, sir?' Jen asked, frowning as she tapped her pen against her notes.

Andrew had promised Peggy that he wouldn't say anything about her connection to the countess. 'Look, just trust me for now, yeah?'

Jen looked unconvinced, which didn't make Andrew feel brilliant.

'I promise that if there's even the slightest hint that Caroline

Winshire is involved, I'll tell you, alright?'

'Alright,' Jen agreed slowly. 'But I'm looking into *everybody* else.'

'Fine by me,' Andrew said, holding his hands up in surrender. 'Every single person on that stage is a suspect until we have evidence that suggests otherwise.'

'Even Lavinia?' Lloyd asked, crunching on the sweet in his mouth.

Andrew looked over at the stage, where Lavinia was waving her arms around dramatically at something that Marion was saying to her.

He sighed. 'Yes, even Lavinia.'

* * *

Peggy closed yet another door with an irritated huff.

They'd tried every room on the first floor that they had access too, and they were already halfway through the second with no sign of Alistair.

'Maybe he's decided to bugger off into the great beyond,' Marnie suggested, scuffing her feet on the carpet, clearly enjoying the fact that she was leaving a trail of disturbed pile, even though it shouldn't be possible. 'Andrew's being more of an arse than usual, by the way.'

'He's right about how bad it would be if anybody found out that you were – *you know.*'

'Dead as a doornail?' Marnie offered. 'Beyond this life? Technically no longer with us?'

'Any of them. *All* of them,' Peggy replied as she selected the next numbered key on the set that Vic had acquired from the manager on her behalf that morning.

'He probably realised that Andrew had absolutely no intention of actually working out what happened to him,' Marnie added, pushing the door open when Peggy unlocked it.

'Marnie, don't say things like that,' Peggy said warningly. 'Andrew will make sure he investigates Alistair's death fully.'

'Yeah, when he's not too busy running around after knock-off Meryl Streep downstairs,' Marnie griped.

'That's not very fair, Marnie,' Peggy said, running her hand along the wall to find a light switch, 'and you know it.'

'What the hell is this room supposed to be?' Marnie asked as the fluorescent tube above their heads flickered to life with a metallic click, bathing them in a jaundiced glow.

Peggy looked around the room as the light warmed up a little more. Storage boxes lined the far wall of the small, windowless room with the face of each one covered in a series of letters and numbers. The handwriting changed a number of times, as did the condition of the boxes. The space strongly reminded Peggy of one of Higson's storage rooms at Tib Street. She'd only been inside them a couple of times, but the dusty, slightly mildewy smell of the rooms had stuck with her.

'An archive maybe?' Peggy suggested as she headed towards the shelves, pulling the closest box down carefully and setting it on the floor at her feet.

Her suspicion was confirmed when she crouched down and lifted the lid. She found that the box was filled with paper files of varying thickness. Each one was labelled with a production name and was filled with documents.

The first file Peggy pulled out had the cast information, programme and box office financial report for the eighty-one production of Shakespeare's *Measure for Measure*.

Marnie wrinkled her nose at the programme Peggy was holding. 'That looks a bit dull.'

'Actually, I think you'd quite like this one,' Peggy said, holding it out for Marnie to take.

'No songs, Peggy,' Marnie said, shaking her head. 'I just can't sit through it without a good song.'

'Actually, many Shakespeare plays have songs in them,' said a male voice.

Marnie squealed in surprise, hiding behind Peggy as Alistair materialised in front of them.

'You can see me too!' Alistair's eyes were wide in surprise. Then he frowned, reeling back slightly. 'Wait, you're not like Miss Peggy.'

Alistair looked absolutely stunned as he pointed his finger at Marnie accusingly. 'You're like *me*.'

'Alistair, this is Marnie Driscoll,' Peggy said, trying to uncurl Marnie's fingers from where they'd clamped around her arm. 'Marnie, Alistair Tunham.'

Alistair tipped his hat politely, even as he looked positively mystified. 'Miss Marnie.'

'Hi,' Marnie replied cautiously.

'I don't understand,' Alistair said to Peggy. 'How?'

'Marnie's my friend,' Peggy explained. 'She's helping me out.'

'There's something different about you though,' Alistair said, his focus solely on Marnie again. 'What is it?'

He caught sight of Marnie's fingers still holding onto Peggy's sleeve. 'That's not possible. That cannot be possible.'

'I'm a bit of a special case,' Marnie replied, looking a little embarrassed.

Even though her reply was light, Peggy knew that Marnie still found it unnerving that she could do things other ghosts couldn't. Truth be told, Peggy found it equally unsettling at times.

'We thought that Marnie might be able to see the other spirit,' Peggy continued when Alistair said nothing. 'Jock.'

'Didn't you believe me?' Alistair asked, looking betrayed.

'No, it's not that,' Peggy replied hurriedly. 'It's just that Andrew – DI Joyce - doesn't know you, and he can't see you either, remember?'

'But he can see *you*?' Alistair asked Marnie in awe.

Marnie rolled her eyes. 'Yeah, he can see me. Doesn't stop him from being a right p-'

'Alright, thank you, Marnie,' Peggy said, cutting her off with a sharp look. 'That's enough.'

'This is absolutely incredible!' Alistair beamed as widely as he had the day before. 'I'm so very delighted to meet you too, Miss Marnie.'

'Cool,' replied Marnie, and Peggy was reminded of Lloyd once more.

The ear-piercing scream that ripped through the air caused Peggy to jump in fright. She stumbled backwards, bumping into Marnie, and looked at Alistair questioningly.

'I have no idea,' he said, shaking his head.

'I think it came from downstairs,' Marnie added, already hurrying through the doorway with Peggy and Alistair right behind her.

'Help!' It was the same voice, high-pitched and terrified.

Peggy and Marnie tore down the staircase as Alistair drifted along next to them.

'Help me! Help!'

'I think that's Lavinia,' Peggy said, as she raced down the hallway towards Cohen's office. 'I think she's in there.'

There was another scream as Peggy rattled the door handle trying to open the door.

'Lavinia?' Peggy called loudly as the door refused to budge. 'Lavinia, is that you?'

'Miss Jones?' Lavinia shouted back. 'Get me out of here! The door's locked and he's going to come back!'

'Who?' Peggy asked, fumbling with the keyring in her hand, looking for the right key in the enormous bunch. The small plaque next to the door said it was room 107.

'I don't know!' Lavinia yelled, sounding like she was crying. 'I didn't see his face! I just heard this horrible voice behind me, and then there was a hand over my eyes and the door locked behind me. You have to get me out! Get me out!'

Lavinia was getting more hysterical by the second, and Peggy dropped the keys on the carpet in her haste to help. 'Bugger!'

Peggy looked up at the two ghosts next to her as she retrieved the keyring. 'Alistair, I need you to go in there and see what's going on. Marnie, go and get Andrew right now.'

Marnie flickered slightly.

'Like a *person*, Marnie!' Peggy yelled, stopping Marnie before she could disappear.

'Oh yeah. Oops!' Marnie turned and sped towards the first set of stage doors, and Alistair disappeared a moment later with a short nod.

Peggy cycled through the keys again. Where the hell was number 107? She had 106 and 108, but no 107. It hadn't been locked earlier when they'd been looking for Alistair, so she had no idea if she'd ever even had the key. 'Lavinia, I'm just looking for the key okay.'

'Well, could you bloody hurry up a bit?' Lavinia shrieked.

Peggy tamped down the immediate flare of annoyance, willing herself to be understanding. Lavinia was terrified right now, and it wouldn't do anyone any good for Peggy to be offended by anything she said in that moment.

'I can't see anyone in there except the screaming lady,' Alistair said breathlessly as he solidified next to Peggy again. 'She seems very frightened indeed.'

'Get me out!' Lavinia screeched again.

'I'll see if I can find Jock anywhere else,' Alistair offered before disappearing once more.

The doors at the end of the corridor burst open and Andrew stormed in, sprinting towards Peggy, with Marnie and Cohen in tow.

'What the hell is going on?' Andrew asked, pulling the bunch of keys out of Peggy's hands. 'Why isn't the door open already?'

'Last time I checked, neither Peggy nor I were locksmiths!' Marnie sniped.

'I don't have the right key,' Peggy said, ignoring Marnie, and snatching the keys back to show Andrew the space where 107 should be.

'Get me out of here!' Lavinia cried frantically.

'Cohen!' Andrew barked. 'Key?'

Cohen tapped his jeans pockets, followed by his blazer and eventually produced a keyring. 'Here.'

Andrew hastily located the correct key and unlocked the door.

The key had barely finished turning in the lock when the door flew open and Lavinia barrelled out of the room, crying hysterically as she launched herself at Andrew.

Peggy hopped out of the way as Andrew lurched backwards, trying to steady himself against the sudden onslaught of hair and tears.

'What happened?' Cohen asked as he looked between Peggy and where Lavinia was sobbing into Andrew's shoulder.

'We were upstairs in some sort of archive room, and suddenly heard Lavinia screaming,' Peggy explained. 'When we got down here the door was locked, but Lavinia said that someone had been in the room with her.'

Cohen paled instantly and for a second Peggy thought he might be about to pass out.

'It was the ghost?' Cohen asked, voice barely above a whisper.

'I don't think so,' Peggy replied. 'Not from the way Lavinia described it.'

Andrew glanced at her sharply over the top of Lavinia's head. 'What do you mean?'

'Lavinia said that someone was behind her, they put a hand over her mouth and then she was locked in,' Peggy explained. 'I don't think she saw who it was.'

'So, it *could* have been the ghost?' Cohen asked, somehow looking even paler.

'Alistair says nobody was in there with her,' Peggy murmured to Andrew. 'So, I can't tell you whether it was Jock or not, but it doesn't sound quite like a ghost, does it?'

'Lavinia, can you tell me what happened?' Andrew asked quietly as he carefully extricated himself from the death grip he was in.

Lavinia, despite her hysterical screaming of only moments earlier, did a superb job of looking rather composed as she stepped back and dabbed at her eyes with her fingertips. 'There was a man. I don't know who he was.'

'Did you see him?' Andrew asked.

Lavinia shook her head with another sniffle. 'No, but I heard him. It was this horrible, deep, gravelly voice.'

'What did he say?'

Lavinia grabbed one of Andrew's hands between both of hers and stared up at him imploringly. 'He said that I was going to be next. He knew my name!'

Marnie rolled her eyes towards Peggy when Lavinia let out another sob and went back to clinging to Andrew's neck.

The doors opened again, and Jen appeared this time. 'Lloyd's got everyone else sitting in the stalls. What's happened?'

'Miss Heathcote was accosted by an intruder of some kind,' Andrew replied, clearly aiming for boss-like and professional, despite the crying woman hanging off him.

Jen raised her eyebrows.

'Mr Cohen, I think Lavinia should probably take the rest of the day off,' Andrew added, untangling himself again.

'No, no, I'm fine, I'm fine,' Lavinia said, standing up straight and wiping her eyes again. 'I just don't want to be on my own.'

'You won't be, I promise,' Andrew said.

Lavinia shot him a watery smile. 'Thank you for getting me

out of there, Andrew.'

'She should be thanking *you*,' Marnie grumbled quietly to Peggy.

'DS Cusack will stay with you for the rest of the day,' Andrew said to Lavinia, nodding towards Jen, thankfully with no suggestion that he'd heard Marnie at all. 'I think a cup of tea might be needed, Jen.'

Peggy thought that Lavinia looked like she might protest, but Jen started herding the actress down the corridor almost immediately.

'Mr Cohen, I think you can restart your rehearsal now, but do not let anyone leave that auditorium this morning, unless they absolutely have to,' Andrew instructed. 'If someone needs to leave for any reason, DC Parker is to accompany them. Understood?'

'Understood,' Cohen repeated.

'I need you to ask some of the theatre staff to do a sweep of the building to check no doors or windows have been damaged or left open, alright?'

Cohen nodded, but he still looked mildly ill as he headed slowly back to the double doors.

'Marnie, I need you in the auditorium too,' Andrew added.

Marnie jerked slightly in surprise at being addressed. 'You want *me* to help?'

Peggy thought that Andrew looked like he might want to make a smartarse comment, but whatever he might have wanted to really say was bitten back in favour of, 'Yes.'

'Alright,' Marnie agreed slowly. 'What do you want me to do?'

'Keep an eye out for any sign of anything that's even the slightest bit unusual, alright?' Andrew said sternly. 'And I mean *anything*. If anything's amiss I want you to come and tell us straight away.'

'Alright,' Marnie repeated, still frowning at Andrew as she turned away and followed Cohen.

'Did you see anyone on this floor when you came down?' Andrew asked, turning to Peggy at last.

Peggy shook her head. 'Nobody. Alistair and Marnie were both with me when we heard Lavinia scream.'

'Is there any way you could have dropped the key to Cohen's office at some point? Left it somewhere for someone to pick up?'

'No,' Peggy replied, feeling slightly offended at the idea.

Andrew rolled his eyes. 'I wasn't suggesting any of this was your fault. You know I needed to ask.'

'That office was unlocked with the door wide open when Marnie and I had a look in there earlier. We left it exactly as we found it,' Peggy explained. 'Why was Lavinia even in there though? I thought the rehearsal had started.'

'Cohen had left some notes on his desk. Lavinia offered to go and get them. Why?'

'So, nobody could have known that Lavinia would be there at that exact moment, right?' Peggy asked slowly.

'Right,' Andrew replied, frowning again. 'Where are you going with this?'

'Well, so far everyone's working on the theory that Lavinia would be the next logical target if there was a curse.'

'There's no such thing as curses,' Andrew interjected.

'Jesus, I said *if* there was a curse.' It was Peggy's turn to roll her eyes. 'How would anyone know that Lavinia was going to be in Cohen's office right at that moment? And why is it that the key to that room is the only one missing from this bunch? Surely her dressing room would be a better bet if you were looking for her.'

Peggy waved the keys towards Andrew.

'Still not entirely sure what you're getting at, Peggy.'

Peggy sighed in frustration. 'What if Lavinia isn't the target? What if it's Cohen? I mean, it's his office that Lavinia was in. Or, what if it's nobody in particular?'

'You don't think Lavinia's being targeted?' Andrew raised an eyebrow. 'Peggy, even ignoring what just happened, her dress was cut to ribbons last week, plus she saw someone outside her dressing room.'

'Yes, I know that,' Peggy replied, still irritated. 'I'm not saying that she's *not* being targeted. But just stop and think for a minute; she wasn't involved in what happened on stage yesterday, was she?'

'No, she wasn't,' Andrew replied grudgingly. 'So, what do you think? It's the production itself being targeted?'

'Maybe,' Peggy said, wrinkling her nose. 'Or do you think it's possible we're dealing with two separate things here?'

Peggy could see Andrew turning the words over in his head.

'An actual haunting, but also some level of human involvement?' Andrew asked eventually, nodding slowly.

'It would explain why Alistair saw Jock on the stage yesterday, but also how Lavinia is certain that it was an actual man who attacked her today,' Peggy replied.

'You don't think this shadow man could be like Marnie? You know, able to appear human, touch things, etcetera?'

Peggy shook her head. 'Alistair said he isn't really like a man at all. Plus, I can't believe that there's anyone, or anything, quite like Marnie.'

'Neither can I,' Andrew replied. He shuddered at the thought.

'What do you want me to do then?' Peggy asked, very aware that everyone else seemed to have been given a job.

'You said there was an archive room, right?'

Peggy nodded. 'Yes, upstairs. Why?'

'I think it's a good bet for finding out a little more about everyone involved, don't you? They've all worked on productions here before.' Andrew shrugged. 'Maybe we can even work out why this play seems to have an above-average death rate attached to it.'

'*We?*' Peggy frowned. 'Is this just you trying to get out of watching that play again?'

'It's mostly me trying to make sure you don't get killed,' Andrew replied.

Peggy bristled. 'Not funny.'

'Not kidding,' Andrew said seriously. 'Come on, let's go.'

'I can look through a pile of boxes myself, you know,' Peggy huffed, heading for the stairs.

'Oh, I know,' Andrew replied mildly, as he followed her. 'But I also know you'd still somehow find a way to attract trouble anyway.'

SIX

Andrew was beginning to think that it actually might have been more interesting to sit through yet another rehearsal of *Lady Bancroft's Rose* than to sift through boxes and boxes of production memorabilia and financial records.

He and Peggy had started by working out which Court productions any combination of Lavinia, Marion, Teddy and Ben had worked on, and then the same for Cohen and Vic. All they'd learned, in Andrew's opinion, was that the theatre world seemed very, very small as main roles seemed to be given out to the same names over and over again.

'There's another note here. This one's from *The Importance of Being Earnest* last year, suggesting that they rehearse Lavinia and Marion separately as far as possible,' Peggy said, passing a piece of paper over the box that sat between them on the floor.

'Another one?' Andrew asked incredulously, taking the note with one hand as he scratched his head. 'Why would you cast them if they can't work together?'

'I think, sometimes, it's possible to have two very different people, and still produce something brilliant in the end,' Peggy said, perhaps a little wryly.

If Andrew thought back over the past year, he'd have to wholeheartedly agree with that statement.

'Anyway,' Peggy continued, snapping the file closed, 'I think we can safely say that the only one of the four main cast members that seems entirely unproblematic is Ben.'

Andrew would have to wholeheartedly agree with that statement too. From what they'd seen in the archives, Lavinia, Marion and Teddy seemed to have problems with each other, or other cast members, or directors, or with theatre staff on a semi-regular basis.

'So, we're only looking at a mile-long list of anyone who might go to extremes to make this production an unpleasant experience for everyone involved,' Andrew groaned, rubbing his eyes. 'Great.'

'And the possibility of Jock compounding the problem,' Peggy said with a sigh. 'Although the fact that there's only one archive box with pre-1945 productions doesn't fill me with confidence that we'll find much about him here.'

'Given how close to the Free Trade Hall we are, I'd say it's likely the Court was hit by bombs too,' Andrew said, dragging the box in questions across the carpet towards him. 'They probably lost any older records they had.'

'Alistair mentioned the bombs when I first spoke to him. I only remember my father complaining about the state of the building, but the possibility it had been bombed never occurred to me.'

'Did they not teach you your history in any of those fancy schools you went to?' Andrew snorted. 'Just before Christmas 1940, our fair city was bombed for two nights in a row. Deansgate was destroyed, all round here was hit – except for the Midland - but the Cathedral was damaged, and further up to Strangeways as well.'

Andrew winced as he finished speaking. That was part of the city they generally avoided talking about, given what had happened there last year.

Peggy swallowed heavily, then pasted a forced smile onto her face. 'Well, I wasn't aware you were a history buff. Miracles never cease.'

'Sorry, I didn't mean to bring that up,' Andrew apologised.

'I have Marnie as a permanent reminder, Andrew,' Peggy replied with a small, self-deprecating laugh. 'Don't worry about it.'

He did worry though. He still sometimes dreamed that they were trapped in that damn burning house, and he'd startle awake with his chest and ribs aching. He'd put good money on Peggy experiencing the same dreams.

'Is there anything there about the 1932 production?' Peggy asked, avoiding Andrew's eyes and gesturing to the box.

Andrew opened the box carefully, mindful of the dust clouds they'd already created in their search so far.

Inside there were only three paper files. It looked like Peggy's lack of confidence may have been warranted after all. He pawed at the paper, hoping for a miracle.

'Ha!' Andrew laughed disbelievingly as he plucked out the bottom file, only to see *Lady Bancroft's Rose – Directed by Richard Sykes – January 1932* written in cursive on the front. He turned it round for Peggy to see.

'Did we actually just find what we were looking for, for once?' Peggy asked, wide-eyed as she crawled around the box to look over Andrew's shoulder as he opened the file.

There were only a few sheets of paper inside, but the top one was a handwritten list of the cast.

'There's Alistair,' Peggy said, pointing to the name listed as standby for Sebastian, under the principal cast.

'And there's Henriette St. Clair.' Andrew nodded towards the bottom of the list, where the actress was listed as Isabella's standby.

Peggy took the folder from Andrew to study it. 'And then fifteen years later she returns to play Lady Bancroft herself at the Palace.'

'Only to end up dead before the second half,' Andrew muttered, shaking his head. He looked at Peggy. 'Why would you come back? Fifteen years after the same production ended in tragedy.'

Peggy shrugged as she leafed through the sheets. 'I don't

know. Maybe the fact that it was being staged somewhere else was enough of a removal from the original for her.'

Andrew shivered slightly. 'It's still creepy.'

'You think everything's creepy,' Peggy replied, rolling her eyes.

Andrew chose to ignore that comment. 'I still can't see how all the deaths are connected; beyond the fact they're all centred around this bloody play. Okay, yes, Henriette St. Clair was *there* when Alistair Tunham died, and then she dies herself during the second production, but what's the connection to the third?'

'What year was it? Seventy-three?'

Andrew nodded. 'Twenty-six years after Henriette's death. Nobody from the original production would have been involved, surely?'

'I doubt it,' Peggy confirmed. 'Like Jen said, you'd probably be looking at a surprisingly sprightly murderer if that were the case.'

'Copycat maybe?' Andrew suggested.

'Does that seem likely?'

'Not really,' Andrew admitted. 'There's always the theory that Henriette St. Clair just fell down the stairs, and Peter McClellan was just a chain-smoking alcoholic who unfortunately had a heart-attack, of course.'

'You forgot the 'malevolent ghost made of shadows' theory,' Peggy reminded him.

Andrew slapped both hands against his face and groaned loudly. 'We're not getting anywhere at all, are we?'

'Come on,' Peggy said, pushing herself to her feet. 'They're going to think we're hiding if we don't go back down there soon.'

'But it's such a terrible play,' Andrew moaned, hands still covering his face.

Peggy laughed and reached down to help pull Andrew to his feet. 'It's not that bad.'

Andrew was about to make a pithy comment about the fact that Peggy was the one who'd fallen asleep during the rehearsal yesterday, but the door slamming loudly behind them startled him into silence.

'What the hell?' Andrew looked around wildly, but there was nobody in the room besides the two of them. 'Did you see anything?'

Peggy shook her head.

'We're leaving right now,' Andrew said, reaching for the door handle.

The door didn't budge. Andrew swore under his breath and tried the handle again.

'Are we locked in?' Peggy asked quietly, cautiously looking around the room as though something terrible might pop into existence at any point.

Andrew supposed that when you were Peggy Swan that was actually always a possibility. 'Keys?'

Peggy handed the bunch of keys over. 'I think this is 208.'

Andrew pushed the corresponding key into the lock and tried to turn it anticlockwise, but the key wouldn't budge. He turned it clockwise instead and heard the barrel roll into place as the door locked. He unlocked it again, but still the door wouldn't open, no matter how hard he pulled on the handle.

'The door's not locked,' Andrew said, keeping his voice as even as possible. 'But it's not opening either.'

'We're on the second floor.' Peggy swallowed heavily. 'Which is where Lavinia saw someone the other night, and where Peter McClellan's dressing room would have been too.'

Peggy didn't explicitly mention Jock, but she didn't need to. Not when the back of Andrew's neck was already prickling in response to an unseen threat.

'Peggy, come here,' Andrew instructed quietly, holding out his hand.

Peggy grasped his hand and allowed herself to be pulled soundlessly against Andrew's side, their backs against the closed door.

'Any chance you could get Marnie up here?' Andrew whispered.

Before Peggy could say anything, an archive box lazily tumbled to the ground from the highest shelf on the opposite wall. The cardboard sides crumpled as the corner hit the carpet heavily and the lid buckled enough to send pieces of paper fluttering free from their files.

'Oh, that's not good,' Peggy muttered as another box followed the first.

'Peg, get Marnie!'

'Marnie?' Peggy called. 'Marnie, can you hear me?'

As if in response to Peggy's shout, another box toppled from the shelves, faster than the first, landing with a much louder thump.

'Marnie! Get up here!'

Two more boxes plunged to the floor with dull thuds, and, unless Andrew was imagining things, there was also now a metallic rattling sound.

Peggy sucked in a surprised breath next to him, and Andrew saw that she had her eyes clamped closed.

Files, which had been inertly lying on the carpet suddenly flew open, untouched by any hand that Andrew could see. Sheets of paper twirled into the air, spinning out of control without even a hint of a breeze in the archive room.

The fluorescent tube on the ceiling flickered violently, and Andrew was immediately back in his kitchen the night before, pleading with Rob to stop.

There was a loud knock on the door behind them, and

Andrew pulled Peggy away from the sound, even as it brought them closer to the maelstrom of paper.

'Boss?' Lloyd called from the corridor. 'Peggy?'

Andrew jumped in surprise when Marnie materialised next to Peggy without warning.

'What the hell is going on in here?' Marnie yelped as a box lid bounced off the back of her head.

'The door won't open!' Andrew shouted to Lloyd. 'It's not locked though!'

Every piece of paper caught in the impossible whirlwind fell to the floor in unison, as though the invisible strings holding them aloft had been suddenly cut.

The door opened.

'How did you do that?' Andrew asked Lloyd in surprise as his DC walked into the room, frowning at him.

'It just opened, sir.' Lloyd shrugged. 'Are you sure it was stuck?'

Marnie crouched so that she could pick up a handful of paper, and only then did Lloyd seem to notice the mess, his eyes widening in alarm.

Andrew looked down to see that Peggy still had her eyes screwed shut, and her fingers were digging into his arm almost painfully.

'Peggy, are you alright?' he asked, squeezing her hand lightly.

Peggy's eyes snapped open and for just a second, she looked as though she were somewhere else entirely. It reminded Andrew of the very first day he'd met her, and he didn't like that expression any more now than he had done then.

'He's angry, Andrew.' Peggy's voice wasn't much more than a crackle of air. 'He's so angry.'

'Did he say anything?' Andrew asked hesitantly. He thought it unnecessary to ask who she meant when the look of horror on her face was enough to answer that question.

'He just kept repeating the same thing over and over again,' Peggy said quietly. She stumbled slightly as she let go of Andrew and shook her head as though clearing it.

'Which was what?'

Andrew's apprehension skyrocketed when Peggy looked at him again.

'*Liars.*'

* * *

It had been a long time since Peggy had felt so out of sorts after encountering a spirit. She'd been fairly certain that the almost-constant presence of both Emmeline and Marnie at Butterton had hugely increased her tolerance for dealing with ghosts again. She'd even managed to walk past the Cathedral a few times in the past couple of months, blocking out the plaintive voices enough to be manageable.

But after what had happened in the archive room earlier, she felt like any progress that she'd made had been unravelled, leaving her with a thumping headache and rolling waves of nausea.

She took another sip from the plastic cup of water that Andrew had refilled and pressed back into her hands a few minutes earlier and blew out a breath of frustration as she stared up at the gilded mouldings that decorated the ceiling.

'I thought you might need this.'

Peggy looked up in surprise as Albany Cohen held a mug towards her.

'That's how it works in England, right?' Cohen grinned. 'Tea solves everything?'

'Something like that.' Peggy put her water on the floor by her feet and accepted the mug gratefully. 'Thanks.'

Cohen, holding his own mug, casually leaned back against the front of the stage and folded one arm across his chest.

'DI Joyce said that you've been working with him for the past year,' Cohen said, and Peggy could tell that he was gently working his way up to a barrage of questions.

'That's right,' Peggy replied. Ultimately, she'd let him ask whatever he wanted, partially because he'd handed her tea that was actually tea-coloured, rather than just lightly tanned milk.

'What did you do before?' Cohen asked. 'I mean, if you don't mind me asking.'

'Accounting, mainly,' Peggy replied, and, well, that was mostly true.

Cohen looked surprised. 'Really?'

'Really.' Peggy smiled slightly. 'DC Parker is a friend of my brother's, so I got roped into helping on a case. It was really supposed to be a one-time thing.'

'And you've always been able to just…' Cohen waved his hands as he trailed off. He gave her a crooked smile. 'Sorry, I'm still trying to get my head around it all.'

'You're doing much better than most,' Peggy replied. 'And yes, it's just been part of my life since I was a child.'

Over Cohen's shoulder, she could see Andrew having a hushed discussion with Marnie; they didn't seem to be at each other's throats, but she was going to keep an eye on them just in case. It amazed her that Andrew somehow still hadn't lost his cynicism, but then again, he was the most stubborn person she knew, so at least part of it would be that he was simply *refusing* to let himself believe in ghosts, even as he held a conversation with an impossible woman.

'And your colleague, Mary, was it?' Cohen asked, gesturing towards the direction Peggy was looking.

'Marnie,' Peggy corrected. 'I met Marnie the same day I met DI Joyce. That was all rather by chance.'

'And she can do what you do?'

'Sort of.'

'Amazing,' Cohen said, and he looked like he meant it. 'Where are her shoes though?'

Peggy paled. The question was innocuous enough, but so close to the very question Marnie had asked Peggy when she'd first encountered her. She could still hear Marnie's terrified voice, even now.

'Are you alright, Miss Jones?' Cohen asked, concerned.

'Sorry, yes,' Peggy replied as she forced a small smile. 'Also, Peggy please, rather than Miss Jones.'

Cohen nodded his acceptance.

'As for Marnie, she just likes to feel connected to wherever we are,' Peggy added. She thought that she might as well pre-empt what would definitely be a question if Marnie returned to the Court the next day. 'She's a creature of habit too; she always wears the same outfit when we're investigating something.'

'Really?' Cohen asked, raising his eyebrows at Marnie's party dress. 'Like a superstition thing?'

'Sort of,' Peggy said again, this time with a small smile.

'Fascinating.' Cohen shook his head. 'You know, I didn't know the police even did this sort of thing.'

'I don't think they usually do,' Peggy replied, taking another sip of tea. 'This is a rather out of the ordinary sort of department.'

'Well, whatever the reason, I'm glad of it,' Cohen said, sighing loudly.

Cohen then laughed, but Peggy thought it sounded more desperate than amused.

'I turned down Broadway for this,' Cohen muttered, taking a gulp of tea.

'Really? Why?' Peggy asked in surprise.

'I needed to get out of New York for a while,' Cohen replied with a sigh. 'I knew the Court wanted me back, so it was the perfect excuse to jump on a plane and get the hell out of there.'

That was more cryptic a response than Peggy would have liked, and whereas Andrew would have continued to prod and pry until he had the answer he wanted, Peggy would just have to let it lie for now.

'I hope you don't mind me asking, but how exactly did you manage to convince anyone to take part in this production?' Peggy asked. 'I mean, it seems like everyone besides Lavinia firmly believes in the curse.'

'Ah, well that's actually a surprisingly easy question to answer,' Cohen replied, rubbing the back of his neck self-consciously. 'It's because of me.'

'I don't follow.'

'I'm putting *Lady Bancroft* on early next year, back home on Broadway,' Cohen explained. 'Once you know that, it's not too much a of a stretch to work out why someone would take on a role in this production.'

'You're taking this cast to New York?' Peggy asked.

Cohen shrugged. 'Honestly, I don't know yet.'

'What about Lavinia?' Peggy asked carefully. 'I know someone else originally had her part.'

Cohen's eyebrows disappeared into his hair. 'How do you know about that? No way did *Lavinia* tell you.'

'DS Cusack was informed by a few people,' Peggy replied, hoping that nobody was going to get into trouble for this.

Cohen, to Peggy's surprise, hooted loudly with laughter. Andrew and Marnie looked over at the sound.

'Oh my God, she'll be so pissed when she finds out that people know!'

'I don't understand why there's so much secrecy around it,' Peggy replied as Cohen continued to grin. 'You told us that she was your first choice, and that she'd been incredible in your show last year.'

'You mustn't get me wrong here, Peggy,' Cohen said as he shook his head. 'Lavinia's a very talented actress, and she'll make a great Isabella, but that doesn't eliminate the reality that she's not the easiest person to work with. I promised her that I wouldn't make a big deal about the fact that I'd cast someone else first, so I hope you can forgive me for giving you the wrong impression yesterday.'

Peggy still thought it was all a little odd, but she didn't get the opportunity to voice that thought as Andrew appeared at Cohen's shoulder.

Marnie had disappeared, and Peggy hoped that didn't mean she and Andrew had descended into yet another argument.

'Mr Cohen, have you made that phone call yet?' Andrew asked, looking between the two mugs of tea as though they were personally offending him.

Peggy rolled her eyes and held her half-full mug out to Andrew. 'Here, you can finish it. God knows you'll be in a worse mood if you don't get some caffeine soon.'

Andrew took the mug, though he twitched in annoyance when Cohen tried to hide a snort of laughter.

'Yes, I have, Inspector,' Cohen said, still smirking a little. 'I've pulled in a few favours, and we've got an alternative rehearsal space for tomorrow morning. Sunday is a rest day anyway, but we'll have to be back here Monday for a full technical.'

'Even one day is better than nothing,' Andrew replied, and finally his annoyance gave way to something that looked more like mild relief.

'I'll get you the address,' Cohen said. He nodded at Peggy as he pushed away from the stage. 'If you'll excuse me, Peggy.'

'No, that's fine,' Peggy said, waving him away.

'Nice chat?' Andrew asked tersely.

'Well, if you define 'nice' by finding out something that might be vaguely useful, then yes, it was a 'nice chat',' Peggy replied, folding her arms.

'What?' Andrew frowned.

'You wanted to know why anyone would take on a role in this production, right?' Peggy raised her eyebrows. 'Well, it turns out that Cohen is planning to stage *Lady Bancroft* again next year.'

It was quite possible that Andrew had never looked more aghast. 'Again? But, *why?*'

Peggy bit back a laugh. 'I think he just *really* likes the play, Andrew. Plus, it doesn't seem to be cursed anywhere else, right?'

'There's still no such thing as curses,' Andrew replied, taking a gulp of tea. 'Where's he putting it on next?'

'Broadway,' Peggy replied, and watched as the realisation dawned on the detective's face. 'There, now you've caught up.'

'They all want him to take them to New York,' Andrew said, looking back over his shoulder to where the actors were preparing to get up from their seats and head back on stage.

'Yes, I'd say so.'

Peggy watched as Marion made a face behind Lavinia's back as she followed her up towards the stage. Teddy seemed to be playing with a Rubik's Cube while Ben ignored him completely as he walked beside him.

'Just be grateful that at least you get to avoid it tomorrow,' Andrew said, turning back to Peggy.

'What do you mean?'

'Well, you and Marnie don't need to come to the new rehearsal location tomorrow morning, do you?' Andrew shrugged. 'No real need, is there?'

'Oh,' Peggy replied, feeling as put-out as she had done the day before when Andrew had just announced that he was cancelling their plans. 'Right, okay.'

'Come on, you don't actually *want* to sit through another rehearsal, do you?' Andrew chuckled slightly, draining the dregs of the tea and setting the mug down right on the edge of the stage.

No, Peggy certainly did not want to sit through another rehearsal, but she did want to feel like she was actually part of the team, rather than an accessory to be picked up and then cast-off again at will.

'Well, I ac-'

'Oh, for Christ's sake!' Andrew hissed loudly, interrupting Peggy, before he stalked past her towards the back of the auditorium.

Peggy whipped around in confusion, only to see her brother waltzing in through the double doors, a smug smile on his face as he met Andrew's angry gesticulating head on.

'Oh, for f-' Peggy cut herself off and hurried up the aisle.

'How did you even get in here?' Andrew was asking Charlie as Peggy reached them.

'Well, I *do* actually own the place, Joycie.' Charlie grinned maddeningly.

'No, you don't,' Peggy sighed, glaring at her brother.

'Near enough, Peg,' Charlie laughed lightly.

Charlie was terrible when it came to joking about their father's mortality. Peggy didn't have much in the way of warm feelings left for her father, but she didn't revel in the same morbid thoughts as her younger brother.

'Look, I only came to make sure that there hadn't been any sightings of the witch herself,' Charlie replied, lips twisting in disdain.

Peggy had momentarily forgotten about her mother's involvement in this whole sorry mess but felt her stomach swoop in protest at the thought.

Andrew, to his credit, backed off immediately at Charlie's explanation, and instead he stopped waving his arms and shook his head. 'No, no sign, and I've already told Cohen to make sure that nobody gets in without advance clearance from me.'

Peggy jolted. 'You have?'

'Well, we can't have just *anyone* walking in here, can we?' Andrew replied, and then he frowned at Charlie again. 'Which begs the question, how exactly did *you* get in here?'

'Would you believe me if I said I have a key?' Charlie asked, grinning widely.

Andrew's mouth dropped open in outrage, and Peggy elbowed her brother hard in the ribs before war could break out.

'He's kidding, Andrew,' she said, holding her hands up placatingly.

Charlie rolled his eyes. 'Nice to see that you're so relaxed, Joycie.'

Andrew scowled.

'Oh, come on.' Charlie laughed loudly. 'Don't you realise what day it is? It's Friday the thirteenth! It's the ultimate day for curses!'

Peggy caught movement out of the corner of her eye. Cohen was heading towards them with a piece of paper in his hand.

'Incoming!' Peggy muttered urgently. 'Charlie, you don't know me, and we're not related, alright?'

'What?' Charlie asked, making a face as though he thought Peggy had lost the plot.

'Well, it's very nice to meet you,' Peggy said loudly, grabbing her brother's hand and shaking it firmly. 'But no thank you, we don't need any assistance at this time.'

'What are you doing?' Andrew asked Peggy, blinking in confusion.

'Same question!' Charlie hissed as he yanked his hand away from his sister.

'Oh, hi there Albany,' Peggy said, far too loudly if the way the director flinched slightly was anything to go by.

'Er, hi?' he replied, before looking at Charlie in confusion.

'This is Charles, Viscount Ashley,' Peggy said, widening her eyes at her brother and hoping that she firmly conveyed that if he didn't play along, she would murder him later, or, at the very least, ask Marnie to sing her West End musicals medley to him. 'He practically owns this theatre.'

Cohen did exactly what Peggy thought he might do at hearing that. He flapped his hand holding the paper towards Andrew without looking at him, smacking the detective in the chest, and then he *almost* bowed in Charlie's direction.

'This is Albany Cohen. He's directing the production of *Lady Bancroft's Rose* that you were so interested in hearing more about,' Peggy added. She ignored Andrew's raised eyebrows entirely.

'Oh yes,' Charlie said, shaking Cohen's hand enthusiastically. 'I'd absolutely love to hear about the play.'

'Perhaps meet the cast?' Peggy suggested firmly.

'Absolutely!' Charlie beamed.

'Now hang on there one second!' Andrew stepped forward as though somehow that might magically derail the situation.

'Mr Cohen, I would *love* to meet the cast,' Charlie continued. 'How about right now? If it's a good time, of course.'

'Oh, absolutely,' Cohen agreed eagerly.

Charlie shot Andrew a smug look before he trotted off towards the stage with Cohen chattering enthusiastically at him.

'What the hell was that?' Andrew snapped at Peggy when the two men were out of earshot.

'Well, I was just thinking about the fact that neither Lavinia nor Cohen told us that there was originally a different actress playing Isabella,' Peggy replied.

'Is that supposed to be an explanation?'

'How many people have you spoken to since we got here yesterday?' Peggy asked. 'Twenty? Thirty perhaps?'

'About that, yes,' Andrew confirmed slowly.

'And yet nobody told you about Lavinia's predecessor,' Peggy replied. 'If someone hadn't decided to break rank and tell Jen this morning, we might not have known at all. For a bunch of people who don't really like each other, they seem to be pretty good at keeping each other's secrets.'

'But what's your brother got to do with it?'

'People tell Charlie *everything*,' Peggy replied, looking over to where Charlie was eagerly greeting everybody on stage. 'If they're hiding anything you can guarantee that he'll be able to weasel it out of them without even trying.'

'He's not police, Peggy,' Andrew protested.

'Neither am I.'

'That's different.'

'It really isn't. Anyway, I've got him out of your way, haven't I?'

'Why are they all so much nicer to him?' Andrew grumbled as they stood and watched Marion and Teddy smiling widely as Charlie shook their hands. 'Jesus, it looks like the receiving line at the Royal Variety up there.'

Peggy snorted. 'Don't tell Charlie you've compared him to royalty. He'll never let you forget it.'

'What does it say about the world we live in when people are more likely to talk candidly to a toff than a detective?'

'Did you just call me a toff?' Peggy asked, slightly offended.

'No. I called *Charlie* a toff. That's different.'

'It really isn't,' Peggy said again. 'But, to answer your question, it's quite simple, really: when people have something to hide – even if it's utterly irrelevant to your investigation - they feel like you're only seeing them as a suspect.'

'People don't feel like that,' Andrew scoffed.

'Of course they do. You're cynical about everything and don't trust anyone; I think people probably pick up on that.'

'I am *not* cynical about everything!'

'No, of course you're not.' Peggy laughed. 'But the point is that people very stupidly tend to trust my brother upon meeting him.'

'I didn't trust him. I still don't.'

'Which is both a credit to you, and also proves my point about you not trusting anyone,' Peggy replied. She pointed at the paper Andrew was holding. 'Now, where are you heading off to tomorrow?'

'I *do* trust people,' Andrew replied, ignoring the question. 'I trust you, and Jen. Even Lloyd, on occasion.'

Peggy thought that the 'on occasion' didn't really apply to just Lloyd, but as she didn't really fancy an argument just then she didn't press the point.

'Are you feeling alright now?' Andrew asked, as though he'd suddenly remembered the events of that morning.

'Fine,' Peggy replied, plucking the paper from Andrew's fingers.

'Actually fine, or 'you just want me to stop asking fine'?'

It was definitely more the latter, but Peggy said, 'Actually fine.'

Andrew obviously didn't believe her, which only further proved her argument about his inability to accept what people told him as truth, but he let it slide.

'And there's been nothing weird since we came downstairs?' he asked.

'Nothing,' Peggy confirmed. She looked down at the paper in her hand. 'This address is on Whitworth Street, so it's just around the corner from the Palace.'

'And your point is what?'

'The Palace is where Henriette St. Clair died,' Peggy said, handing the piece of paper back. She shook her head at herself. 'I can't believe I didn't think about that already.'

'What are you suggesting? Going to the Palace to see if Henriette St. Clair is there?'

'Exactly. Plus, it'll let me see how normal it is for a theatre to be nigh on devoid of ghosts.'

'After this morning, I'm glad this place doesn't have any more.' Andrew shuddered. 'That's not a bad shout though.'

'Thanks.'

'How are you planning on getting them to let you in for a snoop around though?' Andrew frowned as he waved at the assembled actors. 'I've got to stay here with that lot until six. Same for Jen and Lloyd.'

'That's alright.' Peggy grinned as she looked back at the stage. 'I know just the people.'

SEVEN

Charlie had been having enormous fun, right up until the moment his sister had curtly informed him that playtime was over and they were off to hunt for a potential murder victim in a completely different theatre.

'I was *this* close to getting an invitation to Cohen's next Broadway run,' Charlie moaned as Peggy climbed out of the car once they'd parked outside the Palace. 'You could have given me another few minutes. It's all I needed.'

'Yes, you've only told me about three hundred times since we left,' Peggy huffed as she waited for Marnie to join them. 'How terribly sad for you.'

'Just because you don't appreciate the theatre the way I do,' Charlie replied airily as Marnie appeared a few feet away.

Peggy snorted loudly. 'You? Appreciate theatre? Since when?'

'I had a lovely chat with a lady called Lauren back at the Court and she was telling me th-'

'Oh, *Lauren*, was it?' Marnie asked, grinning at Charlie as she nudged him in the ribs. 'Yes, I see why you might be very interested in the theatre all of a sudden.'

'I resent the implication that my interest is anything but honourable,' Charlie replied as haughtily as he could manage. From the looks his sister and Marnie were shooting him he thought that he might not have come across as authentically as he'd been aiming for.

'*Regardless*,' Charlie continued, pushing his sunglasses up into his hair, 'it's neither here nor there when we have a case to crack.'

'Right,' Peggy agreed. 'Come on then.'

Charlie led the way towards the entrance. He rattled the doors, but they didn't open.

'It seems we might have a problem,' Charlie said to the two

women behind him.

'Since when has a locked door stopped you?' Peggy raised her eyebrows.

'Very true,' Charlie replied. He looked through the glass panels in the door and spotted movement inside, and then raised his hand to knock loudly on the door.

The woman he'd seen inside looked over with a frown. Charlie gave her a wave and after only a second of hesitation she headed towards the doors and unlocked one.

'Yes?' the woman asked, polite but wary.

'Hello, there,' Charlie replied, smiling charmingly. 'I was hoping that you might be able to help me.'

'I'm afraid the box office is closed until two,' the woman replied. 'You can usually catch them on the telephone a few minutes before.'

'Oh no, I'm not interested in buying tickets,' Charlie replied.

'You're not?' the woman frowned. 'Then what is it that you want?'

'Actually, I was much more interested in buying the theatre,' Charlie replied simply.

He watched as the woman's eyes bugged for a split-second before she clearly decided that the man in front of her had lost the plot.

'Right,' she replied slowly. 'Okay, well I'm afraid that's not something I could help you with.'

'I'm certain that's not true, Ms…?' Charlie quirked his head in question.

'Stanley. Amanda Stanley,' she replied, still wary.

'Lovely to meet you, Ms Stanley,' Charlie replied ducking his head slightly. 'I'm Charles Swan. I own the Court across town, and I'm looking to add a few more arts venues to my portfolio.'

'You own the Court?' Amanda blinked slowly in confusion. 'Pardon?'

'Well technically my father still owns it,' Charlie shrugged, rolling his eyes. 'You know how these things are.'

'Right,' Amanda replied. 'Sorry, *who* did you say you were again?'

Charlie knew that this was the moment to unleash the titles. 'Sorry, Charles Swan, Viscount Ashley. My father is the Earl of Acresfield. You may also have heard of my mother? Caroline Winshire?'

'Oh, yes, yes, of course! Your mother is so supportive of the theatre community,' Amanda replied, and all hesitation had been replaced by gushing.

Charlie would have preferred that none of that gushing be related to his terrible mother, but there wasn't much he could do about the fact that Caroline had convinced a large portion of society that she was actually a benevolent angel with a heart of gold.

'Right,' Charlie replied, forcing his smile even wider. 'So, you can see that interest in the theatre runs in the family. In fact, may I introduce you to my sisters?'

He heard Marnie make a choking sound behind him, and Charlie had to bite his lip to stop himself from laughing loudly. That would serve her right for telling him to piss off the night before.

'This is my elder sister, Lady Margaret Swan, and our younger sister, Lady Marnibeth Swan,' Charlie replied, and he couldn't contain his slight snort at the end of the introduction.

'Oh, please do come in,' Amanda replied, all smiles as she unlocked the second door. 'I'll see who I can get to come and talk to you if you'd like to just wait in the foyer.'

'That would be wonderful, Ms Stanley, thank you so much,' Charlie replied as graciously as he could when he could feel Marnie's laser glare practically slicing the back of his skull in two.

'Marnibeth?' Marnie shrieked as Amanda left them alone.

'Well, Marnie's not exactly the most aristocratic name out there, is it?' Charlie replied, rolling his eyes. 'I improvised. Anyway, just be glad I didn't say you were called Hortense!'

'Marnibeth's not even a real name!' Marnie made a disgusted face. 'I hate you.'

'Charming,' Charlie replied, laughing again.

'Right, okay!' Peggy cut in loudly, as she often had to do when Marnie looked ready to kill someone. 'Perhaps we should actually get a move on. Amanda's unlikely to be gone long, and we need to take a proper look around.'

'Go on then,' Charlie said, nodding towards the doors to the auditorium. 'Try not to get caught though, alright? There's only so much smoothing over I'll be able to do before they call Father or something.'

Peggy wrinkled her nose. 'We'll do our best.'

Charlie lounged against the wall as Peggy and Marnie disappeared into the auditorium. He was delighted that he didn't actually have to go with them, and he'd happily admit to that. Charlie liked being involved in cases as long as he was dealing with the *alive* end of the spectrum; mostly because he didn't enjoy feeling like he was being left out of a conversation, but also because, despite growing up with Peggy, he wasn't entirely comfortable being reminded how often he was surrounded by ghosts of any kind.

He could cope with Great Aunt Emmeline; given how close she and Peggy were, it wasn't really an option for Charlie to be afraid of her.

The same went for Marnie, and even though he'd joked about her being his younger sister for the benefit of his little ruse, he really had started seeing her like that to some degree. He would never tell her that, of course, because she'd just take the piss for all eternity.

Still, none of that meant that Charlie enjoyed thinking too

hard, or too often, about death. He was much happier using his money and his contacts to make life easier for the Ballroom team wherever possible. After all, even though he wouldn't admit this either, he would be eternally indebted to them for giving Peggy the opportunity to get involved in something that she was actually good at and leave all the crap that had happened to her in the previous couple of years behind.

A few minutes later, a door opened and Amanda reappeared. This time she had a man with slicked back hair and a wide smile walking beside her.

Charlie pushed himself off the wall and stood up straight. It was time to convince people that he was in the market for a theatre. Surely it couldn't be that hard.

'Good afternoon,' the man said, reaching out a hand to warmly shake Charlie's. 'I'm Chris Hunter, the interim manager of the Palace.'

'Pleased to meet you, Mr Hunter,' Charlie replied graciously. 'Now, before we go any further, there is actually one question that I need to ask.'

'Of course,' Hunter replied. 'Ask away.'

Charlie scratched his head and frowned. 'How much does it actually cost to buy a theatre?'

Before Chris Hunter could even *begin* to formulate a reply, the door to the auditorium burst open just a second before Peggy and Marnie ran breathlessly out into the foyer.

'Come along Charles, we must be on our way!' Marnie called in an affected accent, scooting past Amanda and Hunter with the barest of smiles in their direction.

'Oh, right, er, I suppose we'll have to schedule this chat for another time,' Charlie said, hurriedly shaking Amanda's and Hunter's hands.

'But-' Hunter started, looking forlorn.

'So sorry!' Peggy added brightly, gripping Charlie's elbow and steering him towards the door. 'We really do have to leave.'

'I'll have my people call your people!' Charlie shouted as he was manhandled out of the theatre and back towards his car.

He looked at his sister in alarm when she let go of his arm next to the Aston. 'What the hell, Peggy? You were only gone about three minutes!'

'That's all we needed.' Peggy climbed back into the passenger seat as Marnie disappeared. 'We need to get back to the Court right now though.'

'Why? What's happened?' Charlie asked, already turning the key in the ignition and pulling an illegal U-turn to get them facing the right direction for the few minutes' drive back across the city. Oh well, it wasn't like Joyce was there to witness it and then complain.

'If you can wait three minutes, I'll tell you and the others at the same time,' Peggy replied.

'Ugh, fine,' Charlie agreed with a sigh. 'Heaven forbid you tell me anything before Joycie gets to hear about it.'

'Don't be ridiculous, Charlie,' Peggy replied, turning away to out of the passenger window. 'I just don't want to have to repeat myself.'

That wasn't it at all, and Charlie knew it, but he wasn't going to risk an argument with his sister right then by contradicting her. Peggy's allegiance to the Ballroom was unquestionable, but she had a loyalty to Andrew Joyce that existed outside of their working relationship. Charlie wasn't entirely unobservant, regardless of what his sister might think.

'Come on, tell me one thing, yeah?' Charlie tried as they got closer to the theatre. 'Something tiny to make up for the fact that Father is definitely going to hear about me threatening to spend his money. I reckon that Hunter chap is probably already tracking down a phone number.'

'Oh, fine, one thing,' Peggy agreed with a sigh. 'It looks like I was right when I said that a theatre should be teeming with ghosts. I'm not sure I've ever seen so many active spirits gathered in one place before.'

'Oh God,' Charlie whined. 'That's it. I'll never go to the theatre again.'

'That means you don't need to be too cut up about not getting an invitation to New York from Cohen then,' Peggy grinned at him as he parked the car outside the Court.

'Yes, I think I'll live,' Charlie said with a moue of distaste as he followed Peggy up the steps and knocked loudly on the door until Jen emerged to admit them.

Marnie popped in just as they reached the top of the short staircase outside the auditorium, and she was only about two inches away from Charlie when she appeared.

'Jesus,' Charlie yelped slightly in fright. 'You bloody did that on purpose!'

'Of course I did,' Marnie replied breezily, nodding in agreement. 'That's what little sisters are supposed to do, right?'

'What?' Jen asked, looking at the trio in confusion as she opened the door to the auditorium to usher them through.

'Oh, just ignore the pair of them,' Peggy replied, rolling her eyes. 'You know what they're like.'

'You've only been gone about twenty minutes!' Lloyd called as he and Andrew looked over in surprise.

'Apparently that was enough,' Charlie said, holding his hands up. 'Don't ask me, I was just the distraction.'

'You found something?' Andrew asked Peggy as they all congregated in the back row of the stalls. 'Was it Henriette St. Clair?'

'She's not there,' Peggy replied, looking around at all of them. 'No sign of her at the Palace at any point after her death.'

'But Peggy was right about it being weird here,' Marnie added. 'The Palace was chock full of ghosts!'

Charlie was gratified to see that Andrew also looked a little queasy at the thought.

'Really?' Lloyd asked in excitement, practically bouncing on the balls of his feet. 'Like who? Anyone famous?'

Andrew gave Lloyd that same judgemental look he always did when the DC did his best impression of a highly-strung puppy. Lloyd looked immediately chastened.

'We spoke to someone who remembered the night Henriette St. Clair died,' Peggy continued, by now very used to the interruptions. 'A woman named Sally who'd died in the late thirties.'

'She died in the theatre?' Charlie asked before he could stop himself. God, what was wrong with these places?

'No,' Peggy replied. 'But she was heavily involved with the theatre itself, so I guess she found her way there after death.'

Charlie still didn't understand how Peggy could talk so calmly about things like that when it gave him the heebie-jeebies as much now as it had when they were children.

'And yet we don't have really have anyone particularly active besides Alistair and Jock here?' Jen said, shaking her head. 'That can't be right.'

'But that's not even the most interesting thing we found out!' Marnie burst out, clearly unable to hold in her excitement any longer. 'We know what happened to Henriette St. Clair!'

'What, really?' Jen asked in awe.

'Mmmhmm!' Marnie confirmed loudly.

'Well?' Andrew asked impatiently.

'So-' Peggy started, but she was immediately cut off by Marnie bouncing up and down in elation.

'Oh, please can I tell them?' she begged Peggy. 'I can do *such* a good impression of Sally.'

Peggy frowned but nodded slowly, and Charlie nearly laughed at how pained Andrew looked.

'Okay, so what happened was that Peggy asked Sally if she'd also seen the shadowy man that Henriette St. Clair had claimed to see, right?' Marnie explained.

'Right,' Peggy confirmed.

'And what did she say?' Andrew asked tightly, clearly trying not to lose his temper.

Marnie hunched over, raising a finger in front of her face and waggling it up and down as she approached Andrew slowly. Andrew backed away in alarm.

'Oh, I saw him alright,' Marnie said in a croaky voice that sounded nothing like her own. 'I saw him skulking around for days, always looking to give that poor woman a fright.'

Charlie thought it was *brilliant*.

Andrew clearly didn't agree, if the way he was looking at Marnie was any indication.

Marnie stood up straight again. 'And then Peggy asked if Sally had ever spoken to the Shadow Man herself, and she got all confused, asking about how she'd be able to do that what with her being a ghost and all.'

'What did she mean by that?' Lloyd asked, biting a Twix that he'd mysteriously procured at some point during the conversation.

'Peggy outright asked her if she'd seen the ghost go after Henriette St. Clair the night she died,' Marnie added, looking far too gleeful for the subject matter.

Marnie then dropped into her Sally pose again and Charlie bit back a laugh when Andrew groaned in despair.

'Oh no, dearie, that wasn't a ghost,' Marnie muttered in her version of Sally's voice. 'The man that followed poor Henriette St. Clair up the staircase that night wasn't a ghost. He was as human as you are now.'

Lloyd dropped his Twix in surprise, and Charlie concurred with the sentiment entirely.

EIGHT

Before he'd set foot in the Ballroom, Andrew had never really had trouble sleeping. Sure, he'd had the odd night where his brain wouldn't switch off enough to let him settle, but everyone had those.

Since Chambers had sent him to Tib Street, however, Andrew could barely remember what an undisturbed night felt like. At first it had been the questions surrounding the bizarre nature of his transfer, and the even more bizarre nature of DCI Higson and his team that had kept him awake until the small hours. But it was when Peggy had looked up at Andrew's apparently empty house last summer and seen someone looking back that things had really started going downhill.

Rob had been reminding Andrew that he was never quite alone ever since that night.

It had started small. Things like Andrew's keys being a few inches to the left of where he'd left them when he went to grab his coat; or his shoes, which had been set down neatly as a pair next to the radiator after work, being four or five feet apart from each other come morning.

Since December, though, something in the atmosphere had changed, and everything seemed a little more threatening than it had before.

Andrew had come home from the pub on Christmas Eve to find every cupboard door and drawer in the kitchen partially open, as though someone had not quite closed them properly after they'd been rooting around looking for something. He'd stood in the kitchen doorway, dumbly staring at the scene before him for a long moment, before instinct and training kicked in and he'd very carefully searched his house to make sure that there hadn't been an intruder.

As he'd expected, there hadn't been anyone there; at least, nobody that he could see.

A few weeks after that is when the flickering lights had started. Initially, it had only been one or two brief flashes at a time, and Andrew could have easily put it down to dodgy wiring, but it seemed that practice made perfect and for months now Andrew would often have hours of his day disrupted with a light show around the house.

The most unsettling evenings, though, were the ones where he managed to convince himself that he could hear whispering in the middle of the night. Sometimes it was from the far side of his bedroom - from right near the wall he shared with Rob's old bedroom - but sometimes it felt like someone was speaking directly into his ear. He'd thrown himself out of bed, chest heaving and heart hammering more times than he could count.

He'd decided that as long as it didn't affect his ability to do his job, he didn't need to worry about it. He was fairly certain that Rob couldn't - or at least, *probably wouldn't* – hurt him, and so he'd kept it all to himself.

The possibility of a murderous ghost at the Court, however, had forced him to consider that maybe he shouldn't rely too heavily on the assumption that Rob would be a benevolent ghost. Rob had been a brilliant big brother, and he'd looked out for Andrew until the day he'd died, but he'd also had twenty-five years to ruminate on the fact that it was Andrew's fault that he hadn't lived to see thirteen.

So, that, plus Marnie and Peggy's revelation that they were possibly dealing with both a murderous ghost and a murderous man, had shot Andrew though with a larger than usual dose of trepidation as he'd walked up the garden path and unlocked his front door.

The house had been still as he'd pushed the door closed behind him, and even with Andrew straining his ears, there hadn't been a sound beyond the faint humming of the fridge in the kitchen.

His early evening had been without incident, but he'd felt himself unable to relax as he'd hastily made himself an omelette. For the briefest of moments, as he'd stood in front of the fridge staring at the box of eggs, he'd entertained the idea that it probably wasn't too late to call Lavinia back and say that, actually, on reflection, he was indeed free and would be happy to have dinner with her for the second night in a row. Then he'd realised that this might be entirely because he didn't want to spend the evening in his own house, rather than any desire to spend time with Lavinia, and so he'd promptly shut the idea down.

By half-eight he was so on edge that he'd jumped any time there was the slightest noise from outside, and he'd ended up watching *Gardener's World* at such a loud volume that he had the beginnings of a dull headache by the time the end credits rolled.

He knew that he could probably go back into Manchester and track down Charlie and Lloyd. It was Friday night, after all, so he knew they'd be at one of their usual haunts.

He didn't really want to go out though. A night in town with those two would involve Andrew paying for every round, being surrounded by girls who were really only interested in Charlie once they figured out that he was the wealthy one, and Lloyd lamenting the fact that Fiona seemed to have finally broken up with him for good for the tenth time. Andrew really wasn't in the mood to be anyone's therapist.

In the end he'd switched off the TV, trudged upstairs and crawled into bed with the duvet pulled over his head. He'd fallen asleep remarkably quickly.

He really should have known that the peace couldn't last.

Andrew's eyes snapped open, the final fragments of a fractured dream slipping through his consciousness, leaving him unaware of exactly why he was awake, but uneasy enough that his stomach twisted when he pushed himself up onto his elbows. His brain was telling him that he'd heard a sound, but now there was nothing but almost oppressive silence pressing against him in the dark.

A quick glance at his watch told him that it was just after one in the morning. He sighed loudly, running his hands over his face to press his fingertips against his closed eyelids.

Which is when he heard the noise again.

Andrew's skin prickled at the sound of the single staccato tap of a piano key downstairs.

'No,' he whispered into the darkness, pushing back the duvet and tiptoeing out of bed. 'You're hearing things, Joyce. You're just hearing things.'

He paused at the closed bedroom door, palm flat against the wood, holding his breath so as not to miss even the quietest of disturbances should there be another.

The same note sounded again, but it was held for longer that time.

Andrew's head tipped forwards and thumped against the door in resignation. He was going to have to go downstairs, even if it was the last thing he actually wanted to do.

What was he going to do when he got downstairs though? Assuming that it wasn't a burglar who just couldn't resist a tinkle of the ivories – which would actually be preferable – and that it truly was Rob, this was far beyond flashing lights and disturbed cupboards, and Andrew was entirely out of ideas.

He opened the bedroom door as quietly as he could, and soundlessly crept down the stairs, making sure to avoid the creakiest spots.

As his foot hit the bottom step, the note sounded three times in quick succession. Andrew nearly yelped in surprise, and he had to clamp a hand over his mouth lest his lips betray him.

The door to the living room was partially open, just as he'd left it on the way up to bed, and he forced himself to walk towards it slowly, keeping his breathing as steady as possible even as it felt like his heart was about to hammer its way straight through his ribs.

The moment his fingers wrapped around the doorknob, a mass of notes came from the piano, and for a split-second Andrew allowed himself to hope that maybe a cat had somehow entered the house and was walking up and down the keyboard.

The split second of hope was enough for him to push the door fully open using his shoulder.

There was no cat on the piano. There was nobody there at all.

'Jesus,' Andrew whispered shakily. His relief at not coming face-to-face with his brother's ghost was so immense that he nearly sank to his knees in the middle of the living room.

Then the cacophony of notes started again, and Andrew clamped his hands over his ears at the volume. He watched in morbid fascination as the keys snapped up and down in a blur of black and white. There was no finesse to the movements, and it both looked and sounded as though the keys were being struck in anger.

Andrew staggered backwards, and nearly tripped over his own feet in his haste. He struggled to stay upright as he turned away from the room and practically lurched into the kitchen once he was back in the hallway. He was getting out of the house, and he was getting out now.

'No, no, no,' he hissed in desperation as his fingers scrabbled across the kitchen counter, but not finding his car keys. He was positive he'd left them there, but there was no sign of them anywhere.

The volume of the piano seemed to have reached impossible levels, and Andrew briefly wondered if he was going to have Mr and Mrs Parr from next door at the front door asking him just what the hell he was playing at.

He wasn't sure what he'd be able to say to them. *Oh, sorry about the noise, my dead brother's just doing a bit of piano practice.* Yeah, because that would go down well…

The piano lid slammed shut with a deafening crash, followed by the door to the living room doing the same thing. Seconds later the kitchen door followed suit.

Before he really had time to think about what he was doing, Andrew snatched up the cordless phone from the counter, thanked his lucky stars that he'd left the back door key in the lock, and escaped out into the garden.

He didn't care that it was hovering barely above freezing outside, not when every window at the back of the house was suddenly aglow with electric lights. He backed away from the house until he hit the tree at the very bottom of the garden; the same tree he and Rob used to shelter beneath when their mother was on the warpath.

He also didn't care that it was the middle of the night. Right then there was only one person who might be able to help him.

Keeping his gaze fixed on the house, Andrew quickly dialled a number and held the phone tightly to his ear.

'Hello?' Peggy croaked after a few rings.

If Andrew's house wasn't behaving like something straight out of a Stephen King novel, he'd probably have felt bad about the fact he'd clearly woken her up.

Andrew's reply was cut off as the back door slammed shut. Jesus Christ.

'Who is this?' Peggy asked, urgency creeping into her voice now.

'Peggy, it's me,' Andrew replied. He flinched as the door opened again before quickly slamming shut violently. 'Shit, shit, shit.'

'Andrew, what's going on?' Any remaining traces of sleep in Peggy's voice were erased instantly. 'Are you in trouble?'

'I think my brother's angry with me,' Andrew replied quietly, staring at the kitchen window. The way the lights were flashing made it look like the dance floor at Rotters on a Monday night. 'Like, really, *really* angry with me.'

'Your brother?' Peggy repeated slowly. Then her breath hitched in surprise. 'Wait, *what?*'

'Peggy, I'm being haunted,' Andrew replied, and a desperate, hysterical laugh escaped. 'Doors slamming, lights flashing, piano being played by a ghost, *haunted.*'

'Andrew, I need you to tell me what's happening right now, alright?' Peggy's tone had softened, as though she might be scared of spooking Andrew – as if he could possibly be spooked any more than he already was.

There was a dull thudding sound from inside the house, followed by a loud crash.

'I don't-' Andrew's back slipped down the trunk of the tree until he was sitting on the damp grass at the base. 'I don't know.'

Peggy swore quietly. 'I'll be right there, okay?'

'No!' Andrew shouted sharply.

He needed help, he knew that, but he didn't want Peggy anywhere near such a volatile situation.

'Andrew, you know I-'

'Peggy, no.' Andrew shook his head even though he knew she couldn't see him. 'Just tell me what to do, just tell me what I have to do to get him to stop!'

Peggy was silent for a long moment. 'I don't know.'

'Peggy, *please*, I need you to help me,' Andrew replied frantically. 'Just tell me what to do. Tell me how to make him stop!'

'Can you see him?' Peggy asked.

'No, but this is the worst he's ever been. Before tonight he ju-'

'What do you mean?' Peggy asked sharply, cutting him off. 'How long has this been going on?'

Andrew watched as the curtains covering his bedroom window whooshed open violently. 'Since last summer.'

'Why didn't you tell me?' Peggy's tone had shifted into something vaguely accusatory.

Because I didn't want to believe it. Because I knew you'd try and blame yourself for it. Because I didn't want to have to tell you that Rob's death was my fault. Because I was afraid.

'Because I was handling it,' is what he settled on eventually, and it sounded like a poor excuse, even to his own desperate ears.

Peggy's silence spoke volumes.

'It was just little things,' Andrew explained. 'My keys moving around a bit, things like that. But now, I don't know what this is.'

The back door slammed twice in quick succession.

'Jesus!' Andrew yelped.

'Right, that's it, I'm coming over, whether you want me there or not,' Peggy replied, and Andrew could hear her shuffling around her bedroom.

'No, Peggy, please, please, don't come, please.' Andrew was almost begging. The lights in the kitchen were practically strobing. 'I don't know what he'd do if he saw you, and I can't risk that. Please don't come.'

'Andrew, I really think-'

'Please, Peggy. Just tell me what to do.'

'You're too bloody stubborn for your own good.' Peggy sighed loudly. 'Okay, I have an idea, but I need you to trust me.'

'I trust you. You know I do.'

'Give me two minutes,' Peggy replied. 'Just stay put.'

Andrew had no intention of going anywhere. The flashing lights had slowed again, but he was fairly sure that he could still hear the piano every now and then.

Oh crap, the Parrs had just switched on a light upstairs. They'd be hammering on the front door within minutes at this rate.

'Alright,' Peggy said in his ear, making him jump a little in surprise. 'Where exactly are you? Be specific.'

'In the back garden,' Andrew replied, wondering just what on earth Peggy was up to. 'The furthest I can get from the house, beneath the big tree.'

Andrew heard Peggy muttering something, and her voice sounded muffled, as though she were covering the mouthpiece with one hand.

A moment later Andrew squeaked in surprise when Marnie appeared next to him with only the faintest of popping sounds.

'Oh, calm down,' Marnie said, rolling her eyes, before staring in fascination at the light show inside the house. 'Jesus, *what* is going on here?'

'Peggy!' Andrew hissed into the phone. '*Why is Marnie here?*'

'Well, you won't let me come and help you,' Peggy replied, 'and Marnie's probably far more useful than me when it comes to this sort of thing anyway.'

'How did she even manage to get here?' Andrew asked as Marnie picked her way through the dark garden towards the back of the house. 'It's not like she's been here before.'

'No,' Peggy agreed, 'but I wondered if she'd have a connection to you, rather than the place. You called her to the Ballroom once, remember?'

Andrew did remember, much as he'd prefer to forget about that whole day.

'Just let her see if she can help, alright?' Peggy prompted quietly. 'It's the best I can do.'

It wouldn't be fair for Andrew to argue; he'd implored Peggy for assistance, but then refused to let her physically come and help him.

'Can you unlock this?' Marnie called from beside the back door.

The lights inside winked out in unison.

'It shouldn't be locked,' Andrew replied, frowning. 'Hang on, can't you just, you know, *pop in*?'

Peggy snorted slightly.

'I can't.' Marnie sounded slightly unnerved. 'I literally can't get past this door.'

'What's happening?' Peggy asked.

'Marnie's saying she can't get into the house,' Andrew replied.

'Maybe you're too far away from her,' Peggy reasoned.

'Everything's stopped inside,' Andrew said as he clambered to his feet. 'Do you think he's gone?'

'I don't think he's ever left that house, Andrew,' Peggy replied carefully.

'That's what I was afraid you'd say,' Andrew muttered as he walked towards the house. He pointed to Marnie and then the door. 'How about now?'

'Nope.' Marnie shook her head. 'I still can't get in.'

Marnie jimmied the handle up and down a few times, but the door still didn't budge.

'Still not working,' Andrew muttered to Peggy, holding the phone against his ear with his shoulder.

Andrew stood right next to Marnie and reached out to touch the door handle. It pushed down easily and with a gentle nudge from his other hand the door creaked open, swinging gently into the eerily silent kitchen.

'I couldn't open that, I swear,' Marnie said, shaking her head. She looked more serious than Andrew could ever remember seeing her before.

'I believe you,' Andrew replied. Then he turned his attention back to the phone. 'Peggy, we're both going in.'

'Andrew, I'm not sure that's a very good idea.'

'It's not, but I don't have any other ideas right now,' Andrew replied. 'Marnie can't get into the house without me.'

'Alright.' Peggy sighed. 'Please be careful. Both of you.'

Andrew gestured for Marnie to enter the house while he

reasserted his grip on the phone.

'Oh no, after you,' Marnie said, flapping her hand towards the kitchen. 'You must be joking if you think I'm going in there first.'

Andrew wasn't in the frame of mind to even begin looking for the usual type of snarky comment he'd easily be able to dredge up for a conversation with Marnie. 'Fine.'

'I don't like this,' Marnie said as she shuffled into the kitchen behind Andrew. 'Something feels off.'

As much as he really, *really* didn't want to agree with her, Andrew was forced to do just that. The house was still, but the silence made Andrew feel as though he were on the edge of a precipice just waiting to be pushed, rather than swaddling him in the blanketing security of his house being truly empty. The air around them felt charged, and Andrew didn't want to be anywhere nearby when it exploded.

Marnie swore loudly when a door upstairs slammed shut.

'What's going on?' Peggy asked urgently.

'Rob's definitely still here.' Andrew moved slowly into the kitchen, listening for any other sounds. 'I don't understand why he's doing any of this.'

He spied his car keys on the floor by the oven and he tiptoed across the tiles to retrieve them. As he snatched them up the phone line fizzed ominously. 'Peggy?'

"drew? A -ou- ll there?' Peggy asked, words crackling and breaking, leaving Andrew with only an impression of the question she was trying to ask him.

'Peggy?' He tried a little louder. 'Peggy, can you hear me?'

'Andrew?' Marnie called, voice shaking slightly.

'Yeah?' Andrew asked, with no small amount of trepidation.

'I think you'd better come here,' Marnie replied, from where she was standing in the kitchen doorway, looking out into the entrance hall.

The phone went dead in Andrew's hand, but he kept hold of

it as he made his way towards Marnie.

When he reached the hallway, he didn't need to ask Marnie why she'd called for him; he could see it clearly enough himself.

Charcoal fingers of dense mist were weaving in and out of the spindles of the staircase as they descended from somewhere above them.

'What the hell is that?' Andrew whispered, already shuffling past Marnie so that he could get to the bottom of the staircase.

His mouth dropped open in surprise as he looked up and saw the same mist hovering above the carpet at the top of the stairs. It undulated almost like a heartbeat and, as Andrew watched, it seemed to solidify into a shape that was beginning to look frighteningly human.

It took a second for Andrew to realise that the buzzing he could hear wasn't in his head, and it all suddenly felt remarkably similar to the first time that he and Peggy had encountered Marnie in the Lewis's Perfume Hall the year before. That had ended with both him and Peggy covered in glass and perfume, and Andrew had a thin sliver of a scar near his right eye from where he'd been hit by a shard of razor-sharp perfume bottle.

He didn't want to be around to find out what was going to happen in his house.

'Marnie, we need to get out of here,' Andrew said. He was scared enough that he was willing to completely ignore his usual rule of never touching the ghost and nudged Marnie behind him towards the front door.

Marnie didn't move. She was frowning, transfixed by the rippling mist as it rolled down the staircase, faster and faster, swirling around their feet and obscuring the tiles beneath them.

'Marnie!' Andrew shouted as the form at the top of the stairs broadened, coils reaching out from each side like grasping hands.

The loud chirp of the phone's ring surprised Andrew enough that he dropped the handset on the floor. The sound of the plastic cracking harshly against ceramic was enough to spur Marnie into motion and she hurried past Andrew towards the front door.

'You're right! We need to get out of here!' Marnie gulped loudly. 'Leave the phone!'

Andrew paused mid-crouch, no longer able to see the handset for the deepening mist that now covered the length of the hallway.

He gave the figure at the top of the stairs one more glance, and on seeing that it definitely possessed something entirely head-shaped he scurried backwards until his back hit the front door. He reached down with his left hand to twist the key in the lock and put the keyring in his pocket before he spun quickly, wrenched the night latch, and finally pulled open the door.

The pair of them spilled out into the darkened front garden and Andrew pulled the door closed behind them. Without a glance back at the house he bolted down the path and all but threw himself into the Belmont, thanking the universe that he'd had the foresight to grab the car keys.

Marnie popped into the passenger seat and stared at him in horror. 'What the hell is wrong with your house?'

Andrew stayed silent as he flipped on the headlights and accelerated out of Acacia Road as though the devil himself was on their heels.

For all Andrew knew right then, he might have been.

NINE

Peggy knew that Andrew wouldn't appreciate her turning up at the rehearsal space like a sleep-deprived mother hen, and so when her watch informed her that it was finally a reasonable time on Saturday morning, she climbed tiredly into her car and drove to Tib Street instead.

If she'd first detoured down Whitworth Street to check that Andrew's car was there, then there was no reason for him to know about it.

Seeing the Belmont had eased Peggy's worries slightly; if Andrew was at the *Lady Bancroft* rehearsal, it meant that he was far, far away from whatever was tormenting him at home.

When the ring of the phone had jolted her out of sleep the night before, she hadn't quite known what to expect. Nobody called with good news at one in the morning, and the simple knowledge of that had been enough for her to snatch the phone from the cradle and brace herself for whatever came next.

Whatever it was that she'd thought the call would be, she hadn't been prepared to hear Andrew's fearful, shaky exhalation of her name; and she certainly hadn't been prepared for the explanation she'd then received.

Andrew was being haunted by his brother – had been for quite some time, apparently – and he hadn't told Peggy about it. The flare of hurt had burned hot but had been tamped down almost immediately by the more urgent need to see what was going on for herself, despite Andrew's objections to her being anywhere near the house. Asking Marnie to go in her place hadn't seemed like enough to Peggy, but it had been better than leaving Andrew alone to deal with whatever was happening in that house.

When the phone call had abruptly ended though, Peggy had

bolted from her bedroom, propelled by the dread that the sudden silence had ignited. Racing towards the stairs in a blur of panic, she'd barely avoided tripping on the top step, her fingers grasping the bannister for support as she'd yelped in surprise.

In that moment, she'd cared very little for any disturbance that would draw Timothy from within the bowels of Butterton House, and she'd thundered down the stairs without even the slightest attempt to mask her movements with a sense of secrecy. Peggy's sole focus had been on reaching her car and racing out to Gatley as quickly as she could. She hadn't known at all what she'd be able to do upon reaching Andrew, but there'd been absolutely no chance that she was just going to sit in her bedroom and wait to hear from him again.

She'd been halfway to the garages when she'd felt the air shift.

'Peggy!' Marnie had called from behind her, stopping her in her tracks immediately.

'What happened?' Peggy had sprinted back towards the house, only realising that she was still wearing just socks on her feet as she stumbled across the gravel. 'Are you alright? Is Andrew okay?'

'We're fine, Peggy,' Marnie had replied, though her voice had been trembling at the very edges. 'He's fine. I swear. He's not at the house anymore.'

'What happened?' Peggy had asked again, watching carefully as Marnie had rubbed frantically at her arms as though trying to ward off a chill.

'I don't know,' Marnie had replied eventually, shaking her head vehemently. 'There was something in that house that shouldn't have been there. It felt wrong.'

Peggy couldn't help but think back to Alistair's own words about Jock: *Don't you think it's funny that a ghost should be scared of something?*

It was one thing to know that Alistair was afraid of Jock, but another thing entirely to hear that Andrew's house was currently occupied by something terrifying enough to have Marnie on edge.

'Peggy, who's Rob?'

'What?' Peggy had asked, wrong-footed. The only other person who knew that Andrew's house was haunted was Charlie, but Peggy had never told him who the ghost was. She'd never mentioned the name 'Rob' to anyone but Andrew himself.

Marnie had frowned. '*Rob*. I heard Andrew tell you that 'Rob' was still there. So, who is he?'

Peggy had been hit with an overwhelming wave of tiredness then, as the surge of adrenaline had ebbed leaving her just feeling cold and anxious. She'd sighed and pressed her fingertips into her brow bone. 'Rob is Andrew's older brother.'

'What?' Marnie had hissed in pure surprise. 'He has a *brother*?'

'Rob died when he was twelve,' Peggy had explained, hoping that this wasn't a betrayal of Andrew's trust in her. 'Andrew was only nine when it happened.'

Marnie had managed to look even more taken aback. 'But back when you first met him, he said he didn't even believe in ghosts!'

'He didn't.' Peggy had shrugged. 'He didn't know that Rob was there until last summer.'

'Because you saw him.' It hadn't been a question.

Peggy had nodded. 'And he's barely mentioned him since, but when he called tonight, he said that whatever's been going on in the house has been getting worse since then.'

'Peggy, I don't think it was a child in Andrew's house tonight,' Marnie had said slowly. 'I don't think it was a child at all.'

Peggy had swallowed heavily and then ushered Marnie back into the house.

Only when they were safely in the kitchen, with the heavy old door closed tightly behind them as a barrier to Timothy's bat-like hearing, had Peggy let Marnie explain what had happened.

She'd listened carefully to Marnie's account, and by the time she'd finished, the tea in Peggy's mug had gone cold, completely untouched.

Even after lying awake for hours thinking about it all, Peggy had been no closer to understanding any of it. When she'd encountered Rob the previous summer, he'd been much less solid than Marnie, and he'd seemed entirely benevolent. Andrew hadn't shared the full story of what had happened, but from the way he occasionally spoke about his relationship with his brother, Peggy had understood that while there seemed to be heavy a sense of guilt about something, the overwhelming emotions were a tangled mix of love and deep sadness.

Peggy stopped her car outside the Ballroom and ran her hands over her face as she yawned widely. The only way she was going to get to the bottom of it all was to speak to Andrew, and that meant she had a few hours to kill first.

It had started drizzling as she'd left Butterton, but somewhere around the outskirts of the city the sky had darkened considerably and the soft patter against the car's windows had intensified into a relentless downpour. Without the engine running, the wipers lay motionless against the windscreen, and the buildings of Tib Street and beyond were blurred beyond recognition.

Peggy hurriedly stepped out of the car and locked it behind her before sprinting towards the weather-beaten door. The key was in her hand before she reached the door, but it still took a good few seconds of jiggling to get the lock to disengage with a loud clunk. She pushed against the damp wood, and it scraped over the tiled floor of the hallway in protest, as though deeply disgruntled about being forced to work on a Saturday morning. The raindrops followed in her wake and made a good effort at amassing around her feet before she had a chance to turn back and shoulder the door closed.

For just a moment, Peggy stood in the darkened hallway to let her eyes adjust. The small window at the top of the stairs did very little to help illuminate the staircase at the best of times, but it was nigh on hopeless on a miserable grey day. The bulbs in the light fitting had blown long before Peggy had ever set foot in the Ballroom, and she seriously doubted that DCI Higson would ever care enough to replace them.

A few icy raindrops trickled down through her hair and under her collar, and Peggy shivered as she headed upstairs towards the Ballroom itself. She always found that with the doors and windows closed it was entirely possible to briefly forget that she was in the centre of Manchester; it was almost peaceful. Perhaps Peggy would have found it more peaceful if she wasn't always half-expecting the ghost of a former DI to materialise in the corner of the room, or for the still-terrifying Dolly to brandish her bleach bottle in Peggy's direction and make another cryptic comment about her ability to speak to ghosts.

She was surprised to find that the double doors to the Ballroom were wide open; Higson usually wanted them closed to keep the heat in, and Andrew saw them as a deterrent to both Dolly and Charlie. Peggy was rarely in the building by herself, and if she was, it was usually only a short-lived moment when she'd arrived only a few minutes before either Andrew or Jen, but that morning she had been certain that nobody else would be there.

Peggy closed the doors behind her – she was decidedly in Andrew's camp on this one – and shrugged off her damp coat. The rain was pelting off the wall of windows even harder than when she'd been outside, and Peggy was going to have to borrow the umbrella that lived beneath Jen's desk if she needed to go out for anything.

As Peggy turned away from the windows, the answer to why the Ballroom doors might have been open began to reveal itself.

The cushions on the decrepit blue sofa looked even more deflated than usual, and there was a shirt thrown haphazardly over one arm. On the floor, next to the trailing cuff of the shirtsleeve, there was a holdall that looked as though it had been rifled through in haste; the sleeve of a jumper was emerging from between the open zips, and there was a single black shoe resting against the canvas, with no sign of its matching partner.

She frowned as she walked over to Andrew's desk and sat down in the chair. A mug still bearing most of a black coffee was perched right on the edge, and when she pressed the tips of her fingers to it, she found that the ceramic was still warm. There was a ring of coffee around the base of the mug, and no attempt had been made to mop it up.

All of that led her to conclude that when Andrew had told Marnie that he'd had somewhere to go the night before, he'd meant the Ballroom. He'd obviously driven to Tib Street, slept on the sofa, and then headed to Whitworth Street in a hurry that morning.

Peggy thought that she might be getting the hang of this detective lark.

There was a single folder on the desk and Peggy reached out to pull it towards her before settling back into the chair.

'The Court Theatre' had been scrawled on the cover in Lloyd's spidery writing and the totality of the case information was secured inside. If the folder contained more than eight or nine sheets of paper, Peggy would have been surprised, and it was disappointingly obvious just how little they actually had to work with, and just how little time there had been for research outside of shadowing the cast at the theatre.

Peggy flipped through the pages quickly but found nothing she hadn't seen before. She supposed that when it came down to it, making sure that nobody died during the performance was the key objective for the Ballroom team, even if that meant not looking into the previous deaths in as much detail as they normally would.

Perhaps that was something Peggy could change, though. She had a few hours to try and find something useful before she'd need to head over to Whitworth Street, and she decided that she might as well use them wisely.

The archive rooms on the first floor seemed the most sensible place to start, and so Peggy picked up the file before crossing the Ballroom to Higson's desk.

She left her slightly damp report of the encounter with Jock the day before in the centre of the desk and made sure that the Post-it note asking if Higson could get any information on George Bevan - the teenaged theatre employee who'd been accused of tampering with the wiring - was securely attached to the paper. Then she carefully lifted a few stacks of paper and general detritus until she spotted what she was looking for, and picked up the heavy bundle of keys.

As she walked down the first staircase, Peggy tucked the file under her arm and tried to locate the three keys that would give her access to the three separate rooms. The keys had been strung onto the keyring in no particular order, but thankfully she remembered that the ones she needed had, at some point, had small blobs of black permanent marker pen applied to their heads; unfortunately, nobody had ever thought to number them.

Just as Peggy was trying the first of the three keys in the door closest to the staircase, she felt something in the space around her shift slightly out of alignment.

Peggy whipped her head around, expecting to see either DI Benson, or even Marnie, if she'd finally got bored of explaining the finer points of *Neighbours* to Emmeline, behind her. To her surprise, though, there was nobody there.

'Hello?' Peggy asked quietly as she first glanced down the murky second staircase towards the entrance hall, and then along the corridor towards where the other archive rooms lay in darkness. 'Who's there?'

The silence stretched around her; it wasn't outwardly hostile or necessarily threatening in any discernible way, but it felt like a manufactured stillness. The feeling reminded Peggy of playing hide-and-seek as a child, and how the knowledge that her brother had been concealed just out of sight and ready to pounce had always put her on edge, tensing her shoulders in anticipation of the playful scare. This anticipation didn't feel playful though; it felt like someone, or something, was patiently waiting.

It was by no means the first time Peggy had felt that something was off about a place, but it was the first time she'd had a feeling like anything approaching it within the walls of the Ballroom.

'Hello? DI Benson, is that you?'

There was no answer, and Peggy squinted harder, trying to see something that she might have missed in the shadows.

Nothing.

Peggy shook her head and turned the key in the lock, pleased when it clicked open on the first attempt. She ran her hand up the wall next to the doorframe and found the light switch. Unlike in the hallway, the single, exposed bulb in the windowless room was in full working order, and it fizzed to life.

Peggy sighed in dismay when she noted that the archive room looked to be in even more of a disorganised state than the last time she'd been in there. The compact table in the centre of the room had two, towering stacks of old files balanced precariously close to the edge, and a selection of biros in various colours alongside a tray of paperclips cluttered up the remaining space.

She leaned forward to glance at the two uppermost files, but she didn't recognise either of the names or case descriptions on the yellowing labels.

She sighed again as she stepped back to push the door open fully, and then firmly kicked the doorstop into place.

Just as she was about to turn around again, a slow, dawning

sense of dread crawled up Peggy's spine before coming to rest at the nape of her neck. Her skin prickled beneath her sleeves, and she suddenly knew with a sense of soul-deep certainty that whatever she did next, she shouldn't look over her shoulder.

There was no voice, neither in her ear nor in her head, but Peggy still understood clear as day that whatever was behind her wanted her out of that room immediately.

'Okay,' Peggy whispered, surprised that her voice came out as steadily as it did. 'Alright. I'm leaving.'

Peggy reached out for the switch and as the lightbulb guttered out Peggy felt the clutch of threatening silence loosen slightly. Keeping her eyes firmly on the shabby green carpet, Peggy used her foot to loosen the doorstop before she stepped back out into the corridor and pulled the door closed behind her. The key scrabbled against the wood of the door and the handle itself a few times before Peggy finally managed to get her unsteady hand to line it up with the lock and secure the room.

The rain was still coming down in droves, tap-tapping against the window like a hundred tiny hands rapping pleadingly against the glass in the hope of gaining entry.

There wasn't a chance in hell that Peggy was going back up the stairs to get her coat from the Ballroom, and so she forced herself to walk down the stairs as though she couldn't feel unseen eyes boring into the back of her head with every step she took.

When she unlatched the main door, she was relieved that it opened easily in her hand, and she walked back out onto Tib Street.

Peggy hurried across the pavement, swearing loudly when she stepped in a puddle that sent a spray of dirt-streaked water cascading over her jeans.

She yanked open the car door with trembling fingers and dropped heavily into the driver's seat.

Jesus Christ. What the hell had just happened?

Her heart was hammering in her chest as though she'd run up and down the stairs a good few times, and she wrapped her arms around herself to ward off a chill that wasn't entirely from the raindrops that had drenched her hair and cardigan on the short sprint to the car. The rain was beating on the roof of the car and sluicing down the windscreen so quickly it was impossible to see outside.

Before she'd met Marnie, Peggy hadn't really ever considered the fact that ghosts could simply leave one place and appear in another. She'd heard stories to that effect, of course, everybody had; after what had happened in Enfield at the end of the seventies, the newspapers had gone on a bit of a spree with printing all types of accounts of encounters with spirits. Peggy would be the last person to argue that these stories shouldn't be believed, but in her own experience that sort of thing had only happened once.

Now though she was less certain. What if whatever she'd just encountered was down to the same ghostly presence that had caused the disturbance in the theatre's archive room the day before?

Even though Sally at the Palace had claimed that the man who'd followed Henriette St. Clair up the stairs the night she'd died was entirely human, Peggy had to wonder whether a spirit like Jock could transpose himself from one location to another if they latched onto a human being strongly enough. God, she really hoped that wasn't the case. She wasn't quite sure she could bear the thought of being followed home by yet another ghost.

Then again, what Peggy had felt upstairs hadn't been angry in the way Jock's spirit had appeared to be, nor did its behaviour match the description Marnie had given about what she'd seen in Andrew's house the night before. Perhaps this spirit was something else entirely. Whatever was inside the building on Tib Street seemed to be more watchful than anything else. She'd hesitate to say it definitely wasn't dangerous – she'd felt the potential threat after she'd switched on the light, and she'd understood that it wanted her to leave that room – but it wasn't the same obvious slick of spite that had accompanied Jock's manifestation the day before.

Peggy shook herself and turned the key in the ignition.

As the wipers cleared the curtain of rain from the windscreen, she started in surprise when she caught sight of a figure standing slightly further down the road, staring directly at her as though they'd been doing it for some time and had just been waiting for Peggy to notice.

There, beneath a black umbrella, with a long cigarette holder loosely dangling between two fingers, was Dolly, leaning nonchalantly against the wall of one of the few remaining pet shops.

Peggy was left with the unnerving feeling that Dolly had somehow been able to see her through the curtain of rain, and she lifted her right hand in greeting.

Dolly stayed statue-still for a moment longer, gaze calculating, and then with a flick of ash to the pavement she gave Peggy a curt nod of acknowledgement.

For a moment, Peggy wondered if she was supposed to get out of the car and engage Dolly in conversation, but then Dolly turned on her heel and began walking back towards Debenhams as though she'd had no real reason or desire to be on Tib Street anyway.

Peggy still had a few hours before the *Lady Bancroft* rehearsal finished, but she knew she wouldn't be able to bring herself to head back to the archive room on her own just yet. Driving all the way home only to come back into town again seemed a waste of time, and so that left her with only one sensible option for a place to spend the next few hours.

'Right,' she said to herself as she fastened her seatbelt.

She frowned down at her lap when she realised that she still had both the file and Higson's set of keys; neither of which were probably supposed to leave Tib Street, and certainly not in Peggy's possession.

She glanced back at the door and almost instantly decided that she'd just give everything to Andrew when she went to Whitworth Street later, regardless of whether he'd be cranky about it; he'd be even crankier when he found out about what had happened in the archive room anyway.

As Peggy drove away, she avoided looking up at the Ballroom's wall of windows, just in case.

* * *

'Are you alright, sir?'

Andrew continued to firmly press his fingertips into his brow bone for just a few seconds more, before he cracked open his eyes.

Jen was frowning down at him in concern. 'Sir?'

Andrew slowly heaved himself out of his sprawl, rearranging his splayed limbs until he could prop himself up a bit better on the scratchy banqueting chair he'd pushed against the wall when he'd arrived. He wasn't giving much more than a vague nod to the concept of sitting up straight – or to professionalism, for that matter – but it was the absolute extent of what he could manage after the night he'd just lived through.

'I'm fine,' Andrew replied, when he eventually remembered that it was customary to respond to your colleague's questions. He yawned widely, covering his mouth with both hands as his back twinged in an unhappy reminder of just how uncomfortable the Ballroom's sofa was.

He was bone tired as it was, so it certainly didn't help that *Lady Bancroft's Rose* was genuinely the dullest thing Andrew had ever been forced to watch. He still couldn't understand why

Cohen and his small company of actors were all so enamoured with it that they'd risk life and limb to stage the damn thing.

'They've nearly finished.' Jen gestured towards the other end of the function room, which had been set out as close to the play's staging as possible first thing that morning. The duct tape Cohen and Vic had pressed into the carpet to mark the various areas of the makeshift stage had already begun to peel away in a desperate bid for freedom that Andrew could strongly identify with.

Andrew nodded and glanced down at his watch—thirteen minutes to twelve, which meant only thirteen minutes to freedom. *Thank Christ for that.*

The door behind Jen creaked open slowly and Lloyd appeared a second later, clutching a half-empty tube of Opal Fruits in his hand. The expression on his face concerned Andrew immediately; it was an expression that was usually followed by Lloyd telling him something he wouldn't like.

'What now?' Andrew sighed tiredly.

'I just went downstairs to use the vending machine,' Lloyd explained, gesturing at the sweets, 'and I noticed that there was a bunch of people standing around on the pavement outside.'

'It's Saturday morning,' Andrew replied with a shrug. 'Town's busy.'

'Right, sir, yeah.' Lloyd grimaced, 'It's just that two of them had cameras, and I recognised one of the other lads. Jimmy Haworth. You know, from the *Evening News*.'

'What?' Andrew sat up straight immediately.

Lloyd nodded. 'Thing is, he saw me, sir. He looked proper chuffed about it, to be honest. He waved me over, so I went – not much point hiding when he knew I'd seen him.'

Andrew pinched the bridge of his nose again when Lloyd trailed off looking troubled. 'And?'

'Well, he said he'd heard about what's been going on at the theatre,' Lloyd replied guiltily. 'Said he'd been told that the police were investigating a murderous ghost; asked me outright if that were the case.'

'What did you say, Lloyd?'

'I asked him where he was getting his dodgy information from, and then I came straight back up here,' Lloyd replied. He winced. 'Was that wrong?'

Andrew shook his head and blew a loud breath out between his lips. 'No, Lloyd, no, you're alright.'

Lloyd looked relieved and unwrapped another sweet.

Andrew stood up and strode towards the cast gathered on the other side of the room. When he reached them, he folded his arms and waited until Teddy's monologue trailed off mid-flow.

'Sorry, Inspector,' Teddy said tightly, sounding more irritated than apologetic, 'but you're putting me off my lines.'

'Am I?' Andrew shook his head. 'Well, one of *you* is putting me off my job right now.'

'What?' Cohen asked, frowning in confusion. 'What's going on?'

'Someone has been talking to a hack at the *Evening News* and I want to know who,' Andrew replied simply.

Cohen shook his head. 'No. Nobody here would do that. Everyone knows how important it is to keep this quiet.'

Andrew's bark of laughter was harsh and disbelieving. 'Really? Well then Mr Cohen, can you tell me why DC Parker has just told me that there's at least one journalist outside right now? One who knows that we're not at the theatre, even though that's supposed to be a secret.'

'It wasn't one of us,' Teddy said, shaking his head emphatically. 'Do you realise how fucking stupid we'd all look if people thought that we'd called the police because of a ghost story?'

'Though it pains me to say it, Teddy's right,' Marion said, ignoring Teddy's smirk at her words. 'Maybe one of your lot blabbed, Detective Inspector Joyce; probably that odd woman who was at the theatre with you.'

Under any other circumstances, Andrew would have laughed at how absurd it was for anyone to suggest that Peggy would ever go to the papers about anything, least of all anything to do with ghosts and curses, but he didn't feel like laughing just then.

'I trust my team implicitly,' Andrew said as politely as was possible through gritted teeth.

Marion shot him a mocking smile. 'Well, maybe you shouldn't.'

'The papers already knew about the curse,' Cohen said, shaking his head again. 'Back when we first started rehearsing, they asked a few questions, and we waved it all off as nonsense. I told you; the producers were happy about the effect on ticket sales.'

'Opening night is a sell-out, and there's only a handful of tickets left for the rest of the run,' Vic added evenly. 'I'm sorry, Detective Inspector, but there's no reason for anyone here to start spreading stories about a ghost at this point.'

'It could have been someone who works at the Court,' Ben suggested, and at least he had the decency to sound contrite.

'Can we get back to what we were doing now?' Teddy asked, folding his own arms in a mirror of Andrew's stance.

Andrew shook his head. 'No. Rehearsal's over. Everybody, pack up your stuff now, and then you're leaving through the back entrance.'

'I wasn't finished!' Teddy growled.

Andrew shrugged. 'It's over. Everybody out. Now.'

Cohen held his hands up placatingly. 'Inspector, I really-'

'*Now*, Mr Cohen!'

Cohen looked ready to argue, and Andrew was more than ready for it, but Vic reached out and briefly rested her hand on Cohen's arm.

'Albany, he's right,' Vic said quietly. 'It won't do us any good for the press to get any real information about the police involvement. I doubt either the theatre or the charity would be delighted about any negative press, so let's just get out of here as quietly as we can. We can regroup at the Court on Monday.'

For a long moment, Andrew thought that Cohen was going to protest further, but in the end, he just sighed in irritation and shook his head. 'Fucking, *whatever.*'

Andrew gave Vic a brief nod of gratitude.

'Everybody out!' Cohen barked at the cast before he stormed across the room and began wrenching the duct tape from the carpet.

'Jen, can you get everyone down to the staff entrance?' Andrew asked. 'Make sure they actually walk away from the building though. If anyone's parked outside, tell them they need to come back for their car in half an hour or so and don't make it obvious that they have anything to do with the play. I don't want anyone trying to get near Haworth and whoever else is out there, yeah?'

'Sir.' Jen nodded and went to stand next to where Teddy was shrugging on his coat with obnoxious sluggishness.

Andrew rolled his eyes. 'Lloyd, once Jen's left, go back down to the lobby and tell the guy on the desk that we need to get everyone out through the back; he should have the key. When you've done that, I want you to give it a couple of minutes and then walk straight out the front door.'

'Past Jimmy Haworth, sir?' Lloyd looked concerned. 'What if he talks to me again?'

'Just tell him that you have no idea what's he on about and then walk away,' Andrew replied. 'Nobody's going to come out after you, so Haworth can stand there all afternoon for all I care.'

'What if he just shows up at the theatre on Monday morning?'

Andrew grimaced. 'We'll cross that bridge when we come to it. You never know, he might find some *actual news* to report before then.'

Lloyd chuckled, but he still looked unsure.

'Andrew?'

Andrew groaned internally before he turned around. 'Yes, Miss Heathcote?'

'Will we be safe out there?' Lavinia asked, eyes wide and wondering.

'Miss Heathcote, it's a handful of journalists, not a braying mob.' Andrew wasn't sure what he was supposed to think about someone who appeared to be more concerned about men with notepads than she apparently was about receiving strange fan mail all the time.

'I'd really appreciate it if you would walk me to my car,' Lavinia said as she leaned further into Andrew's personal space. 'Perhaps we could get some lunch first, wait for everyone else to leave?'

Lloyd sniggered.

'DC Parker, I think now might be a good time to go down to the front desk,' Andrew snapped, glaring at Lloyd. 'No sense in waiting.'

Lloyd said nothing as he walked away, but his amused silence annoyed Andrew anyway.

'Miss Heathcote, DS Cusack will take you to your car as soon as it's possible,' Andrew said firmly, trying to ignore the way Lavinia's face fell slightly. He had a bloody job to do, he couldn't just go gallivanting off to lunch, even if it sounded like a significantly better option than going back to his godforsaken house.

'Oh.'

'DI Joyce, could I have a word, please?'

Andrew was relieved to see Vic heading towards him, holding a folded piece of paper.

She stopped when she reached him and shot Lavinia a tight

smile. 'Thank you, Lavinia.'

Lavinia looked taken aback. 'I'm just talking to DI Joyce.'

'I believe DS Cusack is ready to take you all outside,' Vic replied, and then the smile fell away completely. 'See you on Monday morning.'

Lavinia looked almost petulant as she glanced between Vic and Andrew in consternation.

'Enjoy the rest of your weekend,' Andrew added, which he hoped would slightly soften the blow of Vic's obvious dismissal.

Lavinia scowled at Vic but didn't add anything else before she flounced over to where Jen was waiting for her, along with her three castmates.

'Can I help you with something?' Andrew asked Vic as he sidestepped Cohen savagely ripping more tape from the carpet.

Vic tipped her head to the left, and Andrew followed her until they were on the far side of the room from Cohen.

'Look,' said Vic when they stopped, 'I don't believe in any of the curse nonsense, and I know you don't either. That doesn't take away from the fact that someone is messing around with this production, and I can't have that. I don't think you've spoken to Emma Allen yet, have you?'

'The actress who was supposed to play Isabella?'

Vic nodded. 'I want you to know that I'm fairly certain that Lavinia is the one who pressured Emma into dropping out, but by the time I'd figured that out we were too far through the rehearsal process to do anything about it.'

'We still haven't got her details from Mr Cohen,' Andrew replied, annoyed that babysitting a bunch of actors all day every day was hampering his ability to actually go out and investigate properly.

Vic handed over the folded paper. 'Albany doesn't think she could be involved in any way, but I'm just saying that if *I* had to watch someone else perform in my place I'd be pretty pissed off.

That's the address of where Emma works.'

'And you think she's the type of person who'd make it her business to terrorise the rest of the cast?'

Vic shrugged. 'I couldn't say one way or the other. She seemed like a sweet girl, but I've seen people change in an instant when they've seen an opportunity taken away from them. This business is cut-throat, Inspector, and I've learned not to trust a single soul I work with.'

Andrew thought that was a fairly depressing way to look at life, even if it fell quite close to his own general suspicion of most people. He took the paper and opened it to read the address before putting it in his pocket. 'What makes you think it was Lavinia who forced Emma out of the production?'

Vic snorted loudly. 'You have met Lavinia, haven't you? When she wants something, she goes after it, and there's nothing anybody can do to stop her. If she forced Emma to drop out, then what's to say that Emma isn't now having her revenge?'

Andrew frowned. What Vic had said made sense, but maybe she too had an ulterior motive. 'And do you believe yourself to be above scrutiny?'

Vic laughed, louder that time. 'Scrutinise away, Inspector Joyce. I'll tell you in all honesty right now that I can't stand a single one of that lot, except for Ben – he's alright – and I don't particularly give a toss who plays Isabella as long as she gets the job done. That being said, if anything happens to any of them, it's my head the blame will lay squarely on, so please do whatever the hell it is you need to do to sort this mess out before opening night.'

Andrew nodded slowly. 'Why is Mr Cohen so sure that Emma Allen isn't involved then? Have you not shared your suspicions with him?'

'Oh, I have,' Vic replied steadily. 'Albany generally thinks he knows better than everyone else. I've worked with him for years, and he's always believed that he's got great instincts when it comes to people; and yet he's cast Lavinia, Teddy and Marion in a play together.'

'Then why work with him?'

'Because he's a phenomenal director,' Vic said with a shrug. 'And he's a decent man. It's just that his intuition is completely fucked. Also, I should let you know that technically Emma is still part of the production.'

'*What?*'

'Emma is the standby for Isabella,' Vic explained guiltily. 'All four roles have a standby just in case anything happens that would warrant someone pulling out of the performance.'

'And nobody's mentioned this before now?' Andrew wasn't proud of the elevated pitch of his voice, but he couldn't help it.

'Normally the standby cast would be part of the rehearsals, but given the rather *hysterical* atmosphere surrounding the production, Albany arranged for the standby cast to rehearse elsewhere a few times,' Vic replied steadily. 'It's unlikely any of them will be needed this close to the production, but they know the whole thing inside out, even if they haven't actually been allowed onto the stage itself this time.'

Andrew fought the urge to yell at the ceiling. 'I'm going to need everyone else's names and addresses as well then.'

'I'll have them for you by Monday morning,' Vic promised. 'The other three standbys are people Albany and I have worked with multiple times in the past, and we approached them directly for the job. Emma's circumstances are obviously very different.'

'You make it sound like you want Emma to be involved,' Andrew stated, and he didn't bother hiding the accusatory hint in his tone.

Vic shrugged. 'I just want an answer, DI Joyce, and between you and me, I'd still rather be working with Emma Allen than I would Lavinia.'

Andrew had nothing to say to that.

'Don't feel as though you need to stay while we tidy up. I'll see to it that Albany leaves through the back.' Vic grimaced as Cohen ripped up the last piece of tape with a particularly vicious tug. 'Try and enjoy the rest of your weekend, Inspector, because I doubt Monday morning will be much fun for any of us.'

* * *

Peggy had hoped that she would arrive on Whitworth Street, triumphantly clutching a wealth of material that would help progress the investigation into the previous deaths at both the Court and the Palace. In reality, the small bundle of paper she had collated thanks to the somewhat sporadic newspaper archive and the photocopier at Central Library wasn't exactly the treasure trove of information she'd hoped to find. She really wasn't sure that it would be enough to soften the blow when she had to explain the bizarre disturbance at the Ballroom that morning.

She'd been pleased enough that she'd found a few reviews mentioning Alistair's name in various venues around the area, but the information she'd managed to amass about George Bevan – the only suspect in Alistair's death – was pitiful to say the least. Cohen and Vic had been right; the police clearly hadn't particularly cared about tracking him down, or about investigating Alistair's death.

The 1932 rehearsal schedule they'd found in the Court's archive room had mentioned an appointment for the cast to be interviewed by a journalist from *The Manchester Guardian*, and she'd been hoping that the library would have a copy of the edition. She'd been disappointed to learn that a significant amount of the newspaper archive was not actually publicly accessible, and she'd had to make a special order at the information desk. She'd then been even more disappointed to find out that it could take up to ten days for her request to be dealt with.

The rain had thankfully stopped by the time she'd stepped back outside, and after spending the entire morning inside, she'd decided that it would be more pleasant to walk to the rehearsal venue. She'd left her car on Peter Street and taken the opportunity of a peaceful few minutes to try and work out exactly how she was going to explain what had happened at the Ballroom without Andrew losing his mind.

Peggy had half-settled on not telling him at all when she rounded the corner to Whitworth Street and only narrowly avoided colliding with Lloyd.

'Peggy!'

'Sorry, Lloyd,' Peggy replied, clutching the folders and keyring to her chest in surprise.

'No, my fault.' Lloyd wrinkled his nose. 'I was just trying to get away from that place as quickly as possible.'

'Why? What happened?'

Lloyd shook his head. 'Nothing much, only some journalists set up camp outside.'

Peggy frowned. 'What?'

'Yeah. The boss reckons one of the actors called the papers trying to drum up a bit of press. They all denied it, of course. Whoever it was told Jimmy Haworth at the *Evening News* that the police are investigating ghosts.'

'Oh.' Well, there went even the slightest possibility of Andrew being in a good mood.

'Yeah.' Lloyd made a face. 'What are you doing over this way though? You're not supposed to be meeting the boss today, are you?'

Peggy shook her head. 'I've just been to the library, and I found a few things about Alistair, so I thought I'd drop them over. Oh, and I wanted to give Higson's keys and this file back. I went to the Ballroom this morning, and I was halfway to the library before I realised that I still had them.'

Peggy was lying through her teeth about the last part, of course, but she didn't want to have to explain things to Lloyd.

'Cool,' Lloyd replied nonchalantly, accepting the explanation as easily as Peggy had hoped he would. Then he held out a hand. 'You might as well just give me the stuff to take back to the Ballroom. No need for you to walk all the way down there; the boss is probably gone now anyway.'

'Oh, has he gone home already?' Peggy frowned at her watch. It had only just gone twelve, so she was surprised to hear that Andrew would have left that quickly.

Lloyd rolled his eyes. 'No. That Miss Heathcote asked him out for lunch again. She said she was worried about getting to her car without being seen.'

Peggy couldn't help but hear an echo of Marnie's 'oh, I *bet* she did' from a couple of days earlier. Even though she thought that she should probably feel that this was perhaps a bit uncharitable towards Lavinia, Peggy found that after another night of no sleep and two – no, *three* – disturbing events in twenty-four hours, she didn't quite have it in her to care enough to do so. 'Oh, right.'

'Yeah, exactly,' Lloyd smirked. He gestured for the file again. 'Do you want me to take that?'

Peggy hesitated. 'Actually, Lloyd, don't worry about it. Surely you weren't planning on going back to Tib Street?'

'Nah,' Lloyd shrugged. 'I was going to get home and try and have a sleep. Out with your brother tonight!'

Great, thought Peggy sardonically. This whole interaction was going to get back to Charlie now. 'Right, yes, exactly, so, no need for you to waste time heading back to the Ballroom. I've got a few things I need to talk to Andrew about anyway, so I'll probably just drop all of this over to Gatley later.'

Lloyd only shrugged again. 'Alright, if you're sure. Though, you might be better off waiting to drop it over to him tomorrow afternoon. Better chance of catching him there by himself if you wait until then, if you get me.'

Lloyd chuckled before he seemed to remember exactly which Swan sibling he was talking to. He clamped his mouth shut so quickly that Peggy would have found it genuinely hilarious if it had happened at any other moment in her life.

'Sorry,' Lloyd muttered apologetically. 'Um, you won't tell him I said that will you?'

Peggy shook her head and sighed. 'No, Lloyd, I won't tell him. Look, just forget about all of this and go home. Enjoy the rest of your weekend.'

Lloyd grinned. 'I'm mostly just going to enjoy almost forty-eight hours without watching that bloody play.'

Peggy couldn't argue with that.

'Bus!' Lloyd announced suddenly, pointing at a bus approaching the stop further up the road.

'Go on then, or you'll miss it!'

'See you on Monday, Peggy!' Lloyd called over his shoulder with a wave as he sprinted up the road.

Peggy waited where she was until Lloyd successfully boarded the bus, chuckling to herself as he waved again when it drove past where she stood.

Then, without even the briefest glance down Whitworth Street, Peggy turned around and trudged back towards her car.

TEN

With the never-ending roadworks of the city centre stalling his progress every few minutes, it took Andrew far longer than he would have liked to reach Chorlton. It was well and truly lunchtime when he parked opposite the small bakery Vic's note had directed him to, and Andrew's stomach growled loudly, reminding him that he hadn't eaten anything since his hastily constructed omelette the night before.

Based on the queue of people snaking out through the open door of the bakery and onto the pavement, everyone else was fully aware that it was lunchtime too. For every person that walked out of the shop, each tightly clutching a white paper bag, two more joined the back of the line waiting to be served by the pair of young women behind the counter.

Popular place, thought Andrew as he climbed out of the car and pulled his jacket on. His back twinged painfully again when he clumsily caught his fingers in the sleeve, and he resolved there and then that he was going to have to go back to Acacia Road; his body couldn't take another night on that damned sofa, even if the alternative meant facing his own personal hell at home.

Andrew jogged across the road, but paused again once he was outside the bakery. The six or seven customers within the shop itself were wedged together like tinned sardines, and Andrew wasn't sure he'd be able to squeeze his way in there without incurring the anger of those queuing for their lunch. The two women serving behind the counter were smiling and chatting with their customers, but even from afar, Andrew could see that they both looked harried beneath the surface pleasantries.

'You'll want to get in the queue, mate.' A bearded man in his late fifties gestured to Andrew and then over his own shoulder with his thumb. 'There's no chance you'll still be in time for a pie, mind. I'd be surprised if they've got any left as is.'

'Yeah, thanks,' Andrew replied as another couple joined the back of the queue. 'I've just got to make a phone call first.'

The man grimaced. 'Taking a risk doing that. They'll barely have scraps when you get back.'

Andrew shrugged with a polite smile and headed over to the phone box outside the pharmacy. There was no way he was going to be able to speak to Emma Allen with a shop full of people around them, but if he loitered around outside the bakery he was going to look like a right weirdo.

Anyway, he did actually have a phone call he needed to make.

He eventually managed to find a ten pence piece in his pocket and blew the lint off it before picking up the handset and pushing the coin into the slot. The coin clattered noisily down the chute before landing heavily in the returned coin box. Andrew swore under his breath, and he had to repeat the process twice more before the internal mechanism finally caught the money.

Andrew dialled, and as the call rang out he watched the bakery queue begin to shorten.

'Hello?'

Andrew pressed his closed fist to his forehead and only just resisted the urge to groan in annoyance. 'Hi, Charlie, is your sister there?'

'Joycie! What are you doing calling on a weekend? *Oh, for God's sake, Marnie, just pause the bloody thing.*'

Andrew sighed loudly as the sound of scuffling continued in the background. 'Charlie. Is Peggy there?'

'No, no she's not. Sorry.'

'Do you know where she is?'

'No.'

Andrew was fairly sure that this was the least informative interaction he'd ever had in his life. 'Right. Do you at least know when she might be back?'

'No, sorry. Why?'

'I just need to speak to her about something, that's all.' Andrew wasn't planning on sharing a single thing about what had happened in his house with Charlie, and he knew he could trust Peggy to have been discreet about it.

'Oh!' Charlie suddenly sounded unexpectedly perkier. 'Hang on, is this about your haunted house?'

Andrew's mouth dropped open in horror. 'She *told* you?'

'Peg? No, of course she didn't.' Charlie's disbelieving eyeroll was practically audible. 'Marnie did.'

Andrew considered just hanging up; he could always pretend that he'd run out of money if asked about it later.

'It sounds frightful,' Charlie continued, oblivious to – or completely ignoring - Andrew's irritation, as usual. 'If I were you, I'd just sell and move somewhere miles away. Even this old place isn't the horror story your house seems to be!'

Andrew experienced one of those sharp pangs of longing for his old, straightforward life in CID. True, his former DCI was likely as corrupt as they came, and Andrew would have probably been packed off to a dead-end role at some point in the future, but at least he wouldn't have been forced to deal with either Charlie Swan, or with a dead woman who enjoyed winding him up at any given opportunity.

'Joyce, are you still there?'

Andrew thoroughly wished that he wasn't. 'Yeah. Look, Charlie, are you sure you don't know where Peggy's gone?'

Charlie laughed, but there was a slight edge to it. 'Contrary to what you seem to think, I'm not my sister's keeper. She's been out all morning, and she didn't mention where she was going. Can't this wait until Monday, anyway?'

Ah. Yes, perhaps Andrew shouldn't really be calling Peggy over the weekend; especially when he'd told her that she wouldn't be needed at that morning's rehearsal.

'I mean, surely you're not planning on going back to your house any time soon anyway, are you?' Charlie asked in surprise.

'Of course I am,' Andrew replied, hoping he sounded more confident about the prospect than he felt. 'I'm sure whatever happened last night was a one-off thing.'

'Right.' Charlie's low drawl managed to convey both scepticism and judgement at the same time. Andrew still wasn't sure how the Swans managed to do things like that with only one word.

'Can you please just tell Peggy that I called?' Andrew glanced at the bakery to see that the queue no longer stretched onto the pavement. 'Tell her not to worry about it though, alright? I'll see her on Monday morning.'

'Alright, but Joycie, I really think you should avoid your house for a few days.'

'I'll bear it in mind,' Andrew replied, while having no intention of actually doing so. 'Thanks.'

Andrew hung up before Charlie could add anything else. The fact that the ten pence then dropped cheerfully into the phone casing without offering up any change did nothing to improve Andrew's mood.

He replaced the handset forcefully and left the phone box with the fleeting thought that maybe he should just transfer to somewhere else in the country entirely; that way he could go back to pretending that ghosts only existed in stories, and he wouldn't be startled into alertness in the middle of the night. The thought soured almost immediately as the sharp sting of guilt jabbed at him with relentless ferocity; he couldn't leave the house knowing that it really would be leaving Rob and everything about their family behind him.

Andrew must have still been scowling when he walked into the almost-empty bakery, because he caught the quick look of amusement that passed between the two women behind the counter when he joined the back of the queue of three.

'You alright there, love?' The shorter of the two asked when Andrew reached the front a minute later. Her hair was scraped back into some sort of complicated plait thing – Andrew didn't have the technical knowledge to define it – making her look quite severe underneath the smile. 'That's some face you've got on there. My Dave looks like that when he's not eaten enough as well. What can I get you?'

Andrew tried to smooth his features out into something approaching professional before he held up his warrant card. 'Detective Inspector Andrew Joyce, Greater Manchester Police. I'm looking for Emma Allen.'

The woman who hadn't spoken to him flinched in surprise and looked at Andrew in open concern. 'I'm Emma. What's happened?'

'It's nothing to worry about, Ms Allen,' Andrew replied evenly. 'I just need a quick word with you about the production of *Lady Bancroft's Rose* at the Court.'

'My sister's got nothing to do with that load of bullshit!' The sudden burst of anger from the first woman was so vehement that it startled Andrew enough that he took one step backwards. He'd been correct about the underlying severity then.

'Jesus, Sue, calm down!' Emma grabbed the other woman's arm tightly and only just about stopped her from rounding the counter towards Andrew.

'Is that snobby little bitch at it again?' Sue snapped, still glaring at Andrew. 'You'd have thought stealing the part from her would have been enough! What's my sister apparently done to her now?'

Andrew pursed his lips. Well, it seemed that it wasn't just Vic who was convinced that Lavinia had pushed Emma out of the production. He nodded at Sue before turning his attention to

Emma. 'A few questions about the circumstances surrounding you leaving the production, that's all.'

'You don't have to talk to him, Em,' Sue added mulishly.

That was technically true, but Andrew didn't want to have to start suggesting options that sounded rather more threatening than he cared for. He would though, if pushed, because speaking to Emma might be the only useful thing he'd have managed to do in days.

'It's alright, Sue,' Emma said quietly. She squeezed her sister's arm before she wriggled past and walked over to where Andrew was standing. 'Go ahead, Detective Inspector, ask away.'

'Thank you.' Andrew was careful to partially direct his gratitude towards Sue as well. He knew how unwise it could be to upset one sibling in the presence of another – he'd dealt with the Swans' ire on enough occasions.

'Hmm.' Sue was still glaring but she began tidying up behind the counter, so Andrew thought that his presence would probably be tolerated for a few more minutes.

'Emma, can you tell me why you left the production?' Andrew asked carefully. 'By all accounts the director, Mr Cohen, thought that you'd make a great Isabella, and you were pleased to have got the role.'

Emma sighed and folded her arms. 'Yeah, yeah, he did say that, and of course I was pleased! There's not been much opportunity for good parts in the last couple of years.'

'Why not?'

'There's been a lot of touring productions in town, so they bring their cast with them, you know?' Emma shrugged. 'I'd love to do all that, but I have to help out here – family business – and I couldn't really afford to leave anyway. It's alright for people like Lavinia; she's loaded, so she doesn't have to worry about whether she can pay for a shit hotel room on tour once the budget's run out.'

Andrew understood that one. He'd never been quite so aware of privilege and the doors it could open as he had over the preceding nine months. He'd also seen the hotel Lavinia was staying at and didn't think anyone would ever be able to describe it as 'shit'. 'So, what happened then?'

Emma shook her head slowly and glanced skywards. Andrew had the awful feeling that Emma might be very close to bursting into tears, at which point he assumed that Sue would likely try to murder him.

'It was a week into rehearsals, and Mum had taken me out for lunch for my birthday,' Emma explained eventually. 'When we got back, there was an envelope waiting for me. I thought it was a birthday card, but when I opened it, it was this horrible letter saying that the play was cursed and that it was Isabella's turn to die on opening night.'

'Do you still have the letter?'

Emma nodded. 'Yeah, it's at home though. Do you want to see it?'

'I do. Do you think you'd be able to bring it to me on Monday? Or I can come back here and get it if that's easier.'

'Yeah, I can bring it to you. Where?'

'Why are you so interested in this now?' Sue called from where she'd come to lean by the counter again. 'Nobody cared when I brought my sister in to see you lot back when it happened. She was shaking like a leaf, and they just laughed her out of the station'

Andrew held his hands up. 'That shouldn't have happened, and I'm sorry that it did, Emma. I work for a special division on Tib Street. If I give you the address, could you drop the letter off there tomorrow, or on Monday for me, please? If I'm not there, you can leave it with anyone else in the building, or just put it through the letterbox, alright?'

'Alright.' Emma held out her hand to her sister and wiggled

her fingers in some indecipherable sibling code that resulted in Sue handing over a white paper bag and a pen almost instantly.

'Thanks,' Andrew said as he took the bag and pen and began to scribble down the Ballroom's address.

'Did Mr Cohen tell you that he's still paying me?' Emma asked. 'To be the standby, just in case Lavinia couldn't go on for any reason.'

'I could give her plenty of reasons,' Sue growled.

'Sue!' Emma threw up her hands exasperated, before looking back to Andrew apologetically. 'Ignore her, please, Inspector.'

Andrew didn't think that Sue's threat was particularly serious, although if he saw her anywhere near the Court before opening night, he'd be inclined to have her escorted off the property just in case. He focused on Emma instead as he handed over the address. 'Yes, I'd heard that.'

'He was really good about it,' Emma added. 'He's paying me the same rate I would have got if I'd performed.'

'He is?' Andrew frowned.

Emma nodded. 'I think he was really upset about the way everything happened. He tried so hard to convince me to stay, but I told him that I couldn't, not when my mum was so upset about the letter as well. He topped up the standby pay out of his own pocket and everything. I think he felt really guilty.'

That was news to Andrew too.

Emma asked as she looked down at the address in confusion. 'Cheryl Richards Dance Studio?'

'Yeah, our office is in a ballroom,' Andrew replied, hoping that didn't sound as mad to the sisters as it still did to him.

'Are you sure you're actually the police?' Sue asked, narrowing her eyes.

'Do you want my details?' Andrew asked, reaching for his warrant card again.

Sue stared at him for a long moment before she shook her

head just once. 'No, you're alright, but you better make sure that little brat faces consequences for what she did to my sister.'

'Why are you so sure that it was Lavinia who sent you the letter?' Andrew asked, hoping that Sue would let her sister answer this one herself.

Emma scoffed. 'You mean besides her criticising every single thing I did in the first rehearsals? Or when she outright told me that she'd make sure that the *right* Isabella would be on stage by opening night? Lavinia always has to be the star.'

Andrew nodded slowly. Emma's belief in Lavinia's guilt would seem to be entirely reasonable.

'Why exactly *are* you here though?' Emma regarded Andrew with suspicion, interrupting his thoughts. 'Has something happened?'

'We're just looking into a few unexplained incidents at the theatre, Miss Allen,' Andrew replied diplomatically. 'Thank you for telling me about the letter. I'll be back in touch next week, once I've had a chance to look at it, alright?'

'Alright.'

'Here.'

Andrew turned his head in surprise as Sue's voice came from much closer to him than he was expecting. She was holding two paper bags out towards him.

'You look like you need them,' Sue said, still far from the significantly more cheerful woman she'd been when he'd first walked in, but maybe slightly less aggressive than she had been moments earlier. 'Get that mardy look off your face, and get some work done.'

Andrew nodded as he gingerly took the bags with a muttered thanks that he hoped didn't sound as flustered to anyone else as it did to his own ears.

Emma gave him a final small smile as she followed her sister towards the back of the shop, and Andrew took that as his cue to leave.

When he was back in the Belmont, he hesitantly unrolled the tops of both bags and was pleasantly surprised to see a flaky sausage roll in one and a Manchester tart nestled in the other, with a garishly red maraschino cherry perched on top. He looked back over to the bakery and found that Sue was watching him once again.

Andrew raised his hand in another gesture of thanks, and Sue gave him one final short nod before closing the door and locking it behind her.

Now that he'd spoken to Emma, and with Peggy nowhere to be found, Andrew realised that he was running out of reasons not to go home.

He looked down at the paper bags again and decided that he'd have his lunch first though.

He wasn't stalling; he was just really hungry.

Honestly.

* * *

'Charlie?' Peggy knocked on her brother's door again. 'Charlie, are you in there?'

'He went out, darling.'

Peggy sucked in a loud breath of surprise as Emmeline appeared next to her. She pressed her hand to her chest and willed herself to calm down; it was her aunt, it was nothing to worry about, and it was nothing to do with what had happened at the Ballroom.

'Margaret, dear, what's wrong?' Emmeline asked in concern. 'You're terribly pale, even for you.'

'Nothing,' Peggy replied, smiling as widely as she could bear. 'I'm just tired.'

Emmeline looked ready to start questioning her further, so Peggy sidestepped her and headed towards her own room instead.

'You said Charlie went out?' Peggy called over her shoulder

knowing that Emmeline would follow her. 'It's a bit early for him, isn't it?'

'I don't make a habit of keeping track of Charles' social engagements, Margaret, as you well know. I still don't understand how he can have so many acquaintances, or why he would even want to.'

Peggy snorted slightly and opened the door to her bedroom.

It was only because she was already half-expecting Marnie to be in there that she didn't jump in fright when she saw that the window seat was occupied; Marnie had taken to sitting there often now that spring was on its way. Peggy didn't know if Marnie could feel the warmth of the sunshine or not, and as she wasn't quite sure whether it would be rude to ask, she'd held the question back.

'Hiya,' Marnie greeted her cheerfully. 'Where'd you get to?'

Peggy knew that Marnie could have tracked her down if she'd really wanted to, but over the past few months Marnie had been trying really hard not to just impose herself on Peggy's day-to-day life. The occasions when she'd just pop up somewhere outside of Butterton had decreased dramatically, and Peggy was genuinely grateful for the effort.

'I just went in to town,' Peggy replied nonchalantly as she hung up her coat and headed over to her dressing table. She wasn't going to mention what had happened on Tib Street. 'Thought I'd get some work done.'

'You didn't go to the theatre on your own, did you?' Marnie asked.

Peggy shook her head. 'No, I went to the Ballroom, and then to the library.'

'Oh, so did you see Andrew then?' Marnie asked, and she prodded at the folder that Peggy had put down so that she could root through a drawer with two hands.

'He was at the rehearsal, so no, I didn't.' Peggy shook her head. 'Why can I never find a pen when I need one?'

'Your policeman called here looking for you,' Emmeline added, perching on the end of the bed.

Peggy frowned. Lloyd hadn't mentioned that. 'He did? When?'

'About an hour ago,' Marnie said, handing Peggy three pens as though she'd produced them from thin air. Peggy couldn't be entirely sure that she hadn't.

'An hour ago?' Peggy glanced at her watch.

'Yes,' Marnie replied slowly. 'What's wrong with an hour ago?'

Well, an hour ago, he was apparently having lunch with Lavinia, Peggy thought, but she wasn't going to tell Marnie that, because she knew exactly what would happen if she did. 'Nothing's wrong with it, I'm just surprised that he called. I thought he'd be busy.'

'Busy?' Marnie raised her eyebrows.

'With the case,' Peggy clarified as she picked up the file, which she'd stuffed her photocopies into on the way up the front steps. 'Why did he call?'

Marnie shrugged. 'Don't really know, to be honest. Charlie told him that he probably shouldn't be calling here looking for you over the weekend.'

Peggy wrinkled her nose. *Great.* Classic interfering brother behaviour from Charlie. They were going to have to have words again. 'And that was it?'

'Well, that and Charlie told him that he probably shouldn't go back to his house for a few days,' Marnie added, and then her eyes went wide as she saw the moment her words clicked into place in Peggy's brain.

'Did you tell Charlie about what happened last night?' Peggy shrieked. She generally tried to avoid shrieking, but felt it was necessary just then. 'Marnie! How could you?'

'Oops.'

Emmeline pretended to be very interested in the other corner of the room.

'For God's sake!' Peggy grumbled to herself as she left her

resident ghosts behind her without another word and headed back downstairs. 'Can nobody in this house keep their mouth shut about anything?'

The feeling of being trapped in an eternal gossipy sleepover settled over Peggy once again, and she wondered, not for the first time, if it wasn't time to just move away from Butterton.

Just then, however, she had more important things to worry about and, for once, being in Butterton House was hopefully going to be more of a help than a hindrance.

Peggy crept down the last few steps of the staircase, carefully checking that Timothy was nowhere in sight before she hurried towards the library on her tiptoes. She was sure that Charlie would tell her to stop being quite so ridiculous in her subterfuge, but Caroline Winshire was already hovering threateningly at the periphery of their lives, and Peggy didn't want to tempt fate by giving away anything to their father's spy. The fact that her father had remained unaware of Peggy's connection to the Ballroom thus far was nothing short of a miracle, and Peggy wanted to keep him in the dark for as long as possible.

When the door was closed behind her, she took care to turn the key in the lock as quietly as she could. A locked door wouldn't keep Marnie or Emmeline out, but it would give her fair warning of Timothy's approach. She shook her head at herself as she put everything down on the desk in the corner of the room – it really was well past time to think about moving out.

'Right, where do I start?' She pushed the sleeves of her cardigan further up her arms and headed towards the shelves that held her father's collection of local history books.

William Swan didn't particularly care about history in the general sense; his interest was only by piqued by texts that mentioned the Swan family or anything connected to the Butterton Estate, and so he'd amassed a collection based entirely on that principle. While Peggy generally found this to be a terribly disappointing way of looking at history, just then she was quite pleased about her father's narrow focus when it came to the task at hand.

If there was going to be anything useful written about the Court, or where Jock might have originated from, then Peggy was hopeful it would be found in her father's assortment of dusty books.

She ran her fingers along the spines, looking for anything that might be a good starting point, and eventually settled on the two most likely candidates. One was a history of the Earls of Acresfield, and the property connected to them, and the other seemed to be a more general book about the city's history, which would no doubt make reference to the Swan dynasty in there somewhere.

As Peggy had stood in the sunshine in St Peter's Square earlier that morning, she'd realised that maybe they'd been approaching some of the case from the wrong direction. While she'd been caught up in trying to understand what had happened to Alistair, Andrew had been trying to ensure that the cast remained unharmed; but perhaps it was the possible connection between both sides of things that needed understanding first – who was Jock? Or, at the very least, where might he have come from?

Andrew had come close to what Peggy thought might have been the right train of thought the day before when they'd been in the archive room at the Court. His brief history lesson about why the theatre's records may not have survived the War had reminded Peggy that she had grown up with a rather constricted view of social and political history, thanks to both her father, and her education. Her 'fancy schools' as Andrew had called them, hadn't devoted much time to history lessons, but there was one event in Manchester's history that was - or at least, *should have been* - inescapable to anyone who set foot in the city.

Alistair had said that Jock had been there since before the Court was built, and what had been there before the theatre had been St

Peter's Field.

Peggy flicked through the history book until she found the chapter dedicated to Manchester in the early nineteenth century.

Halfway through the opening paragraph came the first reference to the Peterloo Massacre in August 1819.

Once, when Peggy had still been very young, her childish curiosity had pushed her to ask Emmeline why so many people had been attacked by soldiers on that day, because weren't the soldiers supposed to protect the people who couldn't fight for themselves?

Emmeline had grown still, drawing into herself, and Peggy had been shocked to see a sheen of tears in her aunt's eyes.

Peggy had sat quietly for a long time before Emmeline had replied with one sentence that Peggy had never forgotten:

'Peterloo is what happens when men who have been given too much power begin to fear those who have been given none.'

Peggy knew that her family, and families just like it, had been part of that problem, and even thirty years after Emmeline's damning conclusion, Peggy still thought that her father was likely to hold a very different opinion on it all than she did. As far as William Swan was concerned, money and power were something akin to divine gifts, bestowed only on those worthy enough to wield them.

She turned the page and saw a map of St Peter's Field; sure enough the Court was well within the boundary.

The other half of the double-page spread was concerned with the victims of the violence. The list of the dead contained quite a few 'Johns' but not a single Jock, although she supposed that 'Jock' could be a nickname anyway. The book also noted that it was unlikely that they'd have a true figure for the number of people killed or injured as a significant number of those involved had concealed their injuries for fear of losing their jobs if they'd been connected to the meeting.

It was entirely possible, of course, that Jock hadn't been involved in the events at all, but perhaps the tragedy that had unfolded in 1819 had scarred the land itself in some way, seeping into the ground and casting a dark shadow over the whole area that could never be truly erased or concealed, no matter how many libraries, or hotels, or *theatres* were built there in the century and a half that had followed.

Peggy sighed as she closed the book again and stared glumly out of the window at the drizzly afternoon.

Perhaps there were some places that could never truly shake themselves free of earlier catastrophe. She thought that might very well be true of her house, and couldn't help but wonder if the same could be said for Andrew's.

* * *

When he'd arrived back from Chorlton, it had taken Andrew quite some time to muster up the nerve to get out of his car. His hand had been forced when he'd realised that Mrs Roberts across the road was staring at him again, teacup in hand. She hadn't had the cup when he'd first parked, so he'd obviously sat there for long enough that she'd had time to go and make tea.

He'd never opened the front door more gingerly in his life, pushing it inwards in increments until it was flush against the wall. Sensing nothing untoward in the hallway he'd then sprinted to the dining room and grabbed one of the chairs from around the table, studiously ignoring the thick layer of dust that coated everything in the room. He'd then placed the chair between the open front door and the door frame in a way that he hoped would make it impossible for the door to be slammed shut while he was upstairs.

Andrew had then repeated the process with the back door.

After quickly checking that the living room appeared undisturbed, he'd made his way upstairs, clutching his house keys, car keys and the damaged cordless phone to his chest as he did so.

When he'd reached the top step, he'd had to stop and take a deep breath. The memory of the charcoal smoke merging into something person-shaped only a foot from where he was standing was terrifyingly fresh in his mind, and a shiver skimmed his spine when he finally stepped onto the landing.

He'd first checked his bedroom, and then the bathroom, but he'd found nothing out of the ordinary in either.

Then he'd made his way to the boxroom that had once been his childhood bedroom, but which now housed a few boxes of paperwork and the odd bits of junk that Andrew felt like he couldn't get rid of but had nowhere else to go.

The first thing that had hit him when he'd cracked open the door was an odd, sickly-sweet smell that reminded him of decaying flowers, but then he'd looked at the walls, and any surprise he'd felt at the troubling scent was robbed from him by a cold wave of dread.

Streaks of what looked like black soot had covered one wall, running up and across the ceiling too, and there were matching marks on the carpet. The posters – the ones he'd so carefully put up himself the summer before Nana Joyce had come and told him that he was going to live with her a bit – had all been ripped in half, right down the middle with a terrifying precision. A box of LPs Andrew hadn't thought about in years had been upended, and shards of black vinyl littered the floor.

Worse than any of that, though, had been the single grey handprint perfectly pressed onto to the wall right by the door,

'Jesus Christ,' Andrew had whispered, wrapping his hands even more tightly around his keys before he'd backed out of the room and closed the door quietly.

He hadn't been brave enough to go anywhere near Rob's old room, so instead he'd hurried back into his bedroom, and pulled an old suitcase out from under his bed. He'd then grabbed as many clothes as he could, shoving everything haphazardly into the suitcase, and then added everything from next to the sink in the bathroom.

Once the suitcase had been filled, he'd awkwardly grabbed the duvet and a pillow from his bed and fled down the stairs. He'd then immediately begun the job of setting up camp by the front door. He was resigned to staying the night, but he wasn't going to stray far from the front door unless he absolutely needed to.

Three hours later, when he was sitting on the sofa cushions he'd pulled into the hall, Andrew was forced to admit that it really wasn't the best plan he'd ever come up with. He'd also have been forced to admit that even the Ballroom sofa would have been more comfortable than his current situation, but he batted that thought away with a palpable sense of resignation. This was his house, and so it was his problem to solve.

He'd closed the front and back doors shortly after returning downstairs as the wind had picked up and the house had quickly become uncomfortably chilly. It hadn't warmed up much since, but as long as the evening and night remained mild, he thought he'd probably be alright.

With no desire to go back to the kitchen any time soon, Andrew was just trying to work up the energy to head out in search of a takeaway for dinner when a sharp rapping sound on the front door behind him almost gave him a heart attack.

He clambered to his feet quickly, ready to yell at whoever was on the other side, if only to make himself feel better about the shrill yelp of surprise he'd let out.

When he wrenched open the door, Andrew's face immediately twisted into an expression of utter bewilderment. 'What the hell are you two doing here?'

ELEVEN

The Railway was as busy as it always was on a Saturday night, which meant that it was far too full of people he recognised for Andrew's liking. He slumped further down into his chair and raised his hand to shield his face slightly when Bill Parr from next door shouldered his way back through the crowd at the bar, carrying a pint and a glass of wine. *Oh God*, that meant Gladys was about somewhere as well. Whereas Bill was a surly older man, unlikely to talk to Andrew at the best of times, Gladys would definitely be wanting a word with him about the terrible noises coming through their shared wall in the dead of night.

'What? What is it?' Lloyd asked from the opposite side of the small table, twisting and craning his neck to try and see what was making Andrew scowl.

'Don't turn around!' Andrew hissed. 'Jesus Christ, Lloyd, do you actually have any idea what subtlety is?'

'Sorry, boss,' Lloyd replied, though he neither looked nor sounded particularly apologetic when he faced Andrew again.

Thankfully, Bill disappeared into a corner somewhere, and so he at least missed the subsequent spectacle of Charlie Swan crossing the pub with three pints balanced precariously between his hands, and what looked like two bags of crisps and a packet of peanuts caught between his teeth.

Charlie put the glasses down in the centre of the table without spilling a drop and then dropped the packets next to them with a grin; the *ta-da* was unspoken but heavily implied, and he reminded Andrew of a particularly self-satisfied Golden Retriever.

'Cheers, mate!' Lloyd reached happily for a pint.

Andrew muttered something approximating a thank you when a beer was nudged in his direction.

Charlie had clearly decided that the correct course of action was to meet Andrew's continued sullenness with obnoxious cheer, and he pushed the crips and peanuts across the table with a flourish, as though he'd achieved something spectacular.

Andrew looked down at the three packets disdainfully. 'We've literally just eaten.'

When Andrew had realised that there was no way he'd get Charlie and Lloyd off his doorstep without agreeing to go out for a pint, the suggestion had been made that they get something to eat on the way. As he'd already decided on going to the decent chippy up by the park when he'd been sitting by his front door, Andrew had offered it up as a suggestion, and they'd both readily agreed.

'It's for soaking up the booze,' Lloyd said, joyfully opening a packet of crisps as though he hadn't just consumed twice his bodyweight in chips and curry sauce. 'Is your house really haunted, sir?'

Andrew started slightly at the abrupt question but didn't reply, choosing to just glower at his pint instead.

'It is,' Charlie confirmed. 'Marnie told me all about. *Terrifying*, she said. Creepy black smoke coming down the stairs and everything.'

Lloyd shivered with a sound of discontent. 'Eurgh.'

'Can we not talk about it?' Andrew grumbled, taking a larger than reasonable gulp of beer. 'I thought that was the whole point of coming to the pub.'

'Sorry, boss,' Lloyd repeated, slightly chastened. 'Got it, no ghosts. Oh, although...'

Andrew pinched the bridge of his nose and groaned loudly. 'What now?'

'Sorry, it's just that I forgot to tell you that I bumped into Peggy this afternoon,' Lloyd explained.

'You did?' Andrew asked at the same time as Charlie.

'Where?' Charlie added. 'In town?'

Lloyd nodded. 'Yeah. I walked right into her when I was heading for the bus. She was heading down Whitworth Street.'

Andrew frowned. 'But she wasn't supposed to be coming to the rehearsal.'

'She wasn't. She was looking for you, boss.' Lloyd shrugged. 'I don't know much about why, but she said she'd been to the Ballroom a-'

'She'd been to the Ballroom?' Andrew asked in mild alarm. If Peggy had been to Tib Street that morning she'd have easily worked out that Andrew had retreated there after the incident in his house; he'd woken up late after very little sleep, and he'd not had time to hide the evidence of his stay. He'd assumed he'd be able to get in early enough on Monday morning to tidy up, thus keeping the whole thing entirely to himself.

'Er, yeah.' Lloyd briefly paused around a mouthful of crumbs and looked at Andrew like he'd lost the plot. 'She said she'd been to the library as well. Oh, and she had Higson's keys.'

Andrew squinted as he slowly processed Lloyd's crisp-mangled explanation. 'Peggy had Higson's keys?'

'Said she forgot to put them back in the Ballroom before she left,' Lloyd said with a shrug. 'I mean, it's fine, isn't it? It's not like the boss is going to want them before Monday. She did say she might drop them over to your house anyway, though, so now I think she probably wanted to talk to you about the thing we're not talking about.'

'Why didn't she just give me the keys this morning?' Andrew frowned. If Peggy had met Lloyd on Whitworth Street, then Andrew would have still been nearby. 'You left before I did.'

Lloyd tipped the final shards straight out of the bag into his mouth. 'Oh, yeah, sorry. I told her that you'd gone out for lunch.'

'Why did you do that?'

'Because I heard La – *Miss Heathcote* – ask you to go out with her again.' Lloyd wrinkled his nose. 'Sorry, was I not supposed to tell anyone that?'

'But I didn't!' Andrew protested at the same time as Charlie's scandalised, 'You went out for lunch with one of the suspects?'

Andrew threw up his hands in annoyance. 'No! No, I didn't. I went to sodding Chorlton to speak to the girl who was supposed to be playing Isabella.' He then glared at Charlie. 'And you know I wasn't out for lunch. I called your bloody house looking for your sister, remember?'

'You could have called from a restaurant,' Charlie replied snootily.

'I was in a phone box in Chorlton!' Andrew argued. 'Jesus! Not that it's any of your business anyway.'

'Hang on!' Charlie held up his hand and then pointed at Lloyd. 'You said *again*.'

'Again?' Lloyd frowned in utter confusion. 'What?'

'You said 'I heard her ask you to go out with her *again*',' Charlie clarified.

'Yeah, 'cos of on Thursday when we were all supposed to...' Lloyd trailed off, looking between the other two. 'Am I in trouble?'

Charlie laughed mirthlessly as he shook his head at Andrew. 'No wonder Marnie's been bad-mouthing you for days!'

Andrew opened his mouth to respond, livid that he was getting it in the neck even though he'd not actually done anything wrong, but when he saw a couple of familiar faces at the bar glance in his direction, he clamped his mouth closed and stared mulishly at a beer mat instead.

'Poor form, Joycie,' Charlie muttered, shaking his head. 'Very poor form.'

And, alright, maybe Andrew was self-aware enough to know that Charlie might have had a point.

'Joyce, mate!'

Andrew looked up, rearranging his face into as neutral an

expression as possible as his former five-a-side coach, DS Mike Lawson approached the table. 'Mike.'

'Haven't seen you around in ages,' Mike said, reaching out to shake Andrew's hand. He gestured at the empty seat. 'Alright if I sit for a sec?'

'Course it is,' Andrew said, and he didn't think he'd ever meant anything less.

It wasn't that he didn't like Mike, it was just that right then he was another barrier to Andrew getting out of the whole situation as quickly as he wanted to.

'Parker, right?' Mike said, gesturing towards Lloyd, unaware of Andrew's discontent. 'You were in Didsbury for a bit?'

'Yeah, that's right. Lloyd.' His reply was cheerful, but Lloyd reached over to pull the second packet of crisps next to his pint immediately, as though he feared that the new arrival might have designs on them.

'Mike Lawson.'

'Cool.'

Mike then turned his attention to the final member of the group. 'Sorry, I don't think we've ever met. Do you work with Joyce?'

'Me? No.' Charlie replied amiably, all hints of irritation expertly hidden away as though they'd never existed. 'I'm Charles Swan.'

Mike looked slightly confused when Charlie didn't offer up any further explanation as to why he and his cut-glass accent were sitting at a table in The Railway with two detectives early on a Saturday evening, but then he seemed to shrug it off and instead turned to Andrew with a worrying hint of mischief on his face.

'So, what's all this I hear about you chasing ghosts?' Mike grinned.

Oh, dear Christ. Andrew was glad he hadn't been drinking in that moment, because he probably would have choked to death in horror if he had. Nobody was really supposed to know how the Ballroom actually operated, and Andrew was more than happy for that to be the case.

'What?' Andrew choked out eventually.

Mike laughed loudly. 'Mate, I can't believe the bollocks they'll print these days.'

'What?' Andrew repeated, even more horrified, as he thought that he might suddenly be putting two and two together correctly.

Mike laughed again, but it quickly tailed off into surprised silence when he realised that nobody else was as amused as he was. 'Shit, don't you know anything about this?'

'About *what*, Mike?'

'Rumour is that Jimmy Haworth at the *Evening News* is writing some crap about the ghostbusting DI,' Mike explained, shaking his head.

'Oh, for fuck's sake,' Andrew groaned, pressing his fingers to his temples. 'How the hell did he even know I was there? I went out the back!'

'Wait, are you saying that you *were* chasing ghosts?' Mike asked in disbelief.

'No, of course I wasn't chasing ghosts!' Andrew sighed, choosing to ignore Charlie's poorly concealed chortle, and hoping that Mike wouldn't read too much into it. 'Look, some actors think that the play they're putting on is cursed, and a couple of them got jumpy about a ghost story, that's all.'

Mike frowned. 'So, you're looking into a *curse*?'

Andrew made a noise somewhere between exasperation and defeat. 'No, because there's no such thing as bloody curses, is there?'

Thankfully, Lloyd held his tongue, even though Andrew could tell that he really wanted to make a comment to the contrary.

'Someone – a wholly alive someone – is mucking about backstage, scaring the cast and the director,' Andrew added.

'That's all it is. We're just trying to find out who it is before it gets any more serious than that.'

Mike nodded, accepting the explanation. 'You might want to get onto Haworth and tell him not to print his story then, because he definitely knows you're involved, whether he's right about anything else or not.'

Great. That was all Andrew needed, wasn't it? As if things weren't bad enough, he'd be the laughingstock of the entire force come Monday. No, strike that, if Mike knew about the story already, it meant that everyone was already getting a good chuckle out of DI Joyce's misfortune. He took another large gulp of beer.

'How'd you hear about any of this?' Lloyd asked Mike, when it became clear that Andrew was too busy wallowing in his own despair to contribute any further.

'I was down the chippy earlier and bumped into Wallace - you remember him, don't you, Joyce?'

Oh, yes, Andrew remembered Wallace, alright; he was the little arse who'd nicked his spot on the five-a-side team when Andrew had first been sent to Tib Street.

'Right,' continued Mike, taking Andrew's scowl as tacit agreement, 'and he said he'd heard it from that prick Kinsella. I didn't quite understand how it got to him, but I think it had something to do with Kinsella's wife, or sister-in-law, or someone who works with Haworth, and they'd seen him this afternoon after he'd apparently tracked you down.'

'I still don't understand how he could have seen me,' Andrew pulled at his collar. 'I was parked up the road.'

'Maybe he didn't see you at all, boss,' Lloyd suggested. 'Maybe it's like you said earlier; someone's telling tales.'

Andrew thought back to the denials he'd been given that morning, and then to what the Allen sisters had told him that afternoon; he had the awful feeling that he knew exactly who the most likely suspect was.

He really was a complete idiot sometimes.

'I knew it was a load of bollocks, Joyce,' Mike said, clapping Andrew hard on the shoulder. 'Don't worry.'

Based on how badly everything in his life had been going all week, Andrew should have realised that it was indeed possible for it to still get just a bit worse.

'Oh, by the way, I saw Roz and Kate the other night,' Mike added, leaning back in his chair and folding his arms.

Andrew's face fell even further. He did not need to hear about his ex-girlfriend and her awful best friend. 'Oh, right?'

'Yeah.' Mike's grin became a leer. 'Still can't believe you chucked her, mate.'

'Nah, he didn't,' Lloyd snorted into his pint. 'She chucked him.'

Andrew briefly considered whether he would actually prefer to go home and be murdered by an angry spirit than to sit through any more of this; he was fairly certain that the answer was a resounding *yes* to death by ghost.

Maybe he'd just send Lloyd in there by himself instead and see what happened.

Mike guffawed loudly. 'She's got herself some new fella now anyway. I think he's a doctor, or a solicitor or something.'

Well, Kate's mother would be pleased, at least, Andrew thought crossly. Mrs Simpson had never been happy that Andrew was 'only' a policeman and had thought that her daughter deserved a significantly greater lot in life; she'd told him that to his face on more than one occasion.

He made only a non-committal sound in response, because he really didn't want to talk about Kate.

'She did ask about you though,' Mike added, rolling his eyes. 'I think she was just fishing for information. Not that I could tell her much, considering you didn't come back when the season started.'

'I told you Mike, I've been too busy with cases,' Andrew said.

He ignored the raised eyebrows from both Charlie and Lloyd. They both knew that he wasn't anywhere near busy enough that he couldn't have tried to find time to socialise if he'd wanted to.

'That's what I told Kate,' Mike said, and then he smirked. 'Though she seemed to think it was because you'd shacked up with some posh bird from work.'

Andrew immediately changed his mind about murder by ghost in his house; he'd take instantaneous death right there in the middle of The Railway if it was on offer.

Lloyd didn't make even the slightest effort to pretend that he wasn't laughing, and Andrew didn't dare glance in Charlie's direction for fear of the expression he'd find there.

'Er, no,' Andrew stammered out eventually. 'No. Kate saw me in here once with a colleague and made up her own version of events. It was nothing.'

'Oh.' Mike looked disappointed that his scrap of gossip hadn't quite panned out the way he'd wanted. 'Never mind, eh?'

'Oi! Mikey, come on, we're off!'

Mike waved over towards the group by the door and then turned back to the table. 'Alright, lads, that's me. Joyce, think about coming back on Thursdays, alright? Have a good night.'

'Yeah, see you,' Andrew replied, sighing loudly in relief when the pub door closed behind Mike and his friends.

The relief, of course, couldn't last.

'Shacked up with some posh bird from work?'

Andrew winced as Charlie repeated Mike's turn of phrase. 'Not my words, alright?'

'So, what happened?'

'Nothing.' Andrew held his hands up. '*Obviously.*'

Charlie leaned back in his chair and made a 'go on' motion with his hands before clasping them on the tabletop, face impassive.

Andrew sighed and dropped his chin to his chest. 'It was last summer; after I went to pick Peggy up from the hospital.'

Charlie's expression darkened, just as it always did when the topic of that day came up, but he remained silent.

'Peggy needed to give a statement about what had happened in the accident, and I didn't want her to have to talk to anyone in CID,' Andrew explained, picking at the peeling corner of a damp beer mat, 'so I offered to take it instead. After everything that had happened, she didn't want to go home straight away, and so we ended up here.'

Andrew scratched the back of his neck self-consciously. 'We were talking about Marnie, and I showed her the engagement ring. Kate saw us, and, well...I'm sure you can guess what story she came up with. Jesus, I told her she had it completely backwards, and so did Peggy!'

Charlie regarded him wordlessly and Lloyd reached for the peanuts.

Andrew would never be able to look back at anything that had happened that day and call it his proudest moment: Peggy had found herself locked in a burning house twenty-four hours later, and Andrew still firmly blamed his own behaviour for that. He wasn't naïve enough to assume that Charlie didn't blame him just as much.

To Andrew's surprise, Charlie's serious countenance cracked, and he sniggered loudly. 'Well, I for one can't wait to tell my sister that she's been causing scandal in Gatley. She'll be absolutely *delighted*.'

'Charlie, no. Don't,' Andrew said firmly. Charlie might have been okay being flippant, but after Peggy had told Andrew how her father had solely blamed her for everything that had happened with Caroline Winshire and that bloody bastard Edgar, there was no way he could be as offhand.

Charlie looked slightly taken back by Andrew's sharp tone. 'Relax, Joycie, I'm joking. As if I'd be stupid enough to say anything like that to Peg!'

Andrew shook his head in dismay.

'At least it's you though. I suppose it could be much worse,' Charlie continued with a grin, but then sobered slightly. 'Though, I'll still be contractually obligated to kill you if you do anything to seriously upset my sister.'

'Charlie,' Andrew growled in warning as Lloyd chortled into his pint glass, 'fuck off.'

Charlie then raised one eyebrow and reached into his pocket to pull out his wallet, which he then held out towards Lloyd. 'Go get another round.'

'We're still on this one,' Andrew protested, looking at his half-drunk pint.

'Another round,' Charlie repeated, waving the wallet towards Lloyd.

'Yeah, alright,' Lloyd agreed slowly, looking between the other two. It was clear that he knew he was about to be excluded from something, but he took the wallet and stood up anyway. 'Same again?'

Charlie shook his head. 'Something stronger, I reckon.'

'What is it, Charlie?' Andrew asked tiredly when Lloyd was out of earshot.

'Look…' Charlie trailed off, looking slightly uncomfortable. 'It's not really my place to say anything but–'

'Well, maybe you shouldn't say anything at all then,' Andrew suggested tightly, knowing that he was going to be deeply unhappy with whatever wisdom Charlie was about to share.

'My sister isn't happy,' Charlie continued eventually. He then made a face that suggested that he was terribly displeased with what he'd just said. 'What I mean, is that for the past nine months I've seen Peg behaving more like herself than she has in years, until this week.'

Andrew shook his head vehemently. 'Charlie, no, I'm not

gossiping about your sister.'

'It's not gossip,' Charlie replied forcefully, prodding at his pint glass and no longer meeting Andrew's eyes. 'I don't want my sister anywhere near any situation that involves either our mother or that utter *wanker*, but I've had to accept the fact that this week there's not much I can do about it.'

'We'll keep them away from her, Charlie, I promise.'

Charlie shook his head again. 'Anyone who doesn't know her would look at Peggy and think that she'd lived an entirely charmed life, but I've seen her belittled, undervalued, heartbroken - at her absolute *lowest* – and I need to know, for her sake, that it won't happen again.'

Andrew frowned. What exactly was Charlie getting at? 'I don't un-'

'You can't just keep Peggy around so that she'll help you with your ghost problem, and then drop her when it's no longer convenient.'

For a long moment, Andrew stared at Charlie in alarm, until his brain eventually kicked in and reminded him that a denial was necessary. 'Charlie, I wouldn't do that.'

Charlie wrinkled his nose. 'But you *would*, Joycie. You've done it this week.'

'No, I haven't!'

'You ditched her and your team when they tried to take you out for your birthday,' Charlie replied evenly, 'but then you made sure that you called her on Friday night when your haunted house was acting up, didn't you? And then you called again today.'

'Look, Ch-'

'I just don't want Peggy to get hurt again,' Charlie interrupted. 'I really don't think you do either, but I'm not sure you appreciate just how attached Peggy's become to the Ballroom, or to *you*.'

Andrew stared back wide-eyed at Charlie's earnest expression.

Jesus Christ. He needed to untangle whatever huge knot of erroneous logic Charlie had got himself into before Lloyd came back to the table. 'Charlie, I think you've got the wrong end of the stick. Peggy is not attached to *me*, alright? Give her some credit, won't you?'

'The self-deprecation schtick isn't necessary.' Charlie rolled his eyes.

'I'm serious!' Andrew put his pint glass down heavily. 'If this is your version of the shovel talk, it's not necessary, alright?'

'I just don't want anyone to get hurt.'

Andrew sighed in despair. 'Look, can we please just talk about something else?'

'Like how the boss is going to kick your arse when he hears about the Haworth thing?' Lloyd snorted as he returned to the table with three glasses of what looked like whiskey in his hands.

To Andrew's utter dismay, over the past nine months Lloyd had learned that his DI was much more likely to let him get away with being a cheeky little git outside of work hours.

Andrew glared. 'You were there too! Haworth bloody recognised you!'

Lloyd shrugged blithely. 'Yeah, but I'm not in charge, am I?'

The cheeky little git was, of course, correct.

'Oh, I'm sure it'll be fine. It's not like anyone would actually believe a word of it.' Charlie waved a hand airily, but then he paused suddenly, face growing ashen.

'What?' Andrew asked, eyes darting around the pub. 'What is it?'

Charlie swallowed heavily. He glanced quickly at Lloyd and then back to Andrew again and grimaced.

'What?' Andrew repeated. 'Charlie?'

Charlie leaned his elbows on the table. 'If we've heard about the *Evening News* thing, then you can bet *other people* have too.'

The very specific emphasis on 'other people' made it clear to

Andrew that Charlie was definitely talking about his mother, and possibly his father too.

Andrew drained his pint and immediately stood up.

'Where are you going?' Charlie asked, baffled.

'Back to the bar,' Andrew replied, already feeling a headache coming on. 'I have a feeling we might need the whole bottle.'

* * *

Peggy blinked up at the ceiling in surprise, shaking her head to try and dispel the sleepy daze she'd been contentedly settling into only moments earlier. She was almost certain that she'd heard a knock on her bedroom door.

'Peggy, are you awake?'

Peggy pushed back her duvet with a slight groan of frustration and rolled out of bed. She shuffled across the room and opened the door to find an unusually timid Marnie on the other side.

'You knocked,' Peggy said in genuine astonishment before she could stop herself.

Marnie gave a tired one-shouldered shrug in response. 'Can I talk to you for a minute? It's important.'

Peggy only barely resisted the urge to check the clock and watch her plan for at least eight decent hours of sleep slipping away with every tick of the second hand.

'I know it's late,' Marnie mumbled, and then she made a terrible hiccupping sound that suggested she might be about to start crying.

Peggy sighed and pushed the door open fully and gestured for Marnie to enter 'Don't worry about it. What's wrong?'

Marnie slowly took her usual seat at the window and turned her head so that she was looking down the darkened driveway when Peggy switched on a lamp. 'I want to visit Rex.'

Peggy flinched in surprise. 'What? Really?'

Marnie nodded, still not catching Peggy's eye. 'I miss him, Peggy.'

Peggy folded her arms protectively across her chest and sat on the end of the bed. She'd never been able to understand what Marnie had seen in her ex-fiancé and given that her own personal experience of Rex Hughes had resulted in her being kidnapped and almost killed, she could probably be forgiven for being hesitant to offer enthusiasm for Marnie's words.

'I know what he did to you,' Marnie continued quietly as she ran her fingers nervously over the cushion she was leaning against. 'And I know that he wasn't who I thought he was, not really, but I still loved him. I want to see him. I want to *speak* to him.'

'I don't think you should,' Peggy said eventually, when it became clear that Marnie would wait for as long as it took for an answer.

Marnie finally looked at Peggy. 'Why not?'

Peggy had a mile-long list of arguments in answer to that, but she knew that Marnie wouldn't listen to most of them. She decided to keep her reasoning as concise as she could. 'Because you don't need him, and he doesn't deserve you.'

Marnie pursed her lips and nodded slowly. 'Right.'

Peggy waited for Marnie to add something, but after a minute or two of strained silence she stood up. 'Okay, well, I think it's time f-'

'I just want to hear the story from him,' Marnie interjected, twisting the engagement ring she still wore around her finger. Peggy still hadn't worked up the nerve to ask her if she still had it because she wanted to keep it, or because it was so impossibly bound to her spirit that she couldn't take it off, even if she wanted to.

'Marnie, you know the story,' Peggy sighed. 'I know you don't like thinking about it, but Rex admitted to working with the

Byrnes, and to being involved in all sorts of terrible things.'

'Terrible things' was putting it mildly, but Marnie was always touchy about the subject of Rex and his true nature, and Peggy really hadn't missed the semi-regular tantrums she'd had to endure in the months following Rex's imprisonment; she was fairly certain that the windows in her part of the house would never open easily again after Marnie had slammed them all shut in a spectacular fit of rage a few days after the events in Wallasey.

'I know you think I'm completely naïve about it all,' Marnie continued, 'but I'm really not. I know what he did, but I still don't understand *why*. I want to know if he really was going to give it all up when we got married – whether he really was going to try and start our new life with a clean slate.'

Oh, Peggy could understand the need to know the truth of a situation. For months after everything that had happened with Edgar and her mother, Peggy had wondered at what earlier moment in her life she'd made the mistake that had sent her hurtling down that ragged path towards misery. It had taken a long time to realise that actually, no, she wouldn't be better off if she knew that, nor would she benefit from wasting any more of her own time wondering what on earth had gone through Edgar's mind when they'd first met, and whether he'd already had an exit strategy in mind right back at the beginning.

'Do you think he'd tell you the truth?' Peggy asked, even though the question ran the risk of a fierce response from Marnie. 'Even now, after everything, do you think he'd actually tell you the truth if he thought it wasn't what you really wanted to hear?'

Marnie's lips twisted and Peggy mentally prepared herself for the screeching that was no doubt coming her way. She'd have to dig out her earplugs as Marnie was likely to resort to playing *The Phantom of the Opera* at full volume again.

So, it came as a surprise when Marnie deflated and rested her chin in her hands, looking far more glum than enraged.

'It's not the same, you know.' Marnie pouted.

'What's not the same?' Peggy asked tiredly.

'What happened with Rex, and what happened with you and Edgar.'

Peggy's fingers clenched involuntarily at the mention of Edgar's name, and she had to fight the urge to just turn around and leave the room.

'Edgar is a complete tosser, and he chose to hurt you on purpose,' Marnie continued as though she hadn't seen Peggy's response to her comment. 'But you've still had the chance to get over it. You're out there trying again, but I won't ever get to do that.'

Peggy tilted her head, taken aback. 'I'm sorry, I'm *what*?'

Marnie wrinkled her nose. 'What do you mean, '*what*'?'

'On what planet am I 'out there trying again', as you put it?' Peggy asked, askance.

Marnie gave a bemused shrug. 'Andrew. Obviously.'

'Andrew?' Peggy yelped, lurching to her feet in surprise.

'Why are you shouting?' Marnie blinked rapidly as she leaned back against the window.

'I'm not interested in Andrew!' Peggy threw up her hands. 'We're colleagues. *Friends.*'

Marnie's expression shifted from nonplussed, to calculating, and finally to outrageously amused in the space of a heartbeat. 'Peggy, are you joking?'

Peggy was *not* joking, and she was going to tell Marnie exactly that in no uncertain terms once she managed to remove the obstruction of her own outrage and regain the ability to form good, sound arguments again.

Marnie's grin grew wider. 'Oh my God! You actually believe that don't you?'

Vaguely, Peggy thought that she should be pleased that Marnie wasn't looking anywhere near as dejected as she had done at the start of their conversation, but it was hard to be pleased about anything when you were being accused of something that was patently untrue.

The phone rang and for a split-second Peggy was struck by a terrible, irrational fear that Andrew had someone heard Marnie's accusation and was now calling to ensure that all allegations had been strongly refuted, or to chastise Peggy for gossiping about him in her free time.

'Aren't you going to answer that?' Marnie asked mildly, still rather too pleased with herself.

'No.'

'*No?*'

'No!'

Marnie frowned. 'But it's nearly eleven, what if it's Charlie and he's got himself into trouble?'

'Don't say things like that!' Peggy snapped, and she was gratified to see that Marnie had the grace to look immediately cowed.

Marnie, annoyingly, was also correct. If someone was calling Peggy at that time of night, it was unlikely to be a purely social call.

With a loud sigh Peggy stalked towards her bedside table and picked up the phone. 'Hello?'

'Peg!' Charlie announced cheerfully as though it were a complete surprise that he'd found his sister at the end of the line, on a call that he'd initiated.

'Charlie,' Peggy grumbled in annoyance.

Marnie gave her a silent look of 'I told you so' and popped out of the room as though she'd never been there.

'Peg!' Charlie crowed again. 'Hi!'

'Hi?' Peggy asked cautiously. Her brother didn't sound like he was in any kind of trouble, but she'd learned on several occasions in the past that this didn't necessarily mean anything. 'Everything okay?'

'*What are you doing on the phone?*'

Peggy's eyes widened in surprise at the plaintive inquiry in the background. Even muffled and disguised beneath the slurred edges of the question that had undoubtedly been Andrew's voice.

'You can have it in a minute!' Charlie shouted, and it took a second for Peggy to realise that the comment had been directed towards Andrew. 'Lloyd! Stop being a baby and come inside!'

Lloyd. Peggy held the phone out in front of her and stared at it for a long second in bewilderment.

'Right, Peg? Peg! Are you there?' Charlie called, and Peggy put the phone back to her ear.

'Yes. Charlie, what the hell is going on?'

'Lloyd and I thought that Joycie could probably do with a bit of cheering up, and we were right,' Charlie replied, and Peggy could practically hear the alcohol sluicing over the explanation. Charlie tended to get very matter of fact when he'd been drinking. 'We thought we should probably get him out of his haunted house, so we went to the pub!'

'Fantastic plan,' Peggy sighed tiredly. 'Right, okay, but why exactly are you calling me?'

'Because he'll listen to you.'

Peggy pinched the bridge of her nose. 'Listen to me about what?'

'About not staying in his house with a murder-y ghost,' Charlie replied slowly as though Peggy were completely dense. 'Obviously!'

The other end of the phone call erupted into harsh whispering and loud scuffling, and Peggy debated the merits of simply hanging up the phone and forgetting that she'd ever had the call in the first place.

'Peggy?'

Peggy grimaced. 'Hi, Lloyd. Everything okay?'

'It's fine,' Lloyd replied, sounding perfectly sober, which was unlikely to be true at that stage on a Saturday night if you'd been out anywhere with Charlie. 'The boss and your brother are having a disagreement.'

'Of course they are.'

The shuffling sounds started again, followed by a pained yelp and an extremely triumphant *ah-ha*!

'It's m'house, and m'phone and m'decision!' Andrew announced into the phone.

At least, Peggy assumed that the final word had been 'decision', though it had been mangled by whatever they'd all consumed at the pub. *Christ*, Peggy hoped Andrew hadn't bumped into too many people he knew, or he'd be in an embarrassed rage about the whole thing by morning.

'I want to stay in my house, Peg,' Andrew slurred. 'Can you tell those two to just go away and leave me alone?'

'I think it might be best if you either all go somewhere else, or all stay there,' Peggy replied carefully. God, she hoped Charlie didn't do something terrible like invite Lloyd and Andrew back to Butterton – Timothy would have an absolute conniption, and Marnie would find some way of being unbearably smug about it all.

'They won't stay here, they're scared.'

With good reason, Peggy thought, but kept it to herself. Andrew had a terrible habit of feeling particularly brave when he was about to something undeniably daft and life-threatening, or when he'd had a bit too much to drink.

'We're not scared!' Charlie's voice came from further away. 'My house has way more ghosts than yours!'

"S'not a competition,' Andrew groused.

'I found rum!' Charlie called. 'At least, I *think* it's rum.'

Peggy looked at the clock and wondered for the umpteenth time if she'd ever get a good night's sleep again. 'Look, has anything strange happened since you got back to the house?'

Andrew paused for slightly too long for his subsequent denial to be believable.

'Andrew, I th-'

'I'm staying here, Peggy,' Andrew replied, sounding far steadier all of a sudden. 'They can stay if they want, but I'm not going.'

'Alright,' Peggy agreed eventually, though she could see absolutely no wisdom in two drunk policemen and Charlie staying in a house with a vengeful ghost overnight. 'But you all need to get out of there if anything happens.'

'Will you come over?'

Peggy made a choking sound. She was glad Marnie had left already. 'What?'

'In the morning,' Andrew clarified as though he hadn't heard Peggy's silent panic at all. 'Will you come over? I need to talk to you about all of this. Properly.'

'Of course,' Peggy agreed. Andrew needed help with a ghost problem, that was all.

A burst of hysterical laughter from somewhere in the background caused Peggy to jump and Andrew to swear loudly in surprise.

'What are you doing?' Andrew asked, clearly not directed at Peggy.

'Ghostbusting!' Lloyd guffawed loudly.

The last thing Peggy heard before the phone call abruptly ended was Andrew grumbling 'You two would be shit Ghostbusters.'

Peggy agreed.

TWELVE

Andrew was in his kitchen waiting for the kettle to boil when there was a soft knock on the front door.

He reached into the cupboard for a second mug and placed it next to the box of Tetley before heading out into the hallway.

Lloyd and Charlie were both still slumped against the under-stairs cupboard doors where they'd eventually fallen asleep around four. Whether the uneventful evening had been because he hadn't been alone in the house, or just that Rob had been feeling more benevolent again, Andrew didn't really care; all he felt was an overwhelming relief that the house had remained silent and still all night.

He stepped carefully over the hollowed crisp packets and the now-empty ancient bottle of rum that Charlie had found in the back of a cupboard and opened the front door to find Peggy on the other side.

'Morning,' Andrew said, pulling the door wide.

Peggy wrinkled her nose at the scene as she stepped inside. 'Did you all sleep down here?'

'Close to the front door,' Andrew replied with a shrug as he turned away and led her towards the kitchen. The shrug was intended to feign nonchalance, but Andrew could feel the tension in his shoulders giving him away anyway. He knew that he wouldn't have fooled Peggy in the slightest.

'Did anything happen?' Peggy asked quietly once she'd closed the kitchen door behind her.

Andrew shook his head as he threw two teabags into the waiting mugs and poured the boiling water in after them. 'Nothing. Even if I'd managed to fall asleep, I doubt any of us would have slept through it if Rob had decided to make an appearance.'

Peggy looked around the kitchen before her attention landed on the tall tree at the very end of the garden. 'Charlie's right, you know.'

'About what?' Andrew asked around a wide yawn he wasn't quick enough to stifle.

'About it being a terrible idea for you to stay here at the minute.' Peggy looked at him knowingly. 'And the Ballroom isn't a good option either.'

Oh. He'd forgotten that Peggy had likely figured out that he'd slept at the Ballroom on Friday night. Andrew grumbled under his breath and turned his attention back to the steeping tea. 'I didn't have any other choice.'

'Isn't there someone else you could stay with temporarily? Just until we work out what's going on here. Didn't you say your grandparents still lived nearby?'

Andrew laughed mirthlessly as he jabbed at a teabag with a spoon. 'And what do you expect me to say to them? *Hi, Nana Joyce, do you mind if I stay here for a bit? Only until your dead grandson stops terrorising me, mind.* Not everyone thinks this kind of thing is normal, Peggy!'

Peggy's face fell, taken aback by the bitterness in Andrew's voice, and he regretted his words immediately. It was the second time in nearly as many days that he'd said something that sounded as though he somehow blamed Peggy for her ability to see ghosts.

'I didn't mean that,' Andrew sighed loudly. 'Really.'

A long moment passed, but eventually Peggy nodded once and made her way to the fridge, all without so much as glancing at Andrew. 'Do you want milk?'

'Please,' Andrew replied stiffly as he scooped out the teabags and threw them in the bin with a sharp flick of his wrist. *Great.* Yet again he was demanding Peggy's help on one hand, and then on the other somehow managing to make her feel bad about it.

Peggy added milk to the two mugs in silence and returned the bottle to the fridge.

'I'm sorry,' Andrew said, handing over a mug as a peace offering. 'It's not your fault. None of it.'

Peggy shrugged. 'I'm not so sure about that, to be honest.'

'What do you mean?'

Peggy put her mug down and leaned back against the counter. 'Think about it logically for a second. Last summer, you were quite possibly the most sceptical person I'd ever met, and now look at what's happening to you.'

Andrew raised his eyebrows. 'I'm not sure that's how this works, Peggy.'

Peggy shrugged again. 'Maybe not, but you have to admit that it could be possible.'

'It could,' Andrew agreed mildly. 'Then again, this all could have happened anyway, and without you I probably wouldn't have a single person who'd believe me. They'd have me locked up by the end of the week.'

Peggy didn't look entirely convinced but didn't try to argue her point further. Instead, she picked up her mug again and cradled it against her chest. 'Do you want to tell me about what happened on Friday night?'

Andrew braced himself, preparing to say what he'd been working himself up to over the course of yet another sleepless night. 'I want to tell you about Rob. All of it.'

Peggy had the good grace to try and keep most of the surprise from her face. 'You do?'

'I do, but I'd prefer not to have to explain it over the sound of those two snoring out there,' Andrew replied, trying to keep his tone a lot lighter than he actually felt. 'Or inside the house. Garden?'

He didn't wait for Peggy to answer and instead opened the back door and began walking towards the tree at the end of the garden; he needed to get this all out before he lost his nerve. If anyone could help him with Rob, it was Peggy; but for her to do that, Andrew knew that he was going to have to share the full story with her first.

He'd already settled himself on the slightly damp grass by the time Peggy approached him. Wordlessly she sat down beside him and waited for him to gather himself.

Andrew was glad for Peggy's silence. He'd run through how to start this conversation so many times, but now that he was faced with the reality of telling her the truth about what had happened twenty-five years ago, his carefully crafted explanation wouldn't come.

'It was Easter weekend when it happened,' he said eventually, putting down his mug and reaching out to repetitively pinch and release a blade of grass next to his knee. 'Good Friday. Agatha - my mother - was as Catholic as they came, so we were supposed to spend the whole day at home. No radio, no TV, and no playing outside.

'Rob was three years older than me, and even though he didn't want to play most of the games I still liked, he would always be up for a bit of a kickabout at the park or back here.' Andrew waved towards the garden. 'We weren't really friends with any of the kids around here, but they loved it any time they could get Rob in goal for them. He was tall and lanky, and almost impossible to score against.'

Andrew paused and squinted up towards the house. How many times had he sat exactly where he was in that moment? How many times had he laughed, caught somewhere between delighted and gently-mocking, when his brother had told him with a childish dead-certainty that one day Andrew would be cheering on his brother in goal at Maine Road?

'He looks like you,' Peggy said quietly. 'Or, I mean, he looks like I imagine you looked at that age.'

Even though Andrew knew full well that Peggy really had seen Rob outside the house the year before, it still came as a bit of a shock to hear that someone he hadn't known back then was aware of the similarities between the Joyce brothers.

'We both looked like our dad,' Andrew explained haltingly, swallowing heavily against the ache of ancient grief in his chest. 'There wasn't much of Agatha in either of us, and I've always wondered if it's the main reason she couldn't really cope with both of us after Dad died; we reminded her too much of him.'

That, and the fact that Agatha had been ostracised from the local community once Jack's less-than-savoury behaviour had come to light after his death. It was in the wake of that loneliness that Andrew's mother had withdrawn from those who'd known her – sons included – and sought a new community where her life before her tragic turn as a young widow could remain unknown and unvoiced. That community had eventually been found at the Catholic church up the road in Peel Hall; St Anthony's was just far enough away that when his mother had reverted to using her maiden name, nobody there would have thought of connecting her to that dead criminal, Jack Joyce from Gatley.

'Rob had been counting on Agatha going to church,' Andrew added, returning his attention to the grass he'd split with his nail. 'There were no services on, but she spent so much time just *in* the church anyway, we thought we wouldn't see much of her. I thought Rob was excited because it meant we might get the chance to sneak out to the park and see if we could get ourselves into a match; Rob had passed the eleven-plus the year before and had gone to the new grammar school over in Marple, which meant I saw a lot less of him outside of weekends and school holidays, so I'd been counting down to Easter weekend because we'd have days to spend together before school started again.

'Any time Rob was out playing football or talking about music he'd heard on the radio, he'd be lectured about how he was wasting his time, and how he should be spending more time reading, or going to church with her. I used to think he was joking when he said that Agatha wanted him to become a priest when he grew up, but I realised later that he was serious.'

Andrew picked up his mug and took a gulp of tea. 'Because of our dad, Rob was a diehard City fan, and he'd been to a few matches when he was small. I doubt he could actually remember any of them, but he used to talk about those afternoons with Dad as though he remembered every single detail. Agatha had banned him from ever going to a match, and I'd always been convinced that it was the one big golden rule that Rob would never dream about actually breaking.'

'But you were wrong?' Peggy prompted when Andrew trailed off into another loaded silence.

Andrew nodded and wrapped his fingers around his mug, hoping to find some warmth to counteract the deathly cold tremor that struck somewhere inside him. 'He'd met a kid in the year above him at school – Ian – who'd told Rob that his older brother worked on the turnstiles at Maine Road, and that he could probably sneak them both in for the match against Sheffield Wednesday on Good Friday.

'So, that Friday morning, Rob was grinning from the minute he opened his eyes.' Andrew pinched the bridge of his nose. 'I was so convinced we were going to have the best day together, and then, after breakfast, Rob told me that he was going to meet Ian up at the park at lunchtime and then go to the City match. I didn't care about football the way Rob did, but the thought of going to a proper match sounded amazing, and I couldn't believe my luck at getting to go to one with my big brother. That's when Rob told me that I wasn't invited, and that I needed to make sure that nobody found out where he'd gone.'

'Oh, Andrew.' Peggy's voice was so soft Andrew wasn't even

sure if she'd realised that she'd spoken aloud.

'Just after Rob told me I couldn't go with him, Agatha came into the kitchen and said that she was going to church, but that she'd be back at lunchtime,' Andrew continued before he could talk himself out of it. 'And that her church friends were coming around at two so that they could all pray together at three o'clock.'

'Three o'clock?' Peggy asked, obviously confused.

'It's the time they believe Jesus died on the cross.'

'Oh.'

'She told us that she wanted both of us to join them,' Andrew added, clutching the mug even tighter. 'Rob would normally just agree to that sort of thing and then try and come up with a way of sneakily getting both of us out if it; he was good at that. But that day he just absolutely lost it.'

Andrew stared down at his tea. He could still hear Rob and his mother arguing, almost twenty-five years later.

'We want to go and see our friends!' Rob had snapped, waving his arms towards the front door. 'We don't want to be stuck inside this stupid house all day!'

'Robert Joyce!' Agatha had barked in reply, a look of stunned fury on her face. 'How dare you raise your voice at your mother! And on this most holy of days!'

'It's because you never listen!' Rob had wheeled around and started stalking towards the front door. 'You never listen to anything either of us have to say. You only care about your stupid friends and your stupid church. Everyone around here already hated us because of Dad, and now they all think you're a loony too. Why are you making it even worse? *Why?*'

That plaintive cry of '*why*' had haunted Andrew every day of his life since that afternoon. Rob's voice had cracked at the end of the question, finally overcome by the frustration and anger that he'd been trying to keep at bay for years.

'Rob shouted at her,' Andrew said for Peggy's benefit. 'Blamed her for our lack of friends. Blamed her for everything, I suppose.

'Rob made to go out the front door, but she grabbed his arm and pulled him back towards the stairs. She'd always had an awful temper, but I'd never seen her look as angry as she did in that moment. She raised her hand right up above her head and I knew that she was going to hit Rob hard enough to really hurt him.'

This was the bit of the story that Andrew had replayed over and over more so than any other incident that day, and he closed his eyes against the phantom lick of pain that burned at his left temple.

He started slightly, eyes snapping open, when he felt the mug being gently removed from the vice-grip of his fingers. A moment later Peggy had wrapped her two hands around his in an unspoken gesture of support as Andrew took another steadying breath.

'I still don't know why I did it,' Andrew added. 'I just saw what was about to happen, and I couldn't let her hurt Rob – not again. I got in the way, and whatever force had been meant for Rob hit me instead.'

Peggy made a quiet sound of distress and tightened her hold on Andrew's hands.

'I don't entirely remember what happened next. I was seeing stars because I'd been knocked into the wall at the bottom of the stairs.' Andrew sighed loudly. 'I remember being bundled up the stairs and then landing on the floor at the bottom of my bed. I remember that she locked the door from the outside.'

Andrew looked up at the back of the house again and wondered if the walls remembered the screaming the way he did. 'I think her and Rob argued for a bit longer and then she locked him in his room as well. Then the door downstairs slammed.'

'She still went to church?' There was so much restrained anger in Peggy's voice that Andrew turned towards her in surprise.

Sure enough, Peggy's eyes were cold and sharp with an ire that was almost frightening in its unfamiliarity.

Andrew nodded. 'I don't know how long she was gone for before I heard the knock at my door. It was Rob.'

'*How?*' Peggy was rightfully perplexed.

'He told me that he'd nicked a spare key months earlier, and he'd hidden it in his bedroom just in case we ever needed to get out of the house,' Andrew explained carefully.

'Your mother had locked you both in your bedrooms before?' Peggy asked in outrage.

'It was almost better when she did that,' Andrew admitted, staring down at his hands. 'At least then we didn't have to listen to her screaming at us.'

'Andrew.'

Andrew shook his head at the sorrow in Peggy's voice. He didn't want her pity in that moment; he just wanted to get to the end of the story before he lost his nerve entirely. 'Rob wouldn't unlock my door, no matter how many times I begged him. He said that I needed to stay there, because he didn't know what Agatha would do if she found out that we'd both left the house.

'I didn't want to be left on my own, but Rob wouldn't budge. He said that he reckoned that Agatha would unlock the doors when it was bedtime so we'd be able to get out to the toilet, but that she was so angry with both of us that she wouldn't actually come in - not with her friends downstairs – but, just in case, he made me promise that I wouldn't tell her where he'd gone if she did find out that he'd left.

'He said that he'd make sure he'd get back for eleven o'clock, because he knew everyone should be well asleep by then. I was supposed to stay awake so that I could creep downstairs and open the back door to let him in. Rob said that he was going to have to come in over the back fence because he wouldn't put it past any of our nosy neighbours, like Mrs Roberts across the road, to see him sneaking in through the front door. He told me he'd see me later, and then he left.'

Andrew looked back over his shoulder so he could see the garden fence. 'He was right about her unlocking the doors without actually opening them. She did exactly that, with a whispered reminder of how much trouble we'd be in if either of us made a fuss while she had her friends in the house, and then went straight back downstairs again.

'I was so afraid that I was going to fall asleep and miss Rob coming back that I just walked around my bedroom, over and over again for hours. Finally, I heard Agatha go to bed. I gave it half an hour or so, and then went downstairs to unlock the door. I came out into the garden and sat right here to wait for him to come back.'

Andrew pulled one of his hands free so that he could rub it savagely across his face. 'Eventually – I suppose it must have been well after midnight – it started raining, and I got so cold that I had to go back inside. I left the door unlocked so that Rob could get in unnoticed, and I went upstairs to bed. I thought it would be okay.'

'Andrew, you don't have to talk about this right now,' Peggy said, almost whispering.

'Rob didn't come down at breakfast time,' Andrew ploughed on. 'Agatha stormed upstairs, and then seconds later she was back in the kitchen, shouting at me, wanting to know where Rob was. I didn't know what to say to her – I was terrified. I think I knew even then that something terrible had happened.'

Andrew squeezed his eyes shut. 'The police didn't come until late that night, and she started wailing as soon as she opened the door to them. She knew what was coming; it was just like what had happened with Dad.

'Nana Joyce – my dad's mother – took me into the kitchen out of the way, but I still overheard it all: Rob had been on the back of Ian's bike, cycling over from Ian's house in Withington, when they'd been hit by a car.'

There was a hitch of breath and Andrew wasn't sure whether it belonged to him, or to Peggy. 'Ian had been taken to hospital with all sorts of broken bones and a serious head injury, and it wasn't until he was conscious hours later that anybody knew that he hadn't been alone on the bike. Rob-'

Andrew cut himself off and all but jumped to his feet, unable to sit still any longer. 'They thought that Rob must have come off the bike first, and that he was thrown further than where Ian and the bike were found. Nobody even knew to look for him until Ian asked if Rob was alright, and by then…'

Peggy stood slowly, mindful of the fragility of the moment, and it was Andrew's turn to reach out and take Peggy's hand.

'The whole time-' Andrew choked slightly and he had to take a long moment to right himself. '*The whole time*, I'd just been waiting for him to come back, and I'd been so pissed off with him for leaving me behind so that he could go and have fun. He left me behind, and I didn't even know that I should have been out there looking for him.'

Peggy wrapped her free hand around Andrew's wrist. 'Andrew you were barely nine years old. You were a *child*.'

Andrew shook his head. 'Don't you remember what you said to me last summer? What message Rob wanted you to pass on to me?'

For a second, confusion creased Peggy's forehead until her whole face crumpled into despair. 'Andrew, I don't think he meant i-'

'How else could he have meant it?' Andrew snapped as grief gave way to decades-old disappointment in his own actions. 'He said I was supposed to come and find him. *Find him*, Peggy. Not just sit there and wait for him to never come home again. It was my fault.'

'Andrew, look at me.' Peggy's tone was gentler than Andrew had ever heard it. 'I need you to understand that what happened to you and to Rob should never have happened. All children make mistakes – and they should be safe to make those mistakes – but you were put in an impossible position. Your loyalty was to your brother, and you did everything he asked you to.'

'But I could h-'

'You couldn't have done anything,' Peggy continued, calmly but firmly. 'You had no idea where Rob would be, so how could you have done anything differently? Andrew, I don't think Rob was angry with you when he said that he wanted to you to come and find him. I think he was a scared little boy who wanted his brother.'

Andrew covered his face as best as he could with one hand, curling his fingers inwards to push against his cheekbones and try and stem the sob that was suffocating him. He felt like a black smudge on the landscape, caught completely out of place between the early spring sunshine and the daffodils that were already beginning to crow for attention beneath the tree. He tried to force the words out, but he couldn't make himself talk about the funeral, or his mother's reaction to it all, no matter how much he knew that he needed to.

Peggy wordlessly wrapped her arms around him, and it was as awkward as it was an entirely appreciated comfort. For an incalculable length of time, no sound passed in the garden, and the two figures sheltered beneath the old tree's budding canopy remained motionless.

Eventually, Andrew heard the back door creak open and knew that whatever peace he had momentarily carved out had reached its end.

Peggy turned away quickly, and she had obviously been successful through silent gesturing, because when Andrew faced the kitchen window seconds later, the room had been vacated.

Good, because whereas he would gladly accept Peggy's company in that moment, he wasn't quite sure he could deal with any sort of reaction from either Charlie or Lloyd.

For now, though, the rest of the story was on pause; the second part to be rehashed and relived at a later date, when Andrew had been given some time to rebuild the defences he'd constructed over the course of twenty-five years.

'Do you want me to have a look around inside?' Peggy asked eventually, releasing Andrew's hand.

Andrew was grateful that she hadn't tried to thank him for sharing the story with her, or to ask him if he was okay when he demonstrably wasn't. Instead, she'd asked the question that Andrew hadn't wanted to ask himself. He'd been so sure that he needed to keep Peggy away from whatever was going on in his house, but now he knew that if he was ever going to get an answer from Rob, then Peggy was his only hope.

Andrew nodded. 'I do. But not by yourself, and we run at the first sign of real trouble, alright?'

He knew that the bar for 'real trouble' had been getting lower and lower since they'd first met, but he was relieved when Peggy agreed with a solemn nod of her own anyway.

Andrew slowly led the way back into the kitchen and out into the hallway. The door to the living room was closed and he could hear Lloyd and Charlie having a conversation at a volume that was just loud enough to be considered unnatural, but he appreciated that they were at least trying to offer him a modicum of privacy.

Peggy kept her hand on the bannister the entire way up the stairs and Andrew suddenly wanted to know if this was because she somehow felt more connected to Rob and the house through actual, physical contact; or if it was a self-preservation instinct adopted by someone who was all too aware that a ghost might just have the power to knock you down the stairs if it so fancied it.

At the very top of the stairs, Peggy paused and looked sharply at Andrew. 'Here.'

Andrew couldn't stop the shiver as he stared back. Where Peggy was standing was exactly where the black smoke had begun to weave itself into the shape of a person on Friday night. 'What is it?'

Peggy shook her head, obviously perturbed. 'I don't know.'

Andrew reached over and gently tugged Peggy away from the spot. 'Don't stand there.'

'Is that Rob's room?' Peggy nodded towards the door to the bedroom at the front of the house as she used her hands to vigorously rub her arms as though she'd been somewhere cold.

'Yeah. I couldn't tell you when Agatha last went in there, but I haven't opened that door in twenty-five years,' Andrew admitted.

Peggy's expression softened again. 'We don't have to open it now.'

'I think we do,' Andrew sighed tiredly, 'but, Peg, please promise me that you'll go straight outside if anything weird happens. I mean it.'

'I promise,' Peggy replied immediately, 'but the same goes for you.'

It took Andrew far longer than he'd be comfortable admitting to, to gather up the courage to even reach his curled fingers towards the door. He blew a loud breath out between his lips and quickly twisted the doorknob before he had another chance to talk himself out if it.

The door opened soundlessly, and Andrew braced himself for whatever it was that he might find on the other side of the barrier he'd kept firmly in place for most of his life.

The sight of the sky-blue and white scarf pinned slightly skew-whiff on the wall behind the bed, exactly as Andrew remembered it, was enough to send him stumbling backwards onto the landing, one hand on his chest as though it might contain the violent hammering of his heart.

With a startled curse, Peggy threw out her arms to stop Andrew from lurching towards the stairs. 'Andrew!'

'I'm alright,' Andrew wheezed, correcting his balance and waving Peggy's concern away. 'I'm alright.'

Alright wasn't even approaching the vicinity of the truth but given that Andrew had half expected jet-black wraiths to come swooping out from the room, leaving only their destruction behind in the final remnants of Rob's life, he'd take the acidic flare of heartache instead.

Andrew slowly approached the door once more and finally allowed his foot to cross the threshold and land on the dark green carpet where Rob had once tried to teach him to play poker, despite being ten and not understanding what poker actually was at the time; the same carpet where they'd sat together as Rob told him stories that grew louder and louder in tandem with the sounds of their parents arguing downstairs; the same carpet Andrew had buried his face into and begged and screamed for his brother to come back until his throat was raw and the house remained stubbornly empty around him. He reeled from the visceral certainty that if he looked around he would be able to tell if even a single item in the bedroom was even a millimetre out of place.

The bedroom was in semi-darkness, with the curtains drawn closed as they had been since the day Rob left. Andrew stilled with his hands on the curtains for a handful of heartbeats before pushing them apart and looking out from a vantage point he hadn't experienced since he was nine. He caught a very surprised Mrs Roberts looking back at him from her living room across the road and he turned away from her calculating stare quickly.

On the other side of the bed, Rob's school satchel was lying half-undone on the floor, and a couple of books had attempted to fan their way to freedom from beneath the unbuckled clasp.

Andrew was sure that the satchel lay exactly where Rob had thrown it in celebration of school breaking up for Easter and he had to ball up his fists against the instinct to go and pick it up from the floor, just as Agatha would have made him do.

'When did your mother leave this house?'

Andrew turned in surprise at how serious Peggy sounded, and he was concerned to see that she looked even more troubled than she had at the top of the stairs. 'What? Why?'

'Andrew, when?'

'December, seventy-eight.'

Agatha had taken her final short journey from the house to her ultimate resting place with Jack and Rob at Southern Cemetery in a torrential downpour, flanked only by her most God-fearing friends and her one remaining son. Agatha's friends had seen the rain as sign of sorrow, but Andrew had only hoped that it would somehow wipe clean his family's history.

As he'd been drenched at the sodden gravesite, his eyes burning with the hollowing knowledge that he was the only one left, Andrew had concluded that no amount of rain would ever be able to wash away the sins of the past.

'And nobody else has been in here in all that time?' Peggy asked

'Not until today, I swear. Peggy, what is it?'

'There's no dust,' she replied. Peggy ran her fingertips over the windowsill and held her hand up for Andrew to see. 'Look.'

Andrew turned in a slow circle to cast his eye over surface, concluding that Peggy was correct. 'What does that mean?'

'I don't know.' Peggy shrugged helplessly. 'He's not here, Andrew, but there's nothing negative about this room. It's nothing like the top of the stairs.'

'I need to show you something else.' Andrew looked around the room one more time before he headed back out onto the landing until he was standing outside his childhood bedroom.

Andrew shivered at the memory of what he'd found behind the door the previous afternoon. 'This was my room. I only use it for storage now, but if you want a room with something 'negative' about it, it's this one.'

Peggy frowned. 'What do you mean?'

'This is how I found it yesterday,' Andrew replied as he gingerly pushed the door open.

The cloying scent of rotting flowers was as pungent as it had been the day before, and Andrew's stomach turned unpleasantly.

'What on earth…' Peggy trailed off as she squeezed past Andrew and stepped into the room.

Andrew had to fight the urge to pull her straight back out of there. Instead, he clenched his fists at his side and watched as Peggy's face grew paler as she stared at the sooty handprint on the wall.

'Andrew?'

The back of Andrew's neck prickled in alarm at the apprehension in Peggy's voice. 'Yeah?'

That awful feeling of being watched by unseen eyes crept up Andrew's spine as the air in the room chilled suddenly, reminding him of cold, wet, winter mornings.

'We need to leave,' Peggy whispered.

Andrew didn't need telling twice.

'Peggy, go!' Andrew barked as he pushed Peggy out onto the landing and slammed the door behind them.

As Andrew's foot hit the top of the stairs, he heard a knocking sound coming from the direction of the box room and he froze. It was nothing more than the light rapping of knuckles against wood, but Andrew would have recognised that sound anywhere.

'Andrew!' Peggy yanked on Andrew's arm hard enough to rip him from his stupor, and they barrelled down the stairs together.

Just as they reached downstairs, the door to the living room burst open, followed immediately by Charlie and Lloyd tumbling out into the hallway.

'What's going on?' Lloyd asked, eyes wide in concern.

'Outside now!' Peggy cried and herded the others towards the front door with an increasingly frantic wave of her arms.

Andrew only just managed to grab his keys before Peggy pushed him over the threshold and pulled the door closed with a resounding thud that rattled the entire house.

The four of them ran across the front garden towards where Peggy had parked her car behind the Belmont that morning.

'Peggy, what the bloody hell is going on?' Charlie asked, staring at his sister in horror.

Andrew began to turn to look back up at the house, but Peggy stopped him with a vice-like grip on his upper arm.

'Don't turn around!' Peggy hissed in panicked warning. 'Any of you!'

The depth of fear on Peggy's face was something Andrew hadn't seen there since they'd driven too close to Strangeways in their pursuit of Rex Hughes the summer before. He knew on a primitive level that he had no desire to ever encounter anything that could put such an expression on Peggy's face.

'But we can't see the things you can see!' Lloyd protested, though Andrew noted that he made no move to disobey Peggy's instruction. 'Other than Marnie, I mean.'

'Take a look at the house across the road,' Peggy said shakily.

Andrew did and inhaled sharply in surprise.

Mrs Roberts was gawking up at Andrew's house, her face ashen and both hands clutched to her chest.

'It's not Rob, Andrew,' Peggy whispered urgently, her entire body trembling as she let go of Andrew's shirt and instead grasped his hand to tow him down the road behind her.

'Then who is it?' Andrew asked even though he thought he might already know the answer. There had only ever been one person who'd knocked on his bedroom door like that.

'I think…' Peggy trailed off, obviously fearful of delivering her verdict.

Andrew closed his eyes and tipped his head back in resignation, skewered by the knowledge that even death hadn't been a powerful enough force to erase the tally of Andrew's supposed sins. 'It's her, isn't it? It's Agatha.'

THIRTEEN

After everything that had happened in Gatley, Peggy had assumed that she would have found it impossible to sleep on Sunday night, so she was more than a little startled to be heaved into alertness by the incessant beeping of her alarm clock early on Monday morning. She blearily reached over to mute the dreadful racket and was hit with the deep suspicion that she hadn't moved an inch since her head had hit the pillow the night before.

A night of completely unbroken sleep should have been an entirely positive event, but the rarity of such an occurrence had Peggy on edge before she climbed into her car an hour later and drove down the long driveway.

When she eventually had to stop at a set of traffic lights, she glanced at the passenger seat where the *Lady Bancroft* case file rested, weighted down by Higson's heavy keyring. It had been hard to remind herself that she was supposed to be assisting on an actual case for the Ballroom when she'd spent most of the day before trying to work out what the hell had happened at Andrew's house.

Shortly after Peggy had realised that Agatha Joyce– or the spirit she was fairly certain was Agatha Joyce – was likely visible to everyone else, it hadn't taken much convincing to send Andrew towards his grandparents' house a mile away; Lloyd had been the one to suggest that the official story should be that Andrew needed somewhere to stay for a day or two, either because he'd had a prolonged power cut or a problem with his water, rather than the inexplicable truth of the situation.

In the chaos of their exodus from the front garden of Acacia Road, Peggy had forgotten that she'd intended to tell Andrew what had happened in the archive room at the Ballroom, something which seemed even more pressing in the light of day.

She'd only remembered once she'd arrived back at Butterton, but as she didn't have a phone number for Andrew's grandmother, she'd decided that it was just going to have to wait until they were all at the Court on Monday morning.

Peggy had wanted to talk to Marnie about it all to see if there were any details Marnie hadn't thought important in her original retelling of what had happened on Friday night, but she'd been nowhere to be seen for the rest of Sunday, and Peggy had gone to bed feeling even more out of sorts than she had all week.

A sharp blare of a car horn from behind her caused Peggy to jump, and she realised that she'd missed the light turning green. She gave a vague wave of apology to the other driver and forced herself to pay attention to the road; she doubted anyone would forgive her if she drove herself into a lamppost because she was too busy thinking about a whole host of ghosts.

By the time Peggy arrived at the theatre, she was well on her way to preparing herself for whatever inevitable disaster was waiting in the wings - both figurative and literal

Lloyd, on the other hand, didn't look even remotely perturbed by anything when he unlocked the door to let Peggy into the foyer and out of the drizzle. 'Morning, Peggy.'

'Hi, Lloyd,' Peggy replied as she shrugged off her slightly damp coat. 'Everything okay?'

Lloyd nodded. 'Nothing much going on, to be honest. The boss isn't here yet, and Jen's talking to Cohen and Vic up in Cohen's office. Oh, sorry, do you want one?'

Peggy blinked in surprise as Lloyd suddenly held out four or five Caramacs clutched between his fingers like a spray of hand-warmed, sugary flowers. 'Um, no thank you.'

Lloyd shrugged and unwrapped a chocolate bar for himself, stuffing the others into his jacket pocket. 'Auditorium's open if you want to go through. I haven't seen anyone else yet, so you'll be safe from any chat about the play for a bit.'

'Thanks. I thought I might try and speak to Alistair if he's around.'

Lloyd, as always, looked caught between interest and apprehension at the thought of Peggy speaking to someone he couldn't see, though certainly less panicked than he had the day before. He nodded and took another bite of chocolate.

Just as Peggy was pulling open the door to the stalls, Lloyd called her name.

She turned back, surprised to see that Lloyd's expression had drifted somewhere closer to concerned. 'Yes?'

Lloyd shifted from foot to foot, clearly working himself up to whatever he was about to say. 'Do you think he's really alright? DI Joyce, I mean.'

Peggy frowned. 'What do you mean?'

Lloyd wrinkled his nose. 'Well, there's his house, obviously, but it feels like that there might be something more than that getting to him. You know what the boss is like.'

Peggy tilted her head questioningly. Yes, she *did* know what Andrew was like, but she was interested to hear what Lloyd's reading of his DI was when it came to this, especially when Lloyd knew nothing about Rob, or Andrew's family history.

'Like…' Lloyd trailed off and shrugged again. 'Like, I don't think he'd really ask for help even if he really needed it, not until it was too late for anyone else to do anything about it. He wouldn't listen to me or your brother on Saturday night when we told him that he should find somewhere else to stay – long before the bottle of rum put paid to the idea – and how long do you think he'll stay away from that house until he thinks it's time he went home? Even after everything that happened yesterday.'

'I'm not sure I'm the right person to talk to about all of this, Lloyd,' Peggy sighed.

Lloyd looked surprised. 'Of course you are. He listens to you.'

'Sometimes.'

Lloyd shrugged. '*Sometimes* is better than never. If I ask him about any of this, or if Jen does, he'll just tell us that it's none of our business. He wouldn't do that to you.'

Peggy almost snorted at that, but at the terribly earnest expression on Lloyd's face she chose to keep her bleak amusement to herself. She'd agree that Andrew trusted her enough to tell her about Rob, and to ask for her help with him, but whether he'd take her advice remained to be seen.

The door that led to the upper staircase opened, and Vic appeared a moment later wishing them both good morning as she headed towards the administrative offices of the theatre.

'Maybe we shouldn't be talking about any of this here,' Peggy suggested. She didn't want Lloyd to think that she was dismissing his concerns about Andrew – they were perfectly valid, and she agreed with his assessment that Andrew would rather get himself into a complete mess before even thinking about asking for assistance – but if anybody overheard them, she doubted Andrew would take at all kindly to it.

Lloyd sheepishly nodded his agreement.

'Actually, Lloyd, when Andrew gets here, could you tell him that I need a word with him, please?' Peggy asked. 'It's work-related. You can tell him that. Oh, and can you take DCI Higson's keys for me? I forgot to give them to Andrew yesterday.'

'Will do,' Lloyd replied, taking the keys and then giving Peggy a quick salute as she turned away and headed for the auditorium.

The stage was empty of the *Lady Bancroft* cast, but Alistair was sitting cross-legged right at the front of the apron again, and he waved at her eagerly when he saw her approaching.

'Miss Peggy!' he called cheerily. 'Good morning.'

'Hi, Alistair,' Peggy replied as she took a seat on the front row. 'No Miss Marnie today?'

Peggy shook her head. 'Not today. She has some business elsewhere.'

Truthfully, Peggy didn't actually know where Marnie was. She hadn't seen her since Charlie had called from Andrew's house on Saturday night, and Peggy could only hope that her friend hadn't actually followed through with her plan to visit Rex.

Alistair frowned and leaned forwards so that his elbows were resting on his knees. 'Are you alright, Miss Peggy? There's something different about you today.'

Peggy twitched slightly at the accusation. 'I'm fine, Alistair.'

Alistair shook his head. 'I apologise, Miss Peggy, my intention is not to offend you. It's just that you seem…'

Peggy gave it a good few moments, but when Alistair didn't continue, she prompted, 'Seem what?'

For a second, Peggy felt like she was under a microscope as Alistair tilted his head to the right and then to the left, scrutinising her.

'Seem what?' Peggy asked again, an edge to her voice.

'There is something darker about you this morning,' Alistair explained slowly, shaking his head. 'It's like you're carrying something of Jock about you.'

Peggy jerked forwards in her seat. 'What?'

'It is not Jock though,' Alistair continued. 'At least, I don't think it is. Miss Peggy, has something happened since you were last here?'

A *lot* had happened in the couple of days that Peggy had been away from the theatre, but she wasn't going to discuss any of that with Alistair. She wasn't thrilled with the fact that Alistair could tell that there was something off about her in the first place – the only person who'd ever made comments like that to her in the past was Aunt Emmeline, and since the events of Marnie's case the year before, Emmeline had redoubled her efforts to try and get Peggy to find new ways to protect herself from being affected by a spirit's energy. It seemed as though everything Peggy had tried hadn't necessarily been as effective as she'd hoped.

'Nothing that has any bearing on our work here,' Peggy replied eventually.

She thought that Andrew would have been impressed with her diplomatic response.

Alistair looked just about ready to launch into a round of questioning, and Peggy knew that she had turn this conversation around.

'Alistair, I want to talk to you about happened back in 1932.'

When Alistair reared back in alarm, Peggy wondered if perhaps she'd been a little too blunt in her desire to divert attention away from herself.

'I already told you that I don't know what happened,' Alistair replied, sorrow crossing his face.

'I know,' Peggy said, keeping her voice soft and even. 'I know you did. I just wondered if you knew why the police named a young man who worked here – George Bevan - as their prime suspect. Did you know him at all?'

Alistair's sorrow became much more pronounced, and Peggy thought that she could *almost* feel it coursing through her own body.

'I knew him as much as would have been possible,' Alistair replied with a shrug. 'Which is to say, not very well.'

'Had you had any problems with him?' Peggy asked carefully. 'Or, had he given you any reason to think that he had any issues with Clarence Wright before you took over the role on opening night?'

Alistair shook his head. 'No, none.'

'Alright, just one more question then: did you ever see him at the Court again in the years after what happened to you?

'I don't believe he ever returned here after my death.'

Peggy sighed loudly. It was what she'd expected, really, but it still made her feel terribly discouraged. She just had to hope that Higson would be able to dig up something useful on the sole suspect who'd ever been connected to Alistair, and maybe, if they were really lucky, a connection to the other two deaths.

'Thanks, Alistair,' Peggy said quietly as she gathered herself and stood up. 'I have some things to do, but I'll be back later.'

'Until then, Miss Peggy.' Alistair tipped his hat and faded out of sight.

'Who are you talking to?'

Peggy turned in surprise to see Marion walking onto the stage, script tucked under her arm.

'You don't really think you're having conversations with dead people, do you?' Marion asked, curling her lips in distaste.

It was amazing how brave people could be when they continued to tell themselves that certain things couldn't be real.

Peggy just gave her a tight smile in reply. 'I'll be out in the foyer. Have a good rehearsal.'

Marion made a noise of disapproval as Peggy turned away, and it reminded her awfully of her mother. She shivered at the thought and hurried out of the auditorium.

* * *

Monday morning was the first time Andrew found himself glad that Higson's car was a coughing, choking rust bucket.

The shrieking wail of distress that the car made as it turned onto Tib Street was loud enough to rip Andrew from his drowsy stupor and fling him straight from the sofa to the wooden floor with a thud that shook every bone in his body.

As his brain tried to process the events that had led to his rude awakening, Andrew dozily glanced at his watch, shaking his head as he struggled to understand why the numbers being displayed didn't make sense to him.

The realisation that he was over an hour late to the theatre smacked him with more force than his tumble from the sofa had done, but it was the slam of the car door outside – overlaid with an unmistakeable squeak of protest from the hinges – that spurred him into immediate action.

'Bollocks!' Andrew scrambled towards the duffle bag he'd left under his desk and hurriedly pulled out a tube of toothpaste, ignoring the toothbrush entirely. Grimacing, he squeezed the toothpaste onto his finger before rubbing it over his teeth and swallowing the remnants with a grunt of disgust.

Why hadn't he listened to Lloyd and just gone to Nana Joyce's house? In no way was the Ballroom a better idea. His grandparents wouldn't have let him oversleep for a start.

As the door slammed shut downstairs, Andrew hastily dipped his hand into the half-empty glass of water next to his telephone and then ran his damp fingers through his hair in the hope that it might make him look slightly more presentable; or at the very least, help to disguise any suggestion that he'd spent another night sleeping at work.

He hadn't quite finished knotting his tie when the door to the Ballroom burst open and he snatched up the nearest case file just as Higson stomped into the room, pausing half-way to his desk when his gaze alighted on his dishevelled DI.

'What in God's name are you doing here?' Higson growled, gesturing towards Andrew with the loaf of bread he was holding in his right hand.

'Paperwork.' Andrew was almost proud of how easily the lie fell from his lips.

Higson, unfortunately, didn't look even remotely convinced as he sat down in his chair and laid the loaf in front of him. 'And you've finished now, have you?'

'Sir.' Andrew nodded. 'I'm just heading over to the Court now.'

'Sit the fuck down, Joyce,' Higson barked, drumming the end of a cigarette packet roughly against his palm.

Andrew pursed his lips. He ignored the chair nearest Higson but deigned to perch on the edge of his own desk, still twenty feet away from his boss.

Higson rolled his eyes as he unceremoniously chucked the packet onto his desk, one cigarette clamped loosely between his lips as he brushed his hands against his various pockets until he located a box of Vestas. 'Oh, I see. We're being a mardy little arse this morning, are we?'

Andrew remained silent. There was no point arguing with Higson whenever he volleyed jibes like that, and more to the point, Andrew knew full well that he *was* being a mardy little arse.

Eventually, Higson leant back in his chair, the box of matches following the cigarette packet into the chaotic heap of paperwork that littered the DCI's desk; neither were unlikely to be unearthed any time soon, and yet Higson would always be in possession of a lit cigarette whenever he needed one. Andrew had wondered on several occasions whether Higson's threadbare jackets were all rigged to always produce fags and matches in some way, like a stage magician's coat with fathomless pockets.

'Right, go on then,' Higson said, gesturing towards Andrew with his cigarette. 'Explain to me how some tosser from the *Evening News* knew to come sniffing round on Saturday.'

Oh, Christ, Andrew had actually forgotten about that. He opened his mouth to reply, but Higson held his hand up again.

'Oh, now, don't worry your pretty little head about the story. Mother Swan has already been on, threatening to sue the bollocks off everyone who works there if they dare print a word.'

Andrew blinked in astonishment. 'You know Caroline Winshire is Peggy's mother?'

'*And*,' Higson continued mildly, ignoring Andrew's question entirely, 'you can also explain why that file you were so engrossed in a minute ago is upside down.'

Andrew couldn't help glancing down at the file in his hand; the file that was the correct way up.

Higson grinned at him and raised his eyebrows. 'And *then* you can tell me why you're about as sharp as a marble this morning.'

Andrew walked towards Higson's desk, reminding himself on the way that he a was fully fledged adult and therefore shouldn't just slouch his way towards his boss, and took a seat opposite the DCI.

'I don't know how the *Evening News* got wind our change of venue on Saturday,' Andrew said when Higson's silence suggested that the explanation better be forthcoming. 'I can't believe that it would be any of us tipping them off.'

'Quite right,' Higson replied, blowing a smoke ring. 'I don't have grasses on my team. So, which of the drama queens at the Court do you think it was?'

'Vic Hill – the stage manager – can't see why anyone would need to call the press at this stage; apparently the show's already virtually sold out.'

'Not my question,' Higson replied lazily. 'I asked who *you* think it is.'

Andrew rubbed the back of his neck. 'If it was any of the cast, I think it's most likely to be Lavinia Heathcote.'

Higson's eyebrows lifted again. 'The supposed target?'

Andrew nodded. 'There's the possibility that *Lady Bancroft* might transfer to Broadway after the run here. No publicity is bad publicity, right?'

Higson stubbed his cigarette out in the overflowing ashtray at the edge of his desk and then folded his hands together just behind the loaf of bread. 'And have you asked Miss Heathcote if she has any little buddies at the news desk?'

'Not yet, sir,' Andrew replied, and then sighed loudly. 'We do have reason to believe that Miss Heathcote might have sent the actress originally playing her part a threatening letter, in order to frighten her into leaving the production.'

'And where's the letter?'

'Here.' Andrew stood to get the letter Emma had pushed through the letterbox the day before. As he headed back to Higson, he surreptitiously glanced at his watch; Jesus, he was so late.

Higson narrowed his eyes as he took the letter, scanning the squat capital letters that covered the page. 'Let me get this straight, Joyce: you have reason to believe this Miss Heathcote has sent a woman a threatening letter, *and* that she might have been involved in leaking details of *your* investigation to the Evening News, but you haven't actually questioned her about any of this?'

Alright, Andrew would admit that when Higson put it like that, it sounded like he hadn't done his job at all. 'Sir, other members of the production have seen evidence of a man acting suspiciously in the theatre, and Peggy has confirmed that there is also a problematic spirit.'

'Yes, I read her report of the encounter you both had with this Jock character,' Higson replied. 'Very detailed.'

Andrew blinked rapidly. 'Peggy wrote a report? *When?*'

'I don't care when she wrote it, Joyce,' Higson snapped. 'I care about the fact that she wrote it up and you didn't. Imagine my surprise when I came in on Saturday afternoon to find a report from Her Majesty, *and* a request for information on a suspect in the first death.'

Lloyd had said that Peggy had been to the library, but Andrew hadn't really considered what she'd been up to.

Andrew didn't know whether he was more surprised that Peggy was apparently conducting her own little breakaway wing of the investigation, or that Higson had just admitted to coming into the Ballroom on a weekend.

'Why were you here on Saturday?' Andrew asked. Apparently, his curiosity trumped any sense of betrayal.

'Working, Joyce, which I can see might seem like a bit of a novelty to you this week,' Higson snarled.

'Working on what?' Andrew asked, unable to keep the question in, even as he saw Higson's annoyance escalating.

'I don't believe that's any of your fucking business.'

Andrew flinched slightly at Higson's sharp response. He'd been wrong: Higson wasn't *annoyed* about something. Instead, there was a flickering flame of pure anger igniting each of his words. Andrew couldn't remember ever seeing Higson behave quite like this before, and he longed to ask what the hell was going on, but he valued his own life too much for that.

He wasn't entirely certain, but Andrew didn't think that this anger was for anything *he* had done, but he'd nodded contritely anyway.

Higson reached for his cigarettes again and sniffed loudly, a defined end to the topic. 'Now, before you get your arse to the theatre, one last thing: where the fuck are my keys?'

* * *

'This definitely isn't what I signed up for when I joined the force,' Jen complained, staring morosely at her empty coffee mug before placing it down on the floor with another loud sigh.

Andrew hadn't arrived at the Court yet, so Peggy had offered to sit with Jen throughout the morning rehearsal while Lloyd took his place backstage.

There was no sign of Lavinia on the stage either, and Peggy was trying very hard not to read too much into the absence of both the actress and the detective; she was very glad that Marnie wasn't around to voice her opinion on the matter.

'I'm not sure I can take much more of this,' Jen added tiredly. 'It just feels like we're not actually getting anywhere.'

Peggy was surprised by the objection coming from Jen of all

people. In the time she'd known the Tib Street team, Jen had never been anything short of completely professional, no matter how difficult a case or a witness had been. If Jen was complaining about something, it must be really bad.

'What happens if this doesn't get cleared up by Wednesday?' Peggy asked. 'Is it enough to bank on opening night being the problem? I mean, the play's on for a week, isn't it?'

'I don't know,' Jen admitted. 'Higson seems to think we'll be done by then, but that only applies if you believe we're dealing with this curse though, doesn't it?'

'And do you?' Peggy asked, as she realised that she was only certain of what Andrew's stance was on this particular technicality. 'Believe in the curse, I mean?'

Jen took her time answering. 'I'm not so sure I do, to be honest. I've seen a lot of things that most people would describe as impossible – most of them since you joined the team, mind – but curses seem like a step too far though.'

Peggy nodded, accepting her answer. She was having a hard time believing in the idea of a curse too.

But then a commotion broke out on the stage, and when Peggy looked up, she thought that she might actually be able to believe in a curse after all.

For a brief, glorious second, Peggy allowed herself to imagine that she must be hallucinating, because there was absolutely no way that her mother was on the stage, was there?

Then the new arrival tilted her chin up imperiously, and the familiarity of that motion hit Peggy so hard that she nearly threw herself to the floor in a desperate bid to conceal herself behind the row of seats.

'Where is Cohen?' Caroline Winshire snapped, the abrupt ice-capped tone instinctively causing Peggy's nerves to jangle in anticipation of an explosion.

'Who's this now?' Jen moved to stand up.

Peggy grabbed Jen's sleeve. 'Jen, no, wait. Please don't go up there.'

'Why?' Jen's confusion slipped into a frown as she looked at Peggy in open concern. 'Peggy, what's wrong?'

'Well?' Caroline added loudly, clapping her hands at Vic and the assembled cast as though she might think that they were entirely beneath her; Peggy was certain that this was exactly what her mother *did* think.

Peggy didn't have a chance to reply to Jen before her worst nightmare played out in front of her and Edgar strolled out onto the stage to stand next to Caroline.

Peggy's breath caught in her chest, lodging sharp and painful behind her sternum.

'Jen, I need to get out of here, okay?' Peggy whispered as she tried to shuffle out to the aisle without standing up.

'Jesus, Peggy, you've gone white as a sheet,' Jen replied, shaking her head in concern but not moving out of Peggy's way in the slightest.

'Margaret?'

Peggy's gasp left her in a rush as her mother's surprised voice cut across the auditorium. Her head snapped up without her permission, and she found herself staring back at an equally astonished face.

'Peggy, who is that woman?' Jen asked quietly. She still didn't move, and just kept her eyes firmly on Peggy.

'Jen, I swear I will tell you everything later, but right now I need you to take this and hide it,' Peggy whispered desperately as she surreptitiously worked the emerald ring off her right hand. 'Please, *please*, look after this for me, and don't let them see it. Either of them.'

'Margaret!' Caroline called again. Her much sharper shout was accompanied by her stalking towards the edge of the stage, Edgar close behind her. 'Where are the bloody stairs? Someone get me some stairs!'

Peggy watched in dismay as Marion and Teddy swarmed Caroline to direct her backstage to the internal staircase. There was no way Caroline would ever do anything as uncouth as climb off the stage.

Edgar on the other hand, apparently didn't have the same qualms, and he practically hopped down into the orchestra pit with a wolfish grin on his face.

'Jen, can you please get everyone off the stage?' Peggy pleaded. 'Even if it's only for five minutes. I don't need an audience for this conversation.'

'What conversation?' Jen asked. She still sounded utterly baffled, but to Peggy's great relief she'd already tucked the ring safely away in her jacket pocket. 'Peggy who are they?'

'Caroline Winshire and Edgar Alexander.' Peggy's heart was hammering in her chest, and she felt as ill as she had done with Jock's voice in her ear. 'My mother, and my ex-fiancé.'

'What?' Jen hissed, and her eyes bugged. 'Your *what*?'

'Jen, please, I am begging you.' Peggy wasn't entirely sure that she'd ever felt so desperate in her life. 'And please just ignore everything I say to them, alright?'

'Alright,' Jen agreed slowly. 'I'll go and see what I can do with the rabble. I doubt I can get you more than a couple of minutes. You saw how harassed Cohen was earlier.'

'A few minutes is more than enough.'

Peggy swallowed heavily as Jen gave her a final look of confusion and headed for the stage, swerving out of Edgar's way as he prowled towards Peggy. Edgar didn't spare Jen even a brief glance; his eyes burned into Peggy, and she forced herself not to look away, even as every fibre of her being screamed at her to run.

Peggy straightened her spine and hoped to God that her racing heart wasn't actually audible. 'Edgar.'

'Peggy.' Edgar smiled as he approached her. 'So good to see you.'

Peggy stumbled backwards as Edgar reached for her, but with nowhere to go she found herself wrapped in his arms a moment later.

Edgar kissed her cheek and Peggy's fingers curled into fists at her sides, body otherwise frozen in horror.

'How are you?' Edgar asked when he eventually stepped away.

His eyes were wide, looking as though he actually cared about the answer, but Peggy knew all too well that he wasn't a man to be trusted, especially when he was looking at her with that carefully cultivated expression of artificial curiosity.

'I'm fine,' she replied eventually, almost shamefully proud of how steady her voice was. 'And you?'

Edgar smiled, and Peggy just about caught the little flicker of cruelty on the edge of his lips before he replied. 'Married.'

It was a direct hit, and for just a second Peggy would have sworn that her heart stopped, leaving her suspended in a glorious peace, until it thudded violently again and she had to reach out a hand to steady herself against the folding seats.

'Married?' The question escaped her lips without permission.

'What in God's name do you think you're doing here? Is this one of your father's schemes?' Caroline snapped as she strode up the aisle towards her daughter. Even with her features twisted in anger she was still strikingly beautiful in that way that had always intimidated Peggy.

Peggy couldn't force any more words out. She couldn't tell her mother why she was really there, but her brain refused to offer up even the flimsiest of excuses. There was a vice clamped around her ribs, making it impossible to take in enough air, and a burning need to escape was simmering just under her skin, racing towards a scalding shock of pure panic

'Well?' Caroline barked. 'And *stand up straight*, for God's sake.'

Perhaps it was the deeply ingrained sense of knowing when to run from one of her mother's moods that spurred Peggy's legs to move, or maybe just a well-honed sense of self-preservation. She slipped past Caroline's confused face with a mumbled 'excuse me' and was halfway back to the stage when fingers curled around her wrist like a vice, and she was yanked to a stop.

Peggy whipped her head back round to see Edgar sneering at her. 'Let go of me, Edgar.'

Peggy tugged, but Edgar's fingers remained fastened around skin and bone that suddenly felt too fragile.

'You were asked a question. What are you doing here, Peg?'

The nickname made Peggy's stomach turn. Only Charlie and, occasionally, Andrew, called her Peg these days; Edgar had lost the right to do so when he'd ransacked her home and sprinted off into the sunset with her own mother.

'Hey!'

Peggy had never been more grateful to see Lloyd in her life, even if his words were garbled around the bite of Toffee Crisp he'd just taken from the bright orange wrapper in his hand.

'Are you alright, Peggy?' Lloyd asked more sharply as Edgar loosened his grip enough for Peggy to shrug him off.

'Yes, thank you, DC Parker,' Peggy replied, pulling her arm to her chest and hoping that the presence of a policeman would be enough to encourage Edgar to back off.

Edgar looked between Peggy and Lloyd, his gaze calculating as he tried to work out exactly what was going on; and how Peggy and Lloyd were connected.

Peggy felt sick all over again when she was reminded of just how close she'd once come to sharing her most fiercely guarded secret with Edgar. If he'd had even the slightest inkling of why Peggy was in the theatre, she knew that he'd already have found a way to use it against her.

'Just two old friends catching up,' Edgar said, his smile a smug, practised quirk of his lips.

'Doesn't look that friendly to me.' Lloyd's eyes were back on Edgar, and Peggy couldn't see even a trace of his usual good humour.

Edgar held up his hands up in mock-surrender, shooting Peggy another sharpened smile before lightly kissing her cheek. 'I'm sure we'll catch up later, Peg.'

Peggy didn't wait for Edgar to make a further move before she turned away from him and practically bolted towards the door at the side of the stage.

'Hey! Whoa, hang on. Peggy?' Lloyd called from behind her just as she cleared the door and reached the internal staircase.

Peggy paused and took a deep breath before she turned around. 'Yes, Lloyd?'

'Are you alright?' He still looked uncharacteristically serious. 'Who was that?'

'I'm fine,' Peggy said, trying, and failing, to smile. 'Really, don't worry about it.'

Lloyd's frown deepened, but any reply he may have made was cut off by Jen jogging down the stairs towards them, looking as concerned as Lloyd did.

Peggy couldn't bear the thought of more pitying looks. She glanced between the two of them and shook her head, knowing that she needed to get away from the theatre. 'I'm going home.'

'Home? But what if Jock comes back?' Lloyd asked, peeking over his shoulder worriedly.

'I'll try and send Marnie over, alright?' Peggy slipped past Jen on the stairs, keeping her gaze on the carpet.

'Peggy, what happened?' Jen asked gently. Thankfully she made no attempts to stop Peggy leaving.

'Nothing,' Peggy replied, her voice cracking as she hurried up the stairs. '*Nothing.*'

FOURTEEN

'For Christ's sake, not again,' Andrew muttered as he carefully guided the Belmont into a space behind the obnoxiously orange sports car parked directly outside the Court. He didn't want to think about what on earth Charlie could have already got up to inside the theatre.

At least there didn't seem to be any bloody 'journalists' around, and just for that fact Andrew was probably going to find it in himself to tolerate Charlie for five minutes or so before he sent him on his way.

He climbed out onto the pavement and slammed the door more forcefully than necessary.

'Andrew?'

Andrew wasn't sure that he managed to completely contain his groan of frustration at the sound of Lavinia's voice, and so he tried to cover up any sound that had escaped with a short bout of forced coughing.

This did nothing to improve the concerned frown Lavinia was shooting him from just outside the theatre doors. 'Goodness, are you alright?'

'I'm fine,' Andrew replied curtly. 'Thank you.'

He turned to head towards the theatre before he stopped and looked down at his watch and then back up at Lavinia. 'Have you only just arrived?'

Lavinia raised one shoulder coyly and smiled. 'Oh, it's not like they can start without me, is it?'

'There you are!' Cohen yelled suddenly as he burst through the doors, looking frazzled. 'Jesus, Lavinia, couldn't you have picked a different morning to be late?'

'What's wrong?' Andrew asked, immediately alert as he stepped away from Lavinia. 'What's happened?'

'Caroline *fucking* Winshire is here, and she's on the warpath,' Cohen hissed, eyes wide. 'That's what's happened.'

Lavinia hurried towards the theatre without giving Andrew another second of consideration, and Cohen hurried through the door after her.

It took Andrew a couple of seconds longer for his own brain to engage fully and realise what Cohen's statement meant for him personally, and when realisation finally dawned, he was through the door quick enough to catch up with the other two before they'd reached the opposite side of the foyer.

'What are you doing, Inspector?' Cohen asked, confused as Andrew barrelled past him, jostling his shoulder violently as he did so.

Andrew didn't reply as he raced up the stairs, flung open the auditorium doors, and all but sprinted down the aisle towards the stage. What the hell had happened?

'You alright there, boss?'

Andrew spun in surprise at the sound of Lloyd's voice.

He didn't quite know what he'd been expecting, but nowhere in the dramatic visions he'd conjured on the five second journey from the pavement to the stalls had he expected to find Jen and Lloyd seated in the middle of the auditorium talking quietly with each other, and with neither Swan sibling anywhere in sight.

For just a second, Andrew genuinely thought that maybe, just *maybe*, nothing had happened, but his heart sank when he caught his colleagues' expressions when they glanced quickly at each other as Andrew approached.

'Sir!' Lloyd said, popping up from his seat immediately like a disturbingly grave-faced jack in the box.

Jen rose to her feet too, more slowly, but she looked no less serious. 'Sir.'

Andrew looked up at the intricate ceiling and sighed loudly. 'Where are Peggy and Charlie?'

'Peggy's gone home, sir,' Jen said, and Andrew's head snapped straight back down sharply.

'Gone home?' he repeated slowly, shaking his head. He'd have thought that she might have taken cover in Cohen's office or something, but not that she'd have left completely.

Wait, that didn't make sense. Charlie's car was outside. He said as much to Jen.

'Charlie hasn't been here this morning,' Jen replied slowly, brows creased.

'Then why the bloody hell is his car outside?' Andrew snapped. He knew that Peggy would only ever choose to drive her own small, unobtrusive car, and even if there were some extenuating circumstances that meant she'd had to borrow one from her brother, Andrew was certain that Peggy wouldn't have chosen such an abominable vehicle.

'The orange one?' Lloyd asked. When Andrew nodded, he added, 'I think that belongs to that posh bloke with the hair.'

'*Who?*'

'I didn't get his name. He seems like a bit of a dickhead, whoever he is.'

'Edgar Alexander,' Jen explained quietly, eyeing Andrew intently enough that it was obvious that she was aware that this information would mean something to him.

Andrew's eyes widened, and he instinctively knew from the look on Jen's face that Peggy must have explained, at least partially, what her connection to Edgar had once been.

'Fuck,' Andrew muttered, pinching the bridge of his nose. That's all they needed, for bloody Edgar to show up right when Andrew needed Peggy to be focused on the case.

And - *worse* - right when Andrew hadn't been there.

'Yeah, well, whatever his name is, he's a complete arse,' Lloyd continued, lacking the vital information the other two had. 'I honestly thought he was toast when he kissed Peggy on the cheek.'

Andrew's reeling thoughts stopped dead. 'He did what?'

He almost didn't recognise the dangerously low, cold voice as being his own. It was the frosty opposite of the rage that already been ignited in his chest at the thought of Edgar being in even the same room as Peggy after what he'd done to her.

Lloyd looked slightly taken aback. 'It's alright, sir, she handled it herself. It looked like she didn't want me to get involved.'

Andrew opened his mouth to ask Lloyd exactly why Edgar still had breath in his body after he'd dared lay a finger on Peggy, but Jen silenced him with a sharp glare.

Right, Lloyd had no clue about the specifics of this particular problem, and Andrew was reminded that he'd promised Peggy to keep his mouth shut about her mother's involvement in the production, and about everything related to Edgar.

'And where have *you* been?' Marion snapped loudly from the stage, startling Andrew into turning around.

In the minute or so he'd been talking to Jen and Lloyd, Lavinia and Cohen had made it to the stage.

'Well, I don't see how that's any of your business, Marion,' Lavinia replied cooly.

'Oh, it's definitely my business, *love*,' Marion sniped. 'We've all been here for over an hour already.'

Lavinia shrugged. 'Oh, get off your high horse.'

Marion snorted angrily. 'I see that Detective Inspector Joyce arrived at the same time. Has he been *interviewing* you again?'

Andrew opened his mouth to deny whatever insinuation Marion was attempting to create, but Lavinia cut him off before he could even start by launching herself towards Marion, her long blonde hair flying out behind her.

'How dare you!' Lavinia shrieked.

Andrew wondered if he should break up the altercation, or whether he should just quietly expire on the spot from embarrassment.

'That is *enough*!' Cohen roared angrily. 'I don't give a flying fuck what anyone gets up to when they're not in this theatre, but right now you're on my goddamn stage, and in my goddamn production, so you will shut the fuck up and do your jobs!'

Cohen's eyes were wide and slightly unfocussed, and he kept flexing his hands as though he might be thinking about just giving something a good clout if afforded half the chance.

Peggy had told Andrew enough about her mother for him to know that whatever Cohen's experience of Caroline Winshire had been that morning, it wouldn't have been even remotely pleasant.

Marion and Lavinia had both been stunned into silence at Cohen's shout and were looking at their feet in embarrassment.

'Get into your fucking places for the final two scenes,' Cohen snapped and held out his hand so that Vic could pass him a stack of paper. 'And if I find out that it was any of you who called the press over the weekend, you'll never work in this business again. I'll make sure of it.'

Andrew's eyes sharpened at Cohen's threat, and he swept his gaze over the cast, looking for any sign of particular discomfort at the words. All four actors looked surprised, but nobody immediately appeared shifty enough to suggest blame. Andrew hoped that this was because none of them had actually called the *Evening News*, and not because he was losing his ability to detect guilt.

The cast made their way to their positions and Andrew wearily dropped into the seat next to Jen.

'Are you alright, boss?' Lloyd asked again, proffering an unopened tube of Rolos towards Andrew.

Andrew, who'd missed breakfast yet again, took the sweets and began peeling back the gold foil. 'Fine.'

'Were your grandparents alright about you staying at their house?' Lloyd asked as he produced another tube of Rolos from his jacket pocket and put two chocolates in his mouth just as the rehearsal began.

Andrew nodded mutely and ran his hands over his face, which only served to remind him that he hadn't shaved.

'Oh!' Lloyd rummaged in his jacket pocket before producing a large bundle of keys. 'These are Higson's keys. Peggy forgot to give them back to you when we were at your house yesterday which, you know, seems fair.'

'Why did Peggy have the keys?' Jen asked. Her lack of questions about why the rest of the team had been in Gatley suggested to Andrew that Lloyd must have filled her in on the events of Sunday morning.

Andrew pursed his lips. 'Peggy's apparently decided to do some investigating of her own. She's been looking into the deaths connected to the play.'

'Oh, that's good,' Jen said, sounding pleased. 'Has she found anything?'

'I have no idea,' Andrew replied curtly. 'She's been requesting files from Higson.'

Jen frowned. 'And that's a bad thing?'

'Yes, because I didn't even know she was doing any of it!' Andrew snapped, and it was only after the words had left his mouth that he realised that this was the truth of it – Peggy had obviously thought that Andrew's investigation was lacking, and instead of talking to him about it, she'd just gone behind his back to request information from Higson.

Jen's frown deepened. 'Are you sure everything's alright, sir?'

Andrew pressed his fingertips into his closed eyelids and scowled. There was something about this bloody theatre that made him feel itchy with irritation, and he drew in the deepest breath his lungs would allow, and then let it out slowly. It didn't make him feel any better.

Everything was distinctly *not* alright, and he hated the fact that he couldn't even fully explain *why*.

Lloyd winced. 'I hate to ask, boss, but do you know if Jimmy Haworth's article is in today's *Evening News*?'

'We don't need to worry about the *Evening News* running any stories about us,' Andrew sighed, morosely staring at the Rolos in his hand. 'Higson told me this morning.'

'What did he do? Threaten Haworth?' Lloyd asked, looking gratified by the idea.

Andrew shook his head. 'He didn't do anything. Apparently, Ms Winshire made it very clear what would happen to the *Evening News* if it dared print so much as a single negative word about the play, or anyone connected to it. The story's dead.'

'Not that I'm not pleased that Haworth's article won't run, but that's not exactly a win for freedom of the press, is it?' Jen sighed.

Andrew agreed with her on both counts.

'She's a right piece of work, sir; that Winshire woman, I mean,' Lloyd added, eyes wide. 'You should have heard the way she spoke to Cohen this morning. I thought he was actually going to burst into tears at one point. You're lucky you missed her.'

'Lucky' wasn't quite the word Andrew would have chosen.

'Where is she now?' he asked. 'The car's still outside.'

'Important business in town,' Lloyd replied in a high-pitched, prim voice. '*Apparently.*'

Andrew caught Jen's eye, and she pulled an unhappy face in return. He needed to talk to her about what had happened with Peggy and Edgar, but he couldn't do that with anyone in earshot.

'Lloyd, can you go and keep an eye on backstage?' Andrew suggested quickly, standing up so that Lloyd would be able to get past him in the narrow row. 'If any of that lot need to go back there, I want you to stay with them at all times. Nobody goes anywhere else without you, alright?'

'Alright,' Lloyd agreed slowly. 'I mean, Peggy's not here, though, so if anything spooky happens I'm not going to be able to do much.'

Andrew shook his head. 'Just go and watch them, Lloyd.'

Lloyd nodded and left them to it.

'What happened?' Andrew asked Jen, as soon as they were alone.

Jen made a face. 'I was sitting in here with Peggy, and the next thing Caroline Winshire came out onto the stage as everyone was getting set up.'

Shit. Andrew grimaced. That meant that Peggy would have had an audience for whatever had happened next.

'Sir...' Jen trailed off, shaking her head, 'Peggy looked like she was about to pass out. I've never seen her look more anxious about anything; well, I hadn't until that man appeared.'

'Fuck,' Andrew breathed, unable to hold it in.

'You already know who he is then, sir?' Jen asked.

'Yeah. Peggy told me about him last year; the day she started in Lewis's.'

Jen screwed up her face. 'Look, sir, I don't know the whole story; only that he and Peggy used to be engaged. But correct me if I'm wrong – *and I really hope that I am* - is Edgar in a relationship with Caroline Winshire?'

Even if Andrew hadn't given a short nod to confirm Jen's suspicion, his face would have given him away.

'Jesus,' Jen muttered. 'That poor girl. No wonder she went home.'

Andrew reasoned that it was actually probably a good thing that he hadn't been in the theatre earlier, because he genuinely couldn't say what he would have done if he'd found himself face-to-face with Edgar, or Caroline for that matter.

Jen reached into her jacket pocket and then held her closed fist out towards Andrew. 'Peggy asked me to hide this from them.'

Andrew lay his palm flat, and he knew exactly what was going to come tumbling into his hand before the familiar emerald ring was dropped there.

He curled his fingers around the band and blew a noisy breath out between his closed lips.

'I thought that maybe you might want to give it back to her,' Jen said as she stood up.

'She asked you to look after it, Jen.'

'And I expect you know far more about what it means to her than I do, sir,' Jen replied firmly. 'I think she'd probably appreciate knowing that we *all* have her back.'

Jen didn't often rebuke him, so when she did, even with delicate subtleness, Andrew still felt a bit like he'd been deservedly slapped.

Feeling suitably chastised, Andrew folded his legs out of the way to allow Jen to shuffle past him and out into the aisle.

He carefully put the ring into the inside pocket of his suit jacket and was struck with the ridiculous thought that somehow the universe had once again thought him the safest bet to look after someone else's horribly valuable engagement ring.

Andrew watched disinterestedly as Teddy entered from the left for the final scene a moment later.

'Where is my angel?' Teddy plaintively delivered his line as he headed towards centre stage. 'Even if the sky were full of stars, I would see her light before all others.'

Andrew had to stop himself from rolling his eyes.

Teddy reached out to press the dummy light switch and the entire auditorium plunged into darkness.

Andrew sprang to his feet as the screaming on stage started. He couldn't have identified the voices if he'd tried.

'Nobody move!' Andrew yelled, running his hand along the row of seats in front of him so that he didn't just topple straight over.

'It wasn't us!' someone yelled from the tech box behind them.

Andrew could still hear panicked movements on the stage.

'Stand still, all of you!' he shouted. 'Jen, are you there?'

'Sir!' Jen replied from somewhere nearby.

'Hang on, I have a torch!' called Vic shakily from the front row.

Andrew raised his hand to shield his eyes when Vic switched on the small torch and managed to shine it directly at his face.

'Sorry, Inspector,' Vic said as she hurried over to hand the torch to Andrew.

Andrew grabbed the torch and ran for the door at the side of the stage. He hurried up the steps, Jen's footsteps clattering along behind him, and burst out onto the stage.

Teddy was standing stock-still where Andrew had last seen him, a terrified look on his face.

'Teddy, are you alright?' Andrew asked as he crossed the stage.

He sighed in relief when it appeared that Teddy was uninjured and hadn't been electrocuted as Andrew had initially feared.

Teddy swayed slightly. 'I think I'm going to be sick.'

Andrew shone the torch around the stage and was surprised to see Marion and Lavinia clutching at each other, with Ben just behind them looking deeply concerned.

'Right, all of you off the stage now,' Andrew ordered. 'Follow DS Cusack and head up the aisle to the foyer. I'll be right behind you.'

Nobody moved, and someone whimpered loudly.

'*Now!*' Andrew snapped, routing the beam of the torch in Jen's direction, so that the cast could shamble over to her.

The door at the back of the auditorium opened and Andrew turned to see someone backlit by daylight.

'There's been a power cut!' the figure shouted.

'Yeah?' Cohen yelled back. 'Thank fuck you noticed, because we obviously hadn't!'

The back of Andrew's neck prickled, and he just *knew* that he was being watched. He spun around furiously, trying to scan as much of the stage as he could with the torch's weakening beam.

He backed away slowly as the range of the light grew shorter and shorter, until it was barely a puddle of light at his feet.

He glanced to the right and saw that the rest of them had almost reached the doors at the back.

Without Peggy, Andrew had no idea what he was up against and, for once in his life, he thought that it might not be the best time to push his luck – not with the way things had been going for him all week.

Andrew turned tail and hastened off the stage, reaching the aisle just as the torch winked out completely.

As he jogged towards the foyer, he could still feel eyes boring into the back of his head.

He didn't quite dare turn around again.

* * *

'Peg, why don't you order something else?' Charlie asked, eyeing Peggy's barely touched plate of food.

'I told you I wasn't hungry, Charlie,' Peggy muttered, pushing the risotto towards her brother. 'Here, you eat it.'

Charlie didn't need telling twice, and he immediately swapped Peggy's plate for his own, which had long since been cleared of his own dinner.

Peggy picked up her wine glass, and then put it down again almost immediately without taking a sip. She felt unsettled, and like she didn't quite fit in her own skin anymore.

'Now that Mother's made her presence known I doubt she'll be back to the theatre until opening night,' Charlie said once he'd shovelled a good few forkfuls into his mouth.

'Charlie,' Peggy groaned, dropping her chin to her chest. 'You promised we weren't going to talk about it. It's the only reason I came out with you.'

That wasn't strictly true; whereas she'd rather not have been back in Manchester sharing a table at Osteria with her brother, the alternative had been trying to hide from Emmeline and Marnie back at Butterton, so, really, it was the lesser of two evils.

'I know I did,' Charlie agreed, somewhat apologetically, 'but I don't think it's a good idea for you to just sit there and stew about it either.'

'I'm not stewing. I just don't want to talk about it.'

'Did *he* dare speak to you?'

Peggy knew that Charlie wasn't going to drop the subject until she'd at least told him the basics of her encounter. *God*, this was going to be excruciating but, knowing the way that her brother was likely to react, it would probably actually be better to drop the biggest of bombshells somewhere public.

Peggy covered her face with her hands, unable to look at anyone. 'They're married, Charlie.'

The fork hit Charlie's plate with such a clatter that Peggy dropped her arms again in surprise.

'They're *what*?' Charlie bellowed.

'Charlie, *Jesus*, keep your voice down,' Peggy replied quietly, furtively glancing around as she noticed that a number of other guests had looked over in obvious interest at her brother's outburst. 'He told me today.'

Charlie's eyebrows had drawn together, and he looked like he might be about to explode in a supernova. Peggy could really do without that happening.

'Charlie, don't, alright?' Peggy sighed. 'It was bad enough living through it all once.'

Charlie's gaze zeroed in on Peggy's right hand. 'Peg, where's your ring? Did that bastard t-'

'Jen has it,' Peggy cut him off, holding her hands up. 'I know she'll look after it for me.'

'At least tell me that Joycie decked him,' Charlie growled, still not pacified.

Peggy shook his head. 'Andrew wasn't there.'

'What?' Charlie had returned to shouting. 'Where the hell was he?'

'I don't know,' Peggy replied truthfully. 'At Tib Street, maybe? Interviewing someone?'

Charlie laughed contemptuously and Peggy blinked in surprise. 'Oh, and was this *someone* blonde and particularly leggy?'

'Charlie!' Peggy berated him. 'For God's sake, stop it.'

Charlie snarled. 'He's supposed to make sure that you're alright.'

'He's supposed to do no such thing!' Peggy argued indignantly. 'I am perfectly capable of looking after myself, and I hope to God that you haven't even *dared* think about telling Andrew that he is in any way responsible for me!'

Her brother's nose twitched, giving her the only answer she needed, and Peggy wanted nothing more dearly than to throw her napkin on the table and bolt out of the restaurant.

'How *could* you, Charlie?' Peggy hissed.

'I'm allowed to worry about you, Peg! I don't suppose you've forgotten what happened last summer, have you?' Charlie asked tightly as he made a motion with his hand in the direction of their waiter.

Peggy's expression darkened. 'Of course I've not forgotten. You can't possibly still blame Andrew for what happened then. It wasn't his fault.'

'It *was* his fault, Peggy,' Charlie countered as the waiter approached. 'Not entirely, but *enough*.'

'Charlie, stop this now, or I'm walking out of here by myself, whether you like it or not.' Peggy folded her napkin neatly and shot the waiter a strained smile.

'Everything alright, Charlie?' the waiter asked.

'All fine, thanks, Luca,' Charlie replied, though his smile looked pained. 'Any chance you could pop this on my tab for me?'

'You don't want dessert?' Luca asked in surprise. 'But there's tiramisu!'

Peggy watched as Charlie's expression crumpled slightly in disappointment, but then he righted himself. 'Not tonight, I'm afraid. We have somewhere else to be.'

'Alright,' Luca replied slowly. 'Well, enjoy your evening, both of you.'

'And don't even bother denying the fact that you've been talking to Andrew about me behind my back, Charlie.' Peggy pushed her chair back and headed for the exit, not waiting for her brother to catch up.

She'd already retrieved her coat from the cloakroom and was shrugging it on by the time Charlie appeared at the door, looking sheepish.

'Sorry, Peg,' he said quietly. 'I shouldn't have said any of that to you, and I shouldn't have said anything to Joycie either.'

'No, you shouldn't,' Peggy agreed as she pulled open the door and stepped out into the night.

'We're going to have to tell Father about this, you know,' Charlie said as they approached his Ferrari. 'Though I can't believe he doesn't already know.'

Peggy's stomach twisted at the thought that her father had likely known that his ex-wife and Edgar had married at some point recently, and yet he'd still kept it from his daughter.

This didn't surprise her at all, but it was never particularly pleasant to be reminded of how little your wellbeing or happiness mattered to your parents.

'Can we at least wait until after opening night?' Peggy asked as she climbed into the passenger seat. 'If Father goes after her about this, you know she'll find a way to blame me for everything.'

Charlie would know that he couldn't argue with that.

'Alright,' Charlie acquiesced, 'but I'm going to see him on Thursday morning.'

Peggy nodded her agreement. 'Please can we just go home now?'

Charlie said nothing in reply; he just turned the key in the ignition and pulled the car out into the evening's traffic.

Peggy rested her head on the passenger window and closed her eyes.

She knew her 'sleeping' act wouldn't fool Charlie in the slightest, but she was thankful that he left her to wallow in silence for the whole drive back to Butterton.

* * *

As he passed the welcome sign at the edge of Butterton village, Andrew found himself mentally counting down the days until he'd never have to set foot in the Court again. In fact, he wasn't entirely sure that he'd ever want to set foot in *any* theatre ever again.

After the power had finally been restored to the theatre that afternoon, and the electrician had confirmed that it was just a power issue rather than any foul play connected to the dummy switch on the stage, Cohen had insisted on going through with the full technical rehearsal as planned.

They'd had to present Marion with a couple of brandies before she'd calmed enough to get back on the stage, but the rest of the day had otherwise passed without further incident.

Andrew knew that he should have been pleased at the straightforward end to the day, but he couldn't help but feel like it had just been a gently mocking proverbial calm before the storm.

The tall chimneys of Butterton House came into view and Andrew slowed to take the turning into the long driveway that would lead to the Swans' front door.

Most of the house was in darkness, and Andrew wondered, not for the first time, why anybody needed so many rooms in any one house; surely by the time you'd managed to switch on the lights in every room, it would almost be time to go back and start switching them off again.

Perhaps that was the only reason William Swan still employed a butler.

Andrew hadn't been a big fan of arriving at Butterton unannounced since the first time he'd encountered the Swans' ancient butler, Timothy, and tonight was no exception.

Thankfully, Peggy and Charlie seemed to be about as delighted with Timothy's constant presence as Andrew was, and so they generally made it their business to answer the door as quickly as possible to avoid involving the butler in their lives at all.

Even so, Andrew drove towards the garages and parked the Belmont as out of view of the main house as he could, just in case.

Once he'd checked that Peggy's ring was still in his pocket, he climbed out of his car and headed for the front door. It was yet another cooler-than-average evening, and he regretted not thinking to grab a warm coat from his house before he'd fled.

Andrew jogged up the steps and raised the large metal ring for the door knocker, before bringing it down heavily twice, just as he always did.

As he waited, he glanced around the darkening grounds, mentally calculating how many times he could fit his house and garden onto just the driveway.

The door opened behind him, and he turned, hoping that it would be Peggy who'd reached the entrance first.

It wasn't, and it wasn't Charlie either.

Andrew schooled his features into neutrality. 'Timothy.'

'Mr Joyce,' Timothy replied cooly, eyes dropping to Andrew's shoes before travelling slowly back up to his face.

Andrew's hands immediately reached to straighten the hem of his jacket, and he was unpleasantly reminded that even though he'd managed to put a tie on in his haste that morning, he was still wearing the jeans he'd slept in.

Well, at least it meant that there was no way that this would be the time that Timothy finally worked out that Andrew was supposed to be a Detective Inspector.

Timothy had made no move to open the door any further.

'I'm here to see Peg- *Lady Margaret*,' Andrew corrected himself hurriedly.

'I'm afraid she's not available this evening, sir,' Timothy said with a threatening degree of politeness.

'Oh.' Andrew frowned. 'Well, in that case, c-'

'Lord Ashley is not available either,' Timothy added, pre-empting Andrew's question about Charlie.

'Oh,' Andrew repeated, somewhat flummoxed. He wasn't sure he'd ever arrived at Butterton and found it utterly devoid of both siblings before.

There wasn't even the slightest chance that he was going to ask if Marnie was around. For a start, he still didn't understand how Marnie's near constant presence had been explained to the butler, and it wasn't anything he wanted to get himself involved in.

'Good evening then, sir,' Timothy said gravelly, closing the door firmly before Andrew could even attempt another enquiry.

Andrew stumbled back slightly in surprise and swore softly as he nearly turned his ankle in an attempt to not tumble down the steps and onto the gravel below.

'Great,' he muttered to himself as he trudged back towards his car. He'd gone completely out of his way to drive out to Butterton, and now he had to go the entire way back to Tib Street with the constant fear of losing Peggy's engagement ring hanging over his head. He'd lost count of how many times his fingers had strayed to his pocket since Jen had handed it to him that morning.

Plus, he now had no chance of speaking to Peggy about what had happened with Caroline and Edgar, nor of telling her about the incident with the light switch.

He tried to ignore the fact that he'd been hoping that speaking to Peggy would have been enough to reassure him that she'd be back at the Court the next morning to keep an eye on all those things Andrew couldn't see. When she'd been absent that afternoon, Andrew had realised just how hamstrung his whole investigation was without her insight, which hadn't done anything to improve his gradually darkening mood as they raced towards opening night.

He tapped his palm on the top of his car twice with a sigh as he opened the door.

As he twisted to climb into the driver's seat, Andrew started in surprise when he saw a flash of pale hair turning away in one of the upper windows. He craned his neck to see better, but only caught a glimpse of the curtains moving slightly.

Andrew's mouth dropped open in surprise.

Peggy was *there*?

Peggy was there, and she'd convinced *Timothy* to tell Andrew that she wasn't available?

Andrew's eyes narrowed, but even the flare of irritation couldn't stifle the sharper crack of betrayal he felt at being left outside.

Right, he thought as he slammed the car door behind him with enough force for the Belmont to shake in complaint, at least now he knew where he stood.

As Andrew approached the crossroads that marked the edge of the village, he spotted a fancy red car in the distance, approaching at speed from the opposite direction. Even though he couldn't see the driver from where he was, Andrew knew it could only be one person.

For a split second, he thought about making Charlie pull over, just to give Andrew the chance to yell at him, but in the end, he decided that he didn't have even the slightest bit of energy available to waste on such a production.

Rather than crossing the road and heading towards his grandparents' house in Gatley as he'd planned, Andrew decided that he no longer had even the remotest desire to see a single one of the Swans that evening, even just in passing, and so he sharply slapped his left indicator and took the turning that would lead him back into Manchester instead.

FIFTEEN

Peggy quietly pushed open the door to the theatre's foyer and immediately stilled, listening carefully. She hadn't seen any sign of her mother or Edgar outside, but one could never be too sure that Caroline Winshire wasn't lurking somewhere ready to pounce. She caught no hint of her mother's sharp voice, but Peggy jolted slightly when she realised that the hint of a papery murmur in the near silence sounded awfully like frenzied whispering if she strained her ears enough.

Suddenly, a blaring boom of a laugh erupted in the auditorium, bursting through the hefty closed doors as though they were nothing more than a thin curtain. It startled Peggy enough that she flinched in surprise.

She recognised the particular brand of explosive mirth and frowned. *What was DCI Higson doing at the Court?*

Peggy swiftly concluded that she'd rather not find out if he was there to talk to her about her disappearing act the day before, and so she fled towards the stairs that would lead her to the dress circle; up there she'd be visible enough to the rest of the team to confirm her presence, but the distance would also allow her to effectively isolate herself.

Peggy opened the heavy double doors that led into the upper rows of seating and almost shrieked in surprise at the figure sitting in the front row, with their feet propped up on the wall just below the balcony railing.

'Marnie!' Peggy hissed when she composed herself. 'What are you doing here?'

Marnie turned her head languidly. 'God, I wish I had some popcorn. Do you reckon Lloyd would lend me a bag of sweets? Just to hold and pretend I can eat them, obviously.'

'What are you doing here?' Peggy repeated in exasperation. 'And where on earth have you been? Emmeline's been complaining that you haven't been around to watch *Neighbours* with her in days.'

'Nowhere. Just around.' Marnie shrugged. 'It doesn't matter. *Now*, tell me all about yesterday. I'll be surprised if this play isn't deader than me by lunchtime! I can't believe it isn't already, to be honest.'

'What do you mean?' Peggy slowly approached the front row, curving her spine unnaturally and hunching her shoulders so that she might remain invisible to the occupants of the stalls below for as long as possible.

Marnie squinted calculatingly. She uncrossed her ankles so that she could set her feet back on the floor and face Peggy properly as she sat down next to her. 'Weren't you here yesterday?'

Peggy willed her face to remain free of any expression at all. 'Yes, but then I had to leave early.'

'Why?' Marnie's eyes narrowed even further.

'It doesn't matter,' Peggy replied with a shrug, using Marnie's own words against her. 'What's going on?'

For a long moment, it seemed to Peggy that Marnie might refuse to accept such an obvious attempt at diverting the course of conversation, but eventually she turned away again and pointed at the stage. 'Well, the obnoxious one with the Rubik's Cube –'

'Teddy.'

'Yeah, him; he's saying he doesn't trust anyone in this place to keep him safe,' Marnie explained. 'The theatre's had to call in all sorts of electricians and the like to get second opinions on the safety of the wiring and stuff.'

Peggy frowned. 'Why?'

'Well, apparently when he touched the dummy switch on the stage yesterday, every light in the whole place went out.' Marnie shrugged. 'Nobody in the tech team had anything to do with it. *Allegedly.*'

'*What*?' Peggy was back on her feet in an instant. 'Have you seen Alistair yet?'

'Nope.'

'I should try and find him. He'll be able to tell us if Jock was involved.'

Marnie rolled her eyes.

Peggy pursed her lips. 'What was that for?'

'Nothing.'

'*Marnie*!'

'Oh, fine,' Marnie sighed. 'I just think there might be something off about him. Don't you think it's awfully convenient that the only person – well, person-*ish* person – that can see Jock, is Alistair?'

'Marnie, that's ridiculous. I really th-'

'What's to say *he* isn't the one parading around pretending to be some creepy, ancient shadow ghost. God, stuck in this stuffy old place he must be bloody *bored* enough to try!'

'That's not fair. He co-'

The rest of Peggy's argument was summarily executed by the unexpected, but terribly familiar, exasperated cry of '*Oh, for God's sake!*' from below, followed immediately by a commotion.

She and Marnie hurried to the balcony railing and leaned forward slightly.

Andrew was striding up the aisle towards the stage, suit jacket flapping slightly in his haste. Even from a distance, Peggy could tell that this was a prelude to Andrew doing something that was likely necessary but also possibly very idiotic.

'I'm really not sure about this, sir!' Lloyd yelped, scampering behind his DI. 'Sir!'

'Andrew, this does seem rather risky,' Lavinia's musical voice followed, though she made no appearance from wherever she was tucked away further back in the stalls.

'Inspector!' Cohen shouted, more hesitant than Lloyd, but with obvious discontent in his voice as he followed in Andrew's wake. 'Inspector, just hold on there for one second, would you?'

'*What's he doing?*' Peggy hissed, and leaned further forward over the metal bar until she caught Jen's eye.

'Peggy!' Jen exclaimed in surprise. 'You're here!'

'What's that bloody moron doing?' Marnie snapped, waving her arm towards where Andrew was disappearing through the door to the left of the stage. Peggy wouldn't have phrased it quite like that, but she couldn't deny that Marnie had got to the point quickly enough.

Higson looked up at the dress circle and grinned like the cat who'd got the cream. 'Oh, good, everyone's here to witness this.'

'Witness what?' Peggy asked, against her better judgement.

'Well, *Miss Jones*, DI Joyce has concluded that the electrical failure yesterday *must be* of entirely earthly criminal origin,' Higson replied calmly, clasping his hands over his stomach, and casually tapping his thumbs against each other. He tilted his head towards the assembled cast. 'Nobody else is too sure about taking his word for it though, so he's gone to prove that he's not about to be electrocuted by a murderous ghost. If this all goes tits up, at least one of you lot can write up the incident report.'

At that moment, Andrew stalked out from the wings to stage right – Lloyd and Cohen close behind - and stopped where the dummy switch was attached to the gaudy yellow wallpaper of Lady Bancroft's drawing room. He turned his head to look defiantly out at his audience, expression twitching ever so slightly out of place for a moment when he noticed Peggy looking down from the dress circle.

Andrew held up his hand and reached over to flip the switch.

Nothing happened.

Andrew clicked the switch back and forth between the two positions a few more time for good measure. He then held his hands up in apparent conclusion, and Peggy finally exhaled.

When Cohen sagged in obvious relief on the stage, Higson

turned impassively to the cast. 'Right, as my DI's still breathing, would you all be kind enough to get your arses up on that stage so that we can get on with finding out who hates one of you enough to engineer all this funny business?'

Marion's indignant squawk was only just loud enough to cover up the finer detail of Lavinia and Teddy's outraged exclamations, and Peggy was fairly certain that Ben was covering a snigger with an affected cough, pretending to scratch the bridge of his nose as he headed towards the stage.

'I'm going to find Alistair,' Peggy said to Marnie. 'Are you coming?'

Marnie shook her head. 'No thanks.'

'Are you going home then?'

'Nope. I thought I might stick around and try to see the 'invisible' ghost.' Marnie rolled her eyes again. 'Just in case.'

Peggy didn't want to get into yet another argument in the bloody theatre, so she shot Marnie a quick smile that might well have amounted to more of a grimace, if Marnie's raised eyebrows were any indication, and left the dress circle.

'Alistair?' Peggy called quietly as she slowly headed for the door that would take her to the first-floor offices and dressing rooms. 'Alistair, are you there? I really need to talk to you about what happened yesterday.'

As she reached the corridor, Peggy felt a gentle shift in the air around her, a split second before she heard a quiet '*Hello*'.

Peggy turned to find Alistair standing near the wall, wearing a rather sheepish expression.

'I'm so sorry about yesterday, Miss Peggy,' Alistair said, all in a rush. 'I tried to find you before Jock interfered with the lights, but I didn't know where you were.'

'So, it *was* Jock's doing?' Peggy gratefully filed away the fact that Alistair had at least missed her rather public interaction with Edgar and Caroline, and focused instead on how Andrew really had just been the biggest idiot known to man. He could have been electrocuted right in front of them if Jock had decided he'd wanted to play dangerous games again!

Alistair nodded. 'Though, truth be told, I don't think he can do much harm to anyone these days.'

'I think the evidence would beg to differ!'

'There was no real danger,' Alistair continued placatingly, and then somehow managed to blanch. 'Even if I personally found the whole trick to be in rather poor taste.'

Peggy wrinkled her nose. Yes, she could imagine that it wouldn't be particularly pleasant to be reminded of the manner of your own death in such a performative manner. 'Alistair, this is the same spirit you described as being the blackest parts of a soul, and the same one that ransacked the archive room. Why are you suddenly so convinced that Jock isn't trying to harm the cast?'

Alistair sighed loudly. 'Because Jock has barely been able to manifest a physical response to anything since around the time Peter McClellan died; almost as if that were his last great hurrah.'

Peggy was certain that the scepticism on her face was so blindingly apparent it would have been visible from space.

Alistair nodded. 'When nobody came in over the weekend, I was worried that they might have finally called off the play. I couldn't bear the thought of that. Not this play again, surely. I went to find Jock; to confront him about what he was doing, and why he wanted to drive people away.'

'And what happened?'

'It's not very easy to have a conversation with Jock,' Alistair replied carefully. 'It's more about an overall feeling than anything else. Honestly, Miss Peggy, until everyone arrived here the other day, Jock has been barely more than a whisper. Still here, still *terrifying*, but people don't think about him like they used to.'

This tallied with Peggy's own working theory that ghosts faded over time as history forgot them and nobody remained to keep their spirits in mind, but based on her own experiences with Jock that week, she was nowhere near comfortable enough to come to the same conclusion as Alistair. 'What did Jock say when you asked him?'

'He couldn't answer me,' Alistair replied with a shrug. 'I remember a time when he could almost *burn* with his fury, but I could barely feel anything from him. Then…'

The sound of a squeaking door hinge, followed by footsteps rendered almost entirely soundless by the blood-red carpet, caught Peggy's attention and she glanced over Alistair's shoulder in trepidation.

'There you are!' Andrew announced as though Peggy had been deliberately hiding from him. He paused, shrinking back slightly. 'Are we alone?'

Peggy shook her head and gestured to her right as politely as possible. 'Alistair's here.'

Andrew's eyes narrowed. 'Right, well is there any chance you could ask Alistair how come he's always here, yet he somehow hasn't seen whoever it is sneaking around the theatre causing trouble?'

Peggy bristled. This was the first time they'd spoken since Gatley, and it was as though the intervening forty-eight hours had robbed them of their sense of mutual understanding. This felt like the conversations they'd had back when they'd first met; back when Andrew hadn't believed a word that Peggy had said. 'Well, I'm sure that Alistair has told us everything he knows. Right, Alistair?'

Alistair grimaced.

'What?' Andrew asked sharply when Peggy's face fell.

Peggy ignored him and focused on Alistair instead. 'What is it? What's happened?'

'I *may* have seen someone hanging around near the director's office yesterday morning,' Alistair explained quietly. 'And she was here a couple of times last week as well. Once, was that first day they arrived for rehearsals, that same afternoon the girl playing Isabella's dress was damaged. I saw her go into the dressing room.'

'Alistair!' Peggy shook her head in disappointment. Andrew was going to be insufferable now. 'Did you follow her? Did you recognise her?'

Alistair shook his head. 'I'm not like Miss Marnie. I find it easier to move around when *you* are here, but I can't just follow people at will most of the time.'

Peggy groaned loudly.

'What?' Andrew asked again, approaching Peggy cautiously.

Peggy held up her hand and focused on Alistair. 'What were you trying to tell me earlier?'

Alistair turned his face away and closed his eyes. 'The light switch yesterday.'

'What about it?'

'It was my fault.' Alistair sighed again.

'How?' Peggy asked impatiently.

'I'm certain that I goaded Jock into it,' Alistair admitted, shamefaced. 'I was so angry that he had driven people away from the theatre again that I called him all sorts of names, Miss Peggy – a good number I could not repeat in polite company, such as yours. I was just so angry at the idea of being alone again.

'He said nothing in reply to my taunts, but then yesterday he recreated that fateful moment. It was to unsettle *me* more than anyone else, I'm sure of it.

'I'm so sorry, Miss Peggy,' Alistair concluded, head bowed. 'It's just that I've really had nobody to talk to in such a long, long time, and I thought that if you knew that Jock wasn't really much of a threat these days, and that it really was just a person causing all of the real trouble that you would have no reason to come back to speak to me.'

'Oh, Alistair,' Peggy said, torn between sadness and frustration,

'I understand, I really do, but you still should have told us about all of that. I would have come back anyway.'

Andrew had narrowed his eyes so much he was almost squinting. 'Peggy, seriously, what is going on?'

Peggy pressed her fingertips to her forehead. There was absolutely no way that what she was about to say was going to be taken well.

'Alistair says that he's seen a woman acting suspiciously in the theatre over the past week,' Peggy explained, and the words left a bad taste in her mouth as she watched outrage bloom in Andrew's expression. 'One time definitely lines up with when Lavinia's dress was damaged, and the same woman was here again yesterday.'

'And why didn't we know this before now?' Andrew's agitation was clear.

Peggy hesitated. She wasn't sure how to express what Alistair had said in a way that would keep her own name out of it.

Andrew was having none of her silence. 'Peggy! Why didn't we know that?'

Peggy braced for impact.

'Because Alistair was concerned that I might not come back if we knew that there wasn't actually any real ghostly involvement to be concerned about,' Peggy said as evenly as she could when she felt slightly mortified about the explanation. 'Also, you were wrong about the light switch – it *was* Jock, but-'

Andrew's eyes widened. '*What?*'

'Sir!'

Peggy and Andrew both jumped at Lloyd's shout.

'Busy right now, Lloyd,' Andrew replied tightly, keeping his attention on Peggy.

'Right,' Lloyd replied slowly, and Peggy could hear him tapping a pencil impatiently against his notepad. 'It's just that the boss wants to see you about something.'

Andrew sighed loudly and ran one hand through his hair. 'Right, of course, obviously Higson needs my opinion on something. Not like he's in charge, is it?'

'Er…' Lloyd faltered. 'Okay. Do you want me to tell him that's what you said?'

Andrew groaned loudly. 'No, Lloyd, *no*. Fine, I'm coming down, alright?'

Peggy glanced at Alistair who, by that point, looked terribly ashamed.

'Stay here and find out if there's anything else you've missed,' Andrew added irritably to Peggy, not bothering to make even the vaguest attempt to include Alistair in his conversation. 'And get a description of the woman he's seen, before someone actually gets hurt while you're too distracted to do your job properly.'

Peggy felt like she'd been slapped, and the blood rushed to her cheeks in a manifestation of the mere idea. So, Andrew *did* know what had happened the day before then. 'That's not fair!'

'Isn't it?' Andrew snapped, shaking his head. 'Fix this now, Peggy.'

Lloyd shot Peggy a sympathetic glance as Andrew barrelled past him, which did nothing to make Peggy feel any better.

Andrew was correct that Peggy was the only one who could speak to Alistair, so the buck stopped with her in terms of getting answers to important questions, but for him to condense the situation with her mother and Edgar - not to mention her preoccupation with Andrew's own safety - down to 'a distraction', was uncalled for, and left Peggy feeling angrier with Andrew than she had in a very long time.

Peggy took a deep breath to compose herself, only to find that Alistair had disappeared.

'Brilliant,' Peggy muttered to herself darkly as she ran her hands over her burning face. 'Just absolutely bloody brilliant.'

There was only one way to fix all of this, and that was to track

Alistair down and make sure that he didn't just pop off somewhere else when the questions got tough; Marnie was just going to have to help with that, whether she liked it or not. Peggy thought that Marnie would probably be pleased to know that she'd been at least partially correct about Alistair's less-than-honest storytelling, and that would go a long way to convincing her to help.

'Peggy!'

'Jesus Christ!' Peggy screeched to a halt in alarm when Marnie appeared only a few steps in front of her. 'Marnie! You're not supposed to sneak up on me like that!'

'I know, but I think I know what's going on, and I need you to come quickly!' Marnie said, grabbing Peggy's wrist and pulling her along the corridor.

'Marnie, slow down!' Peggy cried as they practically ran down the stairs to the foyer. 'Where are we going?'

Marnie stopped suddenly and Peggy only just managed to avoid crashing into her back when Marnie released her arm.

'We're catching the villain in the act!' Marnie hissed. 'Now, keep your voice down or you'll ruin the big reveal.'

'What are you talking about?' Peggy asked in disbelief. '*Who* are we catching?'

'Lavinia,' Marnie replied, voice cold. 'I was in her dressing room having a little snoop around in her handbag an-'

'Marnie! Andrew will fly off the handle entirely if he finds out you did that!'

Marnie rolled her eyes. 'Andrew getting cranky about something? What a novelty that would be.'

Peggy conceded that Marnie might actually have a point with that, but it still didn't mean that she was ready to jump in and start condoning Marnie's personal interpretation of 'investigating', not when she was fairly sure that Marnie had picked Lavinia's dressing room to rifle through entirely because she just didn't like her.

'She's got black lipstick in her dressing room,' Marnie said, holding her hands out in conclusion. 'Just sitting there, waiting to be used.'

'Okay, well, she is an actress, Marnie, so she's probably got loads of stage makeup in there,' Peggy replied firmly. 'What's that got to do with anything?'

Marnie scrunched up her face. 'Are you being serious right now? She's obviously pushing the whole 'curse' thing to get attention! She's the first to say that ghosts aren't real, yet she's the only one who's really seen a ghostly figure here; she's the only one who's *apparently* been locked in a room by an unidentified man; she's the one who's taken it upon herself to distract the detective investigating the case; oh, *and* she's also the one wh-'

'Yes, I get your point,' Peggy snapped crossly.

'*Well*?' Marnie frowned.

'Well, what?'

'Do you want me to go back in there and see if I'm right or not? I won't do it if you really don't want me to, but this could be the only chance we get. She went up there a couple of minutes ago, so I'd say we're already running out of time.'

Peggy sighed. She had a bad feeling about all of this, but then again, she'd had a bad feeling about all of this since she'd first set foot in the theatre. 'Fine, but you can't let her see you. You'd better be right about this, Marnie, because it'll be my head if you're wrong!'

Marnie nodded solemnly and pointed to the auditorium. 'Go find Inspector Joykill and I'll be right back.'

Peggy gave herself one solitary second after Marnie disappeared and then entered the auditorium.

Andrew was standing near the door, intently looking at a piece of paper Jen was holding.

'Can I have a word?' Peggy asked. She wasn't going to say please.

Andrew looked at his watch. 'I only left three minutes ago. Has he told you something useful?'

'No,' Peggy replied. 'Actually, this is about something else.'

'Peggy, we need to find out abou-'

'Andrew, would you just *shut up* for one second, and actually listen to me?' Peggy clenched her fists at her sides. 'I am trying to tell you something important!'

Jen and Andrew glanced at each other, and it would be hard to say which of them looked more surprised at Peggy's outburst.

'Go on then,' Andrew said eventually, suitably reprimanded.

'Right, okay, the thing is, Ma-'

The doors to the auditorium burst open and Peggy whirled around in surprise to find Marnie running towards her again.

'I was right!' Marnie said, grinning triumphantly. 'She's on her way down now. I'd give it five seconds before the screaming starts.'

'What are you talking about?' Andrew asked, looking between Marnie and Peggy in bewilderment.

True to Marnie's estimate, only a moment later Lavinia's piercing scream sounded from somewhere behind the stage before she burst out from the wings with the delicately draped fabric of her costume whipping around her.

Andrew and Jen were half-way to the stage before Peggy had even realised they'd moved, and she raced after them with Marnie on her heels.

Three rows from the front, they passed Higson calmly sitting in the very middle seat, looking for all the world as though he couldn't see or hear the hysterical woman standing centre stage.

'Lavinia!' Cohen was nearly shouting himself as he tried to pry the young woman's hands from her face. 'Lavinia, what's happened?'

Lavinia let out a plaintive wail. 'I'm going to die, aren't I?'

'Nobody's going to die,' Andrew said firmly.

Lavinia quickly turned from Cohen and reached out with another whine of distress; it was clear that Andrew had been her intended target, but her stumble forwards coincided with Lloyd running onto the stage, and so it was the youngest member of the Ballroom team who found himself with his arms full of distressed actress.

The rest of the cast made no move to comfort Lavinia but looked around uneasily. Not for the first time, Peggy wondered how a group of people who cared so little for each other could stand to work together on such a small production.

'Crocodile tears,' Marnie muttered darkly from where she and Peggy stood in the wings.

'I was wrong,' Lavinia said, sniffling delicately as she untangled herself from Lloyd. 'I was wrong about everything! The play is really cursed.'

'What do you mean?' Lloyd asked, eyes wide in wonder.

'There's a message on the mirror in my dressing room,' Lavinia explained, voice trembling. 'Just like what happened to that poor man. Oh, God!'

'Lloyd, stay here with Miss Heathcote and everybody else,' Andrew ordered calmly. 'Jen, with me.'

'Marnie, did you actually see her writing on the mirror?' Peggy asked quietly. 'Are you completely sure that's what happened?'

'I swear,' Marnie said seriously. 'Peggy, I swear on Rex's life.'

Peggy couldn't ask for more than that. She grasped for Andrew's sleeve as he made his way past her.

'Peggy, I need to get up to that dressing room!'

'I know,' Peggy said, releasing her grip. 'But can you just promise you'll listen to me on the way?'

'I'll stay here in case anyone else shows up,' Marnie interjected, gently pushing Peggy in the direction of the staircase.

'Are you alright, Peggy?' Jen asked quietly as the three of them ascended the first set of stairs.

'Fine, Jen, thanks,' Peggy replied, keeping her head down. She had neither the time nor inclination to talk about the events of the previous morning just then, and she had no intention of making a big show of asking Jen for the ring back yet, knowing that Andrew, in the foul mood he seemed to be in, would only label her a drama queen.

'Well, what did you want to tell me?' Andrew paused at the foot of the second staircase.

'Marnie was suspicious about something she found in Lavinia's dressing room earlier,' Peggy said as confidently as she could manage.

Andre's eyebrows shot up. 'Why was Marnie in Lavinia's dressing room?'

Peggy ignored him. 'She found some black lipstick.'

'And?' Andrew folded his arms. 'Surely she's got heaps of makeup in there.'

'Right, but it's *black* lipstick, Andrew,' Peggy continued. 'Just like with the message to Peter McClellan before he died. Look, the thing is, Marnie thought that Lavinia might be planning to write a message herself.'

'*What?*'

'Peggy, why did Marnie think that?' Jen asked calmly, in direct counterpoint to Andrew's obvious fury.

'Marnie pointed out that Lavinia is the only one who's actively stated multiple times that she doesn't believe in ghosts, or in the curse-'

'Because there is no curse!' Andrew threw up his hands in frustration. 'There's *something* playing party tricks, granted, but an actual *someone* has been seen hanging around the theatre, which we would have known days ago if you'd actually questioned Alistair properly.'

'Hang on, what?' Jen shook her head. 'Who's been hanging around?'

Peggy sighed. 'This morning, Alistair admitted that he's seen someone a few times and–'

'And he might have told you earlier if you hadn't decided to be so friendly with him that he lied to get you to come back. It's called maintaining a professional distance, Peggy!'

Peggy reached her limit. 'It's called 'not being a complete dickhead', Andrew!'

'Okay, maybe we should all just calm down a little bit,' Jen suggested placatingly.

Peggy ignored the suggestion. 'Marnie saw Lavinia writing the message on her mirror.'

Andrew scoffed. 'Oh, right, and Marnie would have no reason to lie about that, would she?'

'What's that supposed to mean?' Peggy folded her arms.

Andrew shook his head. 'Forget it.'

Peggy followed him up the stairs towards Lavinia's dressing room. 'No, hang on, what did you mean by that?'

Andrew spun around and Peggy took a step backwards in surprise. 'Marnie's got it into her head that I've somehow slighted you.'

Peggy flinched. 'What?'

'Jesus, Peggy, I forgot we were all supposed to be going to dinner, alright?' Andrew snapped. 'I forgot. You didn't have to go gossiping to Marnie about it!'

'What the hell are you talking about?'

Jen coughed. 'Please, I really don't think this is the place.'

'No, this is the place,' Andrew replied, still glaring at Peggy. 'Jealousy doesn't suit you, Peggy.'

'Jealousy?' Peggy sagged at the accusation.

'Look, it is not my fault that your arsehole ex showed up here yesterday,' Andrew continued unabated, 'so I don't see how your brother can blame me for that as well, but I bet h–'

'My brother?' Peggy blinked in surprise. 'What's Charlie got to do with any of this?'

'Oh, and another thing!' Andrew barrelled on. 'Why the hell are you requesting files from Higson without asking me first?'

'Because Higson is the one with the file, not you,' Peggy retorted sharply. 'And you've barely been interested in a word I've said since we got here. Plus, I *was* coming to tell you about the file on Saturday, but you'd gone out for lunch!'

'I hadn't gone out for lunch!' Andrew cried in exasperation. 'I was questioning a suspect.'

Peggy threw up her hands. 'You are bloody *impossible!*'

'I'm impossible?' Andrew snapped. 'At least I've not been hiding from you!'

Peggy shook her head in confusion. 'What are you talking about now?'

Andrew snorted derisively. 'So, you didn't tell you butler to just get rid of me last night?'

Peggy flinched, taken aback. 'What?'

'I saw you, Peggy! So, what was it? Was I bringing down the tone of the place or s-'

'Sir!' Jen barked harshly, and both Peggy and Andrew looked over to her. 'Perhaps we should actually take a look in the dressing room?'

Andrew cleared his throat, turned on his heel and stomped up the corridor to where Lavinia's dressing room door had been left wide-open. He swore loudly and disappeared into the room.

Peggy took a second to compose herself. What the hell was Andrew on about? She'd gone out for dinner with Charlie the night before, and she'd certainly never asked Timothy to turn Andrew away, not last night, nor on any other occasion.

'Peggy?' Jen prompted quietly.

Peggy nodded, waving her hand. She had a job to do.

As Peggy reached the doorway, her mouth fell open in surprise.

Smudged, oily black words covered the mirror and the walls, letters running so closely together it was impossible to read them at first glance. She looked up in trepidation, and sure enough the smoke-tinged ceiling had scrawls of writing reaching from one end to the other.

'Jesus, what happened in here?' Jen squinted at the writing on the ceiling.

Andrew set his jaw as he looked back at Peggy. 'Are you still going to stand there and tell me that Lavinia did this?'

Peggy swallowed heavily. The ceiling was far higher than Lavinia could have reached; but it was also far higher than anyone else could have reached either. But why would Marnie have lied to her?

'No,' Peggy said. 'But I don't think your mystery suspect did it either.'

'*A false witness shall not be unpunished,*' Jen read slowly, deciphering the spidery scrawls, '*and he that speaketh lies shall perish.*'

Andrew opened Lavinia's handbag and rifled around for a second. 'Nothing. Not a single tube of any lipstick.'

Peggy ignored him and leaned in close to the mirror to read the same words Jen had just recited, repeated over and over again on the glass.

As she stared at her reflection behind the scribbled words, the letters in the centre shifted slightly, and she inhaled sharply in surprise as spidery cracks begin to slowly meander outwards towards the edges of the frame. Peggy shivered as the low-level whispering she'd first heard in the foyer earlier curled around the door and into the room, growing louder with every word.

'We need to get out of here,' she hissed quietly as she walked backwards, keeping her eyes on the mirror.

'Peggy, I'm not in the mood for dramatics,' Andrew scoffed, shaking his head.

One of the lightbulbs on the top edge of the framed mirror flared brightly for a moment before winking out with a quiet pop. It was followed in quick succession by two more.

Peggy watched as Andrew's eyes flickered from the lightbulbs to the mirror, and then finally back to her. '*Oh.*'

The door handle rattled ominously, and Peggy was starkly reminded of how she and Andrew had been trapped in the archive room. She quickly lurched across the room, pressing her back against the open door so that it couldn't suddenly close and lock the three of them inside.

'Out!' cried Peggy as she felt an unseen force pushing against the other side of the door. 'Now!'

Jen and Andrew didn't need telling again, and they hurried out of the room into the corridor.

Unexpectedly, the pressure on the door ceased entirely and Peggy stumbled backwards as the door swung inwards until the doorknob crashed loudly into the wall behind her.

Every bone in Peggy's body rattled with the force of impact and she had to shake her head to clear her thoughts.

Then, with sudden and terrifying clarity, Peggy knew exactly what was about to happen, and she almost tripped over her own feet in her haste to get out of the room and shut the door behind her.

Peggy was still pulling the door closed when the mirror exploded outwards, raining razor-sharp fragments all over the carpet and she yelped in surprise, tucking her face into her shoulder to avoid any of the stray shards that whipped through the narrowing gap before she managed to slam it shut.

'Peggy!' Andrew snapped harshly, though more through panic than anger, as he tugged her away from the door. 'Are you alright?'

Peggy nodded and drew her arm away quickly. 'I'm fine.'

Andrew didn't look entirely convinced, but he didn't press the issue.

'Jock?' Jen asked.

Peggy nodded. She winced as another loud thump sounded from inside Lavinia's dressing room.

'That's it,' Andrew said, with an underscore of finality as he ran his hands through his hair in frustration. 'I'm going to speak to Cohen.'

Jen nodded her agreement.

'What are you going to tell him?' Peggy asked.

'The truth,' Andrew replied. 'This play's cursed.'

SIXTEEN

'The show's still on.'

Andrew looked around in surprise as Cohen stepped into Lavinia's dressing room, glass crunching beneath his boots. 'I don't think I heard you correctly, Mr Cohen.'

'No, you heard me just fine,' Cohen huffed, staring at the scribbles on the wall. His face was drawn, and he looked like he'd aged twenty years in the time it had taken him to make his phone call to Caroline Winshire. 'Ms Winshire won't cancel.'

'Then refuse to do the play. Surely you and the theatre have a say in it.'

Cohen snorted in disbelief. 'Do you honestly think that's true?'

'Of course it is,' Andrew argued. 'Someone might die.'

'My career is on the line here, Inspector. I've already done everything you've asked me to: I've now cut nearly every single member of the crew, and I've let you all poke around wherever you've needed to, no matter how disruptive it's been for my actors. But we open tomorrow, and if I walk now, I'm finished.'

Andrew threw his hands up in irritation. 'Do you think everyone will be clamouring to work with you if one of your actors is murdered?'

Cohen dropped his head in his hands. 'People like Caroline Winshire can't be reasoned with. If I refuse to do the play, she'll just get someone to step in and make sure it goes ahead tomorrow anyway. I don't think you understand the sort of money and influence someone like that has.'

Andrew understood that rather too well, thanks all the same, but he couldn't tell Cohen that without giving away Peggy's secret.

'What if your cast just refused to go on?' Andrew tried, though he knew it was likely pointless.

Cohen gave Andrew a look of despair. 'Haven't you learned a damn thing about them this week? If the threat of ghosts and curses wasn't actually enough to drive them away before now…'

'*Someone could die,*' Andrew repeated through gritted teeth.

Cohen glowered. 'Then I suggest you hurry up and do your job, because if anything happens in this theatre tomorrow night, you'll be as much to blame as I will, if not more so.'

Cohen had left before Andrew found the wherewithal to even begin formulating a retort.

'He's right, *sir*,' Jen said quietly, standing up from where she'd been crouched and putting the department camera back into its case. She'd been snappish with him ever since they'd left Peggy in the auditorium and returned to the second floor. 'The theatre won't say 'no' to Peggy's mother, and she probably *could* just find another director at short notice if she wanted to.'

Andrew groaned loudly and pressed his fist to his forehead. 'What is wrong with all these bloody rich people? It's like they were all born without the ability to care about anyone else.'

Jen wrinkled her nose. 'Not all of them.'

Andrew knew what Jen was getting at, and, *no*, he didn't actually need reminding (yet again) that he'd behaved like an utter arse to Peggy (*yet again*).

Hang on. *Peggy.*

'Caroline Winshire doesn't own the theatre,' Andrew said slowly, as a path to a satisfactory conclusion began clearing its way in his head. 'Peggy's *father* does.'

'What's that got to do with anything?'

'Peggy could ask her father to get the production cancelled,' Andrew said, nodding as his idea sprouted legs. 'There's no love lost between him and his ex-wife, so he might actually go for the idea.'

Jen's expression did not suggest that this idea was as sound as Andrew thought it was. 'Sir, you can't possibly think that's a good idea.'

'Why not?'

Jen looked so genuinely taken aback that Andrew was forced to stop and consider if he really was just spouting nonsense.

'I'm fairly sure I don't need to answer that,' Jen eventually replied, somewhat pityingly.

Andrew made a sound of frustration. Jen was right. Of course Jen was right. He couldn't ask Peggy to lobby her father like that, and he knew what her answer would be if he asked her to. Peggy's involvement with the Ballroom lasted only as long as her father didn't know anything about it; Andrew couldn't afford to take the risk that Peggy would leave; he *wouldn't*. Higson would kill him, for a start, and only if Charlie didn't get there first. Plus, after that morning, he doubted that Peggy would agree to any of his ideas any time soon as it was.

'We should have just sent bloody Marnie to haunt Caroline Winshire into submission back at the beginning of all of this,' Andrew suggested weakly.

'If you don't think Marnie had already suggested that to Peggy - and had already been shot down - then I don't think you know either of them very well,' Jen sighed.

'I'm not so sure I do.' Andrew shrugged. It was an hour later, and he was still finding it difficult to even begin to understand why Peggy would have lied to him about something important just because she was pissed off with him on a personal level. He'd concluded that Marnie must have led her on, but even that didn't make much sense to him; Marnie had never been afraid to be completely straight with people, even if she knew her words wouldn't be appreciated. Marnie and Andrew had often been at odds in the past, but he'd really thought that she was done with meddling in anything Ballroom-related.

Still, it was impossible to argue with the evidence daubed on the walls around him – there was no way Lavinia could have done it, no matter what Peggy and Marnie had said.

'I'm sure there'll be an explanation for it,' Jen said, picking up her notepad from the dressing table. 'In fact, I thought I might go and ask Marnie for a statement about what she saw.'

'Why? We already know it will be complete bullshit.'

Jen looked annoyed again. 'Do you really believe that Miss Heathcote has had nothing to do with any of it?'

'Do you believe that she *has*?' Andrew countered.

Jen said nothing for a few moments, but then she sighed loudly. 'I think the person most likely to have warned Emma Allen away from the play with a threatening letter is Miss Heathcote, which I think we knew even before you visited the Allens; we already have multiple accounts of her criticising Emma's performance in early rehearsals, after all. It would be an easy leap to suggest that maybe she's been causing little bits of trouble here and there to gain some publicity for the play; I mean, she's made no secret of the fact that she wants to go to New York, has she? The same could be said about whoever might have ratted us out to Jimmy Haworth at the weekend.'

'We have no actual proof she was involved in any of that,' Andrew replied, folding his arms, acutely aware that Jen had a point; Christ, he'd come to the same conclusion himself on Saturday.

He didn't want it to be Lavinia behind everything, though, because if it was, he'd allowed himself to be led, and everything that had happened after that first day was therefore his fault. 'Jen, we can't just start accusing people without evidence. Everything needs to be investigated fully before we start pointing fingers.'

Jen nodded. 'Exactly. *Everything* needs to be investigated.'

Andrew grimaced when he heard heavy footsteps in the hallway. 'Any chance that's Cohen coming back to tell me that Caroline Winshire's had a change of heart?'

It wasn't Cohen; it was Higson, and he looked utterly livid.

'Well, Joyce, I hope you're abso-fucking-lutely delighted with yourself,' Higson snapped, his large frame blocking the doorway.

Andrew bristled. 'Why?'

'Because our esteemed blue-blooded colleague has decided that she's had enough of your crap to last a lifetime and has fucked off away from here for good, that's why!'

Jen gasped in surprise and Andrew stammered out a sound that might have been a question if it had contained any real syllables.

'Peggy's gone?' Jen asked in astonishment.

'Don't worry though, Joyce,' Higson sneered, 'she made sure to do your job for you before she left.'

Andrew still couldn't quite find the words to formulate a reply. *Peggy was gone? Permanently?*

'She spoke to that Alistair lad again before she went,' Higson continued, completely ignoring the fact that his DI was finding it impossible to clamber back towards operational from the state of utterly poleaxed he'd found himself in, 'and he's given her a description of the woman he's seen hanging round at various times over the past couple of weeks. She even did you a favour and wrote it down for you.'

Higson swung his meaty palm towards Andrew's chest, and Andrew had to quickly scrabble to recover from the force of the thump and then catch the paper before it fluttered to the floor.

Andrew read Peggy's neat, loopy handwriting quickly and almost-immediately swore under his breath.

'Problem?' Higson asked, producing a cigarette from his pocket and lighting it.

'I think I know who this is,' Andrew replied, pointing at the paper. He then pinched the bridge of his nose. 'I think it might be Emma Allen's sister. I spoke to her on Saturday; they work together in the family bakery in Chorlton. Sir, when you say Peggy's *left*, what do you mean?'

'I didn't say *left*,' Higson snarled, a swirl of smoke rising to unite with the nicotine-stained ceiling tiles. 'I said she'd fucked off away from here. And I meant just that.'

Andrew tried to work out what the difference was.

'Right,' Higson added, pointing at Andrew, 'you can speak to Parker and send him out to see this woman in Chorlton. Or send Jen if he takes too much longer on his coffee date.'

'I can go,' Andrew offered.

'You will do no such fucking thing, sunshine,' Higson barked. 'You're going to go and interview every single person in this theatre again, and then again, and *again*, until you get something useful; and don't piss off Driscoll, because if you do, we'll lose the last chance we've got of knowing what the fuck's going on with things we were relying on Her Majesty to see.'

Andrew twitched. 'Wait, Marnie's still here?'

'She is,' Higson confirmed. 'I think she's waiting for Lloyd to bring the blonde one back from getting a cup of coffee – she apparently needed to go out for a fancy one to *calm her down*. Driscoll wants a word with her.'

'You're going to let Marnie speak to a suspect?' Andrew asked, blinking rapidly. Once his initial disbelief that the Ballroom actually existed had passed, he'd had to very quickly come to terms with the fact that the general workings of things on Tib Street were at odds with usual police procedure, but this seemed a step too far, even for Higson.

'Oh, hang on, she's a suspect again now, is she?' Higson rubbed his nose. 'You had her as a victim an hour ago. No wonder you were fast-tracked to CID with reliable, unwavering instincts like that, Joyce. How you ever expect us plebs to keep up, I'll never know.'

Jesus, Andrew had a headache.

Jen shuffled past, throwing the strap of the camera bag over her shoulder. 'I want to ask Marnie a couple of things about what she saw up here earlier.'

'Now that's a good idea,' Higson said, letting Jen pass. 'Nobody's told her that her version of things is up for debate, by the by. And nobody *will* tell her that until we've also got a proper statement from Elizabeth Taylor downstairs.'

'Got it, sir.' Jen nodded firmly and left.

'You think Marnie's telling the truth? That Lavinia did this?' Andrew asked askance, gesturing to the room around them. 'Even when it's obvious that there's no way that this is the work of a single person in five minutes?'

'The only thing that's obvious is that you're not doing your fucking job properly. Did your fancy courses in Bramshill tell you that you were only supposed to get statements from *some* of the witnesses? Or is that some daft conclusion you've come to yourself?' Higson shook his head and blew a ring of smoke at Andrew. 'Did you hit your head when you landed in the canal last week, or something? You haven't argued with *Miss Jones* like that since all that business with that arsehole Hughes. So, what is it? Trouble in paradise?'

'Trouble...?' Andrew choked on his own surprise. '*No!* There's no trouble. I mean, there's no paradise. Oh, for fuck's sake, you know what I mean.'

Higson smirked as though it had only ever been his intention to make Andrew squirm. 'No, I expect you'd be a lot easier to put up with if that were the case.'

Andrew closed his eyes and reminded himself that this man was his boss.

'Get your utterly useless arse downstairs, Joyce,' Higson growled as he backed away from the door. 'Now.'

He knew it was immature, but Andrew couldn't stop himself from pulling a face at Higson's retreating form. He wasn't however, feeling quite immature enough to just stay in the dressing room and sulk.

He'd only just opened the door to the auditorium when he

saw Cohen practically launch himself across the stage and start yelling at Teddy.

'Do the line again or get off my stage!' Cohen shouted, towering over the actor in question.

Teddy, because he apparently didn't possess a shred of self-preservation, only raised his chin defiantly. 'There was nothing wrong with the line.'

'You're standing ten feet from the goddamn light switch!' Cohen threw his hands up. 'The audience will think Sebastian's developed fucking *telekinesis* if you manage to turn the light on without actually touching it!'

'I'm not touching that thing until someone with a bloody degree in electrical engineering tells me that it's safe!'

Cohen had turned puce in rage. 'Light switch, Teddy, or I swear to God that I'll get your standby here in under an hour. Same goes for the rest of you!'

Teddy stared back for a long moment, but then took a step back and returned to where Andrew knew was his marker for the beginning of the scene. Lavinia was nowhere to be seen.

'The show must go on,' Andrew muttered under his breath as he made his way to where Jen was talking quietly with Marnie in the stalls.

'And I came straight down to tell Peggy that I was right,' Marnie said as Andrew approached. 'So, what now? Are you going to arrest the smarmy little cow?'

'Marnie!' Jen admonished firmly. 'That's not appropriate.'

'Oh, whatever,' Marnie scoffed, 'as if she cares what anybody thinks of her. Except her adoring public, and Andrew, *obviously*.'

'Um,' replied Jen, catching Andrew's eye.

'What?' Marnie asked, and then turned her head and saw Andrew glaring daggers at her. 'Oh, come on, you're not going to try and deny that, are you? She's been following you around with heart eyes all week.'

Andrew scowled. 'That's enough. Now, if you've given Jen your statement, maybe you could go and do something useful.'

Marnie didn't rise to the bait, and instead just rolled her eyes. 'Oh, I will. I just need to find Peggy first. Where is she?'

Oh.

'She left a little while ago,' Jen replied carefully, and from the look she was shooting him, Andrew wondered if he was silently being told to scarper as quickly as he could.

Marnie looked understandably confused. 'She didn't say anything to me. Why'd she leave?'

'Um,' Jen said again and looked to Andrew for assistance.

It couldn't be good that *Jen* was at a loss in looking for the least-terrible way to say that Andrew had called Marnie a liar and then accused Peggy of being both distracted and *jealous,* of all things.

Marnie narrowed her eyes at Andrew. 'What did you do?'

'What makes you think *I* did anything?' Andrew almost cringed at the petulant sound that came out of his own mouth.

Marnie opened her mouth to respond but was cut off by Higson loudly calling her name.

Andrew nearly sighed in relief.

'Keep it down!' Cohen barked from the stage.

Higson held up his hands in a vague and insincere suggestion of apology and then turned his attention to Marnie.

'Miss Driscoll, as much as I would absolutely love to hear whatever bombardment of creative insults you're inventing for Joyce right now, I need you to come with me.' Higson pointed his thumb over his shoulder.

'Me?' Marnie asked in genuine surprise.

'*Her?*' Andrew's own question rooted more in sheer horror.

'Oh, sorry, did one of the rest of you die while I was out of the room?' Higson looked around, unimpressed. 'If not, then nobody else is going to be much use to me. Except for Swan, obviously, but she's not here right now is she, *Joyce?*'

Andrew averted his gaze, suitably chastised.

'Has something happened?' Marnie asked.

Higson's lips turned down in distaste. 'I've just been followed from the stage door.'

'Who by, sir?' Jen asked, alarmed.

'I'm afraid I can't tell you that, on account of the fact that I couldn't see them. Which is where Miss Driscoll fits in.'

Andrew frowned. 'Hang on, if you can't see anyone, how do you know you were followed?'

'Because not all of us need a full haunted house routine to know that we're not quite alone, alright?' Higson snapped. 'And shouldn't you be off interviewing someone right now?'

Higson turned on his heel and strode off with Marnie trotting along behind him a moment later.

'Do you think we should follow them?' Jen asked, nodding towards the foyer.

'And do what? If Higson thinks he's being stalked by an invisible man, how are we going to help?'

There was the sound of brief commotion, and they both looked up in apprehension to see Lavinia being led onto the stage by Lloyd.

'And you couldn't possibly have waited until I'd finished?' Marion waved her arm crossly in Lavinia's direction. 'You're not even in this bloody scene yet!'

'Oh, I'm actually feeling much better now!' Lavinia snapped derisively. 'Thank you *so much* for asking, Marion.'

'I couldn't give a toss how you feel, darling,' Marion retorted. 'Now get off the stage.'

'Marion, please,' Cohen implored.

Lloyd began a slow side-step towards the wings.

'*Marion*, please?' Marion snorted. 'Right, because I'm the one being a disruptive little madam. *Again!*'

Cohen turned towards Lavinia. 'Lavinia, maybe you c-'

'Disruptive little madam?' Lavinia shrieked, ignoring the director entirely. 'How dare you! I could have been *killed* this morning!'

'Chance would be a fine thing,' Teddy added. He then looked over at Andrew and Jen and grinned. 'Obviously, I'm only kidding. Gallows humour!'

Ben rolled his eyes and walked off the stage without saying a word. Vic threw up her hands and hastily followed him, and Lloyd took it as his opportunity for escape.

'Maybe we *should* go after Higson,' Andrew suggested quietly to Jen as the argument in Lady Bancroft's drawing room intensified. 'You know, just in case.'

Jen was heading for the doors before Andrew had finished speaking.

'I can't wait to get out of this place,' Jen said with a loud sigh as they crossed the foyer.

It wasn't like Jen to complain about a case, so Andrew told her as much.

Jen smiled wearily. 'Peggy said something like that to me yesterday. I just don't like this place; it feels claustrophobic. And the cast…'

Andrew gestured for her to carry on when she trailed off with a shrug. 'Go on, don't stop there.'

'They're just so entitled about everything,' Jen replied eventually. 'Well, except maybe Ben, who actually seems alright. But it's not the money thing, or the privilege thing by itself; it's the way that they're all just so bloody convinced that they're special. Take Lavinia for instance. Is she really a better actress than Emma Allen?'

Andrew shrugged. 'I've no idea.'

'Exactly! And we'll never know. Nobody who comes to see this play will ever know what it would be like to see Emma play Isabella. They won't know whether a girl who works in a bakery is any better at reciting someone else's words than a girl who was born with a silver spoon in her mouth, will they?'

It wasn't like Jen to get quite so impassioned about an opinion on a case, and it made Andrew wonder what was hiding underneath her words. Jen got on with Peggy and Charlie like a house on fire, so it couldn't just be the rich thing that was bothering her. Even though he'd worked with her for nearly a year, and socialised with her too, Andrew still didn't know quite where she became more *Jen* than DS Cusack.

Andrew didn't get to ask her just then, though, as suddenly there was a familiar, shrill scream from somewhere upstairs.

'That was Marnie,' Jen murmured, and they both bounded up the stairs together, barely a hair's breadth between them in the narrow space.

When they hit the first-floor corridor, through silent agreement they split up; Jen headed towards Cohen's office and the staircase that led down to the stage door, and Andrew moved quickly towards the row of dressing rooms used by everyone except Lavinia.

'Marnie!' Jen yelped in surprise.

Andrew turned just in time to see Marnie running up the staircase from the stage door. Jen reached out and grabbed her arm, instantly halting her panicked run.

'Marnie, what happened? Where's DCI Higson?' Jen asked. On the surface she sounded entirely calm, but Andrew could see the way her eyes were quickly trying to unravel Marnie's expression and work out what they were dealing with.

'He's outside,' Marnie hiccupped.

'Outside? Why?' Andrew asked, striding over to them.

'We'd just gone down the stairs, and Higson wanted to take a peek out in the alleyway, just to make sure that there was nobody hanging around,' Marnie explained quickly. 'He told me to go and have a look in Cohen's office and the dressing rooms, just in case I could see anything odd. I'd just got back up here when the door to outside slammed. I ran down the stairs to let Higson back in, but I couldn't open the door.'

That sounded awfully familiar to Andrew.

'And so, I was just about to come and find you both when this horrible *thing* appeared next to me.' Marnie swallowed heavily. 'It was like people said. It was like a man, but not really. Just shadows, and anger, and *death*.'

Andrew shivered. 'Right, I'm going to go and check that Higson's alright. You two get back downstairs, because if there is something lurking, you can bet it's probably heading for the stage now that we're all up here.'

'Lloyd's downstairs,' Jen said. Then, when she saw Andrew's expression, added, 'Yeah, okay, I see your point.'

'Maybe I should stay here, just in case,' Marnie suggested to Andrew. 'I'll be in so much trouble with Peggy if you get killed by a ghost.'

'Marnie, go with Jen,' Andrew replied firmly. 'You'll b-'

Andrew was cut off violently as something crashed into him and he stumbled backwards, arms flailing as his hands tried to find purchase on anything they could reach.

Marnie and Jen shouted in surprise, but Andrew couldn't hear them over the pounding of his own heartbeat.

Andrew had barely managed to let out a gasp of alarm before the force hit him again, throwing him off balance as the back of his shoe slipped over the edge of the top step. He tilted backwards dangerously, wavering for a moment before the momentum of the blow sent him tumbling.

Instinctively he threw his hands up over his head protectively, and managed to have one final thought before his shoulder hit the staircase:

This is going to really bloody hurt.

SEVENTEEN

'Margaret, darling, what *are* you doing?'

Peggy cracked open one eye to find Aunt Emmeline peering down at her as though she'd sprouted an extra head.

'And in here of all places!' Emmeline added disapprovingly, glancing around as though the surroundings had made it their personal business to offend her.

'*Here of all places*' was the rusting, skeletal remains of the Victorian glasshouse that had once dominated Butterton House's south lawn and, really, Peggy would have to admit that Emmeline did have rather a valid point. The few panes of glass that remained uncertainly tethered to the frame were liable to hurl themselves to their demise at any moment if given half the chance, and therefore it perhaps wasn't particularly wise to sit on the stone floor directly beneath the most dramatic curved ironwork in a moderate rainstorm.

'*Margaret!*'

Peggy opened both eyes, suppressing the frustrated groan that she knew would just irritate Emmeline, and gave her aunt her full attention. She even managed to paste on what she thought was likely a fairly convincing smile. 'I'm fine, Aunt Em.'

Emmeline had an astounding talent for conveying a whole host of judgemental retorts by simply raising one eyebrow, so when the second eyebrow raised ever so slightly after the first, Peggy knew that she was in real trouble.

'Alright, I'm not *fine*,' Peggy replied eventually, drawing her knees up to her chin. 'I am *alright* though. I promise.'

Emmeline sighed loudly, and then very slowly lowered herself down until she was sitting opposite Peggy.

'Oh, don't look so terribly surprised, dear,' Emmeline huffed when Peggy stared at her in amazement. 'I have sat on a floor before, you know.'

Peggy thought it was probably polite not to point out that the last time Emmeline had rested her backside on anything even remotely floor-like it was when one of the Georges was on the throne (and not the most recent one, mind, nor even the one before him).

'What's happened?' Emmeline asked gently. 'You've been so unhappy lately. You know I don't like seeing you like this.'

Peggy had a nicely abridged version of the week's events ready, but when she began speaking, what came out instead was the entire sorry story.

By the time Peggy had finished speaking, Emmeline had developed a pinched expression around her eyes, and her lips had tightened into a moue of displeasure that always accompanied any story involving Caroline and/or Edgar.

However, when she finally responded, Peggy was surprised that it was about neither of those things.

'Margaret, how could you have gone into that house knowing how dangerous it could have been?' Emmeline was obviously furious.

'What else could I have done? I had to try and help. I think it all might be my fault anyway.'

'How could it possibly be your fault?'

Peggy looked up at the sky. She was unreasonably hoping for some sort of divine inspiration to help her answer the very question she'd been grappling with since Andrew had first called her about what he'd assumed had been Rob, but all she got was the unpleasant sensation of cold raindrops hitting her cheeks.

'Before he met me, Andrew didn't believe in ghosts at all,' Peggy explained eventually. 'The whole idea was inconceivable to him, and even *now* – after everything we've been through with Marnie, and everything that's happened since last summer – he's still pushing back against the idea in any way he can.'

'I fail to see how Andrew's inability to see what's right in front of him could in any way be blamed on you.' Emmeline shook her head.

'That's not what I meant.' Peggy exhaled loudly and ran a hand through her damp hair. 'I just wonder whether Andrew spent so long pushing against the idea that there could be anything beyond normal life, the *beyond* has been pushing back just as hard the whole time.

'So, what if Rob was so desperate to let his brother know that he was there, and that he'd been fighting against Andrew's scepticism since the day he died? Maybe when Andrew's doubt slipped a bit, it was enough to cause something like a crack, maybe; and that crack has only got wider since then. Does that even make sense?'

Emmeline was quiet for a long moment. 'It is an interesting theory; I'll give you that. Yet, even if all of that were true, it still doesn't make it your fault.'

'His mother – or whatever is left of his mother – wouldn't be tormenting him if he'd carried on never entertaining the idea that any of it could even be possible,' Peggy countered. 'If we'd never met, maybe this would never have happened.'

'Perhaps you're correct,' Emmeline said mildly. 'Though have you considered what else could have happened if you hadn't met? Marnie's murder would likely never have been solved, nor would any of those other cases you've helped with, and who knows where your detective would be. Even if I sometimes disapprove of how casually you throw yourself headfirst into all of this police business, I can see the good that you are doing; both for other people, and for yourself.'

Peggy pressed the heels of her hands into her eyes. 'But what if I'm just making it more dangerous? What if the belief people have in *me* is leaving them more open to a spirit that might want to do them harm?'

Emmeline sighed again. 'Margaret, I understand all of this as much as you do – which is to say, not very well at all – but I cann-'

'Oh my God, *there* you are!'

Both Peggy and Emmeline yelped in surprise when Marnie popped into existence right in front of them, looking panicked.

No, *absolutely not*. Peggy did *not* have the patience to deal with Marnie just then.

Peggy pushed herself to her feet immediately and made her way towards what had once been the doorway to the glasshouse.

'Peggy, hang on! Wait, *please*! I wasn't lying to you this morning!'

Peggy spun around and glared at Marnie. 'Really? Because I saw that dressing room, Marnie, and there's no way Lavinia did that to the room.'

'I know!' Marnie said holding her hands up. 'I know, Jen showed me. But I'll swear on anything worth swearing on that I saw her writing on the mirror herself!'

'Marnie, you t-'

'I *swear*, Peggy!' Marnie nodded seriously. 'Whatever happened *after* Lavinia left the room, I can't say, but she did exactly what I said she did.'

Peggy pursed her lips. 'None of it matters anyway, because Andrew doesn't believe a word of it. *And* more to the point, why the hell have both you and Charlie been gossiping about me?'

'What?' Marnie's face crumpled into confusion at the sudden change in topic. 'I haven't been gossiping about you!'

'Yes, you have!' Peggy shouted 'Yes, you bloody well have!'

Marnie flinched. 'I don't know what you're talking about.'

'Oh no, of course you don't,' Peggy snapped. 'So, you *didn't* tell Andrew that I was angry when he cancelled on his birthday dinner?'

'Well, you were angry,' Marnie replied firmly. 'He was being a dickhead, and I thought he needed to be told that. You're my friend, Peggy! I wasn't trying to gossip about you; I just wanted that idiot to know that he was on my hit list.'

'You shouldn't have said anything at all!' Peggy sighed in frustration. 'Look, can you just leave me alone for a bit? Please?'

Marnie's face fell. 'I'm sorry, Peggy.'

'Yeah,' Peggy muttered. 'Everyone's always sorry.'

Peggy shook her head and left the glasshouse. She'd only made it a few steps before something occurred to her, and she turned back towards the glasshouse, where Emmeline was speaking quietly to a very glum Marnie.

'Marnie?' Peggy called sharply.

'Yeah?' Marnie looked over hopefully.

'What was wrong? When you got here, you looked completely freaked out. Why?'

Marnie fidgeted slightly. 'Nothing. Nothing you need to worry about.'

Oh, give me strength, for crying out loud. Peggy sighed yet again. 'Marnie, *what?*'

'Um.' She nervously twirled the engagement ring around her a finger a couple of times. 'Right, it's just that Higson thought he was being followed by a ghost.'

'*Higson?* Why did he think that?' Peggy asked, utterly puzzled. Higson had never made any real suggestion that he was aware of anyone, or anything, he couldn't see.

'Not entirely sure about that,' Marnie replied warily, 'but he was right. I saw *him.*'

Peggy's eyes widened in apprehension; the look on Marnie's face was enough to tell her who she was talking about. 'You saw Jock?'

Marnie nodded, face still paler than usual. 'He's just like Alistair described him, Peggy. It was awful. I understand why someone like Peter McClellan might just drop dead from fright!'

'Is Higson alright?' Peggy asked, alarmed. 'Did something happen to him?'

Marnie grimaced. 'Higson's fine, but Jock *might* have pushed Andrew down a staircase.'

'What?' Peggy cried shrilly, lurching forwards without quite meaning to. 'Marnie, Jesus, you should have *led* with that!'

'Oh dear, oh dear,' Emmeline mumbled faintly, twisting her hands together. 'Is he alright?'

Marnie nodded and then looked Peggy dead in the eye. 'I'm not lying to you. He's a bit bruised but he's fine. And before you get any ideas, Higson doesn't want you to go back to the theatre, alright?'

Peggy felt sick. Admittedly, she was the one who'd left the theatre, despite Higson's objections, but now Andrew had been hurt, and for Higson to bar her from going back now felt li-

'Peggy, *stop!*' Marnie snapped, cutting Peggy's self-recriminations off immediately. 'I can practically hear you telling yourself off! Higson said I'm to tell you – and these are his words, not mine, alright? - that Inspector Smartarse will be busy interviewing everyone at the theatre for the next twenty-four hours, so he wants *you* to carry on looking into Alistair's death in case you find anything that might sort out this – and again, direct quote from Higson – 'steaming pile of utter bollocks'.'

'I can do that at the theatre!' Peggy protested.

'You don't need to be there. I'm going back now, and Higson said I can be there tomorrow too, just in case. I'm not allowed to talk to Andrew though, unless his life is in immediate danger.'

Peggy frowned. 'Why not?'

Marnie huffed loudly. 'Because after it was obvious that he wasn't dead, I found out that he'd told you I'd lied about Lavinia. I told him that he was an utter bastard, and I wouldn't hesitate to throw him down the stairs myself given half the chance.'

Emmeline made a sound that suggested she might be terribly

offended by the whole exchange, and Peggy understood why Higson so often said that Jen was the only adult amongst the lot of them.

'I think it's best if you do what Higson says this time, Peggy,' Marnie said seriously. 'Look, in the morning, why don't you go to the Ballroom, and I'll go to the theatre? That way, if anything happens, you'll only be up the road. Yeah?'

Peggy didn't see what else she could do but agree, no matter how little she liked the plan. 'Alright.'

Marnie nodded and then wrinkled her nose. 'And Peggy? I really *am* sorry about earlier, and for what I said to Andrew last week. It wasn't my place, and I should have just kept my mouth shut.'

Peggy shrugged tiredly. 'It's alright, Marnie.'

Marnie gave her a weak smile, and then her eyes narrowed. 'But Andrew's still on my shit list, and for his sake he better stay on the ground floor.'

Marnie disappeared before Peggy could craft a reply.

'*Jesus Christ*,' she muttered to herself.

'For once, Margaret, dear,' Emmeline said, patting her terribly great niece on the arm, 'I concur.'

* * *

'Thank you.' Andrew carefully accepted the cup of water being offered to him, hissing slightly as he lowered his arm again.

'You shouldn't be here, sir,' Jen said disapprovingly, but sat down next to him anyway. 'You hit your head hard enough that you should really see someone about it.'

'I've interviewed thirteen people,' Andrew replied, looking morosely at the very blank page of his notebook, and ignoring her concern entirely. 'I've got absolutely nothing that we didn't have before.'

Jen sighed and looked over towards the stage where they'd reached the final scene of what Andrew hoped might actually be the last run-through of the day. He really didn't understand why one dress rehearsal wasn't enough. 'Maybe I'll get something useful from Emma Allen's sister. We'll figure something out, I'm sure of it.'

'Hmm.'

'Have you taken a statement from Miss Heathcote yet?'

Andrew frowned. 'Didn't Lloyd do that earlier? When he took her out for that coffee.'

Jen made a face that Andrew didn't quite understand. 'No. Apparently he tried to take her statement, but then they somehow ended up talking about what music Lloyd likes listening to.'

Under normal circumstances, Andrew would feel the need to berate Lloyd for neglecting to do his job properly, but Andrew had experienced Lavinia's witchery when it came to steering the conversation away from any topic she didn't want to linger on.

'Have you read Marnie's statement?' Jen asked.

'Yes.' Andrew didn't particularly want to talk about Marnie after their confrontation earlier – he'd still been quite dazed after the fall, but he definitely remembered her yelling at him, and he thought she might have made a direct threat before Higson sent her on her way. 'She says she saw Lavinia writing totally different words than the ones scrawled all over the dressing room walls.'

'*Her feet go down to death; her steps lead straight to the grave,*' Jen quoted the passage from Proverbs that Marnie had sworn blind she'd seen Lavinia writing in lipstick. 'It doesn't quite fit the pattern of the others, does it?'

'What do you mean?'

'Well, when Alistair died, the note talked about the deceitfulness of the wicked, right? So, assuming Alistair wasn't the target, it suggests that the intended victim had been engaging in deception of some kind.'

'Right.' Andrew nodded slowly. 'Where are you going with this?'

Jen shuffled in her seat for a moment, gathering her thoughts. 'Well, victim number two – Henriette – the verse on the paper in her pocket suggested she had uttered lies; and as for Peter McClellan, I can't remember the exact words, but–'

'*He that gathereth treasures by a lying tongue shall stumble upon the shades of death,*' Andrew interjected. He knew that line well. His mother had been a big fan of wheeling it out whenever she thought either of her sons was attempting to mislead her. When it came to Agatha's favourite fire and brimstone warnings, Andrew was fairly certain *that* one came second only to the one she held so dear to her heart she'd hung a needlepoint of it on the stairs:

The Lord detests all the proud of heart. Be sure of this: They will not go unpunished.

Jen looked surprised. 'Yeah, that was it. So, don't you see, sir?'

Andrew scrunched his eyes shut, irritated by how his thoughts still felt too sluggish. *God*, he really hoped he wasn't concussed.

Jen took pity on him. 'It's always about liars.'

Even through the haze, Andrew could see that Jen was correct. He thought back to what Peggy had heard Jock screaming at her when they'd been locked in the archive room.

'Liars,' Andrew repeated slowly. *Bollocks.*

'What Marnie says she saw Lavinia writing makes no sense,' Jen continued. 'Plus, do you *really* think that Marnie is just walking around with the odd bible quote up her sleeve?'

No, Andrew did not think that. It was becoming abundantly clear to him that he might actually have been horribly, *horribly* wrong about everything.

'Maybe you should be the one to ask Miss Heathcote what was written on the mirror,' Jen said eventually, rising slowly to her feet. 'Nobody's been in that room since we left it earlier, so she either confirms that what we saw is what she saw too, *or* she has the same answer as Marnie. I know which one I suspect it will be, and I hope you do too.'

Jen picked up the camera bag from the floor and gave Andrew one last searching look. 'I'll call into the Allens on the way home and let you know what I find out in the morning. Take care of yourself, sir.'

Andrew wasn't sure how long he sat alone after Jen left, but her words lingered long after her footsteps had been swallowed up by the sounds of the rehearsal on stage.

I know which one I suspect it will be, and I hope you do too.

Admitting that he felt like a complete and utter idiot may have been the biggest understatement of his entire life. He was more than old enough to know that he couldn't always be right, even if he wished he could be. Whether his lack of focus and diligence had been the result of the stress and terror of his experiences at home didn't actually matter – he'd messed up, big time.

At what point in the preceding week had he stopped trusting his team, or Peggy implicitly? And more to the point, *why*?

If he'd been blessed with just a smidge more confidence in his self-awareness, perhaps he could have found his way to the conclusion that this week had shown him that he'd grown to rely on other people – in direct contravention of the way Agatha had raised him to be self-sufficient – and he'd reacted poorly in response to that realisation. He wasn't supposed to need anybody – he was supposed to be fine by himself.

Even ignoring his own stupidity for a minute, nothing about the case made any sense to him. He was almost a week in and, if he was completely honest, he was still floundering when it came to how on earth he could bring it all to a satisfactory conclusion. They'd been tasked with ensuring the safety of the cast, and concluding whether they were looking at any supernatural involvement in the previous deaths or not, and Andrew couldn't hand-on-heart say that he'd been successful in either endeavour.

If he had a hope in hell of untangling the mess that he'd got himself into, he was going to have to go right back to the beginning; right back to the two questions Peggy had posed when they'd been looking through the archives.

'Why this play?' and *'Why only here, in Manchester?'*

They were good questions - key questions – when, if you ignored the presence of passages from Proverbs at each scene, there didn't seem to be any cohesive link between all three previous deaths, nor with the possible demise of a current cast member.

The first death – Alistair's – remained unexplained. Due to the shoddy investigation at the time, beyond the vague suggestion that a teenaged theatre employee *might* have had something to do with it, they didn't actually have any real evidence to even begin to form a real conclusion. The fact that Alistair couldn't remember anything about his death hadn't been hugely surprising, but it didn't make it any less disappointing. Andrew was fairly certain that Alistair hadn't made any suggestion that Jock, or any other presumed spirit, played a part in his death, although he couldn't be one-hundred-percent certain without checking with Peggy, which was now an impossibility.

Then there was death number two: Henriette St. Clair at the Palace fifteen years after Alistair. It was the same play, but a different theatre. They had an eyewitness who'd confirmed that there was no ghostly involvement in Henriette falling down the stairs; instead, just someone who had heard the stories of the Shadow Man and taken to terrifying Henriette in the days leading up to her death. They had no idea *why* she'd been targeted, but they knew she'd been involved in Alistair's production of *Lady Bancroft*.

Finally, Peter McClellan in the seventies. They were back at the Court with that one, and Andrew had stacks of feverish reports from those who'd worked at the theatre at the time, all packed to the rafters with sightings of ghosts and ghouls, and not even the *hint* of a suggestion that there had been any human foul play that time around; just Peter McClellan's health problems exacerbated by a ghost he swore was terrorising him.

So, where did all that leave him when trying to work out what any of it meant for Cohen's production?

Nowhere.

Andrew sighed loudly in frustration.

'Are you alright?'

Andrew's head turned in surprise at the unexpected appearance of Lavinia, and he winced when the movement pulled at his tender shoulder. The stage was empty, so Andrew assumed that he'd missed Cohen winding up for the day.

She was no longer wearing her full Isabella costume, but her hair was still piled artfully on top of her head in a manner that Andrew couldn't quite believe could ever be structurally sound enough to survive a full performance.

He still couldn't understand how a person had the ability to just *sparkle*, but that was the only way he could explain Lavinia if pushed. In stark contrast to when he'd last seen her crying and shrieking in terror at Lloyd, she looked calm, composed, and entirely confident of her own place in the world. Andrew knew better than to assume that just because someone *looked* comfortable it didn't mean that they actually *were*, but no matter how hard he scrutinised her, he couldn't see anything of the troubled victim about Lavinia.

God, he really was an idiot, wasn't he? It was a genuine wonder that Marnie hadn't been the one to chuck him down the stairs after he'd dismissed her accusations that morning.

'Andrew?' Lavinia had obviously been expecting an answer,

and her expression had shifted towards something that might have even approached actual concern for a moment.

Andrew cleared his throat. 'I'm fine, Miss Heathcote, thank you.'

'We've been over this, *Andrew*. Just Lavinia is fine.' She laughed lightly, rolling her eyes. 'You don't have to be so professional all the time. We're friends now.'

No. No, they weren't friends. They weren't anything at all. They certainly weren't whatever the very specific emphasis she'd placed on '*friends*' had implied, nor would they ever be.

Lavinia, as always, took Andrew's silence as agreement and tilted her head coyly. 'I wish I didn't have to be the one to keep asking, but I was hoping you'd like to get dinner tonight, and then maybe tomorrow after the performance w-'

'Lavinia – Miss Heathcote – stop. No,' Andrew said, awkwardly rising to his feet. *Oh God, what was he supposed to do now?*

'No?' Lavinia repeated slowly as though she wasn't used to hearing such a word.

Andrew nodded, which he quickly realised might be misinterpreted as a mixed signal. '*No*. Thank you for the offer, but I'd like to ensure that things are kept strictly professional while I conclude the investigation.'

He could almost hear Peggy trying to contain an undignified snort at such a stilted delivery.

Lavinia frowned, but then almost immediately brightened. 'Oh, right, yes, of course. But the play is only on for a week, and I'll have some time before I go to New Y-'

'Miss Heathcote, can you tell me what was written on the mirror in your dressing room this morning?' Andrew forced himself not to fidget as he watched Lavinia's expression run through an indecipherable sequence of emotions.

'What?' Lavinia appeared completely flummoxed by the

sudden change in conversational direction.

Andrew squared his shoulders. 'This morning, you were very upset to find that a message had been left on your mirror. Could you confirm what that message was, please?'

Lavinia gave a brittle laugh. 'I already told you, and you've seen it anyway.'

Andrew shook his head. 'You didn't tell me anything. You haven't yet given your statement to Constable Parker, and as the lead detective on this case, I'd like to make sure that I'm in possession of all of the relevant facts.'

Peggy would have snorted at that too.

For a second or two, it looked like Lavinia might decline, but then she shrugged. She looked up to the ceiling, just as she had when she'd been trying to recall a line from the script. "Her feet go down to death', and then 'her steps lead straight to the grave'.'

Bugger. Andrew squeezed his eyes shut for a long second. Marnie had been telling the truth, which Andrew would have found out if he'd actually bothered to do his job properly. Christ, Higson was *right* - he was completely useless.

Now he knew that the woman in front of him had been lying to him, *and* that there really was a ghost at work. Not to mention the fact that there was also the possibility that Sue Allen was somehow involved in the entire mess.

'Andrew?' Lavinia looked only moments away from making a fuss about him.

'Right, okay, thank you, Miss Heathcote, that's been very informative.' Andrew reached for his jacket. He briefly considered attempting to pull it on, and then thought better of it as soon as he moved his right arm. 'I expect I'll have some follow up questions for you tomorrow.'

'You're leaving?'

'Rehearsal's over,' Andrew replied firmly. 'It's time I went.'

Lavinia's eyes narrowed, and Andrew realised that he

genuinely could not face yet another argument; there'd been far too many that day as it was, and he just wanted to eat some dinner, go to bed, and get through the next miserable twenty-four hours unscathed, so that he could eventually return to his awful, possessed house and suffer in relative peace.

Entirely alone.

Except for the ghosts, obviously.

The stark realisation of just how much of a shitshow his life had become was so utterly stunning in its clarity that Andrew almost burst out laughing. He managed to reign it in though.

'Why are you smiling?' Lavinia asked, folding her arms, as she finally bestowed Andrew with that same air of disdain she offered to others.

Ah, apparently, he hadn't reigned it in quite enough.

'If you'll excuse me, Miss Heathcote,' Andrew added as politely as he could, 'I really do need to be getting on, so if you'll please allow me to escort you to the front door, we can both get on with our evenings.'

He was briefly struck with the thought that his mother would approve of his manners.

Lavinia, however, didn't seem to appreciate it, if the pitch-black scowl she gave him was anything to go by. 'I'm perfectly capable of seeing myself out *without* your assistance, Detective Inspector Joyce.'

Andrew didn't doubt that for second.

He gave her a full minute to leave the theatre, and then slowly gathered his things and shuffled towards the foyer.

His shoulder hurt, his head hurt, and his ego had taken more than a light thrashing. He was also tired, hungry, and desperately in need of a good night's sleep. He chose not to dwell on the ever-growing list of people who were likely no longer speaking to him as he pushed the exit door open and stepped out into the early evening.

It had rained again, and the threat of another downpour hung heavy in the sky. Any brief hint of spring that had reared its head over the weekend, seemed to have been snuffed out again for the time being. Andrew shivered, and grumbled in equal parts pain and annoyance as he awkwardly tugged his jacket sleeves over his arms.

The St. Patrick's Day revellers didn't seem to be too concerned by the threat of drizzle, and a large group was already spilling out of the door of the pub across from the theatre despite the fact it hadn't yet hit six o'clock.

Knowing that there wasn't a chance he'd find anywhere for a peaceful pint (and that Jen would actually murder him is she found out that he'd gone out drinking alone with a head injury), Andrew set his mind to finding something to eat instead.

Thankfully, there was one place he knew he'd get a warm reception regardless of how busy it might be, and so Andrew turned up his collar against the wind and set off towards Cross Street.

When he pushed open the door to Bombay Palace five minutes later, Arun greeted him with his usual enthusiasm.

'Mr Joyce!' Arun beamed as he heartily shook Andrew's hand. 'I haven't seen you in weeks. Where've you been?'

'Work's been busy,' Andrew replied tiredly.

'Do you want a table? We're fully booked, but I'll sort you out.'

Andrew shook his head. 'Just takeaway tonight, thanks. Work's *still* busy.'

'Fair enough.' Arun looked towards the door and then back at Andrew. 'No Princess Peggy tonight?'

Andrew groaned internally. They *loved* Peggy at Bombay Palace, and Arun always failed to hide his disappointment when Andrew turned up alone. 'No, not tonight. Just me.'

Arun's cheer, as expected, deflated slightly. 'Oh, well. Do you just want your usual then?'

'I'll go to the bar and order, don't worry about it.'

'No, no, no, you stay there,' Arun replied, airily waving a hand. He squinted at Andrew over the top of his glasses. 'You actually look a bit peaky. Are you alright?'

Peaky didn't quite cover the dull pain that seemed to be radiating throughout his whole body, but Andrew wasn't going to share the ins-and-outs of his day with Arun. 'I'm fine. It's just been a long week. A *very* long week.'

'Sit down,' was all Arun said, before striding off towards the kitchen.

Andrew sat on the red velvet-upholstered bench positioned just inside the entrance with a deep sigh. The seats in the theatre hadn't been designed with long legs in mind, so Andrew gratefully took advantage of the space by stretching out as far as he could manage.

He tipped his head back and closed his eyes, thinking that he'd actually be quite happy to just go to sleep there; it was warm, smelled fantastic, and nobody in the building (living or dead) had ever tried to kill him – *perfect*.

Arun, however, did not feel the same.

'Mr Joyce!' he called, shaking Andrew's shoulder urgently. 'I have a party of twelve arriving in the next few minutes, and as much as I value your custom, I cannot have you snoring so loudly in my restaurant.'

'Shit, sorry.' Andrew rubbed his hands over his eyes and then slapped his palms against his cheeks a few times. 'Sorry, Arun. Really.'

'Don't worry, Mr Joyce.' Arun nodded as he held out a large bag of food. 'This will sort you right out. Now, I've popped some extra onion bhajis in there, just in case the princess comes over, alright?'

'She's not coming over,' Andrew said firmly, as he clambered inelegantly to his feet; possibly too firmly if the taken aback expression on Arun's face was anything to go by.

'Mr Joyce,' Arun hissed urgently, '*what have you done?*'

Jesus Christ, there was that bloody question again.

'Nothing!' Andrew replied, outraged at the implication, and also at himself for not being able to come up with a better response.

'Hmm,' Arun said as he released the bag handles into Andrew's grip. 'On your tab?'

Andrew shook his head grumpily. 'No, this one can go on Charlie's.'

'Tip?' Arun raised his eyebrows.

'Oh, a massive one,' Andrew replied, and he felt a bit better knowing that Charlie was going to pay for his dinner.

'Right you are,' Arun grinned. 'See you soon, Mr Joyce, and next time bring-'

'Peggy. Yeah, I know,' Andrew grumbled and slipped out through the doorway just as the large group Arun was expecting arrived outside.

It had, of course, starting raining again while he'd been in Bombay Palace, but despite the bone-tiredness tugging at his every step he managed to hurry just enough to make it back to the Ballroom without getting completely soaked through.

He had to put the bag of food down on the doorstep on Tib Street because he couldn't shoulder his way through the stiff door like he normally would.

'Bloody door,' Andrew grumbled as he eventually closed it behind him, scraping across the floor with a terrible grating sound. He still had no idea who actually owned the building they were in, and therefore still no idea of who would be in charge of maintenance, but he knew without a shadow of a doubt that Higson wouldn't even dream of attempting to fix any of the building's many problems.

He'd just about put his foot on the bottom step of the staircase when he paused, puzzlement settling silently over him; he could swear he could smell cigar smoke. No, that wasn't right; it wasn't cigar smoke, it was more familiar to him than that. It was very similar to the scent of pipe tobacco that had always clung to Grandpa Joyce's jumpers when Andrew had been a child. To be honest, if he hadn't seen his grandpa alive and well only the day before Andrew might have started to panic about what might be waiting for him at the top of the stairs. Two ghostly family members was already two too many for Andrew's sanity.

He inhaled again but he'd lost the scent between one breath and the next. He shook his head, reasoning that it was probably just Dolly smoking God-knows-what while the building was empty; he didn't find it difficult to imagine her rattling around the Ballroom, bleach bottle in one hand, pipe in the other.

Andrew closed his eyes and exhaled slowly. *Please*, he thought in the direction of any power that might listen, *please don't let Dolly be here*. He wasn't afraid to admit that the Ballroom's cleaning lady unsettled him as much as she always had, and if she was lurking somewhere in the building then Andrew was going to sleep in his car.

When he'd satisfied himself that he'd heard no hint of a rattling cough or a smoke-tinged cry of 'Pretty Boy!' he allowed himself to relax a little and continued on his way. The bulb in the light fitting suspended over the staircase - just like the front door - was no longer fit for purpose and Andrew ascended slowly, because ending up in a heap at the bottom of the stairs for the second time in a day would be more than a small step too far.

On the first-floor landing, Andrew had to stop again because the door to the closest archive room was open, and the light had been left switched on inside.

He peered around the door and saw the small stack of files carelessly piled in the centre. He knew Higson had been in and out of the room frequently over recent weeks, so he assumed that the DCI must have nipped in to grab something after he left the Court, but before he went out to – in his own special way with words – *'get suitably ratarsed in the name of my Irish ancestry'*. It wasn't like Higson to leave a door open like that, but Andrew supposed the lure of free-flowing Guinness at The Pelican was stronger than his instinct for nebulous bursts of order.

Andrew reached his hand into the room to switch off the light, and then grabbed the door handle. He automatically gestured towards the bottom of the door with his foot, ready to kick the doorstop out of the way, but looked down in surprise when the tip of his shoe met only air.

That was…odd. The floor to the archive room wasn't entirely level and because of that, the door would always swing closed without a prop; yet there it was, wide open and entirely prop-less.

Andrew tugged on the door handle and his brow furrow further when the door refused to budge.

'Oh, what now?' Andrew sighed in annoyance. Great, all he needed was another ill-fitting, sticky door to deal with. For a moment he thought wistfully of the plans that he'd once seen for the new and wonderfully modern building they were planning to build to house CID.

He pulled on the door handle again, but still it didn't move.

'For fuck's sake,' Andrew muttered darkly to himself, looping the handles of the bag of food over his left wrist so that he could use both hands to pull on the door.

His shoulder throbbed as he heaved the handle as hard as he could manage, letting out a little gasp of discomfort.

'Come on, you bloody stupid piece o-'

Andrew's words morphed into a loud yelp of surprise as the door gave way suddenly and he stumbled backwards as his fingers slipped off the handle. His left heel caught the instep of his right shoe, and his arms windmilled wildly to try and correct his balance.

Unfortunately, the dramatic thrashing didn't help enormously with his balance. He toppled to the floor with a grunt of pain, and the contents of the bag from Bombay Palace came tumbling out before Andrew could gather the wherewithal to try and halt the inexorable disaster.

The foil tray of butter chicken hit him square in the chest, and he flinched as the corner immediately crumpled, allowing hot, orange sauce to seep from beneath the cardboard lid onto his shirt and tie. The container plummeted to the floor, landing upside down as Andrew expelled a colourful cloud of expletives while he scrabbled to right the tray. His fingertips recoiled from the heat of the foil and by the time he'd flipped it over again, the lid had made a break for freedom and was sinking into a puddle of its own making.

Andrew looked at his hands in dismay, both now covered in an oily orange film that was dribbling down to his wrists and seeping into the cuffs of yet another ruined shirt.

Pilau rice covered Andrew's jacket, and even in the dim light of the landing he could see how far the jewel-like grains had bounced and scattered across the floorboards.

He put his elbows down next to him to help push himself back to a sitting position and winced as he heard the distinct *crack* of a poppadom being obliterated beneath his right arm.

With a deep growl of irritation, Andrew stumbled to his feet. His will to live nearly left him entirely when he put his heel down directly on the small polystyrene pot of mango chutney which immediately collapsed, soundtracked by an unpleasant duet of squeaking plastic and disappointed squelching.

If his hands hadn't been covered in sauce, he thought he might have dropped his head into them and wept out of sheer frustration.

Instead, he looked down at the utter state of both his clothes and the landing. The wall beneath the window was speckled with rust-coloured flecks, and Andrew knew that Higson was going to murder him (if Dolly didn't get there first). Even if he managed to clean up the most obvious evidence well enough, the sauce from the butter chicken had already begun seeping through the cracks in the floorboards and would give him away for weeks afterwards.

All that remained of his longed-for dinner was a tablespoon of sauce, and a single piece of chicken just about clinging onto the corner of the tray, tenuously pinched into place by the puckered foil, alongside the small sweaty plastic bag of warmed salad. Miraculously the container of onion bhajis – *Peggy's* onion bhajis – remained intact.

So, it was only after a lengthy cleaning session, and a newly developed hatred for rice, that Andrew found himself sitting at his desk, dipping three onion bhajis into the disappointingly meagre smear of remaining sauce.

He glanced down at his watch and groaned when he saw that it was already nearly ten.

Pushing the empty containers away, Andrew rubbed the crumbs from his fingers and reached over for the letter that Emma Allen had dropped in the day before.

He looked at the handwriting carefully, hoping that something would immediately pop out and identify the author, but no matter how hard he stared at the letters, at no point did a signature mystically appear at the bottom of the page. He'd seen Lavinia's handwriting on her script – all swoops and flicks, as though the letter formation felt it needed to prove itself as prone to drama as the penholder – and it was nothing like the squat, block capitals of Emma's letter. That didn't mean much, of course; it was entirely possible for people to disguise their handwriting, but Andrew didn't have the level of expertise required to be able to immediately tell whether he was being lied to via the medium of ink distribution.

It wouldn't actually matter *who* had written the damn thing anyway if a single thing happened to one of the cast the following night. *That* is what he needed to focus on. Higson may want answers about Alistair's death, and those of Henriette St. Clair and Peter McClellan too, but Andrew knew that those answers were going to have to wait. For now, he just had to hope that the three deaths were entirely unconnected, and the whole sequence of events had been nothing more than chance and coincidence.

Deep down, Andrew knew better than to believe in chance and coincidence by that point, but what choice did he have?

God, he wanted a shower, and a shave, and his bed; he *missed* his bed. Still, there was nothing he could do about any of that in that moment. He really didn't fancy the idea of fleeing from his home mid-shower – Jesus, Mrs Roberts would die of fright, if she hadn't already keeled over from Agatha's appearance at the weekend – so he was stuck with Plan B: sleep at the Ballroom again, and then beg whoever the hell was on the desk over at Bootle Street nick to let him use the showers before he had to be at the theatre for eight-thirty.

He switched off the chandeliers, but the room was still bathed in the jaundiced glow of the street lamps just outside the windows. With a sigh, he flopped back on the ratty blue sofa, pillowing his head with his left arm and trying not to jostle his right shoulder too much in the process.

He closed his eyes and tried to think about anything that wasn't the case, or his house, or Peggy, or Rob, or Jen's disappointment, or –

Andrew growled and rolled onto his side, facing away from the windows, and tried to switch off entirely. However, even though he'd changed out of his shirt and scrubbed his hands, the overpowering scent of ginger and garlic still lingered, and his stomach grumbled in response to missing yet another meal.

He was just about descending into something that was more

of a fugue state than a peaceful slide towards gentle sleep when he was disturbed by the sound of breaking glass. He startled awake immediately, heart rate ratcheting up, even as he reminded himself that he was in the middle of bloody Manchester on St Patrick's night. Christ, if he continued like this, he was going to send himself into an early grave.

He pressed his face into the scratchy blue upholstery, ignoring the fact that anybody had ever sat on this sofa before; his head hurt, and he was too tired to care about whatever the hell his face might be coming into contact with. Maybe he should have taken Jen's advice and gone to see a doctor; it probably wasn't wise to be alone with a possible concussion. At least if he died alone in the Ballroom - which felt disturbing likely with his current string of luck - he'd probably end up stuck in the afterlife with someone he was already acquainted with.

He wondered if Peggy would feel contractually obligated to speak to him.

Wait.

There was a terrible, slow scraping sound that reminded Andrew of nails on a chalkboard, and his mind immediately went to his mother.

The sound wasn't outside.

It was coming from *inside* the building.

Andrew rolled off the sofa, soundlessly dropping into a crouch for a second, straining his ears to pick up anything else.

Very slowly, he rose to standing, pushing his jumper sleeves to his elbows, just in case that would somehow help. He looked at his desk and scowled; there was nothing useful there for fighting either a ghost or an intruder.

He made his way carefully towards Jen's desk and reached beneath the chair to grab the umbrella that was perennially stored there, just in case.

The sound of furious whispering reached his ears, and he

raised the closed umbrella over his shoulder as if it were a baseball bat and moved carefully towards the closed double doors of the Ballroom.

Slowly, ever so slowly, he reached out his hand and pushed down on the handle. The hinges squealed slightly as Andrew pulled the door open and he winced at the noise, which sounded a hundred times louder in the stillness of the night.

He readjusted his grip on the umbrella, fingers flexing and then tightening around the handle.

He stilled, and a silent gasp of surprise stole the air from his lungs.

The dark mass at the stop of the stairs shifted slightly, morphing into something wider and far more terrifying.

And then it screamed.

EIGHTEEN

'Joyce!'

Andrew's head throbbed violently at the shout, and another wave of nausea rolled over him as a prickle of clamminess crept across the back of his neck from shoulder to shoulder. He was mid-shiver when he saw something white hurtling towards his face. He threw his arms up for protection, but he was too late to stop the mass from striking the bridge of his nose forcefully and then slumping down onto his knees.

'Christ, my grandmother can catch better than that,' Higson grunted as he shook his head in disappointment, 'and she's been dead for fifteen years.'

Andrew blinked to clear his head and looked down at the sheaf of paper resting on his lap, barely being held together by the tip of a carelessly utilised paperclip.

'How the fuck you actually managed to clout Swan right in the face in the dark, I have no idea.'

Andrew winced. He had no idea how he'd quite managed it either.

If he was entirely honest, when he'd seen the large black shape on the Ballroom's first floor landing the night before, his first instinct had been to run; to just zip backwards into the Ballroom and barricade the doors behind him.

He'd almost instantly realised that there wasn't much point in trying to barricade yourself from something that likely wasn't bound by the laws of physics, and so he had switched into attack mode.

The shrill scream from the unidentifiable mass had startled him so badly that Andrew had rushed forwards without a second thought and viscously brought the umbrella down in a sweeping arc, in the hope that if the thing was at all corporeal it would be distracted enough by the strike to allow Andrew to race downstairs and fling himself into the Belmont.

The 'thing' had screeched again when Andrew had struck it with the umbrella, which had been the moment that Andrew had realised that perhaps he'd misunderstood the situation.

'Ow, Jesus, *fuck*!' Charlie had cried, plummy voice unmistakeable, even under the alarmed slurring. '*What was that for?*'

Andrew had rocketed back into the Ballroom and flipped the switch for the chandeliers. The golden light had filtered out onto the landing, illuminating a rather startled Lloyd, and an even more startled Charlie, cowering at the top of the stairs.

'Mate!' Lloyd had yelped. 'I mean, *sir*! What are you doing?'

In that moment, Andrew had wondered that himself.

'Put that bloody thing down!' Charlie had whined, pinching his nose. '*Ow!*'

Andrew had looked between Charlie – blood dribbling down his face – and Lloyd, and then allowed his gaze to settle on the now-twisted umbrella, which was back to resting on his shoulder, ready to be swung again as necessary.

'Ah,' Andrew had said, when comprehension had finally dawned. 'Shit. Sorry, I thought you were…'

He'd trailed off, unwilling to finish the sentence.

Charlie didn't seem to care anyway. He'd shouldered past Andrew into the Ballroom and collapsed onto the sofa, pulling a handkerchief from his pocket and stuffing a rolled corner of it into his nostril.

Right, Andrew had thought as he'd moved aside to let Lloyd in and shut the door behind them, apparently he wasn't getting the opportunity to go back to sleep any time soon.

The opportunity had drifted further away when Lloyd had subsequently plonked a bottle of Jameson down on his desk and then gone rifling through Higson's desk drawers until he'd recovered three cleanish glasses.

'Joyce, I'm going to thump you for so many reasons when I can see straight,' Charlie had grumbled as he'd pressed the heel of his hand to his forehead.

'What are you both doing here?' Andrew had asked when he'd managed to scrape up a handful of wherewithal.

'Rotters was crap,' Lloyd had replied, handing Andrew a glass with significantly more than a double whiskey in it. 'Some poncy lot up from London who were just like New Order, except for the fact they were completely shit. Went to the offy instead.'

'Why didn't you just go to a pub instead?' Andrew had asked. 'Or *home*?'

Lloyd had given Andrew a look that suggested he was about to give a very obvious answer to a very stupid question. 'Sick of Guinness, and it's way too early to go home.'

'Right,' Andrew had replied, and taken a large gulp of his drink.

In the dimly lit auditorium of the Court the following morning he'd be hard pushed to tell you what had happened for the rest of the night. He had a vague recollection of Charlie giving him an absolute bollocking for telling Peggy that her brother had been gossiping about her, and for being absent from the theatre when Edgar had turned up. He was also fairly certain that at one point Lloyd had been standing on Higson's desk and telling a very involved story about how he'd first met Fiona, his eternally on-again off-again girlfriend. But beyond that, his brain just shrugged at him unhelpfully.

He'd fallen asleep at some point, because he'd eventually woken, head slumped on his arms on top of his desk, just like he had the morning of his birthday. It had then taken him a long moment to realise that he'd violently started awake because Jen had been shaking his shoulder urgently.

Jen hadn't even tried to hide her annoyance at the state of the Ballroom, nor at the state of her colleagues.

Her profound disappointment in them all, though, had paled in comparison to the thunderous fury on Higson's face when he'd walked in five minutes later and immediately deduced what had happened.

'Joyce, Parker, tidy yourselves up now!' Higson had barked. 'This is supposed to be a department of the goddamn GMP, not a sodding hostel for little idiot boys who can't hold their alcohol!'

Charlie had made the terrible error of snorting with laughter.

'Something funny, Swan?' Higson had asked, terribly calmly even as his beady eyes were sharp as flint.

Charlie had shaken his head vigorously, over and over again.

'Didn't think so,' Higson had snapped, and then turned back to Andrew and Lloyd. 'Get Little Lord Fauntleroy out of here, and then get your arses to that theatre. *Now!*'

None of them had needed telling twice. Andrew had grabbed his still-open duffle bag, and then they'd all three stumbled out of the room, clattered down the stairs, and spilled out onto Tib Street.

As he'd jogged up the road towards the Bootle Street station, hoping that he still had clean clothes in his bag, Andrew's brain had only just enough capacity to remind him to be thankful that at least Higson didn't seem to have noticed anything amiss after Andrew's disastrous incident with his dinner.

'Oi, Joyce!' Higson shouted, and Andrew was dragged back to the present.

'Sir,' Andrew managed to cough in return, and he picked up the stack of paper. 'What's this?'

'*These* are handwriting samples that Cusack thought might be a good idea to take from everyone here yesterday afternoon while you were playing fainting maiden,' Higson replied, folding his arms. 'So, yet another person doing your job for you.'

Andrew pursed his lips but didn't say anything in return. He didn't really have an argument anyway, did he?

He flicked through the pages, looking for anything that even remotely matched the letter Emma Allen had received.

'Well?' Higson held out his hands for the papers once Andrew got to the end of the stack a second time.

'Nothing,' Andrew replied in disappointment.

'What about this one?' Higson handed over a sheet of smaller, notepad paper.

Andrew's eyes widened immediately. The bulk of the writing didn't look anything like the penmanship of the mysterious letter, and, in fact looked like two different authors, but then right at the bottom there was a telephone number, followed by four words written in the same squat capital letters that Andrew had spent so much time staring at he could probably replicate them in his dreams:

ANDERTON - CALL AFTER SIX

'How?' he breathed in disbelief. 'Who wrote this?'

'Emma Allen.'

Andrew looked at Higson in bewilderment. '*What?*'

'Cusack went to see the sister at the bakery yesterday,' Higson explained, sniffing loudly. 'Asked her about where she was any time any of the funny business happened around here.'

'And?'

'Alibis tighter than a duck's arse for every single one of them,' Higson replied, shrugging, and then sitting down just up the row from Andrew. 'Cusack – clever girl – wasn't convinced though, so got her write down a few things to make sure we had her handwriting somewhere. That's her writing at the top there.'

'But you said it was *Emma* Allen, not Sue,' Andrew said, shaking his head at the incriminating handwriting.

'While Jen was speaking to Sue, the phone rang, and Emma answered it,' Higson continued, plucking the paper from

Andrew's hands again. 'It was about a babysitting gig she was wanting. She obviously needed to write a few things down, so she grabbed that paper from the counter while Sue was talking, which is why the writing changes halfway down.

'Right at the end of her phone call she wrote herself that important little note in capital letters. Cusack – did I mention she's a clever girl? – spotted the similarity and sat young Emma down for a nice chat.'

Emma Allen? *Emma Allen?* It didn't matter how many times Andrew repeated the name to himself, it still didn't make any sense. 'Why would Emma Allen send herself that letter?'

'Because Lavinia Heathcote paid her to.'

Andrew turned his head in surprise when Jen's voice came from behind him. He rubbed at his shoulder again when it protested – sleeping at his desk, and smacking Charlie hadn't done his sore muscles any good. He would ignore it all now though, if it meant that someone would just explain what the bloody hell was going on for him.

Jen finished walking down the aisle and came to a stop in front of Andrew and Higson. 'Everything we were told about Lavinia criticising Emma's acting in the initial rehearsals is true, but apparently it wasn't actually enough to get Emma to quit. Lavinia tried everything she could think of, eventually escalating to the stories about the curse and the Shadow Man, and when that didn't work...'

'She paid her to leave,' Andrew groaned in annoyance when Jen trailed off with a knowing shrug. 'Well, Jen I can answer your question from yesterday for you; you know, 'is Emma Allen a better actress than Lavinia?' Yeah, I think she might be.'

'Her sister is furious with her,' Jen added. 'The threat of actually being in trouble scared Emma enough that she was happy to dob in her monied sponsor. The shouting started when Emma pointed out that she'd been getting paid double for doing absolutely nothing. Turns out Sue isn't a fan of a lazy work ethic. I thought I might have to bring them both in just so they didn't kill each other there in the bakery.'

'But Sue Allen saw that letter,' Andrew said, shaking his head. 'Surely she recognised her sister's handwriting.'

Jen shrugged. 'I think people only see what they want to see, sir; particularly when it comes to people they love. Sue had no reason to believe that her sister would ever be involved in something like that, so missed what was right in front of her.'

'Jesus. Great work, Jen.' Andrew shook his head in amazement. 'Have you spoken to Lavinia?'

Jen nodded. 'She's denying everything, of course, and right now we haven't got anything more than Emma's word.'

Andrew splayed one hand across his face and pressed hard on his brow bone with a sigh. Suddenly, his eyes popped open when he was struck by a sudden thought; the kind of thought that could solve everything. 'If we pull Lavinia out of the play for questioning that's the end of the play, right? Surely there's no chance Cohen would bring in Emma as the alternative. If there's nobody to play Isabella, there's no play at all.'

Higson snorted loudly. 'Are you still labouring under the misapprehension that Cohen is the one in charge of anything here?'

Andrew screwed up his face as he realised his oversight. 'Caroline Winshire.'

'Mother Swan wouldn't care if *Parker* played Isabella,' Higson added, reaching into his pocket and pulling out a white paper bag. 'The play's on. At least we'll get to see if we're really dealing with a murderous spirit now, eh?'

'You can't be serious!' Andrew argued. 'We've got the perfect excuse to cancel the performance, and you want to just wait and see if anyone else gets thrown down a staircase?'

Higson rose slowly to his feet, neatly reminding Andrew just how tall and broad the DCI really was. 'In case it's escaped your notice, Joyce, we still have no idea who this mysterious woman is - the one who was spotted at the scene of at least one incident. The mysterious woman, might I add, that you were very keen to impress on us all was much more likely to exist than a homicidal ghost. We also appear to have an unseen force here that's very happy to play silly buggers and try and break my DI's neck, even when his little comrade told Miss Swan that he's not the murdering type, at least not anymore. So, until we know why it's only this bloody play that manages to kill off its cast before it can get through a single performance in *my* city, we're not going anywhere.'

Higson might have had a point.

Andrew looked around the empty auditorium. Nothing had materially changed since the first time he'd walked in the week before, but that morning it felt like there was a current running through the whole building. He couldn't explain the feeling to any degree of satisfaction, but it was as though something was waiting just out of sight. He'd rather not admit it, but the mood of the building that morning reminded him of his own home.

'This place is being locked down until tonight,' Higson said as Andrew turned his attention back to him. 'Bootle Street's giving us six uniforms for the day. I've put two of them on the first floor to make sure nobody goes up to the second, another one in the foyer, and the other three on the exterior doors. Nobody gets in or out without my say-so, capiche?'

'Sir,' Jen agreed, and Andrew nodded his assent.

'Have you told that lot that they're stuck in here for the day yet?' Andrew asked as Cohen, Vic and the four actors walked out onto the stage with the skeleton tech and wardrobe team. It was a fairly pitiful sight for a production.

Higson shrugged nonchalantly. 'Isn't that the sort of thing I employ you for?'

Andrew very nearly rolled his eyes, but quickly remembered that he was still on shaky ground, and it would probably be best not to antagonise Higson for the umpteenth time so early in the day.

'Is Marnie here?' he asked. He actually wanted to ask if *Peggy* was there, but he didn't like the idea of showing Higson just how much the answer to that question would matter to him.

Higson raised one eyebrow shrewdly anyway. 'Driscoll is trying to find Alistair Tunham to see if we can get a better description of this mystery woman.'

'I'll make sure I'm with Marion and Lavinia at all times. I've already told them they'll have to share Marion's dressing room for the day,' Jen said, and her utter lack of excitement for such a task was obvious.

'Good. Joyce, you can babysit the alright one and the little dickhead with the Rubik's cube.' Higson pointed to where Ben and Teddy were watching Lavinia and Marion sniping at each other. 'Where's Parker got to?'

'He's doing a walkthrough to make sure all doors and windows are secure,' Jen explained.

'Should he be doing that by himself?' Andrew asked.

Higson let out a booming laugh. 'Says the man who barely believes in the afterlife.'

Andrew did roll his eyes that time. 'Alright, well I suppose I'd better go tell them that they aren't going out for coffee or lunch today.'

'Good luck with that, sir,' Jen said, and for the first time that morning she gave him a hint of forgiveness.

Andrew did not, however, feel the same level of clemency radiating from Lavinia as he appeared from the wings to deliver Higson's will to the masses; in fact, if looks could kill, Andrew would have been annihilated where he stood.

'Inspector!' Cohen muttered tightly through gritted teeth as

Andrew approached. 'I hope you're bringing me good news.'

'Not quite, Mr Cohen,' Andrew replied with all of the apology he could muster. 'Not quite.'

'Fuck.' Cohen sighed loudly, sharing a pained look with Vic before pressing clenched fists against his eyes. 'Fuck, fuck, fuck!'

Andrew stayed silent, but he really couldn't have agreed more.

* * *

Peggy was digging through her handbag in search of her set of keys for Tib Street when the door to the (former) Cheryl Richard Dance Studio opened in front of her.

'Bit late, ain't youse?' Dolly's gravelly voice filtered out from behind the door before the rest of her followed, tightly cocooned in a cloud of smoke. Her cigarette holder was aloft in her right hand, and her left was resting on her hip in a show of impatience.

'N-n-no,' Peggy stammered, trying to overcome her surprise. 'Good morning, Dolly.'

'Mmm,' Dolly replied, casting her eyes critically over Peggy from head to toe, in a manner that was awfully reminiscent of her mother. 'Pretty Boy left without youse.'

Well, on one hand that statement helped Peggy confirm that Dolly wasn't *actually* omniscient – not always, anyway – but on the other it just reminded Peggy of the gulf that had opened up between her Andrew, which she didn't really appreciate.

'Actually, I'm working on something by myself at the moment,' Peggy replied, and she hated herself a little bit for how snooty she sounded.

Dolly's mouth quirked in what was possibly amusement. 'Are youse now?'

'Yes.' Peggy nodded firmly. 'So, if you'd please excuse me, I really should be getting on.'

Dolly reached over and wrapped a gnarled hand around Peggy's wrist. 'Yer wrong.'

'I need to get upstairs.'

'*Yer wrong*,' Dolly repeated more aggressively. Her grip tightened and her eyes narrowed as she leaned in close enough that a puff of smoke-infused breath hit Peggy's cheek. 'Youse should stay out of the dark. Both of youse should.'

'What?' Peggy asked in alarm. 'I don't understand.'

Dolly's expression softened, and it was like looking at a completely different person. Peggy could feel her anxiety mounting as the seconds ticked by. 'Don't get lost like 'e did.'

For the space of a heartbeat or two, there was absolute stillness and Peggy could feel a mounting sense of apprehension as Dolly continued to stare at her with what appeared to be genuine concern.

Abruptly, Dolly let go of Peggy's wrist and moved out of the way. 'Go on then, away with youse, or youse'll be too late.'

Peggy fled.

She bounded up the stairs to the Ballroom, pushed open the double doors and then slammed them behind her.

'Christ,' Peggy whispered, breathing heavily, hand on her chest as she let her handbag fall to the ground. Dolly often spoke in riddles, but Peggy had never seen her look quite so grave about something before. She shivered even though it wasn't cold and belted her trench coat more firmly around her waist.

What on earth had Dolly been talking about though? What shadows? *Who* had got lost?

On any other day, Peggy would likely have given these questions much more consideration, but her attention had been caught by the state of the room.

'What on earth?' Peggy muttered to herself as she approached the three glasses on Higson's desk, and the empty bottle of whiskey lying next to them, precariously close to the edge. Had she missed some sort of party?

A jumper that she recognised as belonging to Andrew was tossed carelessly over the arm of the blue sofa, so it looked like he was back to sleeping at the Ballroom.

Behind her, the phone on Jen's desk rang shrilly, and Peggy twisted in shock at the noisy intrusion, almost tripping over the mangled umbrella that seemed to have been discarded in the middle of the floor. 'Bugger!'

For a moment, she dithered about whether she was supposed to answer it or not, but ultimately decided that Higson would be more annoyed with her for not taking an important message than for her answering the phone in the first place.

'Hello?' Peggy said as she picked up the receiver, and then panicked that there was a more formal way you were supposed to answer a police phone.

There was a loud crackle on the other end of the line. 'Miss Swan?'

Peggy's eyes widened in surprise. *Who on earth would be looking for her at the Ballroom?* 'Um, yes.'

'Ah, good morning,' the warm voice replied. 'It's Douglas Frost here, from Central Library's information desk.'

'Oh!' Peggy replied far too loudly. Yes, she'd left the Ballroom's number so that she wouldn't run the risk of Timothy answering the phone at Butterton. 'Oh, Mr Frost, I'm so sorry I haven't been back in to see you yet.'

'Not to worry at all,' Douglas replied kindly. 'I just wanted to let you know that I've found the editions you were looking for. I did a sweep over everything we had in print for the following two weeks and pulled out anything I thought would be helpful for your project. The copies are all at the desk in the Reading Room for you, or I can post them out to you if that would be more helpful.'

'No, no, I'll come in and collect them now. Thank you so

much, Mr Frost, I really appreciate it.'

'Not a problem, pet,' Douglas replied. 'Look after yourself.'

When the call disconnected, Peggy replaced the phone.

Well, she hadn't really fancied hanging around on Tib Street after her encounter with Dolly anyway, so the phone call was the perfect excuse to leave and still feel like she was getting something useful done. It may also have been the perfect excuse to avoid going anywhere near the archive room again after the incident at the weekend, but she was fine without admitting that to anyone.

She gave the unusual level of untidiness one final puzzled glance before she went to retrieve her handbag from by the door.

As she straightened back up, she caught sight of movement in the corner of her eye and turned her head sharply towards the far end of the Ballroom.

DI Benson was standing beside Higson's desk, staring directly at her. He seemed to be saying something, but Peggy couldn't hear him over what sounded like bursts of radio static.

'What?' Peggy shook her head as she walked quickly towards him. 'I can't hear you.'

Up close, Benson looked panicked, and he raised a finger to his lips as though telling Peggy to keep her voice down. His eyes were darting around the room, never settling anywhere for more than split second at a time.

'What's wrong?' Peggy whispered as quietly as she could manage.

Benson's eyes only widened, and he pressed his finger harder against his lips.

His message was clear: *shut up!*

Peggy held her hands up in understanding and apology and Benson lowered his hand.

'What's wrong?' Peggy mouthed, silently enunciating each word in the hope that Benson understood the question.

Benson shook his head and pointed at Higson's desk.

'I don't understand.' Peggy shrugged helplessly.

Benson glanced to the left suddenly, and his eyes widened in response to something Peggy could not see.

When he looked back at Peggy she gulped at the blatant fear in Benson's expression. What was he trying to tell her?

Benson said one word, just loud enough for Peggy to hear.

'*Go.*'

Peggy backed away immediately, keeping her eyes on Benson. She'd assumed he wanted to her to leave quickly, but as she was beginning to pick up speed he made a flapping motion with his hands that she interpreted as 'slow down.'

Okay, so whatever the hell was going on, Benson wanted Peggy to act like she wasn't desperate to run out of the Ballroom.

She made a detour to Andrew's desk and pretended to look through the shallow stack of files he'd left there, and then prodded the foil container with half an onion bhaji nestled in the corner in genuine disappointment. She was so determined to get out of there, though, that she almost missed the single blue file bearing a Post-it note with 'Swan' scrawled in what she thought was Higson's spidery writing.

She opened the folder and found two pieces of paper with a few typed lines on each. This must have been everything Higson had managed to dig up on the elusive George Bevan. It didn't look like it was going to be particularly useful after all.

'Right,' Peggy said loudly to nobody while making a show of checking her watch. 'Library time.'

She readjusted the strap of her handbag and made her way out of the Ballroom. As she closed the doors, she caught one final glimpse of Benson through the decreasing gap. He hadn't moved away from the wall and was once again just watching her silently, finger back on his lips.

Peggy crossed the landing to the staircase quickly, averting her eyes from the closed archive room door just in case, and she didn't let go of the breath she was holding until she was outside in the sunshine again.

Clutching the George Bevan file to her chest, Peggy hurried towards Central Library, knowing that when everything at the Court had been concluded, she was going to have a very serious word with Higson about what had been going on in the Ballroom.

Peggy strode up the steps and in through the entrance doors, before making her way up to the Reading Room.

Douglas Frost was at the information desk, and he was already holding out an envelope with a grin by the time she reached him. 'That was quick, Miss Swan.'

'Thank you,' Peggy said, gratefully taking the envelope. 'Yes, I'm on a bit of a deadline with all of this, and this week has already got away from me.'

'Well, you're free to take a seat anywhere you like if you want to stop and read a while,' Douglas said, waving his arm around the fairly empty room. 'It's not exactly packed in here this morning.'

Peggy was seriously considering it as a perfect alternative to reading alone (or not alone, as the case may be) in the Ballroom, but then her gaze ticked up towards the ceiling and settled on the inscription that ran the whole way around the dome:

Wisdom is the principal thing; therefore get wisdom, and with all thy getting get understanding. Exalt her and she shall promote thee; she shall bring thee to honour when thou dost embrace her, she shall give of thine head an ornament of grace, a crown of glory she shall deliver to thee.

'Where's the verse from?' Peggy asked, with just the slightest hint of hesitation.

'Hmm?' Douglas asked before he saw that Peggy was pointing above their heads. 'Oh, it's Proverbs.'

Proverbs. Just like the messages for Alistair, Henriette, Peter and Lavinia, although at least this one had been chosen for its more positive message. Peggy shivered again; it was like she couldn't get away from any of it, no matter where she went.

'Are you alright, Miss Swan?' Douglas asked, eyes crinkling in concern.

Peggy pasted a smile on her lips. 'Fine, thank you. Actually, I think I might read outside while we can actually see the sun for a little while.'

'Aye, it's been a grim week for the weather.' Douglas nodded sagely. 'Off you pop then. Come back and tell me if you ever find out what that young lad in your newspaper reports was up to.'

'I will,' Peggy promised with a smile. 'Thanks again.'

Douglas waved her away with another smile and Peggy left the library again.

It was actually slightly too cold to sit outside comfortably, but she'd made her decision, and she was going to stick to it. She'd turned right without thinking; her feet leading her towards the Court before her brain had caught up with her legs.

She stopped at the edge of the pavement, about to cross Mount Street, and looked over at the theatre only a little further down the road. No, she wasn't going to go there, not least because Higson had told her to stay away.

If Peggy were being entirely honest, she'd be forced to admit that Higson's order wasn't actually the main reason she was hesitant of returning there; his edict ranked well below her fear of encountering her mother and Edgar again, and lower still below the thought of encountering Andrew when she was still caught somewhere between the trust and appreciation that she'd felt upon his sharing Rob's story with her, and the hurt caused by his spiteful words the day before.

Peggy stepped away from the kerb and turned to the right instead, heading for the Town Hall.

Even though it wasn't a particularly warm day, the men tasked with pedestrianising Albert Square had downed tools for a chance to have their tea break while the sun was shining down on them, and Peggy found that she was suitably content to sit on the steps at the base of the Albert memorial and open the envelope that Douglas had given to her.

The first sheet was a photocopied page from the edition of *The Manchester Guardian* that had been listed in the paperwork in the Court's archive. There was a large photograph of the four original cast members, all with serious expressions as they stared out at Peggy, frozen for eternity in black and yellowing-white.

Beneath the cast photo was a second image which showed a significantly larger number of people. The caption suggested that this photo included the director, standby cast and a handful of theatre workers.

Peggy squinted at the slightly smudged figures until she found Alistair at the far end of the front row. It was hard to see his expression in detail, shaded as it was beneath a hat very similar to the one usually perched on his head in the theatre, but the way he was standing, head held high, suggested that he was radiating confidence. There were so many people in the photograph, her hopes rose that something might jog Alistair's memory of that night.

The next few sheets were reports of Alistair's death from different local papers, and Peggy was disappointed to see that in each one, the story was still primarily focussed on how the famous Clarence Wright had cheated death by pulling out of the play at the last moment. All three newspapers had chosen to print a photograph of Wright, rather than the 'unknown' talent.

The penultimate piece of paper was a short article from *The Manchester Guardian*, with the headline 'Hunt for Suspect in Theatre Murder', and Peggy was finally rewarded with a photograph of Alistair. He looked to be in his late teens in the photograph, and he was smiling so widely that Peggy couldn't help but wonder when and why the photograph had been taken, and what had made Alistair beam like that.

She frowned as she read the caption beneath the photo, but no matter how hard she squinted at it, or how close she held it to her face, the words didn't change:

Suspect: George L. Bevan

'What?' Peggy muttered to herself as a horrible swooping sensation rippled through her. *George?* Surely that must be a mistake.

She quickly turned to the final page from Douglas' envelope – an even shorter article from the *Manchester Evening News* - and her heart sank at what she saw there: a short story that informed her that the police had been unable to locate George Bevan and had concluded that he must have fled the city after the murder. This was followed by a smaller version of the same photograph she'd seen on the previous page, right next to a photograph of a man in his mid-twenties with a spectacular moustache and a terribly serious expression. This second photograph was captioned *Alistair Tunham*.

Peggy's shock swiftly morphed into a blinding sense of panic, and she nearly sent all of Douglas' photocopies flying up into the air as she scrambled to her feet and tripped down the steps beneath Albert's feet.

'Alistair' at the Court wasn't Alistair Tunham at all; Peggy had been so keen to find out what had happened to Alistair, and at no point had she considered that she was being lied to. Christ, Andrew was right about her being too naïve for real police work.

'Idiot!' Peggy chastised herself as she raced back towards Peter Street, dodging flustered pedestrians with barely an apology.

Jock had been telling her the whole time, hadn't he?

Liars, he'd said. Even Marnie had seemed to know that there was something awry with 'Alistair'.

Peggy hurried across the road towards the Court's entrance and stumbled to a halt when she saw two uniformed police officers talking together at the doors.

'What's going on?' Peggy asked. 'Has something happened inside?'

The older of the two broke off mid-conversation and turned to Peggy with a look of irritated confusion. 'What?'

'Look, I need to get inside!' Peggy gestured towards the lobby.

The policeman laughed loudly. 'The show's not 'til tonight, sweetheart.'

'Yes, I know that!' Peggy replied, trying to keep her voice at a reasonable level. 'I need you to let me in now though.'

'And why would I do that?'

'Because I need to get a message to DI Joyce,' Peggy said, waving the envelope as though that would help her case. 'Or DCI Higson. He's in there too, isn't he?'

The irritation on the policeman's face transformed into suspicion instead. 'Building's closed.'

'But I just told you that I need to speak to DI Joyce or DCI Higson!' Peggy was shouting by that point. 'It's about the case they're working on.'

The younger policeman raised an eyebrow, 'And what would you know about current cases?'

'I work with them,' Peggy said as evenly as she could manage.

The synchronisation of the two men laughing was perfect enough to *almost* be impressive.

Peggy, however, was not impressed. Instead, she decided to resort to the type of tactics that her brother would employ in such a situation. 'My father owns this theatre!'

The older man guffawed again. 'Right, well at least that's more likely than you know 'igson!'

Peggy narrowed her eyes and made a move towards the door.

She was blocked immediately, and the younger man grabbed her wrist tightly. 'You're not getting in there, love, so I suggest you bugger off, unless you want to spend the rest of the day with the desk sergeant on Bootle Street.'

For just a moment, Peggy considered pushing it. Perhaps actually getting arrested would somehow make it easier to contact Andrew or Higson.

Then she remembered that she wasn't actually supposed to know anything about the Ballroom, and therefore someone was likely to get in trouble.

Peggy narrowed her eyes and wrenched her arm free. 'Fine.'

As she turned away, she heard the two men sniggering behind her, and she desperately wished that she could wipe their smug expressions right off their faces.

However, she didn't have time for that; she needed to be logical about things.

Peggy jogged back towards the library, reaching the phone box just as an opportunistic cloud crept in to cover the sun.

After a quick call to Directory Enquiries, and a frantic search for a pen in her bag, Peggy keyed in the number for the Court's box office and waited impatiently for the call to be answered.

At the click, she opened her mouth to ask for anyone from the police team inside the building to come to the phone, and squawked in annoyance when the recorded message told her that the box office was closed for the day due to a sold-out special event at the theatre that evening.

'Crap, crap, crap,' Peggy muttered as she slammed the receiver back into its cradle.

What the hell was she supposed to do now?

'Idiot!' she yelped at herself again when she realised that she'd had the perfect solution the whole time.

'Marnie!' she called loudly, pleased that she was in a phone box, which at least kept the staring from passers-by to a minimum. 'Marnie!'

After a few minutes, and still no sign of Marnie, Peggy had to accept defeat.

She took a deep breath and lifted the phone to her ear once more as she dug some more coins out of her purse.

'Please answer, please answer, please answer,' Peggy muttered into the phone.

'Hello?'

'Charlie!' Peggy cried into the phone, eminently relieved that her brother had reached the phone before Timothy.

'Jesus, Peg,' Charlie grumbled, sounding inexplicably nasal, 'keep your voice down. My head's killing me, and I've only just got back to the house.'

'I can't get into the theatre!' Peggy ignored her brother's attempt to elicit sympathy for his self-inflicted hangover.

'Well, I don't actually have a key, nor am I in town, so I c-'

'No! I mean, they've got policemen on the doors, and they won't let me in,' Peggy explained.

'So, tell them you need to speak to Joycie.'

'Jesus, Charlie, I'm not completely thick, you know!' Peggy rolled her eyes. 'I *did*, and they still won't let me in. I've tried calling the theatre, but nobody's answering the phone.'

'Why are you so desperate to get in anyway?' Charlie asked, slightly warily. 'I thought you were done with this case.'

Peggy wasn't quite ready to share the reason with her brother. 'Don't worry about why, just tell me what I should do. I've run out of ideas!'

Charlie made some muttered statement about how he was better than a last resort, and then added, 'Marnie?'

'Already tried that,' Peggy huffed. 'She's not answering me.'

'She's probably too busy plotting Joycie's demise. *Oh*, speaking of! He smacked me in the face with an umbrella last night and I c-'

'Charlie, focus!' Peggy snapped, even as she realised that she now had half an explanation for the umbrella she'd nearly fallen over in the Ballroom, and for Charlie's odd tone of voice.

Charlie sighed loudly. 'Right, if they won't let you in, I doubt they'll let *me* in, and short of dragging Father down there to force our way in, I think we might be a bit stymied.'

'Charlie, they could be in real danger,' Peggy replied anxiously.

'Right, okay,' Charlie said eventually, 'I've got an idea. It's not going to get you in immediately, but it *will* get you in. Is that good enough?'

'Yes,' Peggy agreed immediately. 'Yes, what do I need to do?'

'Where are you?'

'In a phone box near the Court.'

'Okay. I'll meet you at the Ballroom in an hour or so.'

Peggy didn't really fancy going back to the Ballroom, but she didn't fancy sharing that with Charlie either. 'Alright. I'll see you then.'

'Do you have a hairbrush with you?'

Peggy frowned. 'No. Why?'

The line went dead.

NINETEEN

Andrew was valiantly resisting the temptation to pull at the collar of his dress shirt for what felt like the hundredth time in ten minutes. It was a tighter fit than he'd have liked, but it was the best Lloyd had been able to come up with when Higson had shipped him out to the shops to try and hire dinner jackets at short notice; and, really, *anything* was better than being forced to borrow clothes from Lloyd's own wardrobe again.

When Higson had first announced the idea, Andrew hadn't been convinced that any amount of dressing up would be necessary for blending in - he had no intention of referring to it as 'being in disguise', despite Lloyd's gleeful attitude towards the whole thing - but when the guests had begun to appear in the foyer, each couple dressed more glamorously than the one before, Andrew had been forced to admit that Higson may have been on to something. This did nothing, however, to make Andrew feel better about being dressed like an awkward penguin.

Lloyd, rather predictably, appeared to be having the time of his life playing dress-up. In direct contrast to Andrew's sullen solitude, he was on the opposite side of the foyer, chatting to anyone and everyone who approached where he was casually leaning against the wall, right next to the door that would lead guests towards the bar for a pre-show drink.

Higson and Jen were up in the first floor dressing rooms, keeping an eye on the cast, Cohen and Vic. It had been made very clear to Andrew that he hadn't been entirely forgiven for his variety of sins over the past few days, and he knew that he was currently suffering through the adult equivalent of being sent to stand in the corner. He would have been more annoyed about his relegation to the foyer, if it hadn't been for the fact that he was pleased to have a genuine excuse to avoid Lavinia. Her short, sharp answers to any question he'd asked that afternoon had been evidence enough for him to conclude that any further suggestions of having dinner together once the whole debacle was over were unlikely to be forthcoming.

As another wave of guests breezed into the Court, Andrew reached out to lift a champagne flute from a passing tray of drinks. He had no intention of drinking it, but he hoped that it might help him to blend in better if he had a prop to hold.

He trudged back up the short staircase that led to the auditorium doors and leaned his elbows on the brass rail that curved around the outer edges of the top step. From this vantage point, he could easily see every member of the crowd being gradually ushered out of the foyer and towards the bar, all loud laughter and hooting compliments.

In that moment, he felt Peggy's absence keenly. She would have been as dissatisfied with the entire event as he was.

The crowd thinned slightly as the steady stream of arrivals paused, and Andrew stood up straighter as he watched a couple of theatre employees hurrying towards the entrance.

There seemed to be a mild commotion occurring by one of the doors; burgundy jackets and waistcoats huddling together and merging into what Andrew could only assume was a polite, but impenetrable, wall designed to block admittance to the foyer.

He looked over to Lloyd, hoping to get his attention and direct him towards the disturbance, and was gratified to see that the younger officer was already on his way.

'No, I can assure you that I really am fully capable of standing here for the entire evening if needs be.' The crisp voice cut right through the cloud of muttering and whispering, and Andrew felt his whole face crinkle in despair.

Oh, here we go, Andrew thought as he watched the theatre manager excuse himself from a conversation in the far corner and head towards the doors, clearly preparing to oust the troublemaker from his event before the evening's patroness arrived.

To Andrew's chagrin, Charlie Swan was admitted to the foyer only a moment later, deep apology etched into the faces and awkward body language of the staff who had - *so rightly* - tried to stop him coming in without a ticket.

Charlie was followed into the foyer by a dress in such a striking shade of bubblegum pink that it took Andrew a few seconds to parse what he was seeing before the realisation dawned that it was Peggy wearing it.

Or maybe it was wearing her. Andrew had never really understood women's fashion.

Either way, even with his limited understanding, he was fairly certain that it could only be described as a ballgown, with a great big, poofy skirt that had probably taken up the entire interior of whatever car she'd travelled to town in. It was the sort of thing that you'd expect to see on the red carpet at the Oscars, not on a typical March night in Manchester.

It took him another few seconds to become very aware of the fact that he was staring. This was absolutely, *entirely* down to the fact that the designer of Peggy's dress had obviously been deeply inspired by a bowl of strawberry Angel Delight, and not at all because he found that the whole look suited Peggy impossibly well.

No, it definitely, *definitely* wasn't that.

'Sir?'

Andrew turned to see Jen looking at him quizzically.

'What?' Andrew asked, clearing his throat as nonchalantly as he could manage.

'Are you feeling alright?' Jen wrinkled her nose. 'It's still not too late to get someone to take a quick look at your head after yesterday, you know.'

'I'm fine.'

'It's just, I've asked you twice if everything's alright down here.'

'You have?' Andrew frowned. Well, that wasn't a great start to the evening's operation, was it?

'Yes, sir,' Jen confirmed slowly.

Andrew ran a hand through his hair. Maybe he did have a more serious head injury than he'd thought. 'Everything's fine.'

Jen nodded her acceptance slowly, even though she looked like she wanted to further check that Andrew wasn't secretly experiencing some sort of breakdown.

'Well,' Andrew added as he gestured towards the entrance, 'it *was* fine.'

Jen looked over to where Andrew was pointing and started in surprise. 'I thought they would have both avoided this place like the plague tonight!'

Andrew looked back to where Peggy was standing a few feet from where her brother was jovially shaking hands with the ushers, glancing around the foyer as though she were looking for someone. She was visibly nervous, and Andrew knew without a shadow of a doubt that only something terribly important would have brought Peggy to the Court when she ran the very real risk of encountering both her mother and her ex-fiancé.

When Peggy looked up towards the auditorium, she finally caught Andrew's eye. Her expression instantly turned serious, and Andrew found himself standing up straighter in response, readying himself for whatever bombshell Peggy was about to lob in his direction.

A dull ache in his ribcage made him flinch and he looked away from Peggy in surprise.

'Sorry, sir,' Jen said, not sounding apologetic at all. She pointed at her elbow. 'Had to give you a bit of a nudge to check you were still with me.'

Andrew thought it best to keep his mouth shut.

'I'm going back up to the dressing rooms now,' Jen added.

'The two electricians have finally signed everything off as safe. The auditorium doors are being opened in twenty-five minutes, and we'll have the cast downstairs and backstage just before then.'

Andrew nodded. 'Once everyone's seated, Lloyd will stay out here. Cohen's managed to reserve a seat for me on the front row, so I'll be just in front of the stage.'

'Very good, sir. I'll head back in.' Jen looked out over the foyer once more. 'I think someone might be looking for you.'

Andrew turned and saw that Jen was correct: Peggy was politely excusing her way through the crowd and heading for the stairs. Every now and then, she stopped briefly to airily wave an arm or bestow a strained smile, and Andrew had to wonder just how much of the crowd below him already knew Peggy from her earlier life in high society.

Only a scant few feet from the bottom of the steps, Peggy was stopped again when a tall, dark-haired man, wearing the only white dinner jacket in the room, rested his hand on Peggy's upper arm as she tried to pass by.

Andrew didn't recognise the man, but he did recognise the expression on Peggy's face as one of absolute horror.

It only took a split-second for Andrew to leap to the conclusion that this man must be Edgar; and then it took only a split-second longer than that for him to realise that the man who'd tried to ruin Peggy's life was finally within spitting distance, and he had the chance to do something about it.

'Hold it there, Bruce Wayne!' Marnie's voice came from behind him suddenly, just as her fingers grabbed the hem of his jacket and tugged him backwards.

'Marnie!' Andrew growled.

'She's got it,' Marnie replied, steel grip not loosening even a little. 'She doesn't need you to swoop in right now, alright?'

Andrew, who was still cycling through satisfying visions of hurdling over gala guests until he reached Edgar, was *not* alright with Marnie's conclusion. Still, he wasn't about to argue with Marnie again – not about this – so he held his tongue in tacit surrender and waited for her to let go of him.

He was gratified to see that Charlie was also glaring daggers in Edgar's direction, but he too was hanging back.

Peggy, however, really did seem to be handling it. Her cheeks were flushed, and she peeled Edgar's fingers from her around her arm with a look of deep revulsion. Andrew couldn't hear what she was saying – he'd always been crap at lip-reading – but Edgar, for his part, looked deeply affronted and just about as surprised.

Andrew felt a deep rush of smug pride, and then immediately felt like a complete idiot for it.

Edgar had turned a rather terrible shade of mauve and he looked like he was squinting at the woman in front of him.

A moment later, Andrew found Edgar scowling in his direction, and so he felt it was only appropriate for him to break out his most severe glare in return, because Marnie couldn't stop him doing that.

Edgar seemed only mildly concerned, until he then looked in the other direction and realised that Charlie Swan was wearing the sort of expression that, if turned on you, might make you wonder if you were going to make it through the evening in one piece. Andrew had been on the receiving end of that look a grand total of twice, and he hadn't enjoyed it either time.

For all his faults, Edgar was apparently not entirely without a sense of self-preservation, and Andrew was gratified to see him back away with his hands raised to his shoulders, before he turned away and melted into the crowd.

When Edgar reached the entrance to the bar, Lloyd didn't open the door for him.

A few moments later, an entirely composed Peggy ascended the stairs. 'I need to talk to you.'

Andrew geared himself up to start on the multiple apologies

that he'd thought he'd have a bit more time to prepare for. 'Peggy, I'm sorry ab-'

Peggy shook her head impatiently. 'No time. Come with me.'

A second later Andrew found himself being tugged towards the auditorium doors, and then down the aisle towards the stage. His apology was going to have to keep for a while longer, as were his questions about where on earth Peggy had found that dress.

When they'd about made it to the halfway point, Peggy let go of his hand, and turned in a slow spin, craning her neck to look up at the dress circle, and then sweeping her gaze over every seat, right into the darkest corners of the theatre.

'What are you doing?' Andrew asked, raising an eyebrow.

Peggy silenced him with a glare and a finger to her lips.

A couple of moments later, she turned her attention back to Andrew. 'I think we're alone but keep your voice down anyway.'

'Peggy, what's going on?' Andrew whispered.

Peggy took a deep breath. 'I was wrong about Alistair.'

'What do you mean?'

Peggy popped open the clasp of the sparkly little bag she'd been holding in her left hand and pulled out a small, white rectangle. She then proceeded to unfold the rectangle until it was an A4 sheet of paper with a grid pattern of sharp lines where it had been meticulously creased. 'Look.'

Andrew took the paper with a quizzical frown. It was a photocopy of an article from the *Manchester Evening News* in July 1932. There was a large photograph, labelled as 'Alistair Tunham', and a smaller shot of another man that Andrew didn't recognise, but assumed from the headline was the suspect in Alistair's death. 'Right?'

'That's who I've been speaking to all week,' Peggy said, tapping the smaller photograph.

Andrew frowned. 'So, what? The newspaper mixed up the photographs?'

Peggy wordlessly handed him another piece of paper. This time there was only a single photograph of the man Peggy had identified as the theatre's ghost, and the caption named him as George Bevan. Andrew looked at Peggy in alarm. 'You haven't been speaking to Alistair?'

'George Bevan,' Peggy replied, sounding furious and dejected all at once. 'He's been lying to us since we arrived.'

'Christ,' Andrew breathed.

This was bad. He'd spent days believing that 'Alistair' was a bit useless, but mostly harmless, only to now have to reckon with the possibility that the ghost had been significantly more calculating than anyone had given him credit for. 'Do you think he's been behind everything?'

'Honestly, I don't know.' Peggy looked about ready to cry in frustration.

'Hey,' Andrew said, and he briefly squeezed Peggy's free hand. 'You couldn't have known he was lying about who he was.'

'I should have done.'

Andrew shook his head. 'Peggy, if we'd gone about any of this case correctly, we might have found these articles sooner – *maybe* – but we were all so focused on the immediate threat to everyone in the theatre, that we – I – didn't think that Alistair's death was relevant enough to investigate thoroughly.'

Andrew sighed loudly. 'I suppose I forgot for a minute.'

'Forgot what?'

'What we do at the Ballroom,' Andrew said with a quirk of his lips. 'We don't work on *current* cases. I really should have known it was always going to come back to the ghost, shouldn't I?'

It was Peggy's turn to sigh. 'We don't know anything about him. George, I mean.'

'Was there anything in that file from Higson?' Andrew asked. God, he'd been so pissed off that Peggy had requested information about George Bevan that he hadn't even taken a second to think that it might be useful, so, of course, that was now coming back around to bite him on the arse.

Peggy shook her head. 'Nothing. Not even a photograph.'

'So, we still don't know if he was involved in Alistair's death.'

'No, and we don't know what he's been involved in since he died,' Peggy added.

'Could he have been pretending to be Jock?' Andrew asked, with the vague hope that they could at least reduce the ghost count by one.

Peggy shook her head again. 'No. Jock and George are definitely two separate entities. I need to talk to George and get him to admit he's been lying to me, and hopefully find out what on earth he's got to do with anything that's been happening here this week.'

'Fine,' Andrew agreed. 'Just let me tell Lloyd what's going on, and then we'll go and look for George.'

'Not you, Andrew,' Peggy said, taking a step backwards towards the stage. 'Even with this, you can't rule out that there are other people involved.'

'We know who else was involved,' Andrew admitted quietly.

'What?' Peggy looked shocked.

'Emma Allen sent that poison pen letter to herself,' Andrew explained. 'Jen figured it out.'

'Why would she do that?'

Andrew tugged at his collar. 'Because Lavinia paid her to, and because Lavinia *did* write a message on her mirror yesterday, even if she's still denying it. Marnie was right, and I should have believed her. I should have believed you both.'

Peggy frowned. 'Does Emma Allen match the description that Alist – *George* – gave to me? Of the woman he'd seen hanging around the theatre?'

'No, she doesn't, but we don't even know he was telling the truth about that. He might not have seen anyone at all.'

'You could be right,' Peggy agreed evenly, 'but you don't know for certain that he *was* lying to us. You need to make sure that there really isn't someone skulking around the theatre waiting to off someone tonight. I can talk to him myself.'

'I really don't think that's a good idea. George really could be a murderer, for Christ's sake.'

Peggy raised her eyebrows. 'And what then, exactly? Are you going to talk to him instead? I hate to remind you, but you can't see him.'

And there, *right there*, was the root of Andrew's problem; he couldn't protect anyone from the things he wasn't capable of seeing. He hadn't even been able to protect himself from being knocked down the stairs the day before, had he?

'I'll take Marnie with me,' Peggy reasoned.

It didn't matter if it was reasonable, Andrew still didn't like it. 'Peggy, please, I don't th-'

'Andrew, can you *please* just trust me to do this?' Peggy asked, exasperated. 'This is what I can do to help, so let me help.'

It wasn't a matter of trust at all, but Andrew knew all too well that he'd given Peggy just cause to doubt the strength of Andrew's belief in her abilities and her reasoning over the past week. 'I do trust you. I still want to come with you though.'

Peggy looked like she might be ready to argue the point, but in the end, she just gestured towards the foyer. 'Then can you first please go and ask Lloyd to do everything he can to keep my mother away from me? If anything happens, she'll be utterly convinced that I somehow set the whole thing up to spite her.'

Andrew winced. He didn't think that Peggy was exaggerating. 'Alright.'

'I'll get Marnie and meet you backstage in a minute,' Peggy said before she turned on her heel and swept down the aisle towards the stage.

'Be careful, Peggy!' Andrew called after her, adding a quieter 'please' when she disappeared through the door beside the stage. She didn't acknowledge that she'd heard him, so he sighed again and hurried back towards the foyer to speak to Lloyd.

Peggy *had* heard Andrew call out to her, but as she wasn't planning on being anything but supremely careful, she hadn't thought it necessary to respond.

'Marnie?' she called quietly as she pushed open the door that brought her into the dimly lit area behind the blackout curtains at stage right. She hoped that this wouldn't be a repeat of earlier that day when Marnie hadn't responded to her - a fact she'd been careful to leave out when talking to Andrew — but her fears disintegrated when Marnie appeared only a few seconds later.

'What's going on?' Marnie asked immediately. 'What's happened? Also, that's a great dress, and you should wear pink more often, but *why are you here?*'

'The ghost we've been speaking to isn't Alistair Tunham,' Peggy replied quickly, needing to get this out of the way as soon as possible. 'He's George Bevan.'

'Who the bloody hell is George Bevan?' Marnie asked, eyes wide.

'The teenager the police thought had been involved in Alistair's death,' Peggy explained.

Marnie was immediately incensed. 'That lying little toerag. If he wasn't already dead, I'd kill him myself.'

'Hang on, Marnie, we don't actually know what happened yet.'

'No, but he's been lying to us. He's been lying to you, even after all his chat about how wonderful you were for being able to talk to him, and for listening to him!' Marnie put her hands on his hips. 'Where is he? I'm going to give him a piece of my mind!'

'That's what I'm trying to find out,' Peggy replied. 'And can you please save the yelling at him part until after I've asked him what on earth has been going on in this theatre?'

'Hmm,' Marnie replied noncommittally.

'While I'm talking to him, I need you to repeat everything he says so that Andrew knows what's going on,' Peggy said as she walked out towards centre stage.

'*Andrew?*' Marnie asked, with similar outrage to that shown for George's deception.

'Yes, Andrew,' Peggy replied, tiredly. 'You know, the detective in charge of this case.'

'Supposedly,' Marnie muttered grimly.

'Come on, Marnie, please. I'll do it without you if I must, but I'd appreciate the help.'

'Hmm,' Marnie said again.

Peggy only just about caught the slight change in the air around her before George appeared in front of her, a relieved smile on his face.

'Miss Peggy! You came back!' George stepped closer as he spoke. 'I was so worried that you were gone for good.'

'Sure you were, bud,' Marnie snapped, folding her arms and glaring.

'I don't understand,' George said slowly, looking between the two women. 'What's wrong?'

'You haven't been telling me the truth.' The words were bitter in Peggy's mouth. 'You've been lying about who you are since we first spoke.'

Several emotions flickered over George's expression, until his face finally settled into something that looked like guilt. 'No, I haven't.'

'Yes, you have,' Peggy replied steadily. '*George.*'

The guilt flared into surprise, and when George's mouth opened to form the inevitable denial, no sound came out. He gawped at Peggy for a long moment, and then eventually his mouth snapped closed again.

'What happened here back in 1932?' Peggy asked carefully.

'Did you kill Alistair Tunham?'

'I did no such thing!' George cried with such vehemence that both Peggy and Marnie took a couple of steps backwards.

At that moment, the door at the back of the auditorium flew open and Andrew came barrelling down the aisle towards the stage access door. 'Have you found him?'

'Yes,' Peggy called back, keeping her eyes on George. 'George is here.'

Andrew sped up, and only a few seconds later he popped out from behind the curtain and onto the stage.

'Marnie, if you rip this jacket, I'll find some way to make you pay for the damage!' Peggy heard Andrew squawk in outrage from just behind her.

'Well, stay put and I won't have to keep grabbing it, will I?' Marnie replied snottily.

Peggy only just managed to refrain from rolling her eyes. Her focus was George, not on the childish sniping of the supposed adults she worked with. 'George was just about to explain what happened back in 1932.'

Peggy didn't actually know that for sure and, if she were to be entirely honest, she was half-expecting George to just pop off into the aether and refuse to answer any of her questions, but perhaps if she stated it with enough confidence, then fact would naturally follow fiction.

'You're correct that I'm not Alistair Tunham, but I did not kill him,' George said eventually. He sighed heavily, removed his straw boater, and ran the back of his hand over his forehead.

'What?' Andrew hissed in confusion.

'Peggy told me to repeat everything Whatshisname says to you,' Marnie whispered back. 'Now, shut up.'

'Can you tell me what *did* happen then, George?' Peggy asked gently.

George, looked up at the proscenium arch and then out into

the auditorium. 'I always wanted to be an actor. Ever since I was small.'

Peggy frowned slightly as she noted the change in George's voice; the crisp edges of his words had slipped, and something decidedly more Lancashire had made its way into his accent. All pretence of Alistair was gone; this was entirely George Bevan now.

'Managed to get meself a job 'ere when I was twelve,' George continued proudly. 'Nothin' fancy, mind. Just sweepin' up backstage to start with, and then, after a while, people used to let me run errands for them, and they'd slip me a few extra pence on the side.

'I got to 'ang around durin' rehearsals and watch what the proper professionals did. You know, the ones who'd been on stage down in London, and even some who'd put on shows in places like Paris and Vienna. Can you imagine that?'

George's face fell slightly as he turned back to Peggy. 'No, I suppose you wouldn't 'ave to just imagine places like that, would you, Miss Peggy?'

Peggy didn't reply.

'Well,' George continued, addressing his invisible audience once more, 'when I was seventeen I 'eard that Clarence Wright was comin' to the Court to put on *Lady Bancroft*. Richard Sykes – 'e were the director – was known for wanting to cast local actors whenever 'e could find good 'uns, and I thought that maybe I'd 'ave a chance if I could just talk to 'im, you know?

'One of the other boys that worked 'ere told me that Sykes and Wright were gonna be at some fancy party they were puttin' on at The Midland a couple of months before the show was due to start, and so I took all me savings – the ones I 'adn't given to me mam – and I bought this jacket from a tailor over in Ardwick. I felt proper fancy in it, and I walked right into The Midland, and nobody stopped me. D'you know what they did instead?'

'I don't,' Peggy replied quietly.

'They called me *sir*, and asked me if I wanted a glass of champagne! *Me*!' George crowed. 'Me mam would barely let me sip 'er sherry at Christmas, and now 'ere I was, swiggin' champagne and talkin' to people who thought I might be interestin', and somethin' more than just some poor lad from Ancoats!'

'Well, what happened?' Andrew asked impatiently when George trailed off into silence.

Peggy turned and made a shushing motion at him before returning her attention to the man she was trying to get the truth out of. 'Sorry, George. What happened at The Midland?'

George's expression darkened. 'Enriette St. Clair.'

Peggy could practically feel the questions radiating from Andrew, so she decided to take control of the conversation before he barged in and scared George away. 'What did Henriette do?'

'She recognised me. I'd bumped into 'er a few times before, and she were a right snob, always glidin' around thinkin' she were better than the rest of us. She 'ad a right good laugh at me in my new jacket, and then told everyone who'd listen that I was just some kid who worked at the theatre, and that I must 'ave sneaked into the party to get drunk and cause trouble!' George's anger was palpable. 'She knew why I was there. She was there for the same bloody reason, after all! The only difference was that she 'ad some fancy invitation, and I didn't.

'I got thrown out of the party after a while. They didn't even let me walk out the front door; I got dragged out through the kitchen and everythin'. Mr McMillan who managed the theatre, 'e let me keep me job because 'e knew I worked 'ard, and 'e knew what sodding 'Enriette was like, but 'e wouldn't let me go near any of the shows for ages. 'E wouldn't even give me permission to stay and watch the performances from the back like 'e'd always used to.

'By the time the rehearsals for *Lady B* started, I'd missed two Shakespeares, an Ibsen, and a Shaw, and I wasn't going to miss the opening night of *Lady Bancroft* when Clarence Wright was right 'ere in the Court!'

Peggy wasn't sure where this story was headed, but she was very aware that she was yet to hear Alistair Tunham's name as part of it yet. 'George, what happened with Alistair?'

George looked up at the ceiling and sighed again. 'Alistair was alright. Turned up when 'e was supposed to, got on well enough with everyone, and 'e weren't a bad actor either. 'Enriette didn't like 'im, of course, but then again, she didn't like anyone; well, anyone except Clarence Wright anyway. Wright didn't like 'er quite as much though, which were the problem in the end.'

'What do you mean?' Peggy asked.

"Enriette followed Mr Wright around like a stray dog,' George replied. 'She wanted 'is attention all the time, but 'e wasn't much interested in 'er. She were right jealous when she found out that Mr Wright 'ad a girl back in London, and then a rumour started that Mr Wright was seen being inappropriate with the lady playin' Isabella — I can't remember 'er name. Jane something, maybe. I knew it must've been 'Enriette that started it because she thought it were really funny when Mr Wright got all upset about it.'

'Did that rumour have something to do with Clarence Wright pulling out of the play?' Peggy asked, thinking back to what Cohen had said when he'd first told the story of opening night.

George nodded. 'The Jane girl's 'usband was mightily upset when 'e 'eard that Wright and 'is wife were apparently *involved*. On the morning the show was openin', Mr Wright 'eard that the 'usband was gonna confront 'im before the performance that night. 'E 'ran back to London like 'e 'ad the devil on his 'eels, even though there were no truth to it. Mr Wright were a right good actor, but I think 'e were actually a bit of a crook and a coward in real life. So, that's when Alistair got told 'e was goin' on that night, and 'e were absolutely delighted about it. Terrified, rightly, but delighted.

'That Jane girl's 'usband showed up just before the play started and was lookin' everywhere for Mr Wright,' George explained sombrely. 'When 'e 'eard that Mr Wright 'ad left, 'e got really angry. 'Enriette was pretendin' to care, but really she was just doin' everythin' she could to try and get Jane to leave so that she could take over as Isabella. She was tellin' this man that 'is wife 'ad eyes for all the men in the production, and now that Clarence Wright 'ad left, it was only a matter of time before she moved on to the next one, which was likely to be Alistair.'

Peggy was struck with the similarity between Henriette trying to force another actress out of the Isabella role, and the way Lavinia had behaved towards Emma Allen. Peggy would have to be fair and declare that Henriette St. Clair's response had been significantly more extreme than Lavinia's, but she had to wonder what the hell it was with this role that seemed to make women lose their minds over it?

'Anyway,' George continued, 'Jane and 'er 'usband 'ad the most almighty row just before curtain up. I was cleanin' up the back staircase when I 'eard it. She told 'im that 'e was an idiot for listening to gossip, and 'e did a load of shoutin' and said that 'e was gonna sort it out for good. *Carter*, that was 'is name. Mr Carter.'

'Sort it out?' Peggy repeated, a sort of cold, sick feeling settling in her stomach as her brain began to make connections.

George nodded. 'I saw Carter talkin' to one of the blokes that did the lights, real 'ush-'ush, like. I don't know what 'e said, but I saw 'im 'and over a great wodge of notes.'

Peggy winced. 'George, if you saw that happen, why didn't you tell anyone?'

George's lips twisted. 'What would I 'ave told them, Miss

Peggy? That I saw a man give another man some money?'

'But surely you must have thought that something bad might happen, especially after what this Carter man had said about 'sorting things out'? You could have saved Alistair's life!'

'Careful, Peg,' Andrew warned quietly, voice strained.

'Maybe I could 'ave!' George cried. 'Maybe I could 'ave, and I've wondered every day since whether it would've made a blind bit of difference if I'd gone to Mr Macmillan, or anyone else, and told them what I'd seen. But I didn't, Miss Peggy, and maybe that makes me every bit the same type of man as Clarence Wright when 'e ran off back to London. Maybe I'm just a coward.'

'What happened next, George?' Peggy asked sharply, not wanting to derail the story by George getting sidetracked by guilt.

'I don't know,' George replied mulishly.

'*George*!'

'Peggy!' Andrew hissed again. Apparently, it was alright if he got stroppy with a suspect, but the same couldn't be said for anyone else.

'I don't *know* because I was all the way at the back of the theatre tryin' to watch the play,' George grumbled. 'Alistair came out to do 'is big line, 'e flicked the light switch and 'e were dead an instant later.'

'If you were nowhere near any of it, why did the police think you were involved?' Peggy asked as evenly as possible.

'Because that evil 'arpy told them it was me!' George exploded, launching forward and waving his arms around.

Peggy stumbled backwards in alarm, colliding with Andrew, who yelped loudly in surprise.

'What's going on?' Andrew snapped as he steadied them both.

'George isn't happy,' Marnie murmured, watching where George was now pacing back and forth.

No, George was not happy. Peggy was fairly certain that George had no way of affecting things around him the way that

Marnie could, or Jock for that matter, but, personally, she was never happy to be around a restless ghost.

'She told the police that I must've left that note in Alistair's dressin' room,' George ranted as he strode across the stage. 'She told 'em I was obviously the type to 'ave those sorts of Godfearin' words up me sleeve, what with me mam 'avin' come over on the boat from Dublin. Mam was as lapsed a Catholic as they came though, and I didn't even know what those words meant.'

'Do you know who did write it?' Peggy asked, still keeping her distance.

George nodded. 'Jock did. 'E told me 'imself years later. The message 'ad been meant for Clarence Wright, not Alistair. Jock's never liked liars.'

Peggy wondered what that meant Jock thought of George's deception.

'Peggy, we've got about fifteen minutes until they open the doors,' Andrew said quietly, and with obvious despair. 'We need to know what we're dealing with here.'

Peggy nodded and took a cautious step back towards the ghost. 'George, can you tell me what happened to Henriette, and to Peter McClellan?

George stopped pacing immediately and scowled. 'That woman got me the sack. I lost everythin'. Mr McMillan wouldn't give me another chance after that.

'After the police came for me I 'ad to run, didn't I? I couldn't stay 'ere and wait to be banged up. I left the city with nothin', and made me way down to London.

'For a bit, I thought it might be alright. It was so much bigger and brighter down there, and nobody knew who I was. I got meself another job in a theatre, and I wasn't 'appy, but at least I didn't 'ave anyone after me. But then the war came, didn't it?'

George looked down at his feet and sniffed once. 'Sometimes I wish I 'adn't seen the end of it, but I did, and thought it would be alright to come back up 'ere after so long. Everyone was gone, 'cept for mam, and I looked after 'er until she died a year later. I stayed in the 'ouse, and maybe things would've been different if I 'adn't seen the news that *Lady B* was being put on at the Palace. The papers couldn't get enough of it, what with what 'ad 'appened with Alistair, but it meant that my name was back out there again too.

'When I 'eard that 'Enriette was starring in the play, I went to the Palace to find 'er. Everyone who'd ever worked at the Court knew the stories about Jock, so I thought I'd give 'er a fright, and try and get 'er to pull out of the play.

'I followed 'er around for a few days, put the wind right up 'er, but she was still there on opening night. I even wrote 'er that note with that bit from Proverbs in it, just like the one Jock left. I only wanted to scare 'er, but those stairs were a deathtrap, I chased 'er up there and she fell right down 'em. I didn't mean for it to 'appen, but it was my fault she died. It was my fault, and I couldn't forgive meself for it.'

Peggy closed her eyes and sighed. George hadn't killed Alistair, but he *had* been instrumental in Henriette St. Clair's death fifteen years later, regardless of his intent. And now, Peggy had a feeling that she knew what was coming next in the story.

Henriette had fallen to her death in 1947, which meant that George would have been thirty-two when it happened. The baby-faced features that Peggy had seen in the newspaper photograph had lingered, giving the impression that George was in his mid-to-late-twenties when he'd died – it was one of the reasons she hadn't thought to question if he'd been telling the truth when he'd said he was Alistair – which meant that he surely must have died soon after Henriette.

'What happened, George?' Peggy asked softly.

George looked directly at Peggy for the first time in minutes, and she was dismayed to see that his eyes had filled with tears.

She always hated this part.

'She screamed when she fell,' George said, in a voice barely above a whisper. 'People came runnin' out, and I knew that I 'ad to leave. I ran straight out of the Palace and down the road towards the canal; I didn't really know what I was thinkin', but the water was freezin', Miss Peggy. I don't even know if I'd changed my mind after I jumped in, but I was too cold to think. It just got darker and darker, and then the next thing I knew I was back 'ere; a place I 'adn't set foot in since I was seventeen.'

'Oh, George,' Peggy said quietly. There'd been nothing in the file from Higson about what had happened to George after the night Alistair had been killed and yet, if what she was being told now were true, he'd died only up the road, and on the same night as Henriette St. Clair.

Nobody had missed him enough to notice.

'Where is he?' Andrew asked quietly as he appeared at Peggy's shoulder.

'Centre stage,' Peggy whispered.

'George,' Andrew said loudly, and George shot him a disbelieving look. 'George, I'm sorry for what happened to you, and I promise that I'll make sure we look into everything you've told us once this case is over. But, right now we're running out of time, and I need to know what's been going on for the past few weeks. I need to know if you've been behind any of it, and if you were telling the truth about the woman you saw.'

'He still can't see or hear you,' Peggy said, when George kept looking at Andrew in confusion. 'He just wants to make sure that nobody else dies because of this play.'

George nodded minutely. 'After the war, the Court was closed for fifteen years, and I watched Jock get less and less powerful, and I could only thank God for it. 'E were awful to the rest of us, terrorising us. I weren't lyin' to you when I said we were all scared of 'im. The others faded away over time; I think mostly because they'd rather be gone for good than to 'ave been stuck with that black soul for whatever eternity we otherwise 'ad.

'By the time they opened the theatre again even I could barely see 'im, and everyone seemed to 'ave forgotten the way the stories of 'im used to scare the livin' daylights outta everyone who ever set foot on this stage. 'E weren't too 'appy about that, but there were nothin' 'e could do if there were nobody around to believe in 'im. I thought 'e might fade away for good, to be honest, but then they went and decided to put *Lady B* on again, and Peter McClellan remembered the stories of the Shadow Man from back when 'e were a young actor. Jock must've found some power in it, because suddenly 'e were more like 'is old self. 'E was followin' McClellan round, repeatin' that verse at 'im; 'e thought it were ever so funny when McClellan dropped dead.'

Peggy swallowed heavily, feeling sick to her stomach at the thought. Andrew shifted uncomfortably next to her.

'Jock were dead quiet again after that. You see, nobody really thought Peter McClellan 'ad been scared to death - not when everyone knew 'ow 'e spent most days drinkin' from dawn 'til dusk - so I really thought it might've been enough for Jock to disappear for good, until this lot turned up, wittering on and on about the Shadow Man and 'ow the play was cursed. That Miss Lavinia was the worst of the lot of 'em, windin' up the others and then claimin' that she didn't believe in any of it.'

Andrew shifted uncomfortably again, and Peggy almost rolled her eyes.

'Jock managed to move a few things around,' George continued, 'paper, keys, little things like that. It weren't until you came along, Miss Peggy, that 'e really got into the swing of things. Both of you actually.'

Peggy frowned. 'Marnie, you mean?'

George shook his head. 'No. Your detective, there. I know the Inspector can't see me like you, but Jock still 'ad enough of 'imself about 'im yesterday that 'e could knock Mr Joyce down the stairs. 'E asn't managed to do that with anyone else.'

Okay, *that* was a troubling thought. Andrew evidently thought the same if the way he inched closer to Peggy until their shoulders were pressed together was any indication. Peggy's niggling worry that she was somehow responsible for what had happened in Andrew's house only deepened.

'But it weren't Jock who locked Miss Lavinia in the office last week. She did that 'erself.' George had the good grace to look ashamed. 'I know I should 'ave told you that, and I'm sorry I didn't. There really *was* a woman 'angin' around though – I was tellin' the truth about that. Do you know who she might be?'

Andrew shook his head as Marnie repeated George's question. 'Not a clue, and I'm not happy about that fact, at all.'

'I'm so sorry, Miss Peggy,' George said quietly. 'It's just that nobody 'ad spoken to me in so long, and when you asked if I was Alistair I knew you were more likely to want to talk to 'im, than you were to talk to George Bevan. I shouldn't 'ave lied to you. It were wrong of me.'

Liars, Peggy thought again. They knew George had lied, and that Lavinia and Emma had lied too. Could they actually trust *anyone* that they'd spoken to over the past week?

'George, where's Jock now?' Peggy asked, even though she wasn't sure she wanted an answer.

'I don't know.' George shook his head. 'I haven't seen 'im at all since yesterday. It must've taken a lot out of 'im to do what 'e did.'

'Hmm,' Andrew muttered gloomily.

'Do you think the cast is in any danger from him tonight?' Peggy asked George.

'I don't know,' George said again, 'although 'e 'asn't seemed interested in doin' much more than scarin' them up to this point.'

Peggy sighed. 'Well, do you think Detective Inspector Joyce is in any danger from him tonight?'

'Not the point,' argued Andrew.

'Yes, it is,' Peggy said, brushing his denial away. 'George?'

George shrugged. 'I'd say it's more likely than Jock 'avin a go at one of the actors.'

'Oh, dear,' Marnie said, false concern dripping from her words, and delivered only just loud enough to ensure she was heard.

'Enough,' Andrew snapped. 'Look, we still don't know who this mystery woman is, so we have to assume that she's out to do harm; specifically to Lavinia, as she's been the one targeted so far.'

'Or she's just another plant Miss Priss has brought in to muddy the waters,' Marnie said.

To Peggy's surprise, Andrew nodded his agreement.

'You could be right,' he conceded, 'but we don't know for certain. I need to speak to Higson.'

'Hang on!' Marnie said, holding up her hand. She pointed at George. 'You said that Jock couldn't be seen by anyone but you these days.'

'I did.' George nodded solemnly.

'Ignoring the fact that I briefly saw him yesterday, that still remains true,' Marnie continued. 'Peggy, you haven't seen him, even when he's spoken to you.'

'Okay,' Peggy said slowly, because she wasn't quite sure where Marnie was going with this.

'So, if Lavinia had been the only one to see the Shadow Man this week, then I'd probably just call her a big fat liar *again*,' Marnie replied. 'But Vic said she saw *something*, even if she doesn't believe in any of it. So how could they both have seen something that should have been impossible for them to see, unless there definitely *is* someone playing silly buggers?'

Andrew frowned as he nodded slowly. 'So, the mystery woman and whoever's been pretending to be Jock could be one and the same.'

'George, can you tell us anything else about the woman you've seen?' Peggy asked.

'No more than I've already told you,' George replied apologetically. 'I never got a good look at 'er face; like I said, she was tall, with long brown 'air, which she 'ad in this fancy twisty plait thing that went right down 'er back. I only noticed 'er because 'er 'air made her look like she'd walked right out of a Shakespeare play. She kept 'er 'ead down, and I never saw 'er talking to anyone.'

'What?' Peggy asked when Andrew screwed up his face.

'When I first heard that description, I immediately thought it was Sue Allen, seeking revenge for her sister, but Jen says she's got an alibi for any time we have a sighting of the woman,' Andrew explained. 'It wasn't her, and it can't be Emma because she's a good half a foot shorter than her sister, and you'd be hard pushed to ever describe her as 'tall'. So, what if it was just Lavinia?'

'Lavinia's blonde,' Marnie sniped, 'which I know even *you* noticed.'

Peggy watched as Andrew fought not to snap back at Marnie – he'd generally been getting better at avoiding the temptation.

'That twisty hair thing on top of her head when she's in costume isn't really her hair though, is it?' Andrew asked, waving his hands over his head to supplement his point. 'I don't know what you'd call it. It's not a ponytail.'

Marnie snorted.

Peggy took pity on him. 'No, it's not a ponytail. It's all clever hairpieces and wigs so that they can do quick costume changes.'

'Do you remember the file we saw for the play Cohen did with Lavinia last year, up in the archive room?' Andrew asked.

'*The Importance of Being Earnest*,' Peggy confirmed. 'Yes, why?'

'Didn't the photograph on the programme have the main cast all dressed up like they could have been performing Shakespeare?'

Peggy thought back to the brief look she'd given that box before Jock had made his presence known. 'I'm not sure. Maybe. But, Andrew, we know that Lavinia was with Vic when they saw a shadowy figure, so that means there could still be two people at work here.'

'So, it's just like Marnie suggested – this man could be a plant,' Andrew replied. 'Look, Lavinia knows where things are kept in this place. She's also good at changing her hair and costume quickly, so it's entirely possible that George has just seen Lavinia with different hair any time he's seen this supposed mystery woman. I'm going to go and check that programme and see if the description matches Lavinia's costume from last year.'

Andrew took a step back and gestured towards the staircase. 'If this whole thing has been Lavinia setting us up, she's not putting a foot on that stage tonight. Peg, I'll even be the one to tell your mother that her play's off and there's nothing she can do about it.'

Peggy appreciated the confidence – and the sentiment – but Andrew didn't have a clue just how formidable a foe Caroline Winshire could be. Peggy knew that her mother could have Andrew's career ruined by midnight.

'No, if it comes to that, *I'll* tell her,' Peggy said firmly. 'She can't ruin my life any more than she has already.'

'Maybe we should get Charlie to tell her,' Andrew suggested with a small grin. 'He'd probably enjoy that.'

'As lovely as it is to see you two being sickeningly nice to each other again,' Marnie griped, making a displeased face, 'can we save all this until after Goldilocks is on her way to a police station, please? Hang about, does this place sell popcorn?'

Peggy was about to tell Marnie off for being a bit too gleeful when a high-pitched scream ripped through the air from somewhere backstage.

The popcorn would have to wait.

TWENTY

Andrew took the steps two at a time with Peggy close behind him.

'That better not be Lavinia again!' Marnie hissed as she followed Peggy and, Andrew assumed, George too.

As they reached the first-floor landing, it became immediately obvious that it hadn't been Lavinia shrieking at all. Instead, Marion and Carly, the usually cheerful wardrobe assistant, were both clutching at each other's forearms, pale-faced and shaking while Jen and Cohen tried to get Marion to stop making a hysterical bleating sound.

Lavinia, for her part was leaning against Marion's dressing room door, features twisted into an expression that appeared closer to annoyance than fear.

'What's happened?' Andrew asked, striding towards Marion, just as Higson appeared at the other end of the corridor from where he'd been holed up in the men's shared dressing room.

'I saw him,' Marion replied in a hoarse whisper. 'The Shadow Man. He went up the stairs to the second floor. Carly saw him too, didn't you?'

Carly nodded. Her eyes were wide, and Andrew saw no hint of deception there.

'Does that mean I'm going to die?' Marion asked in a small voice, with no hint of her usual disdain.

Without giving her an answer, Andrew turned and barrelled up the narrow staircase. If Marion and Carly had both seen someone then it was likely that it hadn't been anything spectral, and this might be Andrew's one chance to catch whoever it was in the act. He supposed that at least he knew now that it wasn't Lavinia in an elaborate costume; although he wasn't sure that such information was particularly helpful to him at that stage.

'Doors are in five minutes, Inspector Joyce!' Cohen bellowed from the bottom of the stairs.

Andrew made a face and chose to remain silent. He had no idea how any of them could still be thinking of the sodding play.

The hallway was empty, and he couldn't hear anything beyond the flustered chattering of the crowd he'd left on the floor below.

He cautiously opened the door to Lavinia's original dressing room first, but all he found were the same lipstick-covered walls from the day before. The shards of mirror crunched beneath his shoes as he checked behind the door, but there was nobody to be seen.

Andrew continued his investigation, quickly moving down the short corridor. The other rooms – a mix of dressing rooms and storage cupboards – remained as empty as the first, albeit with zero instances of angrily daubed scripture.

Finally, the only door that remained was the one that led down to the stage.

Andrew twisted the doorknob and stumbled slightly when the door didn't open as expected. He tried again, rattling the doorknob violently, but the door remained stubbornly closed. It was well and truly locked.

He spun around and barrelled back down the staircase to find that the first-floor corridor was now teeming with people.

Off to one side, Peggy was speaking quietly and calmly to Cohen, obviously trying to sooth the waves of stratospheric frustration that Andrew could practically feel radiating from the director. Just beyond them, a stricken Vic was standing with Ben and a still visibly shaken Carly, while Jen was continuing in her attempt to get Marion to take normal breaths instead of the terrible gulps of air she was sucking in.

Higson was ferociously bellowing down at the uniformed officers still stationed just inside the stage door. Andrew had missed most of the tirade but caught the part where Higson accused them of not having the brains to know their arses from their elbows.

The whole scene was a chaotic one, and it struck Andrew that absolutely everything about the entire week had been rooted in some form of chaos.

How much of that chaos had been engineered by Lavinia, or whoever was now dressing up like an angry spirit?

Hang on.

Andrew looked around, scanning the small crowd. He caught Jen's eye. 'Where's Lavinia?'

'What?' Jen turned slowly in a complete circle, shaking her head in confusion. 'She was here a minute ago.'

'I know,' Andrew replied. 'I saw her. Where's Teddy?'

'He went for a slash a few minutes ago before the screeching,' Higson called as he lit the cigarette hanging from his lips. 'I told him he could piss off and do whatever the fuck he wanted. I'm not too worried about that little prick getting himself killed. If I had to spend five more minutes with him, I'd have strangled myself.'

Marnie's sudden reappearance wasn't quite as subtle as Andrew would have liked, and he sighed in poorly concealed frustration when Marion managed to blanch even further in fright, point at Marnie in a wordless gawp, and them crumple to the carpet.

'Marion!' Cohen cried in horror. 'Shit! What happened? Was it the ghost?'

'No,' Peggy replied quickly, eyes to the floor, 'it wasn't the ghost.'

Marnie looked Andrew dead in the eye, as seriously as she'd looked at him in Gatley on Friday night. 'They're both backstage, screaming at each other.'

Andrew inclined his head in thanks, and then pointed at the assembled crowd. 'All of you, stay here with DCI Higson. Jen, find Lloyd and tell him not to let anyone into this auditorium. I don't care if he has to handcuff Caroline Winshire to the front door to make that happen, but nobody gets into that auditorium until I say so.'

'Sir.' Jen nodded and headed towards the foyer, leaving Vic and Cohen to watch over Marion.

'Find the prick, Joyce,' Higson barked, 'and make it quick.'

'Sir.' Andrew agreed. He held his hand out to Cohen and gestured impatiently. 'Give me your keys. All of them. Now.'

'Driscoll!' Higson snapped as Marnie made to follow Jen. 'Where do you think you're going? You broke the grumpy wench so you can sit there and mop her brow until she comes around.'

Andrew snatched Cohen's keyring and hurried towards the door that would lead him to the stage, leaving Marnie's disgruntled grumbling behind him.

As he'd anticipated, the door was locked, just like the one upstairs.

Andrew quickly located the correct key and pushed open the door a moment later. Immediately, he could hear raised voices in the near distance, but the words weren't clear.

He was half-way down the staircase when he realised that he wasn't alone.

Andrew whipped his head around to see a mass of pink right behind him. 'Peggy!'

Peggy nearly tripped right into him. 'Jesus, Andrew, don't stop on stairs like that!'

'Go back up there and stay with Higson,' Andrew ordered, pointing over Peggy's shoulder.

'Absolutely not.'

Andrew scowled. 'I have no idea what those two down there are up to!'

'You have no idea what Jock is up to either,' Peggy replied plainly.

'He's not my problem right now!' Andrew sighed loudly. 'Peggy, please, just go back up there. Look, if Jock is around, what's to say he doesn't decide to have a go at one of the cast? Or Cohen? Or one of our team?'

'And what if he decides to have a go at *you*?' Peggy folded her arms. 'Marnie's back there, and George too. They can handle it without me. You can't.'

Andrew wanted to argue – there weren't many things that he appreciated less than Peggy throwing herself headfirst into danger – but then there was a further explosive eruption in the raised voices below, followed by a sudden, ominous silence.

'We should move,' Peggy murmured.

Andrew led the way quietly down the final few steps, reaching out to slowly peel a blackout curtain out of the way.

He waited until Peggy was right behind him again and then shuffled slowly into the concealed area of the stage.

'Shit!' Andrew hissed in alarm, bolting towards where Lavinia lay, sprawled awkwardly on her back, with the crimson fabric of her costume splayed dramatically around her.

'Oh my God,' Peggy whispered as she dropped to Lavinia's side. She reached out her fingers to check Lavinia's pulse and flinched back in surprise when Lavinia shifted slightly with a soft groan of pain.

'Miss Heathcote? Lavinia?' Andrew tried urgently to rouse her further, keeping his voice low, lest Teddy be lurking nearby. 'Can you tell me what happened?'

Lavinia blinked sleepily, clearly unable to focus on Andrew as he spoke to her.

Peggy suddenly made a choked gasping sound.

'What is it?' Andrew asked uneasily.

Peggy opened that ridiculous sparkly bag and pulled out a white handkerchief. She pressed it to the back of Lavinia's head and then held up the scarlet-stained scrap of cotton so that Andrew could see. 'That's a lot of blood, Andrew.'

Rationally, Andrew knew that head wounds could bleed an

awful lot, and that what looked like an extraordinary amount of blood wasn't necessarily as terrible as you might initially think. Still, Lavinia wasn't responding much beyond the small whimpers of pain that fell from her lips when Peggy pressed the hanky against the wound again.

'Lavinia, can you hear me?' Peggy asked quietly but firmly. 'Do you know where you are? Do you know what happened to you?'

Lavinia's expression creased in discomfort as she parted her lips, blinking far too slowly to be considered normal and alert.

'Teddy,' she muttered eventually, just before her eyes rolled back into her head and she stilled entirely.

Andrew felt his own blood seize, until Peggy once more pressed two fingertips beneath Lavinia's jaw and sighed in relief.

Andrew looked around, eyes straining to see in the dim light. Next to Lavinia's feet there was a heap of black material, which turned out to be a discarded long black coat once Andrew gave it a bit of a prod. He assumed it was part of the costume Teddy had donned as the Shadow Man.

Just beyond Peggy lay something small and heavy looking, and Andrew frowned as he tried to decipher what it was from afar.

He picked his away towards it, pressing his finger to his lips as he passed Peggy, and then crouched down to take a closer look.

There, with a shiny smudge that looked like oil in the semi-darkness, was the brass carriage clock that usually sat right in the centre of Lady Bancroft's mantelpiece.

It wouldn't have taken a genius to figure out that Lavinia had been hit on the back of the head with the clock.

'Is that the clock from the set?' Peggy asked in dismay.

Andrew nodded grimly. 'You don't have another hanky on you, do you?'

'Sorry.'

Andrew tugged off the infernal bowtie, bidding a silent goodbye to any deposit that had been placed on the hired suit, wrapped the satin around his fingertips and gingerly lifted the clock from the floor. 'I need you to take this up to Higson, alright? Get someone to call an ambulance for Lavinia and tell Cohen his play's stuffed. Then, I want you to get out of this theatre and go home.'

'I'm not leaving you to go after Teddy by yourself!' Peggy rose to her feet and folded her arms.

'I'll be fine,' Andrew replied with as much confidence as he could muster. 'Peggy, I need you to be somewhere else, alright?'

Andrew vividly remembered the last time he'd said those exact words to Peggy: they had just managed to flee the burning wreckage of the old Hughes' house, and Andrew had been excruciatingly aware of the fact that they were face-to-face with someone who had murdered Marnie in a jealous rage, and who would likely not hesitate to do the same to Peggy, if given even half the chance.

Peggy hadn't listened to him then, but he really needed her to listen to him now.

'I can call Marnie down here and get her to give Jen a message,' Peggy reasoned. 'I can make sure tha-'

'Peggy, *no*,' Andrew said firmly, reaching out to still Peggy's hand.

Peggy looked down in surprise.

'You said it yourself,' Andrew added, keeping his tone as light as he could, 'they've got Marnie up there to help them. Jen or Lloyd will make sure Lavinia's okay. I need to know that you're somewhere else; somewhere safer than here. Alright?'

A loud shuffling sound from somewhere beyond the curtain startled them both.

'Peg,' Andrew hissed urgently, '*Please.*'

'I'm sending Jen down after you,' Peggy whispered insistently.

'And Higson. And Lloyd!'

'You can send whoever you want, just go back up those stairs.'

Peggy pulled her hand away, and then very carefully took the clock from Andrew, making sure to keep her fingers on the bowtie. 'Be careful.'

'I will.'

Andrew watched until Peggy had crept quietly to the top of the stairs.

A whining, scraping sound from the direction of the stage almost disguised the quiet snick of the door closing, but as soon as Andrew knew that Peggy was out of range he sprang into action.

He tiptoed to the edge of the stage, keeping himself just out of sight from anyone who might be in the auditorium, and peered around the curtain.

Teddy, in his Sebastian costume, was crouching close to the ground on the opposite side of the stage.

At first, Andrew couldn't work out how Teddy seemed to have his hands inside the stage, but then he realised that there was a square opening in the floor that he'd never seen before. There was a trap door that was usually covered by a large, floral rug that was part of the drawing room set.

Andrew watched as Teddy lowered himself into the opening, keeping his forearms flat on the stage as the rest of his body dropped out of sight.

When Teddy's chin was just above the opening, he reached the fingers of his left hand out to pull the corner of the rug back towards him, tugging until it concealed his head.

A second later, there was a dull thud beneath the stage, and the rug dropped down to lay flat against the stage once again, concealing the hole Teddy had just disappeared into.

'For fuck's sake,' Andrew grumbled as he walked softly across the stage towards the rug. He knew that when he lifted the rug it would let the house lights shine down into the space beneath the stage, and then he'd have very limited time before Teddy realised that he'd been followed.

Based on his weapon of choice in the attack on Lavinia, Teddy seemed to be quite the opportunistic criminal, so Andrew dreaded to think what sorts of things languished under the stage, just waiting for an opportunity to maim him.

Andrew shrugged off his restrictive dinner jacket, letting it slither to the ground, and finally unbuttoned his collar. Then he took a deep breath and braced himself, before clambering to his knees and pulling back the rug.

There was a brief moment of complete stillness when Andrew found himself looking into the void below, with a very surprised Teddy staring right back at him.

'Detective Inspector Joyce!' Teddy's voice was pitched slightly higher than usual as he made an obvious effort to conceal his panic. 'Everything alright?'

'Not really, Teddy, no,' Andrew replied mildly. 'Any chance you could tell me why you attacked Lavinia?'

For a couple of seconds, Teddy stood there with an expression of forced blankness, before his eyes shifted to the right and he darted into the darkness with a muffled curse.

'Teddy!' Andrew barked, making a face as he realised that he really was going to have to follow Teddy into the bowels of the theatre. 'Teddy, stop!'

Teddy, unsurprisingly, did not reply.

'I bloody hate my job,' Andrew grumbled, before very inelegantly lowering his body through the trapdoor.

When he'd been looking down at Teddy, the floor hadn't seemed to be more than seven or eight feet below the stage – not a terrible distance to someone tall like Andrew – but when he was hanging by his fingertips, arms straining, it felt much, much further away.

'Jesus!' Andrew yelped as his injured shoulder protested in a painful spasm and his fingertips slipped from the edge of the trapdoor.

He found himself in free fall for a brief moment, before he landed on a few tarpaulins that did absolutely nothing to cushion his landing.

Andrew rolled onto his knees, hissing in discomfort as he clambered to his feet. It was much darker beneath the stage than he'd anticipated, and it took his eyes a good few seconds to adjust to the change.

He crept backwards until his back hit a solid wall and he tried to orient himself.

He must be at the very edge of the stage, possibly even just beneath the curtains of the left wing. Teddy, however, had bolted in the opposite direction, and Andrew didn't have a hope of seeing where he'd gone without finding a light switch first.

He groped at the wall behind him, shuffling further towards where the front of the stage would be above him. Eventually his knuckles brushed against something metallic, and he realised that it was a door handle.

Andrew pressed the handle down slowly and pulled. The door didn't open.

He tried pushing too, for good measure, but that did nothing either. It was yet another locked door.

He probably had a key for it on Cohen's keyring, but he could neither see the key labels in the dark, nor did he want to alert Teddy to the fact that he had the keys in the first place if he started jangling them around in the lock.

Andrew realised that if there was a door into a dark space then there was likely to be a light switch nearby, so he raised his hands slightly higher and patted around the edge of the doorframe.

He nearly exclaimed in relief when his fingers finally found a promising panel.

With only a brief plea to anyone listening that he wasn't about to electrocute himself, he pressed the switch.

The triumphant smile faded from his face when his efforts were rewarded with the dimmest yellow light he could have imagined.

Still, beggars couldn't be choosers, and at least he had a better idea of where he was.

'Shit,' Andrew muttered as he squinted into the semi-darkness. At least when it had been entirely dark, he hadn't any clue about the absolute disaster maze he'd found himself in.

Machinery for ancient stage traps and lifts filled the room, providing Teddy with perfect hiding places at every turn.

On top of that, the whole area was obviously used as a dumping ground for anything and everything that didn't have a home anywhere else in the theatre, if the assortment of chairs, boxes and what looked to be a severely damaged popcorn machine were anything to go by. It reminded Andrew of his spare bedroom in that respect, though hopefully it was significantly less haunted for the period of time that he was down there.

There was a clattering sound from the other side of the room, and Andrew darted forward hoping to catch a glimpse of where Teddy might be.

Teddy, it transpired, had made his way up a spiral staircase, which Andrew assumed led to another hidden door in the floor of the stage.

'Hey! Stop!' Andrew shouted as he wedged himself through a small gap separating two pieces of machinery that he couldn't have named if you'd paid him.

Teddy pushed more furiously at the ceiling just above his head, and for once Andrew was actually delighted to find that a door in this bloody theatre was locked.

Andrew raced towards the staircase. He leapt over a wooden bench, and then immediately misjudged his own athleticism when he attempted to clear a second, matching one.

His shin hit the bench with an audible crack, and he cried out in alarm as he tumbled headfirst towards the dusty floor.

Andrew managed to fling his hands out in time to save his face from greeting the ground. The sawdust that had coated the floor, now coated his hands, and he choked slightly when a few stray wisps decided to also coat his tongue.

He looked up from his uncomfortable sprawl to see Teddy charging down the steps.

When he reached the bottom, Teddy disappeared for a few moments, before he reappeared clutching a short metal pole.

Andrew scrambled to his feet, only narrowly avoiding tripping over the same bench in the opposite direction.

'Woah, woah! Hang on!' he yelped as he dived behind some sort of hydraulic lift. 'Teddy, put the bat down!'

'This wasn't supposed to happen!' Teddy cried, brandishing his new makeshift weapon. 'All she had to do was hold up her side of our agreement!'

'What agreement, Teddy?' Andrew raised his free hand in a gesture of peace, but he remained behind the lift just in case. He tucked the keys behind his back when he realised that his stupid suit trousers didn't have pockets.

'She owes me for keeping my mouth shut about how she got that other girl to quit,' Teddy snapped. 'And for not telling anyone about how *she* was the one causing all that trouble and then blaming it on bloody ghosts!'

'You mean Lavinia?' Andrew asked, already knowing the answer.

'Of course I fucking do!' Teddy snapped. 'You already know about her paying that other girl off. I heard that WPC of yours tell her earlier.'

'*Detective Sergeant* Cusack,' Andrew corrected him firmly.

'Oh, whatever,' Teddy sniped, waving the bat again. 'What

kind of bloody joke shop outfit are you lot anyway? Lavinia couldn't believe her luck when actual, *genuine* police officers who believe in ghosts showed up. And you even had that mad woman who thinks she can *talk* to them. Lavinia thought she was incredible. Where'd you find her anyway?'

Andrew scowled.

'It was Lavinia's idea to have me parading around pretending to be that ghost they're all so terrified of. She thought it would be better than just her fannying about the place in different wigs,' Teddy continued. 'She said it would get us both to Broadway if we kept it up until opening night.'

Andrew shook his head. 'So, if you care about going to New York so much, why did you attack Lavinia? The play can't go on now, Teddy.'

'I don't give a toss about Broadway!' Teddy was obviously seething. 'I did everything that lying bitch asked me to do, and then she had the fucking nerve to say that she won't pay me because I went off her precious little script.'

Andrew was doing his best to piece Teddy's rant together in his head, but he still wasn't quite there. 'What do you mean?'

'Tonight!' Teddy bellowed, and he stepped forward menacingly. 'I mean tonight! I told her I wanted to give Marion an extra little fright – that cow's had it in for me since the day I met her – and Lavinia got pissed that I'd done that. She's supposed to be the star of the haunting, isn't she?

'She came down to backstage like we'd agreed; it's where she wanted to have her dramatic end scene. She was supposed to scream to get you all racing down – you already know she's got a right pair of lungs on her – and you were supposed to see her standing up for herself against this fucking, stupid 'Shadow Man'. Then I'd disappear off the other side of the stage, dump the costume, and be back through the crossover before any of you even realised that I hadn't been there to begin with.

'Lavinia would be the brave heroine who faced a near-certain death but still opened the show to rave reviews,' Teddy said in a passable impression of Lavinia. He then made a ridiculous 'jazz hands' motion that was entirely spoiled by the fact that he was carrying something that he fully intended to thump Andrew with.

'But that's not what happened...' Andrew trailed off, hoping that Teddy would fill the leading silence with an explanation rather than a sudden bout of violence.

Teddy sneered. 'No, that's not what happened. She came down and screamed at me for wasting time pulling my 'stupid little stunt'. It wasn't stupid though; I thought I'd given Marion a heart attack it had worked so well!

'Lavinia didn't appreciate it though. She was pissed at me, saying it would make it harder for anyone to believe her grand finale performance. Even though I hadn't agreed to whatever the hell she did with the light switch the other day – that nearly gave me a heart attack - and she still continued to deny that she had anything to do with it! We argued, and she said I'd broken the terms of our agreement.'

'What agreement, Teddy?' Andrew asked for the second time, hoping that he'd actually get an answer.

'She owes me twenty grand!' Teddy roared. 'She said she wasn't giving me a penny, and that if I tried anything she was going to tell everyone that *I'd* been the one behind everything, and that I'd threatened her.'

'So, you decided to do one better and attacked her instead?' Andrew snapped. 'You could have killed her!'

'Conniving bitch had it coming,' Teddy replied coldly.

Andrew pursed his lips. 'There's nowhere for you to go. Just put the bat down and make this a much more pleasant experience for both of us.'

'I'm not going to prison, Joyce.'

Andrew would beg to differ on that one.

'So,' Teddy continued, 'why don't you just let me walk out of here? I don't care if you tell them that you almost got me before I gave you the slip. By the time any of you catch up with me I'll have sorted this whole mess out. My family is very well connected.'

Andrew frowned again. 'So well connected that you were willing to kill a woman for twenty grand? Surely that's like pocket change for you.'

Teddy's smarmy smile slipped from his face. 'It's not the money, it's the principle of the thing. I wouldn't expect someone like you to understand that sort of thing though. Look, why don't you save me the trouble of a few phone calls; what'll it take for you to keep your mouth shut? Five grand? Ten?'

Andrew blinked in surprise. 'Are you trying to pay me off?'

'Everyone has a price, Joyce,' Teddy replied evenly, shrugging. 'What's yours?'

Andrew frowned. What was that he could hear?

'Oh my God!' Teddy crowed. 'I didn't think you'd actually *consider* it. This is too good!'

'Shut up!' Andrew snapped.

'Fuck off!'

'No, seriously, shut up!' Andrew held up his hand again. 'Can you hear that?'

'Hear what?' Teddy looked around anxiously. 'I can't hear anything. What are you on about?'

Andrew ignored him and squinted into the gloom. He could definitely hear something that sounded like whispering, but where the hell was it coming from? It couldn't actually *be* whispering, because there was nobody else in the trap room.

Maybe there was a vent somewhere, and he was hearing the others talking upstairs.

Maybe it wasn't actually whispering at all and was just the low-level din of some clever stage machinery.

Or maybe it was something else entirely. Maybe it was something that Andrew didn't want to consider at all.

'I've had enough of this!' Teddy snapped. He lunged towards the gap Andrew had squeezed through.

Andrew scrambled out of the way and leapt behind some tall rolls of what he thought might be old carpet propped against the wall, falling to his knees so that he could crawl through the makeshift tunnel.

He could hear Teddy crashing about behind him and realised that being entirely without backup wasn't the brightest idea he'd ever had.

He knew what he had to do, no matter how much it would gall him to actually do it.

'Marnie,' he hissed as he lurched to his feet again. 'Marnie, I could do with some help!'

Perhaps it was time to try the bunch of keys. Andrew looked down at the keyring as he hurried towards the door he'd found in the dark, flipping through them quickly and trying to read the labels on each. Unfortunately, the keys were only numbered, and Andrew knew that the corresponding number would be on a small brass plaque screwed to the other side of the door. He had no idea which key would fit the lock, and it wasn't like Teddy would give him time to figure it out; he was much more likely to crack Andrew over the head and steal the keys from him instead.

'Marnie!' Andrew shouted. 'For fuck's sake, either get down here, or send everyone else.'

He winced as Teddy swore loudly behind him, and he changed direction so that he was running away from the door again.

'And I don't mean Peggy!' Andrew yelled, realising that it was worth clarifying.

'What the hell are you shouting about?' Teddy snarled. 'Give me those bloody keys!'

'Marnie! Seriously, I know you're pissed at me b-'

Andrew cried out in surprise as he was violently yanked backwards.

For the split second it took to hit the ground, Andrew lived in the hope that it *was* Marnie who'd grabbed him, but then he landed hard on his side with Teddy standing over him, bat raised.

The whispering reached fever pitch and Andrew pressed his hands to his ears, keys digging uncomfortably into his face.

Teddy looked around wildly. 'What's that? How are you doing that?'

The twin lightbulbs flickered threateningly and Andrew really, *really* hoped that at least *that* was Marnie.

'Stop it!' Teddy screeched, bringing the bat down.

Andrew rolled out of the way in panic, just as the lights went out, plunging the room into a darkness that felt heavier than it had earlier.

The bat clanged heavily against the floor.

Holding the keys to his chest, Andrew slowly moved towards where he thought that the back wall might be, careful to stay as close to silent as he could.

'Joyce! Put the fucking lights back on.'

Andrew's fingertips grazed the rough masonry, and he pressed his back to the wall again. He then dropped slowly into a crouch, hoping it would make it less likely that he'd be hit if Teddy started swinging the bat around recklessly in the dark.

The air cooled rapidly, and Andrew knew with a terrifying certainty that he'd be able to see his breath, if he could see anything at all.

He felt something like cold fingers trail over the nape of his neck and he jerked forward in fright, breathing rapidly.

Telling Peggy to leave suddenly felt like a less brilliant plan than it had ten minutes earlier.

'Joyce!' Teddy yelped from somewhere nearby. 'What the hell is this? Are you in it with that bitch? Are you trying to scare me?'

Andrew kept his mouth shut. As much as he wanted to refute Teddy's accusation, he wanted to keep his current location unknown even more.

The whispering stopped dead.

Andrew froze as an icy breeze fluttered over his cheek.

Then, murmured directly into his ear in a hoarse, brittle voice, came the words he'd read every time he'd climbed the staircase at home as a child:

'*The Lord detests all the proud of heart. Be sure of this: They will not go unpunished.*'

Andrew's heart stuttered unpleasantly. He'd thought of those words for the first time in almost a decade only the day before.

That was the final straw.

Andrew decided that he was going to try every bloody key on that keyring until he managed to open the door, any threat from Teddy be damned.

He pelted forward, groping for the door in the near darkness. With the weak beam of the house lights above him he thought that he might just be able to make out the numbers on the keys.

'Joyce!'

Andrew's head snapped up towards the unexpected voice.

Higson.

'Down here!' Andrew yelled. He was happier taking his chances with Teddy when he knew he wasn't entirely alone.

Higson appeared, peering down through the opening, and for one glorious moment Andrew though that he was finally out of the woods.

Then the trap door which had been hanging down into the room snapped upwards and slammed shut with such force, the entire room shook.

Teddy let out a high-pitched scream, but Andrew barely heard it over the cacophony of whispering voices assaulting him from every direction, suffocating him under a thick blanket of sound that made it almost impossible to think.

In the complete darkness it was impossible to see the keys at all, so Andrew tried them one-by-one, only able to feel his way to the lock and use his fingers to separate the ones he'd already tried from the next. His hands trembled enough to make the task even harder than it already was.

'Joyce!' Teddy exclaimed. 'Joyce, what the hell is that?'

Andrew turned around with no small amount of trepidation.

Towards the middle of the room there was a shift in the darkness; a patch of brighter grey that seemed to be shifting and dancing in midair.

'Teddy, get back here,' Andrew ordered quietly.

'What the hell is that?' Teddy repeated.

Andrew didn't have a firm answer, but he was concerned enough about his guess anyway. 'I think it might be that ghost you don't believe in.'

'Piss off!' Teddy replied, though he sounded terribly uncertain.

'Teddy!' Andrew hissed. 'Get back.'

Sudden hammering on the door behind him startled Andrew, and he staggered closer to the nebulous grey haze.

'Joyce!' Higson called through the door. 'Joyce, are you in there? If you're dead, I'll kill you!'

Andrew still had enough about him to roll his eyes.

'Not dead!' he yelled back, silently adding the 'yet'.

The trap room was by then chilled enough that Andrew was shivering, and he wished that he hadn't left his jacket on the stage.

'The keys you've got are useless!' Higson shouted. 'No key for this door. Cohen's gone to find someone who *does* have one.'

'Fuck,' Andrew muttered to himself.

Teddy suddenly bumped into Andrew's sore shoulder as he took it upon himself to run in the direction of Higson's voice and start pounding his fists on the door once he'd found it.

'Get me out of here!' Teddy wailed. 'Get me out!'

'Joyce, Driscoll can't get in to you,' Higson called, ignoring Teddy's plea. 'Vic wants to know if you can see a spiral staircase.'

'Can't see anything,' Andrew yelled back, 'but I know roughly where it is.'

'Then get your arse up it! It leads to a trap door in the stage. Parker's trying to open it.'

'Alright!' Andrew shouted. Now all he had to do was get past whatever the hell that thing was in the centre of the room, and then find a staircase in pitch blackness.

No problem.

'Teddy, we need to go the other way,' Andrew said as reasonably as he could manage when trying to save the arse of a man who'd tried to brain him.

'Fuck that!' Teddy continued hammering on the door.

Andrew held his hands out in front of him, carefully stepping forwards and hoping that he wasn't going to end up arse over tit again.

As he got closer to the middle of the room, the feeling that he shouldn't go anywhere near the distorted shadows just grew stronger.

He had only just realised that he could hear the beginnings of the whispering again when the lights suddenly snapped on above his head.

Andrew blinked at the sudden change in brightness, shaking his head to clear it, and then darted forward to take the opportunity to clear as many obstacles as he could while he still had the benefit of being able to see them.

The lights went out as suddenly as they'd come on and the whispering built to a roar.

Andrew swore. He couldn't have been more than six feet from the bottom of the staircase, but now he was going to have to get past those two bloody benches again in the dark.

The lights came back on, but then flickered off again a second later.

Andrew took a hesitant step, and the room lit up again for a moment.

'What's that?' Teddy yelled, voice shaking with fear. 'Something just touched my arm!'

'It was probably just a spider,' Andrew lied calmly. 'Just come over this way, yeah? They're going to open the door at the top of the stairs.'

What, and just let you arrest me?' Teddy snarled. 'I told you, I'm not going to prison because of that selfish cow!'

'Bigger picture, Teddy,' Andrew hissed through gritted teeth. The lights were flashing, reminding Andrew of when he and Rob had spent an evening switching the kitchen light on and off as quickly as they could while their mother had been out with friends. They'd thought it was enormous fun until Agatha had come home early. Rob had borne the brunt of the blame for that one.

Suddenly, light flooded down the spiral staircase and Lloyd's face appeared; his cheeks flushed from the effort of prising open the trapdoor. 'Alright, boss?'

Before Andrew could reply, Teddy let out a bloodcurdling howl.

Andrew spun around and, to his horror, discovered that the grey shape had been replaced with a figure that looked like it might once have been a man dressed in ragged grey clothes. There was a sneer etched deep into his face, below sunken cheekbones and empty black eye-sockets.

'Jesus Christ,' Andrew breathed in horror.

This only seemed to incense the man further as he raised his hand to point at Andrew.

'Thou shalt not-,' the man snarled before cutting himself off with a harsh cough. 'Thou shalt not take the name of the Lord thy God in vain.'

Andrew backed towards the staircase. This was not good.

'Sir, I think you should get up here,' Lloyd said, sounding panicked.

Andrew agreed entirely, and he was ready to bolt up the stairs when Teddy decided that the best course of action when faced with an angry ghost was to lob a metal bar at said angry ghost.

Jock – as Andrew assumed that's who it was – turned towards Teddy with a growl of rage.

Even with the constant flickering of the lights, it was easy to see the blood drain from Teddy's face as he realised how grave his error had been.

Andrew swore under his breath as he came to terms with the fact that he couldn't actually leave Teddy to get killed by a ghost, no matter how much of a dickhead he was.

'Sir!' Lloyd shouted in dismay when Andrew turned back towards Teddy and Jock. 'What are you doing?'

'Hey!' Andrew yelled at Jock, waving his arms above his head, still clutching the keyring. 'Oi! Over here!'

Jock's attention returned to Andrew, and Teddy went straight back to hammering on the door, screeching for salvation.

There was a series of metallic clangs from behind him and Andrew looked over his shoulder to see that Lloyd was hurrying down the spiral staircase.

'Lloyd, get out of here!' Andrew cried.

Lloyd shook his head. 'Cohen's just got some keys. That door'll be open in about thirty seconds., so that arse can get out that way, alright? You need to come up the stairs with me now, because if that *thing* shuts the trapdoor we're fucked. Er, *sir*.'

Almost as if Lloyd's words had ignited the idea, there was a horrible groaning, creaking sound, and Andrew knew that the door above their heads was about to close, trapping them all in the room until Cohen managed to get the door open.

If Cohen managed to get the door open.

Without much thought for how rational he was being, Andrew reached down and picked up what looked like a yellowing playscript from near his feet and chucked it in Jock's direction.

The creaking stopped and Jock took an odd, faltering step towards Andrew. Jock had no eyes to speak of, but Andrew could feel them boring into his soul anyway.

Andrew threw the keyring after the script.

'Sir,' Lloyd whispered. 'Sir, this is a really, really, *really* bad idea.'

'Just back away slowly,' Andrew murmured from the corner of his mouth. 'Get up the stairs.'

'What the hell is going on?'

Andrew screwed up his face at Marnie's shout. Great, so she turned up *now*. He kept his eyes firmly on Jock, who took another step towards him.

A ceaseless gust of wind, just like the one that had swept through the theatre's archive, raced through the room, picking up anything light enough in its wake and sending paper and sawdust eddying through the air.

The whispering erupted once more, and Andrew had to clamp his hands over his ears again.

Jock's outline flickered slightly, but then resolidified as he moved ever closer to Andrew.

There was suddenly so much clanking and banging that Andrew could barely concentrate on the task at hand. He wanted to squeeze his eyes shut, but he didn't dare take his trained attention off Jock.

Jock reached out his hand again, and Andrew found that he was almost within touching distance.

Andrew didn't want to believe that any of it was happening,

but the evidence was becoming increasingly difficult to refute.

A terribly loud creaking sound from above their heads split the air, standing out from the general cacophony.

Andrew looked up to see what fate was about to befall him when he was suddenly tackled to the ground for what felt like the hundredth time in twenty-four hours, just before the sound of violently splintering wood filled the room.

Andrew's breath whooshed out of his lungs as his back hit the dusty ground, and for one long agonising moment, he thought that he might never be able to draw breath in again; but then he was yanked into a sitting position and a gasp of sawdust-filled air hit the back of his throat. He coughed violently in response.

'Andrew! Are you alright?'

Andrew cracked open one eye and discovered that all he could see was *pink*.

His second eyelid popped open when the pink shook his shoulder roughly.

'I'm not dead,' Andrew croaked hoarsely, pressing his hands to his chest.

'You're not dead,' Peggy confirmed, tilting her face towards him with an expression of deep concern settled between her eyes.

Andrew wheezed in horror as the surprise cleared and reason returned. He looked around frantically, but Jock was nowhere to be seen.

Peggy shook her head. 'I don't know where he went. George has gone looking for him. He disappeared when that fell.'

Andrew followed Peggy's gaze, and his own eyes widened when he saw the enormous counterweight half-wedged in the floor, exactly where Andrew had been standing.

'Nice tackle, Peggy!' Lloyd crowed, and Andrew noted that he looked far more relaxed now that Jock had disappeared.

Lloyd's words registered a second later, and Andrew gawped at Peggy. '*You* knocked me out of the way?'

Peggy shrugged.

'Peggy!' Andrew snapped. 'I told you to get out of the theatre.'

'If it helps, I wouldn't have saved you,' Marnie sniped from nearby.

Andrew glared, ready to ask Marnie why the hell she'd ignored his earlier call for help, but there was a commotion behind him.

'Hey!' Cohen cried in surprise.

Andrew turned just in time to see Teddy push a startled Higson out of the way and then flee through the now-open main door.

'Shit!' Andrew struggled to his feet and raced after Teddy. He could hear people following him, but he kept his eyes straight ahead.

Teddy swore loudly, increasing his pace as he took a sharp right and burst through the door that led to the auditorium, just at the edge of stage left.

Teddy didn't stop, and Andrew had to reach out his hands to avoid being hit by the door as it swung ferociously back towards him, and he shouldered his way out into the auditorium.

Teddy was already halfway up the aisle, ignoring every one of Andrew's demands for him to stop.

Andrew ran faster, finally exploding through the door to the foyer only a few seconds after Teddy.

The uniformed officers at the top of the stairs hadn't recovered from the slightly earlier surprise of Teddy fleeing past them, and they barely reacted as Andrew raced by, hurtling down the stairs two at a time.

'Stop that man!' Andrew yelled, but the baffled guests only stared back in confusion, or jumped out of Teddy's way.

Teddy shot through the front doors and out onto the pavement just as Edgar was helping an elegantly dressed woman out of the driver's seat of that stupid orange car.

Caroline Winshire watched Teddy's approach with pure

surprise written all over her face.

Teddy grabbed the car keys from Caroline's hand and roughly pushed her out of the way. Then he flung himself into the driver's seat and peeled away from the kerb a second later.

Andrew patted his sides, looking for the keys to the Belmont, before he realised that he'd left them in his jacket, which was still on the stage. 'Idiot!'

Peggy appeared at his side in a flash of flamingo.

'Charlie!' she yelled. 'Keys!'

Andrew watched as Charlie reached into his pocket halfway across the foyer, and then threw his car keys in an arc towards his sister, who caught them safely in her right hand.

'Come on then!' Peggy snapped at Andrew before she hurried past her obviously surprised mother and ex-fiancé without sparing either of them so much as a glance, and then darted across the road in the direction of what looked like a white Porsche something-or-other. '*Andrew!*'

Andrew ignored the look of puzzled disdain he received from Caroline Winshire, neatly skipped out of the way of the paramedics who were battling their way into the Court with a stretcher, and ran after Peggy, dodging the early evening traffic.

When he reached the car, only the passenger seat was free. They didn't have time for an argument, so he climbed in and slammed the door shut behind him.

Peggy was trying to tuck the multitudinous layers of skirt out of the way. 'Stupid bloody dress!'

'I like it,' Andrew found himself saying, even though he definitely hadn't intended to *ever* voice that thought.

Peggy looked perplexed for a moment, and then shook her head. 'Fasten your seatbelt.'

Andrew had barely clicked the belt into the socket when the Porsche roared to life, and he was pressed back into his seat as Peggy hit the accelerator and sent them hurtling away from the Court.

TWENTY-ONE

The high-speed part of the chase was never going to last – not in the city centre.

By the time Peggy had whizzed them past Rotters, Teddy was already caught at the traffic lights just beyond the Palace theatre.

If Andrew had been driving the orange monstrosity in an attempt to get away from the police, he'd probably have been a bit more evasive in his driving, and he really wouldn't have cared about keeping the car scratch free.

The traffic lights changed, and Teddy turned left onto Whitworth Street. Peggy had the nose of the Porsche practically touching the car in front, forcing it to go faster, whether it wanted to or not, so that she could nip through the lights just as they turned red.

Peggy, Andrew knew, would likely have ignored the red light anyway. Her driving tended to reach levels of aggression that she didn't often employ in her everyday life. Just then, Andrew really appreciated it.

'What happened? Was Teddy working with Lavinia? I thought they hated each other,' Peggy said, tapping impatiently on the steering wheel as they found themselves only three cars behind Teddy.

'I think they *do* hate each other,' Andrew replied. 'Teddy found out that Lavinia was paying Emma off, and he threatened to expose her if she didn't pay him too.'

'Blackmail?' Peggy asked in surprise. 'What *is* it with this play?'

'I have no idea.' Andrew shrugged.

Teddy turned left suddenly, and Peggy followed immediately.

'Lavinia won't be going to Broadway after this.' Andrew shook his head as he looked out the window.

Peggy scrunched up her nose. 'Do you think she'll end up in prison for any of it?'

'I doubt it. I expect she'll manage to wiggle her way out of ever fully telling the truth.' Andrew made a face at himself. 'She's good at that.'

Peggy hummed in what might have been sympathy, and then swore loudly as Teddy made a very sharp right-hand turn towards Ancoats.

Andrew closed one eye as Peggy followed the orange car, cutting up a couple of other drivers as she did so.

As he approached Great Ancoats Street, Teddy braked suddenly. He then threw the door of the car open and rolled out onto the road.

Peggy slammed on the brakes and the Porsche screeched to a halt.

Andrew was out of the car before Peggy had killed the engine.

As he passed Edgar's car, Andrew reached in and pulled the keys out of the ignition. As much as he'd enjoy seeing Edgar's face after telling him that his car had been nicked for a second time that evening, the thought of throwing the keys back at him was somehow more satisfying.

'What the bloody hell are you doing?' Peggy asked in disbelief as she caught up to him.

'Loads of car thefts around here, Peg.' Andrew grinned even as he took off running again. 'Can't be too careful!'

Teddy was infuriatingly fast, and Andrew was really starting to regret giving up five-a-side; at least it had kept him quick.

On the other side of the main road, Teddy ran past the darkened mill, and Andrew lost him to the shadows.

He swore loudly as he hurried across the road where, thankfully, the traffic was mostly stationary due to the never-ending building work that seemed to be popping up all over Ancoats in recent months, and eventually caught sight of Teddy again as he reached the mill himself.

To Andrew's consternation, Teddy then peeled down to the right, heading for somewhere that Andrew had seen enough of for a lifetime.

'You have *got* to be kidding me!' Andrew hissed as he trailed Teddy up the steps and over the Kitty Bridge to the towpath on the other side of the canal.

'Arthur!' Peggy called from somewhere behind Andrew, just as he tripped off the last step of the bridge.

The shout confused Teddy and Andrew enough that they both stopped and awkwardly turned back towards Peggy.

Andrew quickly realised that Peggy was talking about Arthur Havers, diamond thief extraordinaire. Very, very *dead* Arthur Havers.

Teddy, however, reasonably assumed that Peggy was calling out to another colleague, and so he chose to look around wildly for any extra people on the towpath.

Andrew saw Peggy furiously whispering into what appeared to be thin-air and then, a moment later, Andrew found himself sprawled on the towpath a few feet from Teddy. The car keys flew out of his hand, lost to the darkness.

'Not him!' Peggy yelled in dismay. '*Obviously!*'

Andrew watched in fascination as Teddy suddenly went from standing still to tumbling to the ground with a squawk of surprised outrage.

'Thanks, Arthur!' Peggy called as she crossed the bridge and quickly helped Andrew up.

'Yeah, thanks, Arthur,' Andrew grumbled as he strode over to Teddy and roughly pulled him to his feet.

Teddy's eyes narrowed, and then with startling precision he punched Andrew in the shoulder, right where it already hurt the most.

Andrew hissed in pain as his eyes watered, struggling to hold onto Teddy as the other man twisted violently in his grasp.

'Stop it!' Andrew grunted. The awful shiny material of Teddy's Sebastian costume was an absolute bugger to get a grip on.

Teddy then stopped moving so suddenly that Andrew's momentum sent him stumbling backwards as his fingers slipped from Teddy's arm.

Teddy immediately turned and started running up the towpath towards the main road again.

'Down here!' Peggy shouted, and Andrew looked first at her in confusion, and then in the direction she was pointing and waving at.

Higson and Lloyd were up on Great Ancoats Street, peering down. When they saw Peggy, they both jogged towards the towpath, coming down the steps just as Teddy reached them, effectively blocking his escape route.

'Fuck!' Teddy screeched in annoyance, spinning around again and racing back towards Andrew.

'Maybe try and actually apprehend him this time, Joyce,' Higson called blithely as he lit another cigarette.

Andrew steeled himself, ready for Teddy to reach him, but at the last-minute Teddy executed a bizarre balletic twist that had him skipping past Andrew without incident.

With a shout of frustration, Andrew whirled around and saw Teddy heading straight towards where Peggy was standing by the bridge.

Well, *that* wasn't happening if Andrew had anything to do with it.

He burst into a run, forcing his legs to remember that they used to be capable of darting around a football pitch for the length of a match every week.

Peggy leapt out of the way, just as Andrew threw his arms forward and sent both himself and Teddy tumbling towards the canal in an inelegant but ultimately efficient rugby tackle.

Teddy yelled as they plunged into the murky water with an almighty splash, and when his head emerged again, he was coughing and spluttering in panic.

This section of the canal was thankfully deep enough that they hadn't broken their necks in the fall, but the inability to put his feet on solid ground hampered Andrew's ability to try and arrest Teddy with any of his remaining dignity intact.

Teddy wildly windmilled his arms as he tried to make his way towards the towpath again.

Andrew screwed up his face, spitting out the water Teddy splattered in his face. He kicked his legs and bobbed towards Teddy, grabbing the other man's shoulders.

Teddy cried out in surprise, sending them both under the water for a couple of seconds as he flailed in alarm.

'Edward Smeaton!' Andrew shouted hoarsely as Teddy tried to pull himself free again. 'I am arresting you on t- *argh*!'

Andrew thrashed around, trying to resist when Teddy attempted to push his head under the water. He took in a mouthful of water and choked in surprise, coughing violently as he tried to stay afloat.

'Oh, get in and help him, Parker,' Higson sighed from the towpath. 'Quickly, before Her Ladyship throws herself in and then drowns in her meringue.'

There was a loud splash, and a gleeful Lloyd joined the fray.

Together, Andrew and Lloyd managed to subdue Teddy enough to get him over to the bank.

Higson reached down a meaty hand to pull Teddy from the water by the scruff of his neck, and then dragged him across the gravel as though he weighed nothing.

'Don't even think about running off,' he warned roughly, 'or you'll find yourself with your head so far up your jacksy you'll get to eat your breakfast again.'

'Arrest him, Lloyd,' Andrew sighed as he heaved himself out of the water, shoulder protesting at the movement.

'Really, boss?' Lloyd asked in surprise.

'Really.' It was only fair. Andrew had already failed twice; he didn't want to tempt fate by attempting a third time.

Lloyd beamed in delight.

Andrew unexpectedly found himself with an armful of Peggy, and he staggered backwards in surprise.

'That was really, *really* stupid,' she chastised him, even as she tightened her arms around his neck.

The awkward position was really making Andrew's shoulder hurt, but he ignored it and brought his own arms up to hug her back anyway. 'Peg, I'm ruining your dress.'

'I hate it anyway,' Peggy countered, but she stepped back. 'I don't even know where Charlie got it from.'

Andrew looked down and noticed Peggy's shoes for the first time that evening. 'Are you wearing trainers?'

Peggy shrugged. 'There was a high chance running was going to be involved. I can't run in heels.'

Andrew laughed, and then winced as he rubbed his shoulder. 'Why do I keep ending up in that bloody canal?'

'Oi! When you two've quite finished your little lovey dovey reunion, get your arses back to the Court. Parker and I will dump this dickhead at Bootle Street on the way,' Higson called, grinning wolfishly at them as he dragged Teddy to his feet.

Andrew cleared his throat in mortification, pulling at his disgustingly damp shirt as Peggy nipped past him to follow Higson, Lloyd and a demonstrably unhappy Teddy up towards the main road.

'Shit, keys,' Andrew muttered as he looked around the dark towpath. Great, it was going to take him ages to find them without a light.

There was a small clinking sound of metal hitting gravel, and Andrew looked down in amazement to see the car keys on the ground a couple of feet in front of him.

Andrew spun in a circle, frantically looking for anyone who could have thrown the keys to him.

'Oh,' he breathed, mostly to himself, when realisation dawned. He sheepishly reached down to pluck the keyring from the ground. 'Thanks, er, Arthur?'

He was met with silence, but considering he didn't get shoved into the water again as he jogged to catch up with Peggy, he thought that he'd probably thanked the correct person.

Andrew couldn't quite resist giving Teddy a smug little wave as he passed him, squashed into the backseat of Higson's rusty little car.

Higson shook his head at his DI pityingly, but neither that, nor the fact that his shoes were entirely sodden for the second time in a week could bring Andrew's significantly improved mood down.

Peggy standing next to Edgar's car looking perturbed, however, did deflate his joyful relief a bit.

'My mother is definitely going to blame me for this,' Peggy sighed as Andrew approached.

'It doesn't matter what she thinks,' Andrew replied, nudging her with his shoulder.

Peggy shot him a wan smile. 'You don't know my mother.'

That was true, and Andrew was actually inordinately grateful for that.

'Here,' Peggy said, holding out the keys to the Porsche for Andrew. 'You take Charlie's car, and I'll take the other one.'

'Not a chance,' Andrew replied. He held Edgar's keys behind his back, just in case Peggy made a grab for them, and headed for the driver's door.

'Why not?' Peggy asked.

Because I want to get canal water all over the upholstery of Edgar the Twat's car, Andrew thought.

'Because if Charlie finds a single scratch on his car, he'll blame me for it,' is what he said instead. 'He'd probably bankrupt me.'

That was patently untrue. Charlie wasn't enormously precious about his ridiculous car collection, and Andrew knew that Peggy was well aware of that fact.

Still, in the end she only nodded and headed for the Porsche instead. 'See you back at the theatre then.'

Andrew climbed into the car – which, according to the overly ornate keyring was a Lamborghini – and started the engine. If he then took a few extra seconds to make sure that he was really settled in the driver's seat, squishing his sodden clothes into the leather, then nobody else had to know, did they?

The drive back to the Court was entirely uneventful, and Andrew only fantasised about ditching the stupid car's nose into a pothole twice.

As they neared the theatre, Andrew was pleased to see that the ambulance had left. He was less pleased to see that a crowd had gathered on the pavement outside.

Andrew parked behind Peggy, and then soggily shuffled across the road to the Court.

'Oh, for God's sake,' he muttered as he saw Cohen and Edgar having a row just outside the doors.

'They've been at it since you left,' Jen explained as she came to stand next to Andrew. 'Apparently the Winshire Foundation still believes that the performance should be going ahead tonight.'

Andrew's eyes bugged. 'You're not serious.'

Jen nodded. 'Oh, I am. Sir, pardon me for asking, but have you been for a swim?'

Andrew only sighed tiredly in reply.

From the other side of the crowd, Charlie shot Andrew a grin. Apparently, he was thoroughly enjoying watching Cohen rage at every one of Edgar's ridiculous suggestions.

'Lavinia's going to be fine,' Jen said, nodding. 'She was

conscious and talking when the paramedics got her out to the ambulance.'

Andrew sighed again, this time in relief.

The relief, however, was short lived as unfortunately that was also the moment that Edgar reached his limit and took a swing that collided heavily with Cohen's jaw.

'Oh, Christ,' Andrew grumbled as he and Jen pushed through the crowd. 'Oi! Stop!'

Edgar did not stop. He pulled back his fist and sent it sailing towards where Cohen was already clutching his face.

Cohen thankfully ducked a little better that time, and Edgar's punch flew wide

Just when it looked like Edgar might try again, Jen propelled herself forward and had Edgar's arms behind his back before Andrew could so much as blink.

Edgar struggled, but Jen had him pressed against the front wall of the theatre only seconds later.

Two uniformed officers who had just been enjoying the spectacle up to that point, finally deigned to step in and help when Andrew glared at them.

He could have done without such a public spectacle to conclude the case, but Andrew would admit to being absolutely bloody thrilled to see that complete tosser being herded towards a car on his way to Bootle Street for the night.

Charlie shot Andrew two thumbs up, so Andrew thought that he might now be fully forgiven for the umbrella incident.

Andrew turned to see what Peggy made of it all, but frowned when he realised that he couldn't see her amongst the crowd.

Peggy had kept herself to the fringes of the melee after she'd followed Andrew across the street. She'd seen Edgar and Cohen arguing and known that her mother wouldn't be too far away.

Caroline Winshire would never be so uncouth as to engage in a public row, but Peggy would bet everything she had that her mother would be nearby to ensure that Edgar was doing exactly as she wanted.

She politely squeezed her way through the throng, keeping her head down when she spotted the two police officers who'd refused her entry that afternoon.

The foyer had completely emptied of guests and staff, except for Vic, who was sitting at the bottom of the staircase to the auditorium with her head in her hands.

'Are you alright?' Peggy asked gently.

Vic's head snapped up in surprise. 'Peggy! What happened to Teddy?'

'DCI Higson has him in custody,' Peggy replied with what was, really, the most minimal version of the truth.

Vic returned her head to her hands. 'We'll be finished after this. I'll have to move to New York permanently.'

'Sorry,' Peggy said automatically, although she wasn't entirely sure what she was apologising for. After all, Vic and Cohen were the ones who'd managed to put together a fairly terrible collection of people; Ben excepted.

'Do you know if DCI Higson is going to want to take statements tonight?' Vic asked. 'Because if he doesn't hurry up about it, I'm going to take myself off to a bar.'

'He'll be back in a minute, I'm sure.' Peggy left out the part where she was certain that Higson had conducted multiple interviews in places that also served alcohol. He'd found Cohen in a pub, for God's sake!

'Please excuse me,' Peggy added, shuffling past Vic and up the staircase. 'DI Joyce left his jacket and car keys on the stage, so I'm just going to grab them.'

Vic waved her away without lifting her head again, so Peggy took herself and her excuse off to the auditorium.

She really *was* going to retrieve Andrew's things, but her ulterior motive was that she wanted to try and speak to George one more time before she left for the night.

The house lights had been dimmed at some point in her absence, and the lights on the stage were casting eerie shadows down the aisle and across the first few rows of seats.

Peggy turned slowly as she walked towards the stage, looking for any sign of George, or any hint of trouble from Jock.

She reached the front row without incident, torn between disappointment and relief at seeing neither of the ghosts, and then made her way slowly up the short staircase that would lead her up onto the stage.

'George?' she tried quietly as she bypassed the trapdoor Lloyd had pulled open earlier. She peered down into the gloom below and thought that she'd be happy to live the rest of her life without ever setting foot in that room again.

Peggy crossed the stage to the other side where Andrew's dinner jacket was still lying crumpled on the floor. She picked it up and checked that his house and car keys were still safely tucked within the inside pocket.

The air shifted slightly, and Peggy whirled around, expecting to see George, but finding Marnie instead.

'What happened?' Marnie asked immediately. 'Did you catch that dickhead? Why does Andrew look like a drowned rat again? Why are you damp? Did you see Jen arresting Edgar?'

Peggy blinked, mentally sorting through Marnie's rapid-fire questions. She frowned as the final one registered. 'Hang on, did you say *Jen* arrested *Edgar*?'

Marnie nodded triumphantly. 'Yep! Edgar decked Cohen, and then when he went for him again, Jen slammed him into the wall. It was ace!'

Peggy had a number of follow-up questions, but the will to ask any of them evaporated when the doors at the back of the auditorium burst open and Peggy's worst nightmare strode towards her, swathed in diamonds and a cloud of fury.

'Margaret! What in the name of God do you think you're playing at?' Caroline snapped, coming to a stop right in front of the stage, and folding her arms across her chest.

Peggy tilted her chin up defiantly. 'I'm working, mother.'

'Working?' Caroline asked in disbelief, followed by a harsh bark of laughter.

'Yes, working,' Marnie interjected.

Caroline cast a look in Marnie's direction that suggested that she'd just smelled something foul.

'You shouldn't be in here,' Peggy told her mother, hoping that she sounded more confident than she felt. 'This is a crime scene.'

'Which really begs the question of what my daughter is doing in here, doesn't it?'

The doors opened again to reveal Charlie racing towards the stage, looking apologetic. He mouthed a silent sorry to his sister.

'I really think it might be best if you leave,' Peggy added. 'Surely you'll want to go and make sure that your husband is alright.'

Marnie gasped in surprise, looking outraged on Peggy's behalf.

Ah, she'd forgotten that bit of the story wasn't public knowledge yet.

Caroline's eyes narrowed dangerously. 'Of course that's what this little tantrum is about! You always were a jealous little madam, weren't you? Always wanting people to pay attention to you – that's what all of those ridiculous lies about seeing things that weren't there were about!

'You do not get to embarrass me just because you didn't get what you wanted! I'd really hoped that you'd have grown up enough by now to know your place, but here you are, doing everything you can to make my life difficult, just as you've done since the day you were born!'

Peggy would be lying if she said that hadn't stung. To be accused of being both jealous and a liar for the second time in as many days – in the same location, for that matter – would be bad enough on its own; but for her mother to suggest that Peggy had somehow orchestrated this entire debacle to embarrass her because Peggy was still sore over Edgar was a step too far.

'I want you to leave,' Peggy said firmly. '*Now*.'

Caroline rolled her eyes. 'Whatever you think you're doing, Margaret, just remember that nobody will ever be interested in you; only in what you have, and what you can give to them.'

'Now, really!' Charlie exclaimed.

'Hey!' Marnie snapped at the same time.

Peggy held up her hands to both of them, just as the auditorium doors opened for a third time to admit first Higson, and then Andrew a moment later.

Oh, she'd really rather not have had an audience for any more of this, but beggars couldn't be choosers, and perhaps this would be the only chance she'd get to stand up to the woman who'd tried to ruin her life.

Whether Caroline would actually listen to her was another thing entirely.

'Perhaps that's how people treat you, *Mother*,' Peggy said, staring down at Caroline, 'but I won't allow anyone to treat me like that anymore. There is nothing about you, or your life, that I am envious of. There are so many things that I have in my own life now; things that you will *never* have, no matter how much money you throw at them. I want you to leave.'

Peggy looked up in surprise when the sound of clapping echoed from the back of the room.

'Lovely little speech, Your Highness,' Higson called, stilling his hands. 'Now, *you*, other woman, what the fuck do you think you're doing in here? This is my crime scene, and I don't recall sending you a little engraved invitation.'

Caroline glared at Higson. 'Excuse me, but I'm removing someone who shouldn't be in *my* theatre.'

Higson pursed his lips, unmoved by the glower. 'No, this is not your theatre, and Swan is here on my say so. It's *you* I've got a problem with.'

'You can't speak to me like that!' Caroline squawked shrilly.

'Oh, I'm *terribly* sorry,' Higson replied mildly. 'Let me try it another way: Fuck off.'

Caroline turned to her son. 'Charles, are you honestly just going to stand there and let this *man* speak to me like this?'

Charlie snorted loudly, and then burst into loud hoots of disbelieving laughter.

Caroline shot Peggy one final ice-cold glare, and then she hitched her skirt above her ankles and stormed up the aisle towards the foyer.

Peggy sagged in relief.

'That's a terrible dress, by the way!' Marnie called brightly.

Caroline paused in front of Higson, sneering, and then turned her attention to Andrew. She wrinkled her nose at his dishevelled state.

'I don't know what your game is with *her*,' Caroline snapped, pointing back towards Peggy, 'but whatever it is, it won't be enough to save your career. I'll have your job for all of this.'

'No, you won't!' Peggy shouted, just as Higson and Marnie offered variations, albeit with much more colourful language.

Andrew just smiled benignly in return and dangled Edgar's car keys from his hand until Caroline snatched them in fury.

'Now, for the third time, get out of my crime scene!' Higson barked.

'Get out of my theatre!' Charlie hollered in a cheerful sing-song tone.

'Charlie,' Peggy warned softly.

'Close enough!' Charlie grinned with a nonchalant shrug.

'Peggy?' Marnie said quietly. 'Look, why don't you go home? I'll stay here and see if I can find George, yeah?'

Peggy shook her head. 'I'm fine, Marnie, I th-'

'Peggy!' Marnie said firmly. 'Go home, I've got this.'

After a long moment, Peggy nodded; she knew how pointless it was to argue with her friend.

Marnie grinned. 'Honestly, though, ten out of ten for the dress, although it looked better before *someone* got it wet.'

'Not actually my fault!' Andrew sighed as he approached the stage.

Marnie just rolled her eyes again and popped out of sight as Peggy approached the lip of the stage and sat down on it.

'I'd help you down, but I think I might actually need to see someone about my shoulder first,' Andrew said with a strained smile.

Peggy winced in sympathy. She wiggled forward until she could slither off the stage and drop down onto her feet. She was *not* going to miss the theatre when this was all over.

'You stood up to your mother,' Andrew said when Peggy reached him.

'I did.' Peggy didn't actually feel brilliant about it. She'd hoped that if she ever worked up the nerve to say anything to Caroline, she'd feel both victorious and relieved, but in reality, she just felt a little like she had motion sickness.

Andrew nodded contemplatively. 'I wonder if maybe it's time I stood up to mine.'

Peggy flinched in surprise. 'Really?'

Andrew nodded. 'If I ever want to live in my house again, I think I might have to try.'

'Can I come with you?' Peggy asked, even though she'd be going along whether Andrew agreed or not.

'Yeah.' Andrew nodded. 'Yeah. I'm pretty sure I can't do this without you.'

Peggy was thankful for the display of faith, but she hoped that Andrew had a plan, because she certainly didn't.

TWENTY-TWO

Their drive out of the city was peaceful, which Andrew found surprising, considering both the evening they'd just had, and the fact that they were about to head into a volatile situation that neither of them was particularly qualified to deal with.

Peggy was driving the Belmont because Andrew hadn't done a brilliant job of hiding the fact that he went slightly green any time he lifted his right arm at the wrong angle.

Both Jen and Lloyd had made it clear that they thought Andrew should be going straight to A&E, whereas Higson had suggested a couple of large whiskeys – '*Free pour, Joyce; none of this measuring malarkey*' – and a long sleep.

Andrew and Peggy had left the theatre without telling the others that they were going to go to the hospital, but that Andrew had only agreed to that if he could first have a shower to wash away the Rochdale Canal still seeping into his skin; *oh*, and only after they first tried to rid his house of his malevolent mother.

As they drove past Southern Cemetery, Peggy suddenly spoke, fracturing the comfortable silence.

'What did Jock say to you?' she asked, keeping her eyes on the road.

'He didn't like my choice of language,' Andrew replied, trying to keep his tone light.

'Was that all?'

Andrew hesitated, but ultimately there was no point lying about it. 'No.'

Peggy glanced quickly in his direction.

'He wanted to pass on a verse from Proverbs,' Andrew explained. 'He even managed to pick Agatha's favourite.'

'What?' Peggy asked in surprise.

'*The Lord detests all the proud of heart. Be sure of this; They will not go unpunished,*' Andrew recited tiredly. 'It was framed on the stairs, right next to the *Our Father* in Latin, and a blessing from the Pope from when my parents got married. Couldn't get away from it until the day she died, and then I shoved it in a cupboard.'

Peggy winced. 'Sorry.'

'Why? It's not your fault.'

Peggy readjusted her hands on the steering wheel. 'Just – *well* – I mean, what do you think he meant by that?'

Andrew shrugged his undamaged shoulder. 'I don't know. He thinks I'm arrogant, I suppose. Funnily enough, Agatha thought the same; she used to accuse me and Rob of it all the time.'

Andrew reckoned that most parents would have been pleased if their children did well at school, but if Andrew or Rob ever received particular recognition for something, Agatha had just told them to stop showing off, or to stop trying to make themselves look better than everybody else. She used to tell them that their father had been a show-off, and that they should never forget where that sort of behaviour had got him.

How Agatha had decided that winning a class prize was even remotely the same as coming out the wrong side of an argument after stealing from another criminal, Andrew had never been able to fathom.

'You're not arrogant, Andrew,' Peggy said firmly.

'Maybe.' Andrew sighed again. 'Maybe some people are just destined to disappoint their mothers, no matter what we choose to do with our lives.'

Peggy hummed thoughtfully and let the conversation drop. The car lapsed back into easy silence, which lasted until they drove past the welcome sign for Gatley, at which point Peggy looked as though she were about to ask a question, only to then change her mind at the last minute.

Andrew let her run through the same motions three times before he had to ask, 'What is it?'

'It's nothing,' Peggy replied.

'Peggy.'

'Oh, fine,' Peggy murmured as she turned right onto Acacia Road. 'Why do you think Jock attacked you and nobody else?'

Andrew frowned, perplexed. 'I think we explained that one with his choice from Proverbs.'

Peggy shook her head. 'Even though we know that Jock was directly related to Peter McClellan's death, he didn't physically *do* anything to him, did he?

'George told us that Jack can't abide liars, right? But even though he caused chaos during rehearsals, he never actually physically hurt anyone; not until he got to you.'

Andrew tilted his head as Peggy parked outside his house. 'Are you asking me if I'm lying about something?'

'No,' Peggy replied vehemently. 'No, of course not. I just want to know why you think he targeted you when he had plenty of other people to choose from.'

Andrew ran a hand over his face. 'This sounds like you have a theory, Peggy, so why don't you just tell me?'

Peggy took a deep breath. 'I think it's my fault.'

Oh. Andrew thought back to what Peggy had said the last time she'd been on Acacia Road. 'Not this again, Peggy.'

'Yes, this again! I mean, don't you think it's odd that you had no idea about Rob until last summer?' Peggy asked carefully as she unbuckled her seatbelt and turned to face him. 'He's been there the whole time, Andrew, but you saw no sign of him until *after* I'd told you about him. You had no problems in that house until I came along and I ju-'

'Peggy, stop!' Andrew held up his hand. 'You can't blame yourself for something like that.'

'No, listen to me. I think you were so resistant to believing in any of it, that maybe some spirits have been pushing back just as hard, desperate to get your attention.'

'But why?' Andrew asked. 'Why bother? Why not just leave me alone?'

'I don't know,' Peggy replied eventually.

'Right,' Andrew agreed. 'Nobody knows. Look, all of that's like saying that it's your fault you can see things other people can't see.

'Peggy, I might not like the fact that I have to believe in ghosts these days – and trust me, I don't – but I accept it.' He twisted his lips in self-deprecation. 'Well, most of the time, anyway. I'm not going to accept you blaming yourself for it. My mother would have eventually found a way to make sure she knew I couldn't ever really get away from her.'

'You're being remarkably calm about all of this.'

'Ah, that's just my arrogance showing.'

'*Andrew.*'

'Let's just get this over with,' Andrew said, looking up at his house. 'And before we go in there, I want you to know that I wish you didn't have to come in there with me, but I can't do it on my own.'

'We leave the minute anything dangerous happens,' Peggy stated firmly. '*Both* of us.'

'You sound like me,' Andrew replied as he opened the car door. 'So, now maybe you know how I usually feel.'

Peggy only rolled her eyes and followed him out of the car.

Andrew strode up the path to the front door as though he wasn't about to walk into a situation he'd rather avoid.

Once they were in the hallway, Andrew closed the door firmly behind them, and for a long moment they stood together, just listening for anything out of the ordinary in the stillness.

Andrew had prepared himself for hell, so he didn't quite know what to do when it didn't arrive as expected. 'Maybe nobody else is home,' he suggested with forced levity.

The silence stretched on.

When the first note on the piano finally sounded, Andrew jumped in surprise, reaching out to grasp Peggy's hand. 'To be clear, this is because *I'm* scared, alright?'

Peggy nodded and squeezed back even as she kept her eyes on the living room door, which was only just muffling the sound of a faltering rendition of *Silent Night*.

'That's the only thing she could ever play on the piano,' Andrew whispered, swallowing heavily. 'Dad taught her the Christmas before he died.'

'Andrew, we don't have to do this now,' Peggy said quietly. 'We can leave.'

'If we do, I'm not sure I'll ever come back again,' Andrew admitted.

'Would that be such a bad thing? Sell the house and start again somewhere else?'

Andrew shrugged helplessly. 'Rob.'

Even if he'd never known that Rob was *actually* there, he still probably wouldn't have felt alright about leaving his one remaining connection to the childhood he'd shared with his brother.

The piano playing ceased, and Andrew gestured towards the door. 'I think we need to go in there.'

'You're going to have to speak to her,' Peggy said as they stepped into the room.

'I know.' Andrew took a deep breath and cleared his throat. God, he'd feel like a right idiot if he wasn't so terrified. 'Agatha Joyce, you're not welcome here!'

His shout was met with ringing silence.

'Do you think that actually worked?' Andrew asked.

Peggy looked deeply doubtful.

Everything then happened at once.

The door slammed shut with enough force to shake the entire house just as the TV in the corner burst to life. The volume of the *M*A*S*H* episode reached ear-splitting levels, interspersed every few seconds with bursts of static.

Andrew and Peggy looked up at the ceiling as the sound of thundering footsteps boomed down through the plaster.

Andrew gulped, pressing his hands over his ears to block out the cacophony. 'I think that tactic worked better with *your* mother!'

A photograph of Andrew with Rob at his First Holy Communion, arms around each other as they grinned at the camera, fell off the wall, shattering the glass.

Andrew crouched to rescue the photo immediately, and he ripped the back off the frame, hoping that the glass hadn't scratched it.

'Alright, I think this might be a bad idea!' Andrew yelled. 'I think we should leave!'

Peggy nodded and reached for the door. Her eyes widened in panic when it quickly became obvious that it wasn't budging.

Andrew's efforts were just as unsuccessful. 'Why the fuck can they all do that to doors?'

Peggy spotted the low-level swirls of mist first; smoky fingers of grey and black just kissing the top of the carpet as they lazily rolled through the room. 'Andrew…'

'That's the bit I really don't like,' Andrew said, reaching for Peggy's hand again. 'Have you ever seen anything like it before?'

'No,' Peggy replied just as the TV turned off with a sharp click.

On the mantelpiece, a vase that had belonged to Andrew's grandmother exploded in a shower of green shards, and Peggy and Andrew cried out in surprise, jumping apart to avoid being hit.

Andrew turned towards the curved bay windows as he heard the glass begin to rattle in the frames. Andrew had far too much prior experience with shattering glass to feel even the smallest bit safe.

He moved towards the back wall, as far from the windows as possible. 'Peggy, come here.'

When Peggy didn't immediately appear at his side, Andrew looked over to see her still standing near the door. She'd gone as a white as a sheet, and Andrew recognised the expression on her face.

'Peggy! Peggy, whatever she's saying to you, ignore her!'

Peggy didn't acknowledge that she'd heard him.

Fuck this, Andrew thought. He darted over and tugged Peggy back towards the wall with him. 'Peg!'

'She doesn't want me in her house,' Peggy said in a small voice, eyes slightly wild.

'It's not her house,' Andrew replied indignantly, and then shouted up in the general direction of the ceiling, 'It's not your house!'

Andrew turned his attention to his sofa, and with a great amount of difficulty and discomfort he managed to manoeuvre it away from the wall.

By the time he'd managed to then drag Peggy down to the carpet behind the sofa he was breathing noisily from the radiating pain in his shoulder, and sweat had begun to bead at his temples.

Peggy didn't seem to have noticed that Andrew was about ready to expire, and just continued to look entirely shellshocked.

'Andrew,' she murmured eventually, staring at nothing in such a way as to let Andrew know that she was definitely staring at *something*, 'Andrew, she's so angry. I don't know what's she's going to do. I don't want you to see her.'

'Peggy, don't look at her,' Andrew said, putting his hands on Peggy's cheeks to gently turn her head towards him instead. 'We're going to get out of here now, alright? I'm sorry I brought you into this.'

A high-pitched beeping from the hallway drew Andrew's attention to the door again.

Shit. It was the battery-operated smoke detector that he'd bought the week after the fire in Wallasey, certain that he'd never again sleep peacefully without it.

Andrew left Peggy behind the sofa and ran to the windows, now vibrating even harder in their frames. He tried to ignore the sound as he reached out to try to open the catches. He couldn't say he was entirely surprised when not a single one budged even the tiniest amount.

No. They couldn't possibly be trapped in a house fire again.

It was like Agatha knew exactly what made up her youngest son's nightmares and was thrilled to exploit his fears. Andrew thought of all those times he'd woken since the previous summer, utterly convinced that he could smell acrid smoke.

'Peggy, I'm going to have to break the windows!' he called, looking around for something to throw. 'Stay down there, okay?'

The alarm seemed to have rebooted Peggy, so of course she ignored his request and sprang to her feet instead.

'Do you think we could lift this between us?' Peggy asked hurriedly, pointing at the coffee table. She was very obviously trying to avoid acknowledging the mist twirling around her ankles.

Andrew looked at the table doubtfully. He wasn't sure his shoulder would bear the weight of it, but they didn't really have any other options. He cursed himself for putting the poker and the other fireside tools in the shed, and for not picking up the cordless phone from the hallway on the way in.

'Alright,' Andrew said, bracing himself. 'Lift it on the count of three, alright? Then we'll try and give it a good swing.'

Peggy nodded and moved to the other side of the table to place her hands under the top edge.

'One, two, three!' Andrew hissed sharply as the weight pulled at his arms.

The windows rattled so forcefully that Andrew was certain that they must only have seconds left.

Running feet pounded on the floor upstairs again at an utterly improbable volume.

A flash of movement in the corner of Andrew's eye caught his attention and he turned his head to see what new horror Agatha had conjured up.

What he saw was so impossible that he yelped in pure alarm and dropped the coffee table.

Peggy wheezed in surprise and nearly pitched over entirely as she found herself so suddenly off-balance.

Andrew barely noticed. He was too busy staring in terrified wonder at his brother.

Rob was standing by the window, still dressed in his City kit, looking *exactly* as Andrew remembered him, even if he didn't seem entirely solid.

'*Rob*,' Andrew breathed, and Peggy whirled around in surprise.

'Oh,' said Peggy softly, which was all the validation Andrew needed to be sure that, no, he hadn't lost his mind somewhere in the terror.

Rob was staring back at Andrew in amazement, and he raised his hand in a small wave that was so familiar – and until this moment, dulled in his recollection – that Andrew nearly sobbed.

A second later though, Rob looked away, his gaze drawn towards the door. His expression shifted from stunned curiosity to fear, and Andrew wondered how he'd grown up thinking his brother had never been scared of anything, because right now he looked nothing short of terrified.

Rob had always, always protected Andrew, but he couldn't do that anymore. Andrew wondered if technically he was the big brother now, with Rob eternally trapped at twelve.

Eternally trapped in a house that he'd hated, with the mother who'd never shown him any real affection.

Andrew couldn't let that go on any longer. Even if he didn't know how the hell he was supposed to rid himself of Agatha's long shadow, he had to try something – *anything* – for Rob's sake.

Whatever fear had settled over Andrew when he'd walked into the house burned away in a conflagration of anger.

He stormed across the room and plucked his parents' wedding photo from the wall. Agatha had taken it down when Jack had died, and for years Andrew had thought that she'd disposed of it. When she'd died, he'd found it tucked in a drawer in her bedroom and in a fit of incomprehensible sentimentality he'd decided to hang it in the living room.

With a brief glance at the two stony faces looking up at him out of the tarnished frame he dropped it on the floor and brought his sopping wet shoe down on the glass.

'Get out of my house!' Andrew shouted, stomping on the frame again and watching the glass shatter into even smaller fragments.

The smoke detector beeped more frantically and there was an unnerving hammering on the other side of the door.

Next, Andrew moved to the tall corner cupboard and yanked open the glazed door. He pulled out a pair of wine glasses that had only ever appeared on the dinner table on Christmas Day and Easter Sunday and hurled them against the wall with a growl of frustration.

'I'm not fucking afraid of you anymore!'

'Andrew,' Peggy said quietly standing closer to Rob, 'are you sure this is a good idea?'

Andrew did *not* think it was a good idea – it was barely an idea at all – but he was just so pissed off with people he *couldn't even see* making his life harder than it needed to be.

'I will never, ever forgive you for what happened to Rob!' Andrew roared, reaching back into the cupboard and dragging out the godforsaken needlepoint that had already haunted him that day, before launching it towards the piano. The corner of the frame hit the music stand and then bounced onto the keys with a discordant blare.

He spun around in a frenzy as the hammering on the door intensified, and he saw Peggy inch even closer to Rob, as though she might somehow be able to protect him from whatever horrors Andrew didn't have the capacity to see.

He caught sight of the lighter lying next to the small basket of kindling that had sat unused since Kate had stopped coming over and complaining that his house was always too cold.

Andrew practically flung himself at the hearth to grab the lighter, wrapping his fingers tightly around the cool metal.

'Get out of my house!' Andrew cried again. 'Leave my brother alone! Leave *me* alone!'

He pulled his parents' wedding photograph out of the frame, uncaring as the broken glass pricked and pulled at his skin and glared at it for a final time. He wanted to erase the faces of the two people who'd brought him into this world without any intention of ever guiding him through it.

'We deserved better than you!' Andrew spat, voice trembling as he held the lighter's dancing flame to the yellowed corner of the photograph and watched in morbid fascination as the paper curled and bubbled, fire racing across the image, violently erasing the evidence of Jack and Agatha from existence.

Peggy whimpered and Andrew looked over in concern to see her face contorted in pain and her hands clamped tightly over her ears.

He dropped the burning photograph into the empty fireplace as it disintegrated before his eyes.

'Get out of my house, Agatha!'

Wind whipped through the room, catching the ashes of the photograph and tossing them into the air, and a piercing scream of pure fury rang through the house.

Andrew stumbled backwards, heading towards where Peggy and Rob stood together, as every object in the room rose about three feet into the air, hung suspended for a moment, and then crashed back to the ground with a crack that sounded like thunder.

The piano stool tipped over a second later and the screech abruptly ceased as the living room door exploded inwards, almost clipping Peggy in the back of the head.

Only the harsh sound of Andrew and Peggy's laboured breathing split the silence, and they looked at each other for a long moment, neither of them quite sure that they'd actually made it through all of that entirely unscathed.

Andrew curled his fingers as the cuts from the glass stung sharply.

Alright, *almost* entirely unscathed.

'Are you okay?' Peggy asked, her voice hoarse as though she'd been screaming,

Andrew only nodded silently and reached for her hand again. He looked around the room, but he could no longer see any sign of Rob.

He led Peggy out into the hallway and gaped at the mess. Every framed picture on the staircase was lying at the bottom of the stairs, and the already damaged telephone was now just a mangled mess of plastic and exposed copper wiring.

The smoke detector was silent, but blackened and misshapen. Thankfully Andrew couldn't smell any hint of smoke.

They picked their way through the mess into the kitchen.

Andrew couldn't be sure whether he or Peggy swore first.

Not a single drawer or cupboard door remained closed, and the contents of each had been deposited on the floor.

Broken plates, cups and glasses littered the route from the fridge to the back door, interspersed with shards of Cornflakes and grains of rice.

The fridge door was open, and the light inside was flickering ominously, as though it were threatening to give out at any moment.

The glass in the top half of the back door had a crack running from the top left to the bottom right corner, and Andrew through that the whole thing might give way with even the slightest slam of the door.

The whole place was like a bomb site, and Andrew was willing to bet that upstairs hadn't fared any better.

'Oh my God,' Peggy breathed in shock as she surveyed the wreckage.

'Is Rob okay?' Andrew asked, clearing his throat when his voice cracked. 'I can't see him anymore.'

'He is,' Peggy replied softly. She closed her eyes for a long moment. 'He's relieved.'

'Is she really gone?'

Peggy sighed. 'I don't really know how to be certain of that, but Rob says that he can't find her. He says he's known where she's been every day for twenty-five years.'

Andrew swallowed heavily at the implication of that and felt an almost overwhelming urge to cry in a mixture of relief and devastation.

He turned away and headed towards the cupboard under the sink. 'I should get this cleaned up.'

Peggy wrapped her fingers gently around his wrist, stilling his arm as he reached for the dustpan and brush. 'Leave it, Andrew. Go and have a shower.'

Andrew didn't have the energy or the mental capacity to argue with her. He ached all over and he thought that he might need to sleep for a week – or possibly never sleep again, if he continued to be haunted by that awful final scream.

He nodded tiredly and trudged up the stairs, hoping that his mother hadn't completely destroyed his bathroom.

As soon as Andrew had left the kitchen, Peggy tiptoed back towards the hallway and stood still as she listened carefully. Once the bathroom door clicked shut and the sound of the shower echoed down the stairs, she returned to the kitchen and furtively opened the back door so that she could step out into the cool darkness of the garden.

'Jesus Christ,' she muttered, running her hands over her face, fingers still trembling from adrenaline and fear. She thought that the preceding five minutes might actually have been the most terrifying moments of her life, which, considering what had happened on her first case with the Ballroom team, was really saying something.

Once she'd composed herself, she straightened up and quietly called, 'Marnie?'

Marnie didn't immediately reply, and Peggy wondered if whatever it was that had stopped Marnie from hearing her outside of the theatre earlier was still at play.

Her concern was alleviated only a second later when Marnie popped into existence a few feet away.

'What's up?' Marnie asked, glancing around the garden in confusion. 'I thought you were taking Andrew to the hospital.'

'Slight detour,' Peggy replied, and she saw Marnie's gaze trail disinterestedly over the back of the house, before her eyes widened.

'Shit! What happened?' Marnie asked in horror, hurrying towards the open back door and gawping at the mess in the kitchen.

'I'll tell you properly later,' Peggy promised, holding up her hands when Marnie looked ready to argue. 'Please, Marnie. Look, I don't want Andrew to know you're here just now.'

'Then why *am* I here?'

'Is everyone still at the theatre?'

Marnie nodded. 'I haven't seen hide nor hair of George, or Jock for that matter. Higson and Jen are still interviewing Vic and Cohen. Your brother and Lloyd are making noises about going out, because apparently they didn't get rat-arsed enough last night.'

Peggy wrinkled her nose. 'Well, can you please tell Charlie that he's *not* going out, and that he's coming over here to help clean up and then give me a lift home. You can tell Lloyd to come too. I don't want Andrew to have to deal with this himself.'

For once, Marnie didn't make a joke or a snarky comment about being used as a messaging service. She nodded, clearly understanding that whatever had happened, it wouldn't likely be classified as 'good'.

'Oh,' Peggy added as Marnie was about to leave again, 'and can you maybe just lay off popping up *just* to scare Andrew for a little while? I think it might actually give him a heart attack after tonight.'

Marnie looked at Peggy for a long moment, calculating gaze raking over her face before she nodded once more. 'I'm still not sure he deserves you, Peggy.'

Peggy flinched in surprise, but Marnie had disappeared before she had a chance to ask what on earth that was supposed to mean.

Peggy traipsed back inside. She closed the door as gently as possible behind her, but the glass still rattled ominously.

She picked up the dustpan and brush, and found a roll of bin bags nearby, before crouching in the middle of the floor, assuming it was as good a place as any to start.

After a few minutes, where the mess didn't seem to be diminishing even as the bin bag filled up with jagged mug handles and smashed jam jars, the lights dimmed gently and Peggy tensed.

She relaxed again only when she saw the figure standing by the back door.

'Hi, Rob,' she greeted him quietly.

Rob gave her a little wave, and Peggy was overcome with a wave of sadness, both for the young boy, and for Andrew.

'Was your brother always terrible at asking for help?' Peggy asked, the question slipping out without much consideration.

Rob looked thoughtful for a moment, and then nodded once.

'He didn't tell me about any of this,' Peggy continued, gesturing at the house in general, 'until it could have been too late.'

Rob wrinkled his nose and nodded again.

'Do you remember what you wanted me to tell him last year, when I first came here?' Peggy asked carefully.

Rob immediately looked at his feet, and Peggy could practically feel the shame radiating from him.

'I don't think you meant it in the way that Andrew took it,' Peggy clarified. 'And it was my fault too. I shouldn't have behaved so poorly to either of you, really.'

Rob shook his head. His lips moved, but even trying as hard as she could, Peggy couldn't hear anything more than an unintelligible whisper.

'I know what he said to your mother tonight, but he still blames himself for what happened to you,' Peggy continued, putting down the bag and leaning back against the counter. 'I don't think he's ever *not* going to blame himself. You know him best; how do I get him to understand that it wasn't his fault?'

Rob frowned, considering Peggy for a few seconds before he closed his eyes as though he were concentrating.

'Make him talk about it.'

The words came through so clearly, Peggy stumbled forwards slightly in surprise. 'I heard that properly.'

Rob smiled proudly, but his next words were much, much softer. 'Keep telling him that it's not his fault. *Please.*'

'I will, I promise.' Peggy looked around when there was the sound of movement somewhere else in the house, and then surveyed the kitchen again in utter dismay. 'Hey, Rob, any chance you could help me clean this mess up?'

Rob reached out his hand towards a broken plate on the counter, and his fingers went straight through it harmlessly. He shook his head and then grinned at Peggy.

He looked so like Andrew in that moment that it broke Peggy's heart a little.

She forced a smile onto her face for Rob's sake. 'Typical.'

Rob laughed, which helped Peggy's smile grow more truthful.

Peggy turned back to pick up the bag she'd dropped and jumped in surprise when she saw Andrew leaning against the kitchen door.

She really hoped that he hadn't overheard anything she'd said, but from the indecipherable look on his face she had a feeling that he probably had.

Andrew walked over and took the bag from Peggy, so that he could set it on the floor.

'I think this can wait for a bit,' he said quietly.

'Are you ready to go to the hospital?'

Andrew shook his head. 'I don't know about you but I'm starving. We didn't even get a chance for lunch today.'

Peggy's traitorous stomach rumbled at the mention of food, and Andrew laughed.

'Come on, let's go get some dinner,' he said, pointing towards the door.

Peggy looked down at her ridiculous pink dress and then raised her eyebrows.

'The good people of Gatley should get to see that outfit.' Andrew grinned. 'You'll be the talk of the town.'

Peggy rolled her eyes and pushed past him into the hallway. 'Alright, fine. Where do you want to go?'

'Well,' Andrew replied, drawing the word out as he twirled his house keys around in his hand, 'I did get dunked in that bloody canal again, so I think that only leaves one option.'

Peggy laughed as Andrew opened the front door. 'Chips it is then.'

TWENTY-THREE

Peggy curled her hands more tightly around the mug of coffee that Lloyd had presented her with twenty minutes earlier. She hadn't yet taken a sip, but instead was using it to try and leech some warmth from it into her cold fingers. It was a fairly mild spring day, but Peggy had been cold enough when she'd stumbled out of bed that she'd wrapped herself up as though as though it were the dead of winter. She hoped that she wasn't coming down with something.

The pounding headache, she'd unfortunately expected. On the – thankfully – rare occasions she encountered a particularly volatile spirit, she was always left feeling a bit like she'd been clubbed over the head. Although, calling Agatha Joyce 'volatile' was the biggest understatement Peggy could imagine.

Even once Lloyd, Charlie and Jen had arrived to help tidy up, it had taken hours to return Andrew's house to a liveable state. The realisation that he was going to have to replace a significant number of his possessions had set in for Andrew fairly early on, and all of the easy smiles over chips – albeit tinged with pain – had twisted into a significantly more pinched expression.

Jen had taken the sulking as a sign that Andrew really couldn't wait any longer to get his shoulder looked at, and she'd bundled him into her car and driven him to hospital at some point well beyond midnight.

Charlie had then taken Peggy back to Butterton, remaining uncharacteristically uncommunicative. He'd looked like he'd wanted to say something important to her as they'd parted at the top of the staircase, but in the end, he'd only bid her goodnight and disappeared into his bedroom.

Peggy, for once, had been dead to the world within seconds of her head hitting her pillow, but her dreams had been scarred by visions of swirling mist and hungry flames.

She hadn't felt even remotely refreshed when she'd woken late, and it had taken her until after lunch to work up the energy to drive back to the Court. She'd dragged Charlie with her, because she wasn't entirely sure that she'd have any case for admittance if she didn't bring the future owner of the theatre with her.

She'd also been slightly concerned that her mother might make an appearance, although she'd kept that particular worry to herself.

Peggy shivered and held the mug closer to her chest. She glanced around, but nobody seemed to have noticed that she was out of sorts. She was grateful that they were all engrossed in Lloyd's dramatic reenactment of Teddy's arrest. Even Andrew, arm resting in a sling, looked amused by Lloyd's impression of Teddy being tackled into the canal.

In the car on the way home from Gatley the night before, Charlie's silence had given Peggy far too much time to think about George, and about how he'd died alone and unrecognised. Nine months on Tib Street had done nothing to dampen Peggy's bleeding-heart tendencies, and it was why she'd felt compelled to return to the theatre that morning: nothing about George, or his death, felt resolved.

Charlie had thought she was putting too much pressure on herself to try and do something about a situation where nothing could actually be done.

'Peg, he died forty years ago,' Charlie had said as they'd opened the auditorium doors and walked towards the stage. 'He had no family. There's nobody left to tell.'

'I know,' Peggy had replied quietly.

'Maybe it has to be enough that we know what happened,' Charlie had suggested. 'I know he didn't kill that first chap, but he *did* cause that woman's death, Peggy. This isn't like what happened with Marnie.

As though he'd summoned her, Marnie had popped out of nowhere, arms folded as she'd rested her back against the stage.

'What are you two doing here?' she'd asked. '*Please* tell me that the case really is over, and nobody has to sit through that awful play just because your even more awful mother wanted them to.'

Peggy had agreed with Marnie's sentiment entirely, but she'd let the comment go without further remark. 'Have you managed to speak to George?'

'No. Not a peep from anyone all night. Honestly, if I hadn't seen it all for myself, I wouldn't have believed that this place had a ghost at all.'

'Maybe he's gone off to wherever he's supposed to go next,' Charlie had offered.

Marnie had snorted loudly. 'Is that how you think this works? Peggy provides the ghost with an opportunity for something like closure, and they just head off into the deathly equivalent of a sunset at the end of it?'

'Maybe,' Charlie had replied mulishly. 'Just because you decided to stick around doesn't mean that's what everyone wants to do.'

'What's that supposed to mean?' Marnie's eyes had narrowed, ready for a fight.

'Stop it, both of you,' Peggy had snapped sharply, and they'd both looked at her in surprise. 'This bloody place seems to bring out the worst in everyone, so just stop before one of you says something that you can't take back.'

They'd both looked suitably chastised, but Peggy had only realised the truth to her words after she'd spoken them.

Ever since they'd walked into the theatre nearly a week earlier, everything seemed to have taken a turn for the worse, and Peggy would do her damnedest to stay out of the Court in future, no matter what her brother's plans for the place turned out to be.

'Look,' Peggy had sighed tiredly, 'could you two maybe just

give me a few minutes? Let me see if I can find George. Then we'll head over to Tib Street, alright?'

Marnie had nodded mutely, and Charlie had uttered a quiet agreement. He'd had that look on his face again – the one from the night before. Peggy was fairly certain that whatever it was he was on the cusp of sharing, she wouldn't want to hear anyway, and so she'd turned away and headed for the door that would lead her up to the stage.

She'd been gratified to see her brother and Marnie actually leave the auditorium, as she'd half expected the pair of them to just take a seat somewhere nearby.

Peggy had walked out onto the apron and sat on the lip of the stage, swinging her legs over the edge so that her heels bounced against the black painted wood below.

She couldn't have been there for more than a minute or two before she'd heard someone clear their throat quietly from somewhere behind her.

She'd immediately turned her back to the stalls, pulling her feet up so that she could sit cross-legged, and found George standing before her, straw boater in hand.

'Miss Peggy,' he'd said softly, 'did you catch that man?'

Peggy had nodded. 'Inspector Joyce apprehended him.'

'And Miss Lavinia, is she alright? I saw what that man did to 'er.'

'I think so,' Peggy had replied as confidently as she could at the time. Truth be told, she'd only heard Jen's brief update the night before, where she'd learned that Lavinia had quite the concussion, but was unlikely to suffer any lasting damage.

'And you, you're alright?' George had been growing more obviously anxious with every question. Peggy had reckoned that it was likely to have stemmed from a sense of guilt about his own small part in the proceedings.

'We're all fine, George,' Peggy had stated firmly. 'Everyone's fine. Where've you been? Marnie was here all night.'

George had deflated further and then taken a seat next to Peggy. 'I'll be honest, I was 'iding from 'er. She weren't too 'appy with me.'

Well, that had been the truth, hadn't it?

George had fidgeted with the hat in his hands for a long moment. 'I'm sorry, Miss Peggy. I never should 'ave lied to you, not about who I was, or about the things I'd seen – or not seen – around 'ere.'

Peggy had nodded her acceptance. 'What about Jock? What happened after we left last night?'

George had shrugged. 'I don't know. After what 'appened beneath the stage, 'e just weren't there anymore. Do you think 'e'll come back?'

It hadn't been lost on Peggy that multiple people had asked her a variation on that question over the preceding twenty-four hours. She couldn't answer George any more or less truthfully than she'd answered Andrew the night before. 'I don't know.'

'I didn't mean for anythin' really bad to 'appen to 'Enriette,' George had added after an even longer pause. 'I didn't mean for 'er to fall. I just wanted to scare 'er, and make 'er feel 'ow I'd felt when I'd been forced to leave.'

'I understand that, George,' Peggy had replied evenly.

'Then you forgive me?' George had asked, naked hope in his voice.

Peggy's stomach had twisted unpleasantly. 'That's not really my place.'

The words had tasted sour, not only because she was uncomfortable with the question, but because her mother's words from the previous evening had reared up again:

'I'd really hoped that you'd have grown up enough by now to know your place.'

What exactly *was* her place?

George had seemed perplexed by her answer. 'Why not?'

He hadn't given Peggy any time to formulate a response before he'd risen to his feet and begun pacing. 'Well, what am I supposed to do then? What? Am I stuck 'ere forever? I said I was sorry!'

Even though George had been in his thirties when he'd died, Peggy had suddenly been able to see the seventeen-year-old in him so clearly. She could see the shame he'd felt at being embarrassed by Henriette, and the fear he'd experienced when the police had named him the key suspect in Alistair's death.

It felt like George's life had stopped in 1932, and even though he'd aged, he hadn't actually matured.

'I can't stay 'ere forever!' George had cried, throwing his hat on the ground. 'I can't be trapped with 'im forever. I wasn't a bad person; I just made a mistake! Why can't you understand that?'

'I do understand, George, b-'

'Then why won't you forgive me?' George had exploded, and Peggy had never been more grateful that George hadn't shown any ability to physically affect things. '*Why?*'

'I can't.'

George's whole body had been shaking, fury and disappointment drawing his eyebrows together. 'Then what's the point of you? If you can't *do* anythin', why are *you* the one I can speak to? Why did you even bother coming back 'ere?'

'Because I wanted to make sure that you were alright,' Peggy had replied, but the words had died as they were still crossing her lips.

George had laughed then, and it had been a grating, cold sound that didn't at all align with the way he'd behaved up to that point. 'So you can walk away feeling good about yourself? Walk away while you leave me 'ere? What 'appens to me, 'ey? If I stay 'ere long enough, do I become like 'im? Like *Jock*?'

Peggy had wanted so desperately to say 'no', but George must have seen some hesitation in her face because his expression had shuttered entirely.

'Get out of 'ere, Miss Peggy,' George had snapped, hard and bitter. 'Get out and mind that you don't set foot in 'ere ever again.'

George had disappeared and left Peggy staring at the empty stage, feeling bereft.

The doors at the back of the auditorium had opened to admit Marnie and Charlie, both wearing matching looks of concern. Marnie had obviously heard George's shouts.

'You alright?' Marnie had called.

Peggy had clambered to her feet and waved away their unease. 'Fine. Thanks.'

She'd almost sighed in relief when Cohen had then appeared from stage right. At least dealing with him had given her the opportunity to shake off any immediate questions about George from the others.

'Peggy?'

Peggy blinked, shaking her head to clear it as Andrew called her name, pulling her back to the Ballroom. 'Sorry, what?'

Andrew frowned. 'Are you okay?'

'Fine,' Peggy replied, forcing a smile onto her face. 'Could do with sleeping for a week, that's all.'

Even though Andrew nodded at her and turned his attention back to Higson, Peggy could tell that he didn't quite believe her.

From her vantage point, Peggy studied the line of Andrew's shoulders; even with his injury, he seemed far more relaxed than he had all week, and Peggy hoped that he would be able to start seeing his house as a home again at some point soon.

She wished that she knew whether Agatha was really gone for good, but as George had so astutely pointed out to her that morning, there wasn't really anything Peggy could do about any of it, was there?

Peggy sighed quietly. She and Andrew seemed to have rediscovered their usual equilibrium, but that didn't negate the fact that they had behaved poorly towards each other over the course of the week.

Andrew had accused her of being jealous, and as much as Peggy would love to refute that charge, she knew that she would have to – *privately* - accept that he'd been correct.

She couldn't, however, accept Andrew's claim that she had somehow encouraged Timothy to turn him away from Butterton House, yet no matter how she looked at it, she couldn't understand why Andrew would have said something like that if he didn't really believe it.

Which, of course, begged the question, why was he so certain that he'd seen Peggy at the house?

And, because that was entirely impossible, who exactly had he seen?

A burst of laughter from Lloyd startled Peggy enough that she flinched in surprise. She pretended that she couldn't see Charlie's questioning gaze.

'Right, enough of that, Parker. Jen, you can go and question the delightful Miss Heathcote again tomorrow,' Higson said, patting his wiry beard and dislodging stray fragments of Eccles Cake. 'Take Parker, but don't let him get distracted by her fancy words again.'

Lloyd looked down at his shoes, but the rosy blush high on his cheekbones was obvious to Peggy, even from the other side of the room.

'She alright then?' Marnie asked, not sounding even remotely sympathetic. 'Did getting clocked on the head knock all the lies out at last?'

Lloyd snorted at 'clocked', and Higson sighed in despair at the two of them.

'She's copped to convincing Emma Allen to leave the production, and to co-opting her into a little scheme to scare people for *publicity purposes*,' Higson explained, looking like he found the 'publicity' part the most abhorrent. 'Apparently, she has no knowledge whatsoever of any plot dreamed up by that twat Teddy though. She very conveniently can't remember much about the past week, and has no idea why uniform found a long, brown plaited wig stolen from the costume department in her dressing room drawers, right alongside copies of keys to the administrative parts of the building. *Allegedly.*'

Higson narrowed his eyes and zeroed in on Andrew. 'Maybe we should send Joyce in instead. See if she remembers *him*, hmm?'

Andrew's face went as beetroot as Lloyd's.

Children, thought Peggy, shaking her head, *the lot of them*.

'I hope you understand the trouble you lot've caused me,' Higson added, picking up a matchbox and opening it, only to close it again immediately. 'I've had three phone calls from Bootle Street already, complaining about the quality of scumbags they've been babysitting for us. One posh dickhead was already one too many, so you can imagine their delight when an even posher dickhead was sent their way not ten minutes later.'

Peggy's stomach rolled. She'd been trying very hard not to think about Edgar at all, but she could imagine the level of fuss both he and Caroline would have been causing.

'I have no doubt that the Chief Constable has already been contacted by the delightful Countess of Acresfield who would, no doubt, like my balls in a vice,' Higson continued, surprisingly unbothered. 'As I happen to be quite attached to them, each and every one of you is going to write up the most pristine reports anyone has ever had the pleasure of reading.'

'Sir,' came the response as a perfect chorus.

'Did you speak to George?' Jen asked, looking first to Peggy, and then to Marnie.

Peggy shrugged as nonchalantly as she could.

Jen's eyebrows knitted. 'I was just thinking that once this is all wrapped up, it might be worth looking through our files to see if we have anything on unidentified deaths in the canal. Maybe it would help to give him some kind of resolution, or something.'

Peggy tensed and tried to force another smile. 'Yes, I think that's a good idea.'

Jen nodded slowly. She'd obviously been expecting a more positive response.

'If I were him, I'd definitely get out of that place,' Lloyd announced as he reached over for another chocolate digestive. 'Imagine if you had to sit through all of the rehearsals for that bloody play again in the future.'

'I'm not sure any theatre in Manchester will touch that play with a bargepole,' Andrew countered, rubbing his shoulder lightly.

God, Peggy hoped that were true. If she never heard another word about *Lady Bancroft*, it would be too soon.

A flicker of something in the corner of her eye had her turning her head towards the back wall immediately, but she found nothing out of the ordinary.

Peggy put her coffee down on the floor next to the blue sofa and leaned forwards so that she could glance around the entire room.

'What's up?' Charlie asked quietly as the rest of the team descended into an animated debate about which part of the play was the worst.

'Nothing,' Peggy replied with another shrug. 'Stiff neck.'

'You look a little peaky, you know.' Charlie wrinkled his nose.

'Thanks.'

There was another brief flash of movement and Peggy looked again. Once again, nothing was out of place, and there wasn't even the slightest hint of anything ghostly.

Oh shit. Benson.

In the chaos of the preceding twenty-four hours, Peggy had forgotten to tell anyone about her bizarre interaction with Benson, or about what had happened in the Ballroom's archive on Saturday morning.

Peggy opened her mouth to interrupt the conversation but was struck with a sudden sense of uneasiness about sharing any of that information with anyone while in the vicinity of Tib Street.

She swallowed heavily and decided that it could keep until morning.

A quick glance down at her watch told her that it was time to leave, and her eyes trailed towards the double doors.

As she turned back to tell Charlie that she was going to head off, she caught Higson staring at her, an unnervingly calculating gaze sharpening his eyes.

Peggy pointed towards the doors, silently asking for permission to be excused.

A long moment later she was rewarded with a single nod and vague wave of Higson's hand.

An argument had broken out between Lloyd and Marnie, concerning which of the two of them could do a better impression of Marion delivering Lady Bancroft's final monologue. Andrew and Jen were pretending that they weren't both highly amused *and* deeply invested in the result.

'I'll see you later, Charlie,' Peggy whispered to her brother.

'Are you sure you're alright, Peg?'

'I'm fine,' she said yet again, this time trying to imbue the words with a brightness she really didn't feel. 'Don't make a fuss, alright?'

Peggy quietly made her way to the doors.

Just before she turned the handle, she looked back towards where the rest of the Ballroom team sat together near Higson's desk.

Know your place, her mother had said.

Peggy had naïvely thought that she might have found it, but now she wasn't so sure.

Maybe George had been onto something. What was the point of her 'ability'? She knew she wasn't the only one who could do what she could do – Higson had outright told her that – so perhaps there was a better fit for the Ballroom out there somewhere.

Peggy opened the door as quietly as possible and slipped out onto the landing.

Andrew heard the Ballroom door click closed and looked over in surprise. He then immediately turned in the opposite direction, frowning when he saw that the blue sofa now only held *one* of the Swan siblings; and not the one he'd prefer.

Charlie shrugged and held his hands up, clearly not wanting to get involved.

'I thought it was just your shoulder you'd clobbered,' Higson said pointedly, cutting over Lloyd to speak directly to Andrew. 'If I'm not mistaken, your legs are fine and you might still have a brain cell or two left in there, so I'm not sure why your arse isn't already following Her Maj down the stairs.'

'What?' Andrew asked, feeling somewhat stupid as everyone looked at him.

Higson steepled his fingers on the desk. 'Granted, I told you that she'd had enough of your bullshit and was fucking off away from here for the last time *before* you got chucked down the stairs, but I thought you'd not let a little nugget of information like that get smacked right out of you.'

Andrew blinked. Surely none of that mattered anymore, did it? Everything was fine. Peggy hadn't actually meant what she'd said.

Right?

He'd apologised for being a complete tit.

They'd apprehended a suspect together.

They'd gone for *chips!*

435

He didn't say any of that to Higson, of course.

The door onto the street clanged closed downstairs.

'Off you pop.' Higson curled his lips into a smug smile and waved towards the door as Andrew stood up.

He paused to pick up his jacket and house keys, squashing them together in one hand, and left the Ballroom without another word. He was taking Higson's decree as the end of the workday, whether it was meant as such or not.

He clattered down the stairs and awkwardly pulled open the door.

Thankfully, Peggy had stopped to button her coat and so was only a few feet away.

'Oh,' she said in surprise. 'Hi.'

Andrew shifted the grip on his keys and clumsily draped his jacket over his uninjured arm. It was actually a little bit chilly, but he wasn't quite in the mood to work out how to wear his jacket over a sling.

'How's your shoulder?' Peggy asked.

'It's alright.' Andrew twisted his lips. 'Not delighted I can't drive for a couple of weeks. It might be a good excuse to actually take some time off.'

Peggy looked at him in genuine astonishment.

Andrew rolled his eyes. 'Yes, Peggy, even *I* understand how to have a holiday.'

Peggy's expression didn't change.

'Oh, I forgot!' Andrew announced, making a face at himself as he inelegantly unfolded his jacket and produced Peggy's ring from within the pocket. 'Jen asked me to give this back to you.'

Peggy stared at the ring for a long moment, and then reached out to gingerly pluck it from Andrew's outstretched hand. She nodded, which Andrew thought might have been in thanks, and then slid the ring back onto her right hand.

'Drink?' Andrew asked, tilting his head towards Market Street.

'Not tonight, Andrew.' Peggy didn't quite meet his eyes.

The crease between Andrew's eyebrows deepened. This wasn't the first time Peggy had declined an invitation from him, but something about this was different, and Andrew felt immediately unbalanced.

'Oh,' he replied eventually, certain that it was a much safer answer than anything else buzzing around his head at that moment.

'It's just…' Peggy trailed off and stared at her feet for a long moment, before her eyes suddenly snapped up to Andrew's, laser focused. 'Look, it's not your fault, I just want you to know that. It's me. It's definitely me.'

'What?' Andrew asked, baffled. 'What's not my fault?'

Peggy seemed to close in on herself slightly, and she dropped her gaze. 'It was brought to my attention that maybe I've become a little too attached to the Ballroom, and everything that goes with it.'

She looked down at the pavement and Andrew tried not to fidget impatiently as he waited for her to continue

'This - the Ballroom, the cases, everything - all came along when I needed something to ground me,' Peggy continued after a long moment. 'I think that I've relied on it, and on you, like a crutch of sorts, but maybe it shouldn't be the *only* thing in my life.'

Andrew was a bit confused about where this was going, but he had the creeping sense that he wasn't going to like the conclusion when Peggy finally arrived at it. He *really* didn't like how close to Charlie's own words it sounded.

'Peggy, what are you actually trying to say?' Andrew asked, irrational fear sharpening the corners of the question.

'I think I need some space from the Ballroom, and the Ballroom needs some space from me,' Peggy explained to Andrew's tie. 'You know, to see if this whole situation really is working.'

Andrew's brain had fizzed slightly at the mention of 'space.' 'You're *leaving*? Peggy, no, I th-'

'Please let me finish?' Peggy asked quietly, wrinkling her nose, clearly unhappy with herself.

Andrew nodded once. What else was he supposed to do?

'I'm not leaving,' Peggy continued, taking a deep breath through her nose. 'Not yet anyway, but I think that there needs to be less of *this*.'

She gestured vaguely between the pair of them. 'You know, less of the dinners, and drinks, and sharing deep, dark secrets at two in the morning.'

'I don't understand what you're trying to say,' Andrew replied plainly.

Peggy looked at him shrewdly. 'I'm *almost* positive that's not true.'

Andrew shook his head, a spectre of slight desperation crawling up his spine. 'Peggy, I really don't understand.'

Peggy smiled sadly. 'Well, that's probably for the best.'

Andrew's frown deepened.

'Look, I need to go,' she added, glancing down at her watch and holding the face tightly as though it was steadying her. 'I bumped into Albany at the theatre this morning. He asked if I'd meet him for dinner, to explain what actually happened last night. He's still a bit lost about the whole thing.'

Andrew stared, and he feared that the surprise he felt was radiating from him. 'Oh. Right.'

Peggy ran a hand through her hair, strands getting caught between her fingers as she cycled through a series of facial expressions that Andrew couldn't read.

Finally, she took a step towards Andrew, but then seemed to change her mind about the intent almost instantly.

In the end she just graced him with an awkward little half-wave as she turned away and headed for Market Street.

Andrew stood in the middle of the road, house keys hanging limply from his right hand as he watched Peggy disappear around the corner.

Shit, Andrew thought. That niggling little notion that had been chasing him around for months barrelled into him with all the subtlety of a wrecking ball, and he suddenly felt cold all over.

Shit, he thought again, blood rushing in his ears as he blinked stupidly at the empty space in front of him; the space that somehow his body and mind had just assumed would always be filled by Peggy.

'Shit,' he said, aloud this time, as his mind whirred backwards through everything Peggy had just said to him; through the way that he'd behaved towards her over the past week, about the case, about Edgar, about Lavinia.

Jesus Christ, Charlie had been right after all; someone's feelings had been about to get hurt, but he'd been wrong about whose feelings they'd be.

Peggy wasn't the one who was overly invested in their relationship, nor was it Peggy who had twisted the boundaries of their friendship and partnership into something else - Andrew had seemingly done that all by himself.

Peggy had been right there the whole time, and he'd been too stupid to appreciate that fact. Now she wanted space from him because he'd finally been too much of an utter, utter arse.

She'd let him down far more gently than he'd deserved, and then gone off for coffee with a successful, wealthy New Yorker, leaving Andrew standing alone in the middle of Tib Street, with only a slightly crap Vauxhall Belmont and a haunted house to his name.

This was not the sort of realisation that he was prepared for in any way.

'Shit!' Andrew shouted at nothing in particular.

'Are you alright there, boss?'

Andrew whirled in surprise at the unexpected interruption to his breakdown.

Lloyd was looking at him like he thought that Andrew might have actually lost the plot this time.

Jen appeared equally concerned, but it was the slightly calculating stare he got from Charlie that worried him the most. Thankfully there was no sign of either Higson or Marnie.

'Shit,' Andrew repeated, this time in embarrassment, covering his eyes with his left hand for a few seconds.

'Did you manage to catch Peggy?' Jen asked, looking around as though Peggy might just be hiding somewhere, and at any moment she'd pop out again.

'She's gone out with Cohen,' Andrew replied, words bitter, and voice devoid of any sort of warmth.

Jen and Lloyd exchanged a surprised glance, quick as lightning, and Andrew had the disconcerting realisation that perhaps his grand epiphany of a minute earlier might not have been as recent an epiphany for anyone else. *Oh my God*, he was such an *idiot*.

'Sorry, old chap,' Charlie said, patting Andrew twice on the shoulder.

He did sound almost terrifyingly apologetic, which didn't make Andrew feel better about anything.

'I'm going home,' Andrew said, utterly mortified, as he shrugged Charlie off. 'I'll get the bus back to Gatley, Jen, don't worry about it. I'll see you all in the morning.'

'Absolutely not,' Charlie said sternly. 'We're going to the pub, and you're coming too.'

'I don't want to go to the pub,' Andrew muttered.

'Come on, sir, it'll help take your mind off Pe-' Lloyd snapped his mouth shut, and then forced a grin. 'It'll take your mind off *people*. And things.'

Andrew opened his mouth to argue, but it was Jen's turn to

cut him off, with a look that was more concern than pity.

'Sir, it's been a rough week,' she said, nodding encouragingly, 'and I think we could all do with a break.'

'Didn't you two have enough of a break on Tuesday night?' Andrew asked, fixing Lloyd and Charlie with a half-hearted glare, even though he could already feel his resolve weakening.

'Come on, sir,' Lloyd repeated. 'Charlie's buying.'

Andrew blew a loud breath out through his lips. It wasn't like he had anything else to do. 'Oh, alright, fine.'

'That's the spirit,' Charlie said in what he obviously thought was an encouraging manner. 'Where to?'

'The Pelican,' Lloyd replied immediately. 'Higson refuses to go in there on Thursdays.'

'Why?' Charlie asked.

'No idea.' Lloyd shrugged.

'Why does Higson do anything he does?' Andrew sighed loudly. 'Alright, The Pelican it is.'

Andrew gestured for the others to lead the way.

They'd closed a case, caught a criminal, and nobody (else) had died, but Andrew was feeling neither proud nor triumphant as he slowly trudged along behind his team as they headed up Tib Street.

Instead, he thought that he might actually be feeling just a little bit cursed.